BOOMSTERS

An Unexpected Adventure

DAVID MARKS

Boomsters: An Unexpected Adventure

Copyright © 2023 David Marks. All rights reserved. No part of this book may be reproduced or retransmitted in any form or by any means without the written permission of the publisher.

Published by Wheatmark®
2030 East Speedway Boulevard, Suite 106
Tucson, Arizona 85719 USA
www.wheatmark.com

ISBN: 979-8-88747-080-1 (paperback)
ISBN: 979-8-88747-081-8 (ebook)
LCCN: 2023907831

Bulk ordering discounts are available through Wheatmark, Inc. For more information, email orders@wheatmark.com or call 1-888-934-0888.

Cover design by Sierra Corona

The story and characters in this novel are fictitious. While certain historical events, figures, and agencies are mentioned, their purpose is solely as a backdrop for the characters and their actions—all of which are entirely imaginary.

All proceeds from this book will be donated to non-profit organizations benefitting senior war heroes.

rev202301
rev202402

ACKNOWLEDGMENTS

I never meant to write a book, but with retirement came more free time than I knew what to do with.

Sure, I did all the things you're supposed to do when you retire—travel, pick up golf, etc. But I wanted something more. My business career was built on my creativity and imagination, so retirement was traumatic because I suddenly had no purpose. It's a jarring feeling to suddenly not feel consequential.

One morning, I imagined a man in a similar position—a former businessman who retired and tried to figure out what to do with his life.

And that's how this journey began.

Computers and I have never gone well together, but my iPhone rarely leaves my side. I'm a pretty good texter, so every morning for four years I spent a couple of hours tapping at my phone to bring this idea to life, my thumb racing to keep up with my thoughts.

There were many people who helped along the way.

Thank you to Mary for your support, inspiration, and for introducing me to a talented young content strategist and writer named Marc Zarefsky. Marc took my initial draft of the story and refined it—keeping the good stuff, establishing clear timelines, ensuring everything was well-structured, and enhancing the character development throughout the story.

Thank you to my kids, who smirked every time they heard I was writing a book. And thanks to my grandkids, who giggled every time they heard Poppy was still writing his book.

Thank you to my parents, who taught me I could make the impossible possible.

I'd also like to thank America's senior war heroes, who have always been role models to me. My father served, and I've had the good fortune to meet hundreds of women and men who sacrificed so much to serve and protect our country. Any profits that come from *Boomsters* will be donated to non-profit organizations benefiting senior veterans.

Perhaps most importantly, thank you to *you*, my readers. Publishing *Boomsters* was never the goal. The journey was truly the destination. This story was challenging to put together, but let me tell you, it was entertaining. This story gave me direction. It gave me purpose.

Put bluntly, *Boomsters* made retirement fun.

Hopefully, this book encourages you to find your own joy, whether you're currently retired or have dreams of retiring one day. Discover your hidden talents, find your passion, and make retirement the best years of your life.

And never forget—when you create your own journey, the destination will come naturally.

1

"We are gathered here today before God and in the company of loved ones to celebrate life," Rabbi Rabinowitz said. "The life of—" He paused. "The life of—" Another pause. Finally, he pulled a notecard from his pocket. "We are here to celebrate the life of Melvin Weinberg."

I adjusted my tie as I leaned toward Mary. "More like celebrating his death," I said. She rolled her eyes as she listened to the rabbi.

"Melvin, or Mel, as most of you probably knew him, was a husband and a father, a man whose life was cut short at the age of fifty-six. The world will not be the same without him."

"Yeah, it will be safer now," I whispered to Mary, who responded with an elbow to my left kidney. "What? Clearly this rabbi never met Mel."

Candidly, I had never met Mel either, but I was confident I knew more about him than any of the two hundred or so people at the funeral. My guess was most were here not because Mel would be missed but because so many people wanted to confirm he was dead.

When you're in your seventies like I am, you become familiar with funerals and the certain routine that comes with them, but it was easy to see nothing was routine about this one. Sure, the rabbi forgot the dead man's name, but now he was extolling Mel's virtues. Mel had no virtues. He was a murderer, a rapist, and a gambler. You can't live life as a jerk and die a mensch. Clearly the rabbi was officiating as a favor to someone.

But that wasn't all that was off. Those in attendance were also peculiar. First, a half-dozen FBI agents patrolled the room. Sarah Cutler—the woman expected to be Chicago's next mayor—was sitting in the front row for all to see. Scattered throughout were members and employees from the West Coast Club, a fitness center I've worked out at for more than twenty years and a place I know Mel was no member of.

Then there was the crowd in the back row. On one side sat associates of Tony Santori, the head of the notorious Italian crime family. Santori expanded his family's corrupt and dishonorable reign from New Jersey to the Midwest six years ago, and although he wasn't in attendance, his presence was certainly felt. On the other side were members of the Deli Boys, a pack of Jews who'd owned Chicago's streets for decades, at least until Santori arrived. Solomon Feldman was their leader, though he, too, was not present. A line of uniformed Chicago police officers blanketed the room's back wall, there primarily to keep the peace between the two families.

Keep the peace? At a funeral? Like I said, the whole scene was bizarre. Then again, I guess it was fitting for the unique set of circumstances surrounding Mel Weinberg's death. Why they were there was a legitimate question, as was this: As a retired businessman who spent fifty years selling trinkets like light-up Christmas necklaces and pens that sang "Yankee Doodle Dandy," what the hell was I doing there?

To answer that question, I needed to take a step back.

David Blazen is my name, born soon after World War II ended at eight pounds and who cares how many ounces. Growing up,

I loved to watch Saturday morning television, where Superman stood for justice and Captain America defended our country from evil. All the shows I gravitated toward appealed to me because they focused on doing the right thing, no matter if the hero was a rifleman or a collie. I liked when bad people were caught and justice prevailed. When I couldn't find the right story on our black-and-white TV, I'd find it in my piles of GI Joe comic books. Before I fantasized about girls, I dreamed about being GI Joe.

The best education I got came from my World War II-veteran dad, a navy man who was the smartest person I knew, even though he never made it past fifth grade. From him I learned how to be human. His motto was simple: "It's nice to be important, but it's more important to be nice."

I went to Wright Junior College in Chicago, but saying *I went there* is a loose term. I only showed up when I wanted, which wasn't often. I wanted to learn to be a salesman, so when I wasn't in class, I was practicing my craft. At that time, I sold personalized pens. I decided I learned all the school could teach me three months into my freshman year when I sold Wright Junior College ten thousand pens emblazoned with the school's name on them.

After my brief stint in college, I started my own business. I sold creative impulse merchandise of all kinds—things people decide they can't live without, like an extendable back scratcher or holiday-themed ice trays. Those who knew me then would call me creative and fast-paced, and I would agree. I had a zest for being zestful. My creativity was not stymied by what others did or what books said, only by the limits of my imagination. Every day, I challenged my brain to think outside the norm.

I got married to an incredible woman, and we raised four incredible children. I lost her to cancer far too young, before she could see any of our ten adorable grandchildren.

I retired after five decades at the helm of my company and issued my declaration of independence—I call it that because I truly felt independent for the first time in my life. No parents or teachers telling me what to do. No customers to worry about. No colleagues to manage. When I got that gold watch at my farewell party, it wasn't just a sign of gratitude; it meant I was on my own. The irony was I didn't have anything to do; who cared what time it was?

When people asked about my retirement plans, I joked I'd figure something out, but really I didn't have a clue. One advantage was I wouldn't be completely alone. My girlfriend, Mary, retired from her forty-year business career the day after I left mine, and we entered this new world enthusiastic to travel, relax, and enjoy our lives with one another, like those hokey life insurance commercials with aging couples hugging on a boat, grateful to have time together.

It took us four days to realize we didn't like boats and there was only so much hugging to do.

We went from leadership positions where others counted on us for direction to spending virtually every waking minute together. It used to take only one of us to squeeze the tomatoes at the produce counter, but now it's a two-person event complete with discussion and, in most cases, a concession on my part. I was no dummy, though; bigger decisions would be needed at the avocados. What used to be short trips now became extended outings. Lunch was another discussion, followed by a compromise. Everything we did was a discussion, then a compromise.

The one thing we agreed on was we needed a new plan.

Step one was to have me rejoin the West Coast Club (WCC). I'd always been in good shape, but in the months leading up to retirement, I was too preoccupied with work and fell out of my regular exercise routine. In my pre-retirement life, the gym provided nothing more than a workout and quick shower before I scurried off to run my business. I never had time to enjoy the relaxation of a good steam or a nice hot sauna. Now, though,

I had nothing but time. Seriously. Mary and I decided I would spend my mornings at the WCC and then we'd meet for lunch. I wasn't quite sure how I'd fill five hours at the gym, but I assumed I'd meet new friends, explore all the place had to offer, or just steam a lot. I was confident I'd figure it out.

I've always been a people-watcher, so when I wasn't working out, I watched everyone else in the club. Some might call this obsessive; others might call it being extremely bored. I'd say yes to both. I learned a whole lot about the people I shared the club with. I quickly realized you can't buy a good-looking body, and in my first six weeks back, I uncovered three different affairs. Frankly, if I didn't spend so much of my morning naked, either showering or steaming, I'd keep a diary.

After all, the WCC quickly became my life.

Even when I wasn't at the club, it was most of what I thought about. On day forty-eight of retirement, Mary and I had lunch with friends we hadn't seen since we stopped working. They told us about a two-month cruise around the world they just took, Mary talked about her Pilates classes and her newfound passion for golf, and I told them about the WCC. For some reason, they weren't impressed by the affairs I'd sleuthed out. Apparently, I needed to work on my delivery.

The next day, Mary and I met for our routine post-workout lunch and had our traditional conversation about nothing and everything on our minds. I told her about my personal best of four minutes and thirty seconds in the steam room, and to say she was uninterested would be an understatement. She has the incredible gift of simultaneously looking at me in amazement while dozing off with her eyes open—it is a remarkable talent, and one she had practiced a lot during the past few weeks. As I started to tell her about a woman who always pretended to work out, she cut me off.

"Sweetie, you need to do more with your life than hang

around the club," Mary said. "Look at what one of my girlfriends dropped off." She pulled a book out of her purse. It was called *101 Things to Do in Retirement Years*.

Mary had always been sweet to me, but not once when I was a successful businessman did she call me *sweetie*. Was this new term higher or lower on her scale of endearment? I faked interest in the book and put it to the side. I didn't think I needed anything else to do. I had the WCC.

Day sixty-two of retirement began like any other day. I arrived early at the club, showered, steamed, worked out, and showered again. Afterward, I did a lap around the place, looking to see if I could find anything of interest to fill my time. I meandered into the weight room and toward the row of five punching bags on the opposite side of the room. I always gravitated toward the bag all the way on the left; when you peer around it, you have a great view of the entire room, and the darkness of the corner makes it virtually impossible to be seen. Or so I thought. I settled into my prime watching position, and as I started browsing the room, I locked eyes with Betty, the club's CEO, standing thirty feet away from me. Despite her title, Betty was extremely hands-on with the club's day-to-day operations. Everybody knew Betty, but having been a member for so long, I felt she and I had a special connection. Watching me stare from behind the punching bag, she forced a smile as she signaled for me to come her way.

What could she want? Maybe to say how great it was to see someone my age so committed to his health and well-being? If only that was her message. Betty didn't greet me as I approached her. She turned and walked out of the room, so I followed to her office.

"Mr. Blazen, please close the door," she said as I walked in.

I gave a slight laugh. "Mr. Blazen? Betty, we've known each other for decades. I don't think you've ever called me by my last name. What's this about?"

She paused, waiting for me to close the door and sit in one of the two red leather chairs facing her desk. "Mr. Blazen, I know you've been spending a lot of time here the past few months, and, well, we've received a number of complaints about your behavior, particularly your obsessive snooping."

Something in those words made it sound like she was describing a psycho. Obsessive snooping? That didn't sound like me. Or maybe it did.

"Punching bags are for punching, Mr. Blazen, not hiding behind, and bench presses are for lifting weights, not sitting on so you can watch everyone else work out," she continued. "This is a place for people to exercise, not to meddle. We're not in some reality TV show here. I'm going to need to ask you to change some of your daily practices immediately."

My cheeks were as red as the chair I sat in. How embarrassing!

As bad as Betty's admonishment was, I couldn't help but notice an added tension in the room, like she was trying to say something to me without saying it. It was as if she was warning me of something, like if I kept snooping around, as she called it, I might see something I wouldn't be able to unsee. Was that what this was all about? The whole idea seemed strange, but so did the conversation. Maybe I was just having retirement paranoia. Either way, if the WCC was going to continue to be part of my daily routine, I'd need to work on fitting in more.

In short, my health club was no longer healthy for me.

Driving home, I felt as little as could be. In two months, I'd gone from an international businessman to a peeping Tom. Mary was already worried about me, and now I had to at least consider that her worrying was legitimate.

I took four days off before returning to the WCC. From the moment I walked in until the time I left, I felt I was being watched. Surely there must have been internal gossip about the weirdo snooping around the club. I steamed, worked out, and showered, then sat down in the ground-floor café near the lobby. Table 16 was my go-to spot, positioned just to the side of the café counter. Prior to my uncomfortable meeting with Betty, that was one of my favorite places to people-watch. With my back to the counter, not only could I see everyone who came in and out of the building, but I also had a great vantage point to see the free-weights room, the basketball courts, and a squash court. I could also overhear conversations at the café counter. There were few better places to see so much activity. But today was different. I had to show my routine was changing and that I wanted to simply fit in, so instead of my normal seat, I sat on the opposite side of Table 16. What better way to show I had no interest in people's business than by literally turning my back to the club's activity?

During my self-imposed four-day break from the club, I thought a lot about what Betty said. I thought about the worsening strain between Mary and me these past few weeks. I worried she was getting bored with me. Hell, I was getting bored with myself. I decided I'd look over the *Things to Do in Retirement* book, so I tossed it in my gym bag. Now, sitting at the WCC, my back to the hustle and bustle of the club, I pulled it out and started to read, ready to be inspired by something new.

#1: Learn to knit.

I was not going to learn to knit.

#2 Write a book.

Give me a break. I could barely read a book, let alone write one.

#3 Build a model airplane.

#4 Travel.

#5 Plant a garden.

This was going to be even harder than I thought.

#16 Lecture on what you know best.

That's an interesting idea. Maybe I could talk about business to college kids or professional associations. I'd have to come back to that one.

#20 Join a health club.

Ugh. I closed the book, satisfied I made it through twenty suggestions yet thoroughly unsatisfied that only one even remotely piqued my interest. I put the book down and was about to get up and stretch when I saw the stairs. Not the stairs I'd gone up and down thousands of times over the years but a separate set of loft-style ones hidden deep down near the end of a long hallway. I'd never seen those stairs before. I hadn't even realized the hallway was there; I just thought it was a way to access the café kitchen. Where could those stairs go? I picked up my book and pretended to read but instead remained locked on the stairs, curious to see if someone I saw going up or down might indicate what could be found at the top.

Over the course of the next hour, I saw a total of four men in suits go up the stairs and none come down. Each was big, not in a muscular way but more like it was surprising to see them make it up the stairs at all. They clearly were not going to work out. So what was going on?

The next day, I returned to my new perch at Table 16, determined to learn more about the mystery stairs. As I waited for anything interesting to happen, I kept glancing down at my book. It was meant to be a decoy, but I wanted to see if anything else would interest me.

#21 Become an artist.

#28 Collect stamps.

#35 Take cooking lessons.

None of those sounded appealing. I was in the middle of reading about remodeling your house when a hard box rammed into my leg. "What the hell?" I shouted as I looked up to see a smaller-sized man with glasses carrying what must have been a three-foot-long black case in his right hand.

"I'm sorry," the man said, "I didn't mean to surprise you. My name is Jack, and I couldn't help but see you're reading my favorite retirement book. It has been a lifesaver for me."

"Really?" I asked, surprised, still rubbing my leg in pain.

"That's right. Thanks to that book, I'm learning the sweet sounds of the trombone," he said, holding up his case. "Plus, check out this winter hat. I knitted it myself!"

Jack pulled out a brown hat with streaks of orange and pink and two puffed balls on top. He put the hat on his bald head and beamed with pride. I looked at the eighty-something-year-old carrying a trombone and boasting about a hat that looked like an orange and a pomegranate that had been soaked in shit, and I realized if that's what this book thinks retired life should look like, I would no longer have any use for it.

"Your hat looks nice," I said, "but if you don't mind, I'm actually late for an appointment."

I gave a quick nod, put my book in my gym bag, and began walking down the mystery hallway to the even more mysterious stairs. I didn't have a plan, but I couldn't spend any more time with Jack. I wandered down the hall and discovered a door at the base of the staircase with a keypad on it. That only made me more curious. As I got close to the door, a refrigerator-shaped gentleman stepped out and, with one look at me, closed the door quickly.

"Who the hell are you?" he asked.

This did not seem like someone I wanted to give my real identity to, so I ignored his question.

"I'm sorry sir, I'm looking to find a room here, and now I can't remember the number," I said.

"It's not this one," Mr. Refrigerator said, blocking the door.

Something interesting was going on up those stairs. But what?

"I didn't mean to intrude, sir. If you don't mind," I said, fidgeting in my pocket, pretending to try to find a scrap of paper, "let me see if I can find that paper."

Out of the corner of my eye, I saw another man coming toward the door. I moved to the side and pulled out my wallet, looking for a paper I knew wasn't there. The new man approached and gave Mr. Refrigerator a head nod. He went to the door and typed 49651* into the keypad. Once he walked through the door, I looked back up at Mr. Refrigerator.

"Oh, I remember. It was room eighteen. Do you know where that is?"

"Do I look like a map?" Mr. Refrigerator asked.

His shape would make for a nice globe, but I kept that to myself.

"Fair point. Thanks anyway."

I turned and walked back down the hall toward the café, a smile on my face almost as big as Trombone Jack's.

I had a new project.

49651. 49651. 49651.

I repeated that code hundreds of times the rest of the day. Something was happening beyond that door, and now I had the digital key to find out what it was. Tomorrow, I planned to get to the gym early and check it out. I remembered that inkling I had while talking with Betty that she was hiding something from me, and I wondered if the two were connected. I'd find out soon enough.

The next morning, I wore my finest dark suit rather than my normal gym garb. I figured if I got to the club early, the door would be more likely to be unguarded, and even if there was someone there, so long as it wasn't the Fridge, I wouldn't look out of place. Fortunately, Mary was still sleeping, so I didn't need to explain the odd attire. I got in the car, the sun still not up, and began the drive to the WCC. 49651. On the way, I thought about all the possibilities beyond that door.

Before I retired, I'd never do something like this. I had my purpose in life, and that was that. Now, though, what was my purpose? There must have been some reason I saw that code. 49651. Maybe whatever was going on beyond that door was connected to my larger purpose in life. Maybe it was some grand mystery that only I could solve. On the other hand, maybe it was nothing at all. There was only one way to find out.

My mind wandered to detective heroes from 1980s television—Magnum PI, Kojak, and Columbo—as I wondered how they'd handle this situation. Unfortunately, my daydreaming got the best of me, and just three minutes from the WCC, flashing lights startled me back to reality.

"Pull over!" I heard over a loudspeaker.

Shocked it could be me the policeman was addressing, I looked and realized there was no other car in sight. I pulled over and sat for at least ten minutes as the officer called in my license plate. Finally, he got out of his car and approached me.

"Good morning, sir," the officer said. "Did you know you were driving sixty in a thirty-five MPH zone?"

Truthfully, I had no idea. "I'm sorry, Officer; it won't happen again."

He slapped me with a $150 ticket and told me to pay more attention while behind the wheel. That ticket was more than a fine. It was a wakeup call. What the hell was I doing? I was dressed for an important business meeting when, really, I had no business being where I was trying to go. This was all a stupid idea.

Mary was awake when I got home, confused by my outfit and why I left my gym bag.

"A cheap friend scored his final deal with a 20-percent discount on his funeral so long as it finished before 8:30 a.m.," I said.

She looked at the clock. It was now 8:42 a.m. She looked back at me. "He cut it pretty close."

I couldn't tell if she believed me, but that wasn't my biggest concern. I was worried about myself. What was I thinking trying to sneak up the guarded stairs? Had I lost all sense of reality? Was I depressed? Did I need to be medicated? Those were the questions that lingered all day and that I fell asleep to. Sadly, they were still waiting for me in the morning. My fall from grace was steep, and my zest levels had never been lower. To put it simply, I was in a bad place. I lost my interest in the WCC. Really, I lost interest in just about everything. I started going through the motions of life with no purpose.

My slump took a toll on Mary, and our relationship began to fracture. I knew she was worried about me, but her disappointment in me was truly concerning. We both retired with dreams for this happy and relaxing next chapter of our lives. She held up her end of the deal, but what was I doing? She and I started to bicker more, less in the joking way we used to and more with a hint of anger.

I'd always had direction in my life, something I was trying to achieve or go after. Now, though, I was lost with no compass in sight. I got together with a couple of friends over the course of the next two weeks to try to answer that question. Bless Mary, she reached out to them and said I needed their support, and while it was fun catching up, none could shake me from my funk.

On day ninety-two of retirement, I once again cracked open the book endorsed by Trombone Jack. Maybe I'd skipped something good the first time around. That night, I sat in bed and glanced through the list again.

#83: Search for gold or pennies.

#91: Take up beekeeping.

#101: Golf.

I stared at #101. I'd never been interested in golf. It seemed like a waste of time chasing a little ball around with a stick. If I wanted that kind of frustration, I might as well get a metal detector and search for gold. At least with that I had the chance of a reward. What do you get with golf? The ball goes in a hole, and then you repeat the whole stupid routine all over again. No thanks. I tossed the book to the side and opted for some TV before going to sleep.

"Mary, give me the remote," I said, still annoyed at the idea of golf.

"Get your own damn remote," she said, turning her back to me.

I could have pushed, but it was easy to see Mary had no interest in me that evening. I walked around the bed to her side and grabbed the remote. My kids gave me the complete DVD set of *The Streets of San Francisco,* and I was still making my way through the first season. I flipped the show on and forgot all about my retirement doldrums. The episode had a love triangle that saw a father and son unknowingly have affairs with the same woman. The story was twisted, but as always, the detectives figured out who to blame for the woman's death.

That night, I dreamed I starred in the show as the good guy trying to catch the city's riffraff and protect the general public. I was in the middle of a car chase, me behind the wheel of one of those classic early 1970 Ford sedans, when, suddenly, I jolted awake. It was 3:12 a.m. on February 10, and I knew what I wanted for my retired life. I was going to be a detective!

I wanted to wake Mary up and share the big news, but I used my detective skills to determine that would not end well. I tried going back to sleep, but it was useless. I was wide awake. I got out of bed, energized like I hadn't been in months. Between my interests in solving problems and my recent sleuthing, being a detective made perfect sense. How did my retirement book overlook this perfect option? I grabbed some breakfast and was back in the bedroom to get dressed for the day ahead, even though it was still pitch black outside. I kept the lights off and tried my best to get ready, but I stubbed my toe on the doorframe as I went for some socks. I did my best to mask the pain as I cursed and grabbed my foot in agony, but I wasn't quiet enough. Mary rolled over and opened one eye to see me hopping up and down holding my foot.

"David, what the hell are you doing?"

"Oh good, you're awake." I stopped hopping and tried to forget the sharp jolts of pain in my smallest toe. "Mary, I figured it out. I figured out what I'm going to do with my life. I'm going to be a detective!"

I'm not sure what I thought her reaction would be. I wasn't expecting a loud cheer or for her to jump out of bed and give me a big congratulatory hug, but I guess I hoped for some sort of encouraging response. Instead, she smiled and rolled back over.

"Great, sweetie, you do that," she said before falling back asleep.

That sounded like approval to me. It wasn't even 5 a.m., and already I had a victory under my belt.

At 5:02 a.m., I sat down at the desk in my home office for the first time in months. Now with direction, I was ready to become a detective. My first assignment? Figure out how to become a detective. I opened my laptop and searched online for *How do I become a detective?* The first few entries made it clear that to be a detective, you needed years of training, certification, and often to be sponsored or employed by a larger entity. Hmm, saying I used to run the company that made battery-operated squirt guns that light up and make noise probably wouldn't count. I kept searching.

I wondered what it would take to join the FBI but quickly had to rule that out due to the age requirements. I guessed Homeland Security and Border Protection also were not looking for seventy-year-old high-school graduates. Being in the Secret Service would be fun, but I wasn't going to leap in front of the president and take a bullet for him, not because I approve or disapprove of the guy but because I couldn't leap anymore. Back to the internet search. There was a job opening for a gate guard at our local senior community center, but I'd rather knit a quilt or maybe one of those stupid hats Jack had. I didn't want to do security. I wanted to follow in my heroes' footsteps and focus on the battle of good versus evil.

I kept hitting the next button in hopes of finding something that would jump out at me, and then, on the sixth page of the search results, I found it: *Become a Private Investigator in just 3 months for $289*. That sounded promising. I sat up straight with my shoulders back and proudly announced myself. "David Blazen, private investigator." It had a nice ring to it. I wondered how long it took Thomas Magnum to become Magnum PI. "Blazen PI" sounded even more compelling. There was just one problem. Three months was still too long. I clicked the link anyway and was taken to the Metro City Internet College (MCIC) website. I poked around a little bit but was interrupted by the front door slamming. I got up in time to see Mary drive away, off to another day of golf and Pilates. I'd tell her about my research later.

I went back to digging around on the MCIC website. The college was easy to find online and learn about, but I found it impossible to locate a phone number. Many people in my position might have given up but not this budding private investigator. I just had to get creative. I tried other searches about the college but still could not find contact information. My next stop was a rating website where I discovered the school was not held in high esteem by the majority. One inspiring five-star rating from a guy said the three-month course built the foundation for his lifetime career as a detective, but after that, there were dozens of unfavorable ones. I quickly lost count of the one-star reviews, people who said the program was a sham and didn't give them what they thought they would get out of it. *They must not have been motivated*, I thought, thinking back to that five-star review. All you need is motivation. As I continued to scroll through the one-star reviews, I found one of interest:

> *I was looking for a career for my husband, Calvin, and found this online certification to become an official private investigator. He lost his job from the bus company, and we didn't have the tuition money, but my parents were kind enough to lend it to us. What a waste! The class consisted of useless online classes that simply repeated the eight pamphlets provided as course material. You guys are crooks, and we couldn't be unhappier. Shame on you, Metro City Internet College! Sincerely, Jennifer Talbert, Rockford, Illinois.*

I found Jennifer's phone number online and gave her a call. I explained I was trying to locate the number for the online school, but I also said I was sorry for her husband's bad experience. She passed along the number but cautioned me against contacting the school. I heard her warning but chose to ignore it. I was a man on a mission. I hung up with Jennifer and called MCIC.

"Good evening," the voice on the other end of the call said, "my name is Sanjay."

"Evening? It's not even noon."

"I'm sorry, sir, it's evening here in India. Thank you for calling the Metro College for Internet City. I mean the Metro Internet College City. No, the—"

"Metro City Internet College?"

"Yes, that's the one. How may I be of assistance?"

"I'm looking for more information on your private investigator program."

"Ah, the private investigator program! A good choice. I'll take your credit card info when you're ready."

"No, I'm not ready to pay for it. I want to know more about it," I said, quickly getting frustrated with Sanjay.

"Oh. Well, a private investigator is someone who looks into—"

"Sanjay, I know what a private investigator is. What I don't know is how your program works. Will I be an official PI once I complete your program?"

"Please hold."

I waited five minutes for him to return.

"Thank you for waiting. What was your question?"

"Are you kidding me? Will I be official once I complete the program?"

"Oh yes, sir, you'll have a certificate and everything."

"What does 'everything' mean?"

"Please hold."

Five more minutes went by.

"Thank you, sir. 'Everything' means all things. Now I'm ready for your credit card information."

"Goodbye, Sanjay."

I got off the phone annoyed, but a new idea came to mind. I called Jennifer Talbert back. "Hi, this is David; we spoke just a few minutes ago about MCIC and your husband's experience with it. Did you happen to keep any of his reading materials from the class?"

"Hold on," she said. "Gizzey, stop humping the table." A few seconds passed before she returned. "I'm sorry, who is this, and what do you want?"

Now I had all sorts of new questions, but I stayed focused like any good PI would. "Hi, Jennifer, this is David. I just spoke to you about your husband's MCIC class. Do you still have any of the assigned work he was given for the class?"

"All we have are those stupid pamphlets. I don't even know why we kept them."

"That's perfect," I replied, struggling to mask my enthusiasm. "Would you take a hundred dollars for them?"

"A hundred dollars? I would have given them to you for free, but sure, I'll take the money. Poor Gizzey desperately needs to be neutered, so you'd be helping me out."

I took down her address and said I could be there in ninety minutes.

Just by talking with Jennifer, I understood money was in short supply for her and Calvin, but pulling up outside their two-room house made it all the more apparent. The only personalization was a sign in the dirt that read *A dog lover lives here*. I couldn't tell if it was a nod to someone in the house or someone buried in the ground—I hoped the former.

I knocked on the door and heard Gizzey's high-pitched bark. No need for a doorbell with that thing. Jennifer opened the door and invited me in. I hadn't made it three steps before Gizzey introduced himself to my left leg. I did my best to ignore the eight-pound fluff ball going to town on the side of my leg. I asked Jennifer if she had the pamphlets, and she handed me a brown envelope. In it were all eight pamphlets, as well as a certificate made out to *Calvin Talbett*.

"Are you sure your husband doesn't want this?" I asked, pulling out the certificate.

"Please, just take it all. Calvin was a different man before he took that class. He didn't drink much then. He was frustrated about losing his job, but at least he still had a little motivation. I think his only goal now is to see how early he can get thrown out of the bar. I blame that damn MCIC for that." She looked at the certificate. "Damn school couldn't even spell his name right."

I genuinely felt bad for them, but it was hard to be empathetic as Gizzey humped my leg from behind. I put the certificate back in the envelope and gave her the hundred dollars. She kicked Gizzey aside and thanked me. I gave her another fifty and thanked her. Two more minutes of that dog on me and I would have neutered the mutt myself with one big kick.

I drove home, parked the car in the driveway, and flung open the front door. "Mary, my dear, it's official. Your very own private eye is here. I've even got the certificate to prove it!"

There was no answer. The house was quiet. Too quiet. Mary's car was in the driveway, but where was she? My stomach quivered as I thought about the possibilities. Had she been kidnapped? This must be the feeling private investigators get when they arrive at a crime scene—something's wrong, and they must be the one to fit the pieces together.

I leaned against the entryway wall, hiding myself from view in case any attackers were still in the house. I rounded the corner and flung open the guest bathroom door. Nothing. I crept to the kitchen and looked everywhere I could think, including in the cabinets and drawers. Why I thought Mary or an attacker would be in either of those places, I wasn't sure, but as a PI, I had to be thorough.

I climbed the stairs as quietly as I could. I made it to the bedroom, and there I saw it, a folded note lying on the center of our bed. Oh my God, she was kidnapped, and there's the ransom note!

I looked around the room, confirming I was the only one there. I slowly made my way toward the bed. I grabbed Mary's tweezers and carefully picked up the note, making sure I didn't leave any fingerprints. I looked it over and then put it back on the bed, prepared to find out how much the bad guys thought Mary was worth. I took a breath, then used the tweezers to open the note.

Went to the mall with Nancy. Be back at 5.

I exhaled. Thank goodness Mary was okay!

I went back downstairs, grabbed my newly acquired internet college materials, and entered what once was my home office. Now that I was official-ish, it would be known as *headquarters*. I sat down at the desk and emptied the folder from Jennifer. There were the eight pamphlets, plus a bonus summary chart, and, of course, the certificate. I separated the items into neat piles. I found a piece of masking tape and proudly attached "my certificate" to the wall. Satisfied with my organization and decoration, I grabbed a sheet of paper to jot down a list of supplies I'd need as an official PI:

- Business cards
- New suit
- Paper clips
- A pocket-sized notebook
- Pens (not from my imprinted pen pile)
- Zip top bags for evidence
- Mary's tweezers (maybe I should buy my own)
- A picture frame (for my certificate)

That night, I had another dream. This one was a Western crime saga. A card scandal in the local saloon led to an all-out brawl that left three people dead. The sheriff called the Lone Ranger for help on the case. As always, the hero figured out how the murders happened, caught the outlaws, and ultimately saved the town. With the case closed, he hopped on his white horse and galloped away. He pulled off his black mask as he turned to look back at the town, but it wasn't the Lone Ranger behind the mask.

It was me.

I brought my horse up onto his back legs and shouted, "Hi-yo, Silver" as we turned and rode out of sight.

The next thing I heard was "David!" My eyes flung open to find Mary sitting up next to me, her face with a look of pure disgust.

"Who the hell is Silver?" she asked.

"What?"

"You just screamed out 'Hi-yo, Silver' and woke me up. I thought someone was being attacked."

I started to explain that Silver was the Lone Ranger's noble companion, but as soon as Mary heard Silver was a horse, she threw the covers over my head and got out of bed. "David Blazen, we need to talk."

"Okay, dear. Let me have my morning coffee, and I'll see you in headquarters."

"David, shut up and be in the kitchen in five minutes," she shouted as she slammed the bedroom door.

When I got to the kitchen, she was pacing. Once I sat, she stopped and turned toward me, fear in her eyes. "David, who are you?"

Was that a trick question? "What do you mean, Mary?"

"I'm trying to gauge your level of sanity. I'm worried about you, David. I'm worried about us. We were supposed to be having the time of our lives during retirement, remember? The carefree lifestyle. The travel. The time together. That was our dream. But look at you now. You were warned about being too much of a creep at the WCC, you got a ticket for speeding, and now you're talking about being a detective and dreaming of life as a cowboy."

I almost stepped in to say calling the Lone Ranger a cowboy was an insult to his bravery and heroism, but I held my tongue.

"And I don't even want to know why you have a private investigator's certificate with someone else's name on it hanging in your office. David, what's happened to you?"

I started to answer but realized the question was rhetorical.

"I told my friend about your behavior these past three

months," Mary continued, "and she said her neighbor's husband retired from a long, fulfilling career, and within two months, he convinced himself he was a cocker spaniel. She said he saw a therapist, and talking to someone helped him. David, I want you to go see that therapist too." She leaned against the counter and stared straight into my eyes as tears began to fall from hers. "David, I'm worried I'm losing you. Forget this detective thing and do something normal. Come to the club and play some golf with me. Please, David, come back to me."

I held out my hand, and she weakly put hers in mine. She looked so defeated.

"Mary, my love, I'm right here. I haven't gone anywhere, and I promise, my sanity is intact. What retirement has taught me so far is that I need mental stimulation. For fifty years, I was a businessman, and my mind was constantly busy. Once I retired, there was nothing pushing me. I had nothing to put my attention toward. Constantly watching others at the WCC gave my mind something to do, and that's what I think this PI work can do. I'm not looking to make it big. I just want to do something that allows me to show some creativity and exercise my brain. If I get to solve a couple of cases, great, and if I don't, that's fine too.

"And I hear you," I continued. "Give me the therapist's number, and I'll give them a call. In the meantime, let's travel. Let's keep going to dinner with friends. Let's do everything we wanted to do in retirement. I just want to keep my mind fresh, and right now, I think I can do that with this PI stuff."

Mary remained quiet. "Do you really think anyone will hire you?" she finally asked.

"Would you hire a seventy-year-old private eye with no experience and questionable credentials?"

"Probably not."

"So what do I have to lose?"

More silence. "Okay. But David, I still have one question." She walked down the hallway and looked at me as she pointed into headquarters. "Who the hell is Calvin Talbett?"

I got up and gave Mary a hug and a kiss on the top of her head. "That, my dear, is a long story."

2

I breathed a sigh of relief as I sat down in headquarters. Mary left for a round of golf, and while she did not understand my new passion, she seemed to be tolerating it. With the house to myself, it was time to work. I looked at my list of things a good PI needs. First up were business cards, so I took out a sheet of paper and played around with possible designs.

David Blazen
Private Investigator

That looked boring.

David Blazen
Private Detective

That looked a little better. Detectives and investigators both investigate, so why not say *private detective*? And why be private? My business would be for everyone.

David Blazen
Detective

Now we were getting somewhere, but something still wasn't right. I thought about some of my crime-fighting heroes. Columbo. Starsky and Hutch. Magnum. They all went by one name. *David* was a little nondescript, and *Blazen* wasn't very memorable. Then I had an idea.

BLAZE

Bingo! *Blaze* would be my detective name. Just like James Bond, I'd be Blaze, David Blaze. Happy with my new name, I called my friend Lew, who had been my company's go-to for business cards for decades.

"Hey, Lew, I'm starting a new business and need some cards," I told him. "It should be simple. On the front, right in the middle in all caps, I want it to say *Blaze*. On the back toward the bottom, have it say *Detective*."

Lew was silent. After a few seconds, he finally asked, "What else?"

"What do you mean?"

"How is anyone going to get in touch with you? You need a website, an email address, Twitter handle, etc."

Hmm. I hadn't thought about that. I didn't have or want a website, and honestly, I didn't want emails either. At my business, I always preferred phone calls or face-to-face conversations. When I talked with someone, I could read how they were feeling and figure out the best way to close a deal. With email, there was no emotion. There was no feeling. No thanks.

"That's a great point, Lew. Put my phone number under *Detective*."

"No Twitter?" Lew asked.

"No Twitter. I'm starting out small and not expecting high demand, so I think I only need about forty cards."

"Oh, David, you've been so good to me over the years. Let me do more than that. Tell you what. It's just as easy to print a thousand as it is to print forty. I'll get working on it right away and get you them within forty-eight hours—on the house! Consider it my going-into-business present."

I crossed business cards off the list. Next was a new suit, but I'd get that the next day with Mary at Bloomingdale's—it was triple-points day, after all.

That was enough supply work for the moment. I promised myself I'd study my PI pamphlets, so I picked up the top one and began to read about crime scenes. The pamphlet informed me that scenes deteriorate over time, and it's important to photograph a crime scene and commit all aspects of it to memory as well. Witnesses are the most important source of information at crime scenes, and because of that, it's critical to document everyone present. I also read about widening the playing field in terms of settings and suspects. Many crimes are organized and developed in a different place than the ultimate crime, so it's important to be open-minded.

February 11 began like any other day for Mel Weinberg—with a hangover and alone in an abandoned basement after a late-night gambling binge. Mel was a slouch, barely five-foot-eight with a receding hairline and a bulge around his waistline. Gambling was pretty much all Mel did the past few years, but he wasn't very good. He was a self-appointed authority on all sports, from basketball and football to cricket and box hockey, but he always doubled up until he eventually lost more than he had.

It didn't take long for Mel's debts to pile up by the thousands, and with little money to his name, he needed a way to get some cash. That's how he first met Carter, a six-foot-four muscular force with biceps as big as watermelons. Carter would proudly introduce himself as a bookie, but really, he was a collector.

When someone owed Tony Santori money, they gave it to Carter. When someone didn't pay, Carter turned to Mel.

Mel was fronted whatever money he needed in exchange for doing Santori's dirty work. The pay scale was dependent on the degree of violence Mel inflicted. Put a gun in someone's mouth to scare them? If they paid their debt, it earned Mel five hundred dollars. Break someone's fingers? That's two-fifty a finger or fifteen hundred dollars for the whole hand. If he killed someone, that could get him upward of fifteen grand. If that kind of violence wasn't enough, Mel also made a habit of tying and gagging his victim's loved ones and forcing them to witness his abuse. He took joy in hurting others—and he was good at it.

But that morning, Mel felt lousy—and not because of the hangover. Gambling took Mel away from his family—both of his families, in fact. Mel had a beautiful four-year-old daughter with his wife, Amber, and two adult children he never saw from a previous relationship. There was no future for him and his older children, but Mel dreamed of a life with Amber and Summer, a little girl with an infectious smile and a commanding personality. He got clean when Summer was born, but within months, he was back on the streets and now only saw his wife and daughter once or twice a year. But he wanted more. Maybe it was the alcohol, but he imagined the three of them running away and starting a new life together. The only way he could do that was to pay off his debts.

Mel shaved thirty thousand dollars off of his debt two nights before when he strangled two men who tried to keep money from Santori, but he still owed well over a hundred grand. With only twelve hundred dollars in the bank, Mel knew he'd need a miracle to ever make his freedom dream a reality.

Just then, he got a text from Carter: *Got a job for you and it's a biggie*, it read. *Need it done tonight. NBWYD & WE.*

NBWYD stood for "Not breathing when you're done," meaning this was a kill job.

WE was what shocked him. Those two letters meant "We're even," as in Mel's debts would be paid. Mel couldn't believe his luck. Maybe he could have that dream life with Amber and Summer after all.

Mel was confident the universe was saying now was the time to do right by his family. He'd reach out to Amber once the job was done and he was in the clear, but before that, he wanted insurance for them, just in case something happened. He cashed out his bank account and walked into the offices of Ricky Schwartz. Mel didn't know Ricky, but he'd seen his billboards all over town:

Looking for an agent who can help with your plan?
Insurance or real estate, Ricky Schwartz is your man!

"I need some insurance," Mel said bluntly as he shook hands with Ricky. "I want my daughter Summer to have money if I die."

"She must be a honey," Ricky said, "so let's get her some money."

The two negotiated a deal that set Mel up with a $250,000 plan. He paid $1,000 upfront, which included a rushed physical, and another $100 to have the paperwork completed by Valentine's Day.

Mel left the building with a single Ben Franklin. He wished he had more cash to get out of town that night after the job, but he felt he was doing the right thing. He couldn't remember the last time he put someone else's interests ahead of his own. A realization like that could have made him depressed, but instead, he started to smile.

I've got a future, he thought. *One more job and I'm out of here.*

With my reading done for the time being, I turned attention to my team. Every good detective had one—an elite group of individuals available at a moment's notice to serve the community and the common good. This team needed to be dedicated and committed to the cause. The problem was I didn't know anyone who fit that description, so I'd have to think through my friends and train them with extensive pamphlet reading instead.

Any elite team of mine had to have Marc on it. We'd been friends for more than sixty years, and he'd always been there when I needed him, like when I flunked second grade, and he made sure to do the same. He was currently a busy guy in the packaging industry, but I knew he'd make time for me. Besides, with him onboard, I'd have unlimited access to zip-top bags and all kinds of boxes for evidence.

Next on my list of all-star teammates was my brother, Jeffrey, who recently retired from his import business and found happiness as an Uber driver. Jeffrey's biggest gift was he could talk to anyone about anything—current events, sports, fine wines—you name it, Jeffrey had an opinion on it. For my purposes, his greatest value would come from his car as access to transportation could be key if I needed to leave a crime scene or get somewhere quickly. Plus, if I ever had to follow a suspect, there would be no better way to stay undercover than from the back of an Uber.

I was sure Jeffrey would say yes, but I texted him about grabbing dinner tomorrow, just to make it official. I made a mental note not to tell him about potentially adding Marc to Team Blaze. My lifetime of watching crime shows taught me that I shouldn't tell everyone on my team everything about each other, just in case one of them is a double agent. True, Marc and Jeffrey had known each other since the Lyndon Johnson administration, but you could never be too careful.

Two days as a detective and I already had a cause and the makings of a team. Oh, and business cards on the way. Everything was falling into place, and I realized just how much fun I was having.

With Mary and me back on track, I hoped sex might be in my future. Ever since I retired, whenever I'd brought it up, Mary always said she'd take a raincheck. What the hell was I supposed to do with twenty-seven rainchecks? Did they have any value? Did I get to bundle them in exchange for something more amazing?

The problem with getting older is you've got to plan for that kind of thing more, and those twenty-seven rainchecks had cost me twenty-seven blue pills. My hope was this time would be different. I went to the bookshelf and grabbed my hollowed-out copy of *Gone with the Wind*, which housed my pills and reminded me of the past twenty-seven times my libido had gone with the wind. Feeling optimistic, I grabbed one of the long-lasting ones and swallowed it down with water and one of the only phrases I remembered from my teenage days in Hebrew school: *Baruch atah Adonai, eloheinu melech ha'olam, aneh hen le lohvet var mezel*, which roughly translated to "Blessed are you, our God, Ruler of the universe, please let me get lucky."

I grabbed my cell phone and set an alarm for thirty-six hours to remind myself when I'd no longer be in the mood.

Mel didn't know anything about that night's victim other than he'd be the last one working at the Hi-Flier Nightclub. Mel never asked about his victims; he just wanted to get in and get out.

Mel snuck inside the club's staff entrance late that night and waited for the place to empty. He watched partygoers leave, followed by the staff and bartenders. When only one person remained, Mel struck. He crept up from behind and quickly slit the man's throat. The man fell back into Mel's arms, and it was then when Mel realized he should have asked more questions.

Without thinking twice about it, Mel had murdered Charlie Myers, the owner of the nightclub and nephew of Sol Feldman, leader of the Deli Boys, the most vicious gang in all of Chicago. Many missing souls could be traced back to the Deli Boys, and now Sol's nephew lay dead in Mel's arms.

All Mel's excitement and enthusiasm for a new life with Amber and Summer were gone before Charlie and the knife hit the floor. Mel had committed hundreds of awful and unlawful crimes but nothing as bad as this. He'd murdered Chicago royalty.

At that moment, Mel only had one thought: *I'm a dead man.*

3

Good morning, Chicago. It's Monday, February twelfth, and here's your local news. If you're commuting into downtown, expect delays. A Brown Line train and Purple Line train collided just south of the Belmont stop, injuring twelve and bringing rush-hour commuters to a grinding halt. In Lincoln Park, police are investigating the death of nightclub owner Charlie Myers. And a fire at the Harold Washington Library destroyed a rare collection of books housed on the building's ninth floor.

I turned off the news as the weather report informed me it would be cold and gray, a fair prediction for February in Chicago. I went to headquarters and grabbed a pamphlet to skim. A section called *Interpretation of Information* jumped out, and I learned that as a private investigator, it was my job to prove any information I had received, whether it was spoken or written. I always thought of written words as being more valuable, but I guess with the rise of the internet and social media, anyone could write anything, and hearsay could quickly become fact. It was my job to not only find the truth but prove it.

A PI is more like an accountant—I must live in a world where precision and exact details matter. Does a can of tomato soup really have 120 calories? Is my morning orange juice really 100 percent juice?

My thoughts were interrupted by the doorbell. My business cards had arrived! I opened the box and grabbed three for my pocket and one for my wallet. Detective Blaze was getting more official by the day.

Back to my pamphlet. I read about needing to stay attentive during conversations and always reading between the lines of everything anyone says. You never knew when a witness might be exaggerating. Being a businessman, I knew all about exaggerating and stretching the truth to make a sale. Almost every advertisement or commercial is less about fact and more about selling the brain on an idea.

The section ended with an ominous four words: *Everyone is a suspect.*

Sarah Cutler was less than two months away from being voted the next mayor of Chicago, but the unexpected death of nightclub owner Charlie Myers presented a problem to her campaign.

Cutler rose through the ranks of city government in the past eleven years under current Mayor Mitch Paulson, whose three terms in office had brought the city enormous economic and educational gains. For all Mayor Paulson did, the one thing he couldn't get a grasp on was crime, and it decimated the city. Sarah had built her campaign on the promise to cut crime and make Chicago safe again, and the public had eaten up her political promises.

Small in stature but overly assertive, Sarah was used to getting what she wanted. She enjoyed overpowering anyone in her way and had no problem coloring outside the lines of ethics if it meant a positive outcome for her.

Much of the violence inflicted during Mayor Paulson's tenure stemmed from the Deli Boys, the Jewish gang based out of a

South Side delicatessen and led by Solomon Feldman—Myers's uncle. Sarah had met Sol before she launched her candidacy and promised him greater control of the city if he would support her—both strategically and financially. To win, Sarah needed to reduce tension levels among Chicago's gangs, and that started with Feldman, whom she figured would be out for blood.

She texted him her condolences.

Thanks, he wrote back. *Whoever is responsible for Charlie's death's gonna pay.*

Sol, we need to talk ASAP, she texted.

Come by the deli at 6:30 tonight.

That's too early. I can't have anyone see me.

Fine, come at 10 after we close.

Deal. And Sol, don't do anything stupid before then.

Mary and I arrived at Bloomingdale's later that morning, ready to make me look like an official detective. I went straight to the Zegna section, while Mary meandered over to the sunglasses. I fit nicely off the rack and found three suits I liked. I bet Bond wore Zegna, but did he shop on extra-points days?

Somehow I finished trying on three suits faster than Mary could pick out a pair of sunglasses, so as I waited, I practiced my people-watching. So many people today spend their time with their heads down staring at their phones. I'd much rather take in the sights, even in a department store. Today my eye was drawn to a young Asian woman pushing an oversized baby stroller with a Shih Tzu puppy inside. Bringing a dog into a store was strange enough, but why such a big stroller? She could have fit seven of those dogs in that thing! People are weird.

I kept looking around and discovered two Asian men also had their eyes on the same woman, but they weren't guessing how many Shih Tzus she could carry. The stockier man standing by the exit gave a hand signal to the shorter one creeping in the women's clothing section. He then relayed the signal to the Shih Tzu lady. Seconds later, they each left through a different exit.

Mary finally returned with a new pair of Tom Ford sunglasses. "Sorry it took so long," she said. "You wouldn't believe it; security requested to look through my purse. They said lots of merchandise has gone missing lately, including sunglasses."

"And they thought you were a thief?" I joked. "Apparently law enforcement needs more help than I realized."

Mary playfully jabbed at my arm as we walked to grab a handful of ties, a trench coat, and a fedora to complete my wardrobe. We left feeling victorious with twenty-four thousand more Bloomingdale's points than we started. We celebrated with a walk through the brisk outdoor mall. Five minutes into our stroll, I saw the Shih Tzu woman again, only this time without her puppy and its throne on wheels. Fifty feet behind her were the two men I had seen. Why were they following her? And where was the dog?

I told Mary to get some toys for the grandkids and that I'd meet back up with her in a few minutes. Instinctively, something felt wrong about these three, and I figured I could do some quick reconnaissance and be back before she was.

Just as Mary left, the two men split up, one toward the mall's east exit and one to the garage to the west. I didn't see where the woman went, so I chose the one heading west and did my best to inconspicuously follow him.

By the time he made it to the garage, I had closed the gap between us to about twenty feet. He took the stairs up to the second floor, with me still a few seconds behind. I worried this guy was going to get away—what he was getting away with I didn't know, but he was up to something, and it was up to me to stand in the way. He was halfway down a row of parked cars when two watches with price tags fell from his pocket.

That was when I made my move.

"Stop, you're under arrest!" I shouted in my most authoritative voice. The man stopped and turned around. I flipped open my wallet, pretending there was a badge. He started to backpedal, so I patted my belt like I was concealing a gun. He stopped and put his hands up. I'd always been a bullshitter, but this was taking it to a whole new level.

"Put your hands on the car," I demanded as he sheepishly turned around and rested his hands on the trunk of a run-down Toyota Corolla. I patted him down and discovered four Mont Blanc pens in his pocket. "You, sir, are in serious trouble. I want some information, and I want it now!"

Just then I realized I hadn't yet made it to the store for many of my much-needed supplies. You must be resourceful when you're in the field, so I reached into my pocket and found the Bloomingdale's receipt. I grabbed one of the Mont Blanc pens and prepared to take notes. After all, I needed to be thorough when gathering details.

"Okay, kid, what's your name?"

"Cheng," he replied, still facing the car. As I wrote that down, he took one hand off the trunk and turned around. Instinctively, I reached to my hip for my make-believe gun.

"Get your hands back on the car!"

Cheng turned back but began to talk. "Please, mister. Please, you have to help me! I don't have money and am not here legally. I can't get arrested. If I do, my wife and child will be deported. Please, you have to help."

I thought about the pens and what Mary said about missing merchandise. Was this guy responsible, perhaps part of a larger operation? With as fast as he had pleaded for help, he couldn't be the ringleader. There had to be someone bigger. Something bigger. I kept digging.

"Where were you going with these pens?" I asked.

"I was going to bring them to the drop-off in twenty minutes. That's where I was going."

"Where's the drop-off?"

"The storage lockers behind the Big Happy Chinese Restaurant."

"What about the sunglasses?"

"Zhang Yong has them and will be there at the same time. So will Li Xiu and the phones she pocketed from the cell phone store. Please, mister, you have to help me!"

Was being a detective really this easy? He'd just given me the names of his associates and their crimes, but who was running this operation? I felt obligated to find out.

"Give me the keys," I told Cheng. "We're going to the drop-off. Keep being helpful, and I'll pass along a good word for you."

Who that good word went to I had no idea, but it was good enough for Cheng.

"Just hurry up," he said, "or else we'll miss the drop, and they'll know something is wrong."

Who were *they*? What else would be at the drop-off? How could I make sure he wouldn't harm me while I was driving? Those were the questions running through my head, along with a mental note to buy handcuffs. I undid my belt and had him put his hands behind his back. I tied the belt tight, then sat him down in the passenger seat before I hopped in behind the wheel.

As we left the garage, I called 911 to make my report. "This is Detective Blaze, and I'm reporting an active crime scene. Please send backup to the storage lockers behind the Big Happy Chinese Restaurant off Lake Street."

After a few seconds of "Wait, who is this?" the dispatcher said the police would be there within five minutes. We were fifteen minutes away. I wondered if the police would wait for me or leave. My next thought was what in the world to do for the fifteen minutes I was driving this suspect's car with him riding shotgun.

Do I turn on the radio? Ask him how his day was going? Find out what he orders at Big Happy? I decided to ask him about his family, and within minutes, I heard his life story about coming to the United States and getting caught up in this elaborate fencing scheme. He told me the scheme was just one of many illegal operations run by a man named Andy Wong. The storage lockers were his, and though Wong didn't technically own the restaurant, he apparently owned the man who did.

Before I knew it, we were behind the restaurant, where eight police cars surrounded a row of storage lockers. I got Cheng out of the car and tried to walk closer to see what was going on, but before we'd made it ten steps, we were blocked by an Officer Mully.

"Sorry, folks," he said, "this is an active crime scene."

"I know. I'm the one who called it in." I made Officer Mully the first recipient of one of my business cards. "Blaze. Detective Blaze," I said confidently. Officer Mully looked at me, down at my card, then back at me.

"Well, Blaze, thank you for your work. We've heard rumblings about an underground Chinese syndicate selling stolen goods in the area, but we never had any proof. Those lockers have hundreds of thousands of dollars' worth of merchandise stowed away that would have been sold on the black market."

He handed me his card and told me to call him if I discovered more about the case. Then he took Cheng off my hands and escorted him into a squad car. I saw Zhang Yong and Li Xiu in a nearby car while another officer tried to calm down the adorable Shih Tzu.

"Thanks, Mully," I said as he closed the car door. "Hey, go easy on that one."

Mully nodded in approval, stared at me for a couple of seconds, then shook his head as he left to take the dog off the other officer's hands.

A press photographer overheard our conversation and asked

to take my picture. I was riding an adrenaline high as I smiled widely for the camera. I walked away to call Mary, whom I knew would be pissed but I also hoped would be proud. If nothing else, she should appreciate my special present for her—a Mont Blanc pen—to soften the blow.

Before she could even say hello, I started talking a mile a minute.

"Mary, you won't believe it; the most incredible thing just happened. It was like I was in my own crime show and solved a mystery the police couldn't. Oh, I was so amazing and daring, and the whole thing was—"

Before I could go further, I finally heard her trying to get my attention.

"David. David! Where the hell are you?"

"I'm sorry, Mary. I just can't believe it. I'm a natural at this detective thing! I saw evil going on, and I stopped it, Mary. I stopped it! I brought down the bad guys. I'll tell you all about it when I see you. Can you pick me up at the Big Happy Chinese Restaurant, you know, the one off Lake Street? Are you still at the mall?"

"Of course I am. That's where you're supposed to be."

"I know. I'm sorry, Mary. I promise it will make sense once we talk."

Mel Weinberg did his best to stay in the shadows, but he knew he couldn't live like that. He tried calling Carter a dozen times, but every time it went straight to voicemail. He feared Feldman had already gotten to him, and if that was the case, Mel knew he was next.

He had to get out of the city. But how? He had no money. No way to buy a plane ticket and escape.

He thought about calling Amber for cash or shelter but decided against it. He owed her and Summer the respect of not getting them involved. He wanted to start over with them, but he couldn't drag them back into his life right then.

He had to do this on his own.

Driving home with Mary, I recounted the entire sequence of events. The hand signals. The chase. The phony handgun. I told her everything except the details of the Mont Blanc pens—I didn't want to blow my cover. She listened to me go on and on and at least feigned interest.

"I'm glad you were able to step in, David," she finally said, "but you put yourself in serious danger over a hunch. Is that what you're going to be doing with this detective stuff? Do I need to worry about your safety? Or your sanity?"

"I promise my mind is clearer than ever. And look, this was a once-in-a-lifetime situation. I had my date with destiny, and I won. Right now, I just want to enjoy that."

Just then, my phone buzzed. "Hi, Mr. Blaze, my name is Tom Lexington of the *NorthShore News*. We are working on a series of stories about retail theft in the area, and I was given your name as an authority on the subject. Would you be willing to write a guest column for us about how the public can protect themselves?"

Apparently, the *NorthShore News* did not validate the credentials of their "authoritative sources."

"Hi, Tom, thanks for the offer. Can I come by your office tomorrow, and we can talk more?"

"Sure, Blaze, that sounds great. See you at 10 a.m. We're excited to have you on our team."

"Who was that?" Mary asked as I hung up the phone.

"Just a reporter looking to talk to me."

"Okay, dear. You're still going to see the therapist I mentioned, Dr. Gassman, right?"

"I will. I'll call tomorrow and take his earliest available appointment."

We got home, and I quickly changed before Jeffrey came to pick me up for dinner. One of the best perks of having an Uber driver for an older brother was when we got together, I got a free chauffeur. Jeffrey picked me up, and I let him choose the restaurant. He told me we were going to Stafani's downtown, knowing I'd never say no to Italian.

I grabbed a gin and tonic at the bar while Jeffrey parked. When he got back, he tapped me on the shoulder repeatedly like a little kid with something very important to say. He whispered in my ear, "Santori's here."

"Who?"

Once we were seated, Jeffrey filled me in.

"Tony Santori is one of the meanest men on the planet," Jeffrey began. "He and his family are based in New Jersey and illegally own much of the East Coast. Think of the nastiest Italian mobster you've ever seen in a movie, and then multiply his evil by ten. That's what Tony Santori is."

"What's he doing here?"

"He and his underlings made Chicago their number-two territory six years ago. In that time, they quickly became one of the city's dirtiest syndicates thanks to their involvement in drugs, extortion, and gambling. Right now the only group that competes in power is the Deli Boys and Solomon Feldman."

Another perk of having Jeffrey around was he knew current events better than anyone. He went on for most of the meal about Santori, saying he was one of the reasons crime in Chicago was worse than it had ever been.

I finally asked Jeffrey to point out Santori to me, and as I glanced across the restaurant, I did a double take.

"I know that guy," I whispered to Jeffrey.

"You know Santori?"

"No, not him—the big guy sitting next to him. That's Mr. Refrigerator from the WCC!"

"Mr. Who?"

With all of Jeffrey's talk about Santori, I realized I hadn't told him anything about my new endeavors. The drain of the day was catching up with me, so I cut the story short and figured I'd fill in the details later.

"Jeffrey, remember Saturday mornings growing up watching all those crime stoppers on TV?"

"Of course. We had our matching cowboy hats, sheriff badges, and toy guns. All we wanted to do was get the bad guys."

"Exactly. Well, I've become a detective and want to stop crime in this city. I broke a big case today and am in the process of building my team. Want in?"

"You know it!"

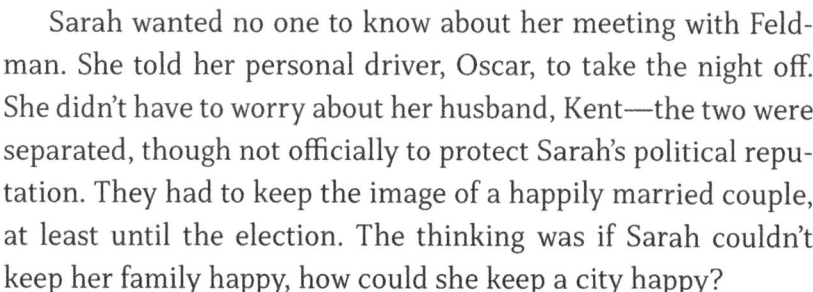

Sarah wanted no one to know about her meeting with Feldman. She told her personal driver, Oscar, to take the night off. She didn't have to worry about her husband, Kent—the two were separated, though not officially to protect Sarah's political reputation. They had to keep the image of a happily married couple, at least until the election. The thinking was if Sarah couldn't keep her family happy, how could she keep a city happy?

She left her condominium a little after nine with no makeup, dressed in a poofy black jacket and black baseball cap to hide her identity, and walked several blocks in the frigid Chicago cold before hailing a cab to the South Side deli. Once there, Sarah walked around the building to its back entrance, took a breath, and entered the home base of Solomon Feldman and his Deli Boys.

Nearing six-feet tall, Sol had more hair on his chest than his head. He routinely wore his top three shirt buttons open and proudly displayed a gold chain adorned with a Star of David. Sol did not deal in small talk, and that night was no different.

"What do you want?" he said as Sarah entered his office.

"I want a truce," she said. "I know you loved your nephew, and I know you want revenge on whoever was responsible for his death."

"You're damn right I do," Sol interrupted, standing up and slamming his fist on the desk. "I'm not agreeing to any truce. Besides, I already know it was one of Santori's men."

Sol informed Sarah the Deli Boys had already put out $100,000 contracts for Carter and a guy named Mel Weinberg.

"It sounds like Carter put the hit out, but Mel was the one who killed Charlie. They'll learn no one messes with the Deli Boys or our family and gets away with it," Sol said. "Then, once I deal with them, I'm going after Santori himself."

"What does Santori have to do with those two?" Sarah asked.

"They both work for him," Sol explained. "At least Carter does. I don't know who the hell Mel is, and frankly I don't care. I'm putting out a two-million-dollar contract on Santori. He's not taking Chicago from me." Sol walked around the desk and got right in Sarah's face. "How dare you come here and ask for a truce? You may be running for mayor, but don't ever forget I'm the one who runs this city!"

This was about as far off from Sarah's intended goal as could be. She needed to think fast and get creative. If the Deli Boys started killing Santori's men, the city would be in turmoil. Then she had an idea. She wanted to show Sol she cowered to no one, but she also wanted to show her support. Most people would have backed down after having the city's most ruthless criminal threaten them—but not Sarah. She stood straight and looked directly into his eyes.

"What if you and your boys don't seek revenge?" she asked. "What if Santori delivers Carter and Mel to you on a platter?"

Sol stepped back as he thought through that option. "That's an intriguing offer. I'm interested. I'll give you three days. They can kill Carter, but I want Mel alive. You hear me? I'm going to make that bastard suffer." Sol walked back to Sarah, mere inches from her face. "If he's not here in seventy-two hours or if Santori kills him without me, I'm going to hold you personally responsible. If I don't get to punish Mel, I'll punish you instead. Are we clear?"

Sol stared fiercely at Sarah. She took a deep breath, then nodded in agreement.

She walked out of the deli and almost collapsed. What was she thinking? She had just promised Santori would deliver two of his own men, and she'd never even met the guy before. The way Sol threatened her played over and over in her head. She shivered from the fear of his words and the gusts of cold wind on her face.

Standing on the dark street corner on the city's South Side, Sarah felt powerless and alone. She'd been independent her whole life, but at that moment, she needed to be consoled. She needed a shoulder to rest her head on. Kent wouldn't do. She needed someone who would listen and not judge her. She pulled out her phone and texted her friend Annette, who said she could come over.

With no taxis in sight at 11 p.m., Sarah resorted to Uber and hoped the driver wouldn't recognize her. When the car arrived, she quickly ducked in and pulled her hat low over her face.

"You Sarah?" the driver asked.

"Yeah," she whispered. "West Coast Club Condos, please."

"No problem. I'm Jeffrey, by the way."

Sarah did not respond. She had been to the West Coast Club Condos before but only for meetings. Riding up the elevator to the penthouse, she nearly hyperventilated, worn down by the added pressure of her new task. She got out and found Annette waiting, arms out, ready to console her friend. They walked inside and over to the couch, where Sarah fell into Annette's arms. Sarah didn't know how long they were there just sitting in silence, but she didn't care.

"Do you want to talk?" Annette eventually asked.

Sarah smiled as she sat up and told her friend about her encounter with Feldman. She explained her predicament with Carter and Mel, but Annette cut her off.

"Wait a minute. Mel Weinberg?" Annette asked.

"Yeah. Why? Do you know him?"

"Know him? That bastard raped me—twice!"

Annette went on to explain how she was in her twenties and naïve when she first met Mel. Her parents tried to dissuade her from spending time with the man, but she was hooked. She thought it was love. Then he raped her. Nine months later, a son was born. The same thing happened two years later.

Annette's tumultuous relationship with Mel left her numb in every regard. She swore off dating once she and Mel split, and she dedicated the next twenty years to raising her two boys as best she could.

When she met Jerry Meade a decade ago, it was a major turning point in her life. Jerry was a self-made man, good-looking, and kind. He built a successful plumbing business over the course of three decades and remained busy with a staff of more than one hundred employees and trucks running all over Chicago. You couldn't miss the trucks—*Plumbco on the Go* plastered on the side with a picture of Jerry's face smiling underneath.

Jerry's success afforded him the opportunity to purchase the penthouse suite atop the West Coast Club Condos. He was generous with his money and provided Annette with stability and comfort, two things she'd never experienced. She had no need to work, so she always had an eye out for unique volunteer opportunities.

That was how she and Sarah first connected.

Annette had met Sarah at an early campaign rally, and she listened to Sarah's goals and felt they aligned with her own vision for Chicago. Annette volunteered for the campaign and took on more responsibilities as she and Sarah got to know each other. The two became friendly as they talked through strategy and tactics. They joked with one another and began to talk and text outside of work as a friendship quickly developed.

"Anyway, back to your predicament," Annette said.

"I don't know. Now I want to kill that son-of-a-bitch Mel myself for hurting you."

"Thanks, but that won't help with your Feldman problem."

The two talked through possible scenarios, but neither saw any other option besides Sarah pleading with Santori to do as Feldman wished.

With Jerry out of town at a plumbing conference and it being past midnight, Annette invited Sarah to sleep in the guest room.

"Thanks for coming over," she said as they parted.

"My pleasure," Sarah said. "Thanks for being a great listener."

That night, I dreamed about Dick Tracy comic books. Talk about a guy always on a quest for finding the bad guys. My dream took me back to my childhood, to my mom smiling as she handed me a new comic book and lovingly patted me on the head.

Suddenly, a blaring alarm started ringing. Was it in my dream? I opened my eyes and still heard the repeated chirping. I jumped out of bed to check the doors. The ringing continued. What was going on?

I went back to the bedroom, and that was where I found it.

My cell phone was mockingly reminding me it'd been thirty-six hours, and my sexual mood was over. Mary asked what the ruckus was about, and I said I mistakenly set an alarm for the middle of the night.

"Everything is fine, dear," I said. "Go back to sleep."

I lay down, ashamed and annoyed. *Twenty-eight pills wasted. What an idiot!*

My dreams eventually took me back to my mom. I was in my bedroom, and she was in the doorway watching me read my new comic book. She stood watching for who knows how long. Then she was lying next to me, giving me a warm hug that felt like it could last forever.

Then things got weird.

Her hands moved to my chest as she began to kiss my neck. What was happening? How did this dream turn into a nightmare? I opened my eyes and realized it was Mary doing the hugging and kissing. She was all over me! I looked at the clock and discovered I was in a new nightmare. It was 7:23, three hours and twenty-three minutes past my mood's expiration! What should I do? Could I stall for the quick-dissolving pill? Could I get up and kill twenty minutes waiting for Mr. Wonderful to jump into action? I didn't keep many secrets from Mary, but my pill artillery was one, and now I was stuck on the front lines defenseless. I would have to fend for myself.

Mary's lips moved from my neck to my mouth, and I tried to keep her there as long as I could. She pulled away and started slowly kissing down my chest. I figured I had about twenty seconds before my secret was exposed, so I enjoyed the last kisses before confronting the reality of life as a seventy-year-old man. Just as she made it down to my stomach, mere inches from seeing Mr. Wonderful looking not so wonderful, she came back up and whispered five words in my ear that sprung my body into action in a way I'd never felt before:

"Take me, Blaze. Take me."

I heard those words and thought, *Blue pills be damned.* I felt like I could conquer the world as I took Mary on the ride of a lifetime and cashed in every raincheck.

Afterward we collapsed in each other's arms, and Mary leaned in closer for an after-lovemaking snuggle. Lying naked in our bed, I couldn't help but wonder if the pill had still left me with some juice post-expiration or if that was all me, an idea that brought a proud smirk to my face. I gave Mary some pecks on the top of her head and told her how great she was. I gave her a hug and a wink as I got up to complete my victory lap. It was off to the showers and then time to start a new day.

4

I did some quick pamphlet reading before heading to my meeting at the *NorthShore News*. I grabbed my supplies list and planned on purchasing everything after my visit to the newsroom.

I hadn't looked at my cell phone since it had woken me last night and was stunned to see nearly a dozen voicemails waiting for me. Most had the same flavor of surprise that I was a detective. My friend Wilt said he was happy I finally added some excitement to my post-retirement life. My brother, Jeffrey, said he read the *NorthShore News* article about my act of heroism yesterday in exposing the theft ring and confirmed his commitment to Team Blaze. My favorite message was from Bloomingdale's security wondering if I was interested in an open position on their team.

I thought about Wilt, a lifelong friend who could be a valuable addition to Team Blaze. He had free time and was not afraid to go to extremes to find a solution to a problem. He was also retired, although I'd never been sure what he retired from. The fact he read the article and was proud of my work showed he recognized this detective thing could be for real. I texted to ask if he wanted to join the team.

Sure, he wrote back. *I'm retired and bored to death. Why not become a detective?*

I was greeted at the *NorthShore News* by an attractive receptionist who was probably in her forties, and her black-framed glasses couldn't hide her eyes scanning me up and down. Her top was tight, and her skirt hugged her long and slender legs. I took a breath and said I was Detective Blaze, there to meet with Tom Lexington.

She looked seductively at me before picking up her phone.

"Mr. Lexington, a Detective Blaze is here to see you. Okay, I'll send him in."

The receptionist eyeballed me again before gesturing to a door to her left. Two women were standing in front of it, and they, too, stared at me as I walked toward the door. Was this what life would be like as a detective? Feeling debonair, I straightened my tie and puffed out my chest.

One of the women motioned for me to come closer.

God, I love being a detective, I thought as I approached her. She leaned in to whisper in my ear.

"Your fly is open."

Dammit.

There wasn't any way to play that off, so I thanked her as I quickly fixed my zipper and made my way into the newsroom. Tom Lexington was waiting by his office door with a copy of that day's paper, and there I saw my face smiling back, just above the fold. He handed the paper to me as I gave him a Blaze card.

He motioned me to his couch and waited as I read the story about yesterday's crime bust. In fifty years as a businessman, I never once had a newspaper story written about me. My name never even made it in the paper. At least now my first appearance wouldn't be on the obituary page.

"This is a great write-up, Tom, really nicely done."

"Thanks, Blaze. I'm glad you appreciate good writing. That's what I want to talk to you about. But first, tell me more about you. How did Blaze become Blaze?"

"Mr. Lexington," I began.

"Please, Blaze, call me Tom."

"Okay, Tom. I've built my career on the simple ability to observe people. It sounds boring, but the general public's observation skills have numbed thanks to technology and cell phones in particular. People are spending millions of dollars for homes with a view only to sit on their couch looking at their devices. Candidly, no one stops to smell the roses anymore. I challenge you to take a walk later today and leave your phone in your pocket or here at the office. Just walk and look around. Take in the sights. You'll be amazed how liberating it feels and how few people are doing the same thing."

"Well, your observations are really what I want to discuss," Tom said. "Our readership is worried about the rise in crime in our area, and I think many of our readers could be reassured with advice from an expert like yourself. What do you think about writing a weekly safety column for us?"

I sat silent for a few seconds. "Tom, I appreciate you considering me for that important role, but I must pass, primarily because I'm looking to increase my caseload. I would, however, be willing to write one piece for you on why I think theft has become more prevalent in our retail stores."

"I respect your honesty, Blaze. Go ahead and send it when you have it ready, and we can go from there."

I stood up and shook Tom's hand. "It's my pleasure. I'll have it for you later this afternoon."

"Thanks, Blaze. And thank you for helping keep our community safe."

I smiled and walked out of his office, through the newsroom, and past the receptionist, who I'm pretty sure winked at me.

Across the street from the newsroom was an office supplies store, where I got almost everything from my supply list. Paper clips? Check. Pens? Check. Notebooks? Check. I even found a frame for my certificate. I approached the checkout with a shopping cart filled with supplies when I thought of a late addition.

"Excuse me," I said to the woman at the register as I started to pull my purchases out of the cart. "Do you sell handcuffs?"

The woman looked at me. She looked behind me and to her sides, as if hidden cameras were trying to capture her being pranked. She finally looked back at me, I think more confused than offended.

"No, sir, we do not sell handcuffs. But there's a store around the corner that does." With a suggestive smirk, she leaned toward me. "They sell great vibrators too."

Tony Santori stared at his office's full-length mirror, straightening his sport coat and adjusting his signature pink pocket square. His six-foot-three frame cast a menacing presence, accentuated by his sharp jawline and slicked-back hair.

He nodded approvingly at his reflection, then went next door to lead his daily briefing. In the room were nine of Santori's soldiers talking about the next day's Valentine's Day plans or last night's big money-making All-Star basketball game. When Santori walked in, all conversation stopped. All movement stopped.

Everything stopped for Tony Santori.

It had been six years since he'd first come to Chicago, but his reign in the Windy City was thirty years in the making. The Santori family came to power in New Jersey decades before thanks to their involvement in drugs, extortion, and gambling, and Tony Santori's father had the foresight to plant a seed in Chicago should the family ever want to expand its operation. That seed was the West Coast Club.

The Santoris became anonymous investors when the pristine facility was built, and today it doubled as the family's Chicago headquarters. Santori had his own private wing of the massive complex, complete with meeting rooms, an office, and an underground apartment.

"Good morning, men," Tony said as he sat down at the head of the table. "As you know, I came here six years ago to help spread the reach of my family's power, and in that time we've put a near stranglehold over this city."

"Hell yeah," several men shouted.

"All that stands in our way now of total city control is fuckin' Feldman and his delinquent Deli Boys," Santori continued. "But their reign will end, and it will end soon. The day is approaching when we will rip this city from Feldman's dirty hands and own Chicago for ourselves!"

The men's enthusiasm began to rise. "Damn straight," shouted one. "Fuck Feldman," yelled another.

Tony had his group inspired. They were ready to do whatever he asked of them. "You know the goal now," Tony said. "Keep that goal in mind and be ready. This town will be ours!"

The men erupted in cheers. Santori then went over the previous day's profits and introduced the crew to his cousin Enzo, an accomplished illegal money manager from New Jersey who would help further expand the family business. The meeting was followed by an elaborate brunch catered by the WCC.

Tony picked up his fork to dig into his South Side Scrambler when Vito, a guard set up outside the room, entered and tapped him on the shoulder.

"Hey, boss, you know that woman running for mayor, the Cutler broad?"

Tony stared at Vito; he looked at the eggs, bacon, and peppers on his fork, then back at Vito, wondering why this knucklehead chose now to ask about city politics.

"Yes, Vito, I've heard of her. Now can I enjoy my eggs, please?"

"Boss, she just called and said she needs you to call her right away," Vito said. "I promised the bitch I'd give you her number, but then I said that Tony Santori calls who he wants when he wants." Vito was clearly proud of this last line as he stood up and puffed out his chest. "Here's her number."

Tony put his fork down and grabbed the scrap of paper. The rest of the conversations around the table quieted. Tony looked at the number. Frustrated, he pushed back from the table and went to his office to call. The audacity of Sarah Cutler to tell a man like Tony Santori what to do had him annoyed but also intrigued. If that lady had the courage to make such a demand, then she just might be someone he should get to know a little more. After all, having the future mayor of Chicago as an associate of his could only mean good things for business.

He dialed the number and waited.

"Hello?" Sarah answered.

"Tony will see you," Tony said of himself with his deep Italian accent. "Come to the West Coast Club at 3 p.m. You will be escorted to Tony's personal area."

I needed a monotonous task to clear my mind and prepare myself to write my *NorthShore News* article. Counting my business cards seemed like a good option, so I began stacking them in piles of ten. Fifteen minutes later, I stacked the last card and discovered a problem. Not only did this last stack only have seven cards, but I only had ninety-six stacks. I was missing thirty-three cards! *Did someone break into headquarters and steal my cards?* Everything else seemed untouched. *Okay, Blaze, slow down. There has to be a logical explanation for this.*

Knowing that a PI needs to be exact, I went back and counted each stack and determined the explanation: Lew shortchanged me. That son of a bitch only gave me 967 free cards! I was going to have to call and give him a piece of my mind.

Feeling cheated, I was readier than ever to write about theft in society. I turned to my computer and pounded at the keyboard in frustration.

IF WE DON'T LOOK AT OTHER PEOPLE, HOW CAN WE LOOK OUT FOR THEM?

Like all of you, I live on the North Shore and have noticed a rise in retail theft. My professional studies prepared me to become a detective and to better understand human nature, and what I tell you is there is a global crisis going on, and it's called self-absorbance.

I'll put it simply: we are all selfish. That's right, I said it. You are selfish, and so am I. Society has become selfish. We don't care about other people like we used to, and honestly, I don't know that we even notice other people anymore. We're all too obsessed with ourselves and specifically our smartphones.

I used to love being able to walk down the street and have a conversation with someone, whether or not I knew them. I got to learn so much by interacting with new people, and I know I grew as a person from those random interactions. Today, though, people don't want to be bothered. Their individual physical space has become far more private, even as their digital lives become more public. People share the most intimate pictures of their children and the insides of their homes on social media, yet ask that same person on the street what they think about the weather, and they'll give you a side eye.

I don't mean to make you feel bad, but it's all our fault. My goal here is to make you stop and think. Now you may wonder what this has to do with safety. Well, I was asked to offer advice on how not to fall victim to the recent string of thefts in the community. As a detective, my most important skill set is my ability to observe, and what I can tell you is society is not observant anymore. We don't look at other people, and if we don't look at them, how can we look out for them?

Where I grew up, my friends and I always had each other's back. We helped no matter the problem. Society doesn't do that anymore. The days of open doors are behind us. When we don't look out for each other, we can't protect or defend one another. We don't see when something bad happens to someone, or we don't notice if someone is in imminent danger. We're too busy looking down at our electronics. The bad guys depend on our self-absorbed society, and as we have closed our doors on each other, we've conveniently opened them to more crime.

As a provider of justice, I will always be looking out for, observing, and protecting our community.

Why have there been so many thefts recently? Because we're not paying attention. How can we feel safer? Next time you go out, don't look down at your phone. Look up at the world around you, and you can be a crime-stopper too.

Blaze. Detective.

I read over the story and sent it off to Tom Lexington. Next, I gave Dr. Gassman's office a call and scheduled an appointment for the following day. They asked for an emergency contact in case something bad happened. *What the hell could go bad while lying on a couch talking to this quack?* I gave in and told them Mary's cell, then hung up and returned to my pamphlet reading.

I learned how imperative it was to avoid personal interest in clients or witnesses. Emotional involvement can hinder facts, so a good private investigator removes all personal feelings from a case. I wondered if there were any exceptions but guessed not after reading that even a simple emotion such as compassion could alter a PI's gut feelings and ultimately the direction of an investigation. The more accurate your gut feelings were, the more successful you'd be.

My pamphlet said you can train your gut by strengthening your other core senses. The pamphlet had pictures of each sense and exercises to further develop them. A good private investigator must be able to address each of their senses individually when on duty. A great PI can do it in their daily life.

I looked over the training techniques for each sense and decided to practice. I grabbed a blindfold, ear plugs, and nose clip, then sat confidently in my comfy corner chair: It was time to begin.

A flurry of questions went through Sarah Cutler's head as she approached the West Coast Club. What should she tell Santori? Should she talk about the Deli Boys' contract on his head? Did he already know about Feldman's demand for Carter and Mel?

For the first time since Sarah had begun her campaign, she wondered if the mayoral seat was worth it. Making promises about what she could do for the city was one thing—she had an incredible team of staff and volunteers who could help accomplish her goals. But this mission—bringing Mel and Carter to the Deli Boys and preventing a feud from escalating between the two gangs—had to be done by herself.

Sarah was met by a tall, rotund man three times her weight. He escorted her down a back hallway, through a locked door, and up a flight of stairs to a mysterious hallway. Sarah had been a member of the WCC for well over a decade, but she'd never seen this part of the club before. She was led into a room where five husky men were playing cards and drinking scotch. She walked uncomfortably past their glaring eyes, noticing each was armed. Sarah had heard tales of Santori's financial involvement in the WCC, and this secret area all but confirmed those stories.

Sarah was led through another door, where she came face to face with Tony Santori, who sat behind his desk as two other men sat back on a couch across the room.

Santori made no attempt to greet Sarah. His face was expressionless and cold, the light casting a harsh shadow over his sharp cheeks. Sarah could tell Solomon Feldman was playing with fire—a big, blazing fire—by putting a contract out on Santori's head. This guy did not seem like one to be messed with. This could get very ugly very quickly.

One of the men on the couch got up and smiled, an act both jarring and refreshing to Sarah. His name was Vince, and he was thinner than the poker-playing goons. He asked what Sarah needed with Mr. Santori. She took a deep breath and began her best effort at brokering a truce. She just hoped Santori wouldn't shoot the messenger.

"Mr. Santori, thank you for seeing me on such short notice, and I'm honored to finally meet you in person," she began. "I wish this meeting were under better circumstances, but I am actually here as a messenger for Solomon Feldman and his Deli Boys."

Sarah watched Tony's fist tighten upon hearing Feldman's name. She took another breath and continued.

"Your men took down Feldman's nephew two nights ago, and Feldman wants you to know he was a good man, a family man. In his eyes, revenge is inevitable. He's already told his boys he'll pay two million dollars to whoever is able to kill you first." Sarah expected Santori to start fuming on hearing this news, but he took it as a compliment and flashed a small grin. She worried that was an even scarier reaction.

"I've asked Solomon to remove the contract from your head and hold off any sort of revenge if you would willingly deliver a peace offering to him."

Vince spoke up. "Why you?" he asked. "Why are you in the middle of this?"

"As you know, my mayoral campaign is built on a pledge to reduce violence in this city. The last thing I want to see is more bloodshed. I know there is a budding turf war between you and the Deli Boys, but I think I know a solution where we all can win."

Sarah's confidence began to grow. She had always been able to read her audience and craft her message to align with their interests. She was transforming into Candidate Cutler before their eyes, sharing the idealism that already inspired so many of her followers.

"Chicago is up for grabs right now, and I believe I can deliver a city where we all can flourish—me, you, and Feldman. There is a lot of money out there just waiting to be taken, and I believe I can give your family the notoriety you crave while still making Feldman feel he's king of the city. I can't do that, though, if you both are at war with each other."

Sarah had Santori's attention. Now it was time for a big gamble. She asked if she could give her personal take on the situation, and Santori nodded in agreement.

"I've heard stories about the Santori family's rise to power in New Jersey, and I've witnessed your quick ascension here as well. You are clearly methodical in your pursuits and deliberate in your actions, but this murder was really stupid. Why in the world would you kill off someone who was literally family to Feldman?"

The other man who was silent thus far jumped up and shouted, "You bitch, who the hell do you think you are, coming here—"

Tony held out his hand for the man to shut up. He gestured for Sarah to continue.

"Tony, if I may call you Tony, do you have a niece or nephew? Imagine what you would do if an enemy took their life. That is what your men did. Your boys Mel Weinberg and Carter slaughtered Charlie Myers, but why? What good came from inciting a war with the top dog in town?

"Anyway, I presented this peace-offering idea to Mr. Feldman, and he agreed that if you deliver Mel and Carter, he'll remove the contract and not seek any further revenge. His only request is that Mel be alive on delivery. Is that something that can be arranged?"

The room was silent. Sarah looked for any sort of reaction from Santori. After a minute, he stood and addressed her for the first time.

"Ms. Cutler," he said, "you have some big balls coming in here and talking to Tony this way. Tony respects that. Not many people can call Tony *stupid* and live to talk about it. Tony's heard your message and will take it under advisement." Santori gestured toward the door.

"Do we have a deal?" she asked.

Santori again gestured to the door.

Sarah thanked him for his time and turned to leave. As she opened the door, she heard Santori start talking with the two men from the couch.

"I don't give a flying fuck if Feldman thinks he's king of the city," Santori said. "That man will regret putting a hit out on me."

Sarah left the room more unsure than when she entered it. Had Santori agreed to the deal? Had this worked, or did she just make more of a mess? Calling Santori *stupid* to his face was not part of her plan, and as she was escorted out of the club, she realized two crime families might now be looking to kill her.

Sarah called her driver, Oscar, and asked him to pick her up. She then made a call she hoped she'd not regret, a common feeling from the past twenty-four hours. She speed-dialed her son, Lance, a lieutenant with the Chicago Police Department, but as usual, the call went straight to voicemail.

"Lance, honey, I need a favor, and I need you not to ask me why," she said after the beep. "Please keep an eye on your daily reports of bodies showing up, either explained or unexplained. I need to find a Mel Weinberg and a Carter..." She paused, realizing she didn't know Carter's last name. Oh, well. "Anyone named Carter. Please do not ask my reasoning; let's just say it's a newly developed campaign strategy. Love you."

As she hung up, she worried Lance might find her name in the report instead.

That night, Mary and I shared dinner and a bottle of Cabernet. I told her I was meeting with Dr. Gassman the following day.

"I'm proud of you for opening up about your post-retirement blues with someone," she said.

Retirement blues? I've never been happier than I am right now. "Who knows?" I joked. "Maybe he'll tell me I'm perfectly normal."

Mary rolled her eyes. "Maybe."

Mel Weinberg, now two days removed from murdering Charlie Myers, was officially freaking out. He'd called Carter fifty times by then and not one response. Carter always told Mel to assume he was dead if he didn't respond within twenty-four hours, which is what Mel now found himself doing. The two men had a good run, but Mel was not mourning Carter's death so much as dreading his own.

If Feldman got to Carter that quickly, why hadn't he taken Mel out yet? Mel feared the answer.

Desperate to get out of town, Mel pulled a scrap of paper from his wallet. His associate had given it to him when they first started working together and said to only use it if there was an emergency. On the paper was a phone number that apparently belonged to Tony Santori. Mel was sure Santori had no idea who he was, but he had no other options. He figured he'd tell the boss he was a longstanding colleague and ask for help disappearing.

Mel dialed the number and was met with a grunted "huh" as someone answered.

"Hello," Mel whispered, "I'm looking for Mr. Santori. My name is Mel Weinberg."

"Hold on," the man grunted back.

Mel wasn't sure what he was holding on for, but after a forty-five-second wait, he found out.

"Mel, this is Tony Santori," a surprisingly jovial Tony Santori said. "Sorry for keeping you waiting. How can I help you today?"

How did Tony Santori know who he was?

"Hi, Mr. Santori. I know we've never met, but I was told to call you in an emergency, and, well, I need a favor. I need some money and a plane ticket. Maybe some new clothes too. I've been in Chicago for too long and need to get out of here. Need to start somewhere new."

"Mel, you're family," Santori replied. "Anything you need, I'm happy to provide."

"Family? Really?"

"Of course! Why don't you meet me tomorrow afternoon at the West Coast Club? Come here early before the sun rises so no one sees you. We'll leave fresh clothes for you in a bag under the name Mike Paselli. I'll have someone come find you a few minutes before our meeting."

Mel was speechless. Who knew his work was so appreciated?

"Thank you, Mr. Santori, I really mean it. You have no idea how stressed I've been. I'll see you tomorrow."

"It's my pleasure," Santori responded. "Enjoy your morning at the gym. Relax, take a shower, and have a good steam. You'll feel better."

5

I woke up ready to conquer a new day, even though I had no interest in seeing Dr. Gassman. Hearing his name made me think I was seeing a lower GI doctor, which frankly sounded more exciting than talking with a shrink, but I told Mary I would, and I'm a man of my word. I decided to start my day with some pamphlet reading, followed by a trip to the West Coast Club for a workout before facing the Gassman.

Before I could start, my phone rang with an unrecognizable number.

"Hello?"

"Mully here."

"Oh, hi, Detective Mully. It's Detective Blaze."

"No need for the formality, Blaze, just call me Mully."

"Gotcha, Mully. How are things going with the Chinese theft case?"

"Blaze, thanks to your quick wit, we've got nine members of the crew. The rest of them ran, my guess all the way back to China."

I couldn't tell which surprised me most: the fact my work led to the arrest of nine people or that Mully thought someone could run to China.

"What about the big guy, Andy Wong?" I asked.

"Blaze, we almost had him. We stormed his hideout and missed him by five minutes, at most. I don't know if he's laying low here or heading back to China, but we'd never been as close as we got, and that's all thanks to you."

"Just doing my job, Mully."

"Blaze, I do have to warn you, though. While we were searching Wong's place, we found a piece of paper with your name on it. I don't know how he knows about you, but be careful. Andy Wong is not someone you want as your enemy."

"Thanks for the heads-up, Mully. I'll watch my back." *I always wanted to say that.*

"No problem, Blaze. Happy Valentine's Day."

Shit.

With all my investigating, I forgot it was Valentine's Day! If Mary found out I forgot, she'd hold it over me for months. I had to plan something big; otherwise, those rainchecks of hers would return, perhaps permanently. I made a reservation at Gibson's, then texted Lester, my jeweler for decades, and told him I needed one-carat diamond earrings for Mary, and I needed them today.

The fact I damn near forgot Valentine's Day confirmed I had too many things going on. I wanted this PI thing to help keep my brain sharp, but I needed to make sure I could still use it for everyday things—like, you know, remembering Valentine's Day. My plan to head to the West Coast Club later in the morning could not have come at a better time. In fact, I decided to just go right then. I'd dedicate time to reading my pamphlets in the afternoon.

I was excited to put all thinking on pause as I entered the WCC and simply use the time for relaxation and rejuvenation. That was what this place used to give me, and I was excited to not investigate and not look around. This was me time, and I was ready to enjoy it.

I walked in and intentionally ignored the café where I used to sit and the hallway that led to the mysterious stairs. Detective Blaze was off duty. My schedule for the morning was simple: shower, short steam, and then the weight room.

I showered off and made it to the steam room door at the same time as a short, grungy man whose belly had never seen a sit-up before. His face looked like a battered boxer's, worn, ragged, and drooping like his gut. This man was clearly out of place. *Forget it, David. Blaze is off duty.*

I held the door open to let him enter first, and he took a seat right by the door, giving me more reason to take my preferred seat on the opposite side of the room, as far away from him as possible. He leaned his head back against the wall, his arms outstretched atop the seats.

The steam was thicker than usual, making it easier to get lost in the warmth. I, too, leaned back to relax, but just as I was closing my eyes, a figure appeared in front of the mystery man. There was movement, and then seconds later, the figure was gone. *What just happened? Dammit, David, forget about it. This is supposed to be you time!*

I tried to relax but kept wondering where the mystery figure went. I finally gave up and decided to get to my workout. I walked out with a "Take it easy," grabbed some water, and made my way upstairs to the weight room. Picturing that man's stomach hanging like a watered-down balloon was all the incentive I needed to do some extra core work and sit-ups.

Waking up with a honey by his side was typical for Tony Santori. Her name was Honey, but all the girls' names were Honey since he never bothered to know more about any of them. Hookers were part of his culture, but he never called them that. He never called them *prostitutes* or even *call girls*. These honeys were escorts. The only difference between the hookers of the past and the escorts of now was about a thousand dollars. Same tricks, just more money. The Santori family was never into prostitution because it was never that lucrative, plus most pimps looked and behaved less dignified than Tony Santori believed himself to be. Tony had his honeys, though, and when he was hunkered down in his secret hideaway beneath the West Coast Club, he routinely was with one—or multiple—of them.

As he gave today's honey a pat on the ass and told her to scram, he put a little extra oomph into the pat, for he knew it was a special day. Sure, it was Valentine's Day, but Tony couldn't care less about all the hearts and lovey stuff. He'd sent flowers to the women in his life with his signature *We are family* greeting because it required zero effort and kept the Italian tradition of strong families intact. But on this day, there was only one person on his mind: his hero, Al Capone.

It was the anniversary of the St. Valentine's Day Massacre, the day that represented Capone's ultimate rise to top gangster in Chicago. It was widely believed that on that day, Capone orchestrated the murder of seven of his enemy's men, signifying he would stop at nothing to become the big guy in Chicago. Tony idolized Capone for his brashness, but more recently he'd grown to respect the authority he carried. Tony wanted to control Chicago like Capone did, and he knew he was getting close.

Tony's grasp on Chicago came from selling money with high interest rates and then turning the profits into legitimate enterprises, like the West Coast Club. Santori also made a sizable portion of his income from the unique assistance plans he offered businesses across the city. Essentially, Santori offered "protection" to small retailers to prevent them from being taken advantage of. It was common knowledge that if a storekeeper rejected the assistance, harm would assuredly come their way.

As a result, businesses were left with a choice: pay the Santori family or get hurt by the Santori family. More than 3,700 businesses across Chicago subscribed to the Santori Protection Plan.

Tony was building an empire, and the only obstacle left to overcome was Sol Feldman and the Deli Boys. Tony knew that on the anniversary of Capone's big day, his own handling of Mel Weinberg could go a long way in dictating his own fate and legacy.

That morning's touch-base meeting with his team was small, with many of his men fulfilling their Valentine's Day duties, but the show must go on. *Capone didn't take days off*, Santori thought to himself, *and neither will I*. The first item on the agenda was the money the family made off gambling debts. Mid-February was the slow time of year when it came to sports betting. The Super Bowl was over, baseball was still months away from starting, and basketball was in a lackluster stretch. Tennis and soccer were underway, but neither of those brought in much dough. Hockey was going on also, but unless it was the Stanley Cup Finals, there wasn't much money to make on the ice.

Debts from Super Bowl bets were beginning to pile up, and the longer they remained unpaid, the greater the total balance would become. Tony's concern was the increased debt combined with high interest rates might make it unrealistic to ever see his money, and that idea did not sit well.

That would have to wait because the immediate concern was this Mel and what should be done with him. Should Tony deliver Mel to Sol as an act of good faith? Should he make sure his team took care of Mel for themselves? Should he do nothing? As of now, Tony didn't know, and that bothered him. He was sure Capone would know what to do.

One of Tony's guys told him Mel already arrived at the WCC and received the bag left for him. Tony wanted his men to keep an eye on Mel but from a distance. Tony's men were instructed to escort Mel to Tony's office just before 2 p.m. He wanted to look this scumbag in the eye and then decide who would make him breathe his last breath.

Tony became more agitated by not knowing what to do, and it began to show. "Any other shit I need to know?" he shouted.

"There is actually something else, boss," said one of his sergeants, "and it ain't good news."

"What?" Tony snapped back.

"You remember Andy Wong?"

"Of course I remember the son of a bitch," Tony said. "He's been on our payroll since almost the beginning of our time here in Chicago."

"Well, apparently Wong's gotten greedy. He built up his own crew and was stealing stuff from department stores in the area and then reselling it on the black market."

"What the—"

"That's not all, boss. Apparently, in addition to the theft, he's been smuggling in people from China to help his operation. His scheme got busted two days ago, and although he got away, his name is out there. If he gets caught, our own protection plans may get exposed as well."

"How many people know about this?" Tony asked.

"Unfortunately, this story is too far along to get swept away. The *NorthShore News* had a story about it yesterday. Some guy named Detective Blaze blew up Wong's side hustle. And today he has his own story about how the public can protect itself from crime and danger."

The underling handed Tony his phone with the news story on it. Tony read the headline about the importance of looking out for each other and couldn't help but laugh as he tossed the phone back.

"I'm not worried about some detective. The real concern is Wong. We've got to find him and help get his story straight. He'll pay for his greediness, but right now, let's make sure he can't bring us down."

Tony ended the meeting and sent everyone away. He'd let his crew work on the Wong situation. Today, Tony's focus was Mel. As he paced around the now-empty room, he kept repeating the same question: what would Capone do?

Valentine's Day was jam-packed for Sarah and the Cutler campaign. The mayoral election was a month away, and although Sarah was leading in the polls, she knew one wrong move could be the difference between Mayor Sarah Cutler and Sarah Cutler, the woman who ran for mayor.

Sarah had spent an hour on the phone the previous night with Annette, telling her about her face-to-face with Santori. She feared she'd placed a target on herself by angering him, but that fear subsided when he texted to say he would talk to Mel at the WCC and then be back in touch about her request.

Annette, happy to support Sarah but uninterested in hearing anything about Mel, focused on the campaign's busy Valentine's Day. Sarah had three rallies scheduled for the day, each of which was to focus on the genuine feeling that people wanted change.

Chicago had been ridden with violence during the current administration. Each weekend, the city's streets were blanketed with blood, and the public was growing increasingly frustrated with the mayor's inaction and inability to control the crime. Sarah was confident a campaign built on reducing crime was her ticket to the mayor's office. Her goal from then until the election was to drive home that point.

Sarah had never clearly explained how she would make the city safer, but acknowledging a problem existed was the first step to recovery. Personally, she knew the only way to follow through on her campaign promises was to keep Sol Feldman and Tony Santori happy, and in less than a day, she had made bold promises to both men, promises she had no idea how to keep.

The first rally of the morning was outside a local hospital, where hundreds of medical personnel waved "Safer with Sarah" signs and shouted cries of "We want change."

"I want change too," Sarah responded from the podium. "I want a city I feel safe in. I want a city where we can walk around and not have to constantly look over our shoulders. I know some of my competitors are running on claims to cut your taxes. I'll be honest. That's not what I'll do. But what I will do is repurpose that tax money and use it to promote more positivity in our city. Updated parks. New cultural events. With a safer city, we can all come together and enjoy Chicago once again. To do that, I need your help. Vote for me, and we can all feel safe again. Thank you, Chicago. I love you and happy Valentine's Day."

In her limo on the way to the second rally, Sarah got a call from her son. Thinking it was him just wishing her a happy Valentine's Day, she let it go to voicemail. But when he immediately called back, she knew something was wrong.

"Hi, Lance, I'm almost at my next rally. Is everything okay?"

"Hey, Mom, you know those two guys you told me to look out for? Well, one just showed up dead."

"What!? What do you mean?"

"We just got a call a minute ago from the West Coast Club that a Mel Weinberg had died in their steam room. The WCC is in my precinct, and we've got guys on the way."

Sarah's car pulled up to the rally as her mind raced at top speed. "Hold on, Lance," she said.

Her job was to deliver a living Mel Weinberg to Sol. Now what would happen? And how did he die? Too many questions took over her thinking. What if Santori went ahead and killed him as retribution? What if Sol had broken his promise and sought out revenge of his own? Either way, the other would not be happy, and that might just be the start of a cold-blooded war—the last thing she needed.

Sarah heard a knock on the window and saw Annette trying to look in and see what the holdup was. Sarah lowered the window.

"Just a second, Annette. I'm finishing a call with Lance."

She rolled the window up and returned to her son. "Lance, do you know how he died? And who is in charge at the scene?"

"All the caller said was a guy was dead in the steam room. They said his face looked like the guy wanted in that nightclub murder. As for who is on the scene, Skip is running point. He should be getting there right now."

Sarah knew Skip well. He and Lance were good friends as kids. Skip missed a lot of school in order to go fishing with his uncle, and some kid—maybe Lance—gave him his nickname. All these years later, it still stuck.

"Lance, who all knows about this?"

"Just me and our receptionist, who personally brought me the information."

"Okay, Lance, that's good. Real good. Now, baby, I need to tell you something. I'm so proud of you for all you've done as an officer and for this city and for getting where you are today. But you need to sweep this one under the rug. Call it a suicide and let it be."

"Mom, I can't do that!" He brought his voice down to a whisper. "I could lose my job for that. What the hell is going on?"

"Sweetie, you know I wouldn't ask unless it was important. This guy was bad, and a lot of people will be happy he's gone. The world is a safer place than it was an hour ago."

"Mom, I need more than that."

"Lance, I'm telling you, to protect this city from a civil war the likes of which we've never seen, we need this to disappear."

"We?"

"Yes, son. We. If we don't handle this correctly, you and I both could be in a lot of trouble."

"Hold on."

Sarah waited for several minutes as the crowd outside her car began chanting her name. She was getting impatient. Finally, he returned.

"Okay, Mom, it's done. Skip is there, and he'll call it an assumed suicide, but we won't confirm it until later."

"Oh, son, that's perfect. I love you. You have no idea how much this means to me."

"You're right, Mom, I don't. I expect you to tell me more later. Oh, there's one more thing."

"What is it, Lance? I really have to go to this rally."

"Skip said he found a syringe."

"Make it disappear."

Sarah hung up, fixed her hair, took a breath, and walked out of her limo with a politician's smile as the crowd of hundreds chanted, "Safer with Sarah."

Vince spent the past six years working his way up the Santori family ranks and was now considered the most trusted member not related by blood. God forbid, if Tony were ever taken down, it would be Vince who'd be chosen to take his place. Tony's trust in Vince was secure, although misaligned, as his right-hand man was an undercover FBI agent. Vince was dedicated to this role from the outset, and it had cost him any semblance of normalcy. No family. No friends. No day-to-day life beyond the Santori family.

Vince appreciated that Santori headquarters were at a health club and routinely filled his free time jogging on the quarter-mile indoor track. His position in the family afforded him unique knowledge about the facility, such as the fact that four security cameras focused on the track, but only three worked. His understanding was that ownership thought four cameras for such a small space was overkill but never took down the extra one. He was grateful for that since it meant he could use an alcove off one corner of the track to meet with a fellow undercover agent. This was the best way to keep Vince's people on the outside informed about the happenings of Vince's people on the inside.

Today, Vince had a lot to share. He told the agent he didn't have a good feeling about the ongoing hatred between the Santoris and the Deli Boys. He was worried Tony would try to stage an all-out blitz to destroy the Deli Boys and make Chicago his for good. He also said he'd heard rumblings that some war council would take place soon and include the senior-most leaders of some other shady Italian families. Lastly, he told the agent about Mel, who apparently murdered Charlie Myers and was wanted by both families. He shared that Mel was at the WCC and scheduled to meet with Santori at 2 p.m.

Approaching sirens put an end to the conversation. As Vince tied his shoe, ready for another couple of laps, he asked the agent to investigate Mel and see if there was any useful info he could share before the afternoon meeting.

"On it," the agent said as Vince turned to continue his jog.

The next time Vince passed their meetup corner, he saw the agent mouth Mel's name, then pretend to slit his own throat.

Marc was worried about his best friend. David invited him to join Team Blaze, but Marc didn't think it was going to be anything serious. He figured they'd get together on Friday nights and watch *Perry Mason* reruns or something like that—not do actual detective work.

Instead, David had gone off and risked his life to stop

criminals selling stolen goods, and now he was writing in the newspaper like he was some sort of authority on crime. How far was this detective thing going to go?

Worried about the safety and sanity of his long-time friend, Marc called Mary and discovered she, too, was concerned.

"The good news is I was referred to a psychiatrist about David's situation, and David has agreed to visit with him later today," Mary said. "Apparently, in rare cases, people who retire can suffer from DVP."

"DVP?"

"Delusional visionary perception. Imagine a guy who is hypnotized and told to believe he is a famous singer. That guy can not only overcome forms of shyness but can pull on an inner talent hidden deep within him to sing."

"You mean like those people who are in distress and find a way to pick up cars or other heavy objects that wouldn't be possible unless they were in some sort of trance?"

"Exactly."

"Well, how long do these trances usually last? I'm worried David is going to get himself hurt."

"Me, too," Mary said, "but we have to let it play out for now. I talked to the psychiatrist, and he specifically told me not to break this obsession of David's, for without proper medication, the depression associated with his real reality of being retired could make him suicidal. The doctor asked me to find something else he would enjoy. David told me we're going to dinner tonight, and I'm going to tell him I just booked an exciting Mexican vacation for us to get away from everything and just relax. Hopefully after this appointment, he will have been prescribed meds."

"I hope so. Where is David now?"

"At the West Coast Club. He decided it would be good to work out before seeing the doctor, and I agree. Besides, how much trouble can he get himself into there?"

I finished my workout and had just enough time for a shower before my meeting with the shrink. A large crowd prevented me from getting to the locker room and showers, so I quickly went to the lobby, where I found Henry, a fortysomething-year-old who'd been an attendant since he was in high school and who was always a fun source of gossip.

"Henry, what's going on over there?" I asked.

"You didn't hear? A guy offed himself in the steam room. I don't know all the details, but apparently, he'd been trying to hide from the cops and just couldn't take it anymore."

I darted back to the locker room just in time to see the man I shared the steam room with be carted off on a stretcher. I saw part of his face as the white sheet put over him stuck to his stomach bulge. I found a police officer, introduced myself as Detective Blaze, and was met with immediate respect. Instantly, I thought back to my pamphlet reading.

"Who is in charge here, and why haven't we roped off the area yet?" I asked.

"My name is Detective Skepper, but you can call me Skip. I've been instructed by my boss, CPD Lieutenant Lance Cutler, to clear the scene as quickly as possible. No roping off this one."

"Why?"

"Look, man," Skip said with a whisper as he leaned in close, "I'm just doing my job and following orders. This is an elite club, and apparently management didn't want to disturb its members any more than this incident already has."

I kept Skip talking, trying to get as much information as I could. "So who was the guy?"

"His name was Mel Weinberg. He was wanted for the murder of that club owner Charlie Myers. We'd tried to take him down for past crimes but never were able to. You never want to hope a guy dies, but this one was a lowlife. From what I understand, he had a wife and a daughter. You've got to feel for them, but what are you going to do? I guess he thought suicide was better than a life in jail."

"You don't need to give me all the details, but between cop and detective, how did he do it?"

"Assumed suicide. Let's just say he overstayed his welcome in the steam room."

My gut feelings were on overdrive—something was seriously messed up here. First, who kills themselves by staying too long in a steam room? What a long and agonizing way to go. I'd have to check the autopsy to confirm how he died. Second, what was the rush? I get the desire to appeal to the clientele, but a guy just died, and already officers were clearing the area, and the janitorial staff was cleaning up the evidence. Did anyone take pictures?

"Were there any witnesses?" I asked.

"None that we know of. He was the only one in the room when a custodian found his body."

"Skip, you've been a big help. Thanks so much. Hey, would you mind giving me the wife's contact information? I always make a point of offering my condolences to loved ones."

Skip didn't bat an eye as he gave me the phone number for Mel's wife, Amber. I ran to my locker to get dressed and grab my phone to take pictures, just to make sure I had an accurate visualization of the crime scene. I skipped the shower and quickly changed as I got a call from Gibson's confirming my reservation for that night.

I was back to the steam room in ten minutes, but by then, the whole scene was cleaned up. You'd have had no idea a dead guy was there less than an hour before. The steam room was already in use again, which meant I'd have to return later for pictures; taking them as guys sat around naked would go against my vow to act more normal at the club.

I needed to sit down and process everything for a minute. It was almost time for my shrink appointment, but forget Dr. Gassman. I had more important things on my mind. I went to reliable Table 16 and tried to think through everything that had happened.

The suicide story sounded ridiculous, so that meant Mel must have been murdered. *Wait a minute! I saw that figure in front of him. I bet that was the killer!* The steam was so thick, I bet they didn't even see me there. But if he was killed, why was it being called a suicide? And why the rush to clean up the scene? I thought back to my pamphlets. Investigators get more accurate information immediately after a crime takes place as opposed to a few hours later. I needed to talk to a witness, but right now the only witness was me. I pulled out my notebook and jotted down as many details as I could remember:

- *Someone appeared in front of Mel.*
- *The mystery man seemed to put his left hand over Mel's mouth and had something in his right hand.*
- *It was hard to see, but I guessed the mystery guy was about six feet tall.*

I was going to need more information, so I returned to the front desk to talk with Henry, my trusty source for club intel. I gave him a handshake with a fifty-dollar bill inside and asked if he could tell me more about the victim.

"I'd never seen him before, but he was already in the locker room when I went in a couple minutes after 6 a.m. He was just sitting in there like he was waiting for somebody."

"That is weird. Did he have any belongings with him?"

"Well, it's interesting. When I got to my desk, there was a duffle bag with a note that said, *Mike Paselli is my guest. Please leave this bag for him in locker 232.* That seemed a little odd, but you wouldn't believe all the odd things I've seen at this place. There was this one time—"

"Henry, what about the duffle bag?" I interrupted, although on another day I'd have loved to hear more of Henry's tangent.

"Oh, yeah, so I went to the locker room, and this guy was just sitting on a bench. I asked if he was Mike Paselli, and he said yeah, so I gave him the bag and a lock. I know the note said locker 232, but this guy seemed pretty slimy, and I wanted to keep my eye on him, so I gave him locker 202, which I can see by looking through the reflection in that hallway painting." He gestured to the bland painting on the wall. "You know I take pride in my work here, Mr. Blazen, so the last thing I wanted was someone causing trouble. And now look what happened. He killed himself. I told you I didn't have a good feeling about him. Plus, why the hell did he say his name was Mike Paselli? I heard the police say his name was Mel. That's strange, isn't it?"

"That is strange," I agreed. "Did you tell any of this information to the police?"

"That's another weird thing. No one asked about anything, including the locker."

I reached into my pocket and pulled out a hundred-dollar bill. "Henry, I need a favor. Can you keep a secret?"

"I guess so."

"Henry, I've been dabbling in detective work. You've pointed out several things that seem odd about this case, and it would really help if I could look inside that locker."

"No way, Mr. Blazen. I'll lose my job."

"You can call me Detective Blaze, and you don't need to do anything, Henry. Just leave the master key on the desk here and bend down to tie your shoe. I will take the key and head to the locker room just like I would any other day. I'll leave all the clothes and the bag itself. All I want to see is if there are any nondescript items that may help piece some of these weird details together."

Henry looked right. He looked left. He looked right again. Then he slowly reached toward the board of keys underneath his desk. He looked both ways again, daintily put the key on the desk, then frantically ducked out of view. Acting was not in his future.

I grabbed the key and checked out locker 202. In the locker, I found the duffle bag, and in the bag, underneath a shirt and pants, I found a wallet, gun, holster, and a small black leather notebook with a few scrap sheets stuffed inside. I grabbed everything but the clothes and stuffed them in my bag, then left and placed the key back on Henry's desk. I assumed Henry wasn't there, but it turned out he was still bent over, tying his shoe for the eighteenth time. I passed him my phone number and told him to call if he remembered anything else.

My brain was going in so many directions as I left the club and got in my car. Just one month ago, I had sat in this parking lot wondering what the hell I was doing after getting pulled over daydreaming about being Magnum. Now here I was with a dead guy's wallet and gun, and I found myself asking the same question: *What the hell am I doing?*

I looked in the mirror, took a breath, and then smiled. I knew exactly what the hell I was doing. I was doing what I was destined to do. I was the good guy taking on evil. Something was not right, and I was going to figure it out. This was no fantasy, dammit—this was real, and I was right in the middle of it.

6

Sol Feldman sat on his throne inside Morry's Deli with half a pastrami sandwich and a potato pancake in front of him. Usually his lunch would be twice as big, but that night he'd be sitting *shiva* for Charlie Myers, and afterward, he and the family would feast in honor of his nephew. Sol had the sour-cream-covered pancake on his fork when his cell phone rang.

"What do you want?" he grumbled.

"Boss, they killed Mel! Santori's crew took him out at the West Coast Club."

"What?"

"Boss, I thought you said that Cutler broad was going to have Santori deliver him alive."

"She was."

"Well, what are we going to do? We're not going to just let them get away with this, right? Those bastards killed Charlie, boss."

"You don't need to remind me, asshole. Just let me think."

Sol hung up the phone. He pounded his fist on the table before flipping it over with rage. He didn't know who he was more pissed off with, Tony Santori or Sarah Cutler. He had lifted the contract off Santori's head because Cutler said she could get him to deliver Mel alive. Now there was no way for Sol to bring justice to his nephew's killer.

He walked out of the dining room and into his back office. He needed to think this one through. He and his boys would surely retaliate, but in what way? Sol wanted to be strategic with his planning. He also wanted to honor his nephew. After a few minutes, he grabbed his phone and called his crony back.

"Don't do a thing right now," Feldman said. "I'll get a plan in place, but today is about Charlie. Let's celebrate his life, and tomorrow I will get my revenge and rip the guts out of Tony Santori myself."

Tony Santori rarely left the club, but that morning's updates combined with the questions about Mel weighed on him, making him feel claustrophobic. He took his private exit onto the roof of the club to enjoy a few minutes of refreshing February Chicago air. He could not figure out the right move with Mel. Sure, he could do what the Cutler woman suggested and have the future mayor be indebted to him, but doing that would look weak. It would look like a peace offering with Feldman, and Tony didn't want a peace offering. Tony wanted the city to himself.

"What would Capone do?" he asked himself. Then he grinned. "I know what Capone would do. He'd kill the bastard. That's what Capone would do, and that's what Santori will do. Forget Cutler. What's she going to do to me? I'm Tony Santori, and I make the rules around here."

After his stirring pep talk, he called Vince. "Vince, I've made up my mind. After our meeting with Mel this afternoon, take him out of here and kill the son of a bitch."

"Um, boss," Vince said, "we have a problem."

"Oh, for fuck's sake. What now?"

"Mel's already dead."

"What? How the hell did that happen?"

"I don't know, boss. I'm trying to find out more now. In the meantime, you better lay low."

"Call everyone back to the club now. I don't care if it's Valentine's Day. Family meeting in one hour!"

Tony ducked inside and back into his conference rooms, fuming. The room quickly filled as Tony paced back and forth, thinking through the optics. Someone invaded Tony Santori's space and made a fool of him, and Tony Santori would not stand for that.

"Okay, so what the fuck happened?"

Jermaine stood up. He was Tony's top security detail. "Boss, the police are calling it an assumed suicide. He was found dead in the steam room. No weapons, no witnesses, just a dead body."

"Who the fuck kills themselves in a steam room?" Santori shouted. "And what's an assumed suicide? I want answers, and I want them now. Find out who dared to shed blood in our space, or you'll all die from assumed suicide. Now go!"

I was still sitting in my car outside the WCC when I pulled out my phone and noticed two voicemails that represented the highs and lows of this Valentine's Day. The first was Lester, who said he had several magnificent pairs of earrings to show me. The second was from Gassman's office. A monotone lady who sounded like she'd rather watch paint dry than call me said I missed my appointment and that I would be charged nonetheless. She went on to say my emergency contact—Mary—was notified and that both she and the doc were concerned this critical introduction was missed. The doctor I wasn't worried about. Hopefully, Lester's magnificent earrings would help tide Mary over.

I went to the jewelers and hoped to get this showing over with as quickly as possible. I brought my gym bag inside to keep its illegal contents as close to me as possible. We went into Lester's office behind the showroom for a more VIP experience. Out came a tray of earrings that all looked the same to me. Lester knew I'm sold with words, so he started telling me about the marvelous pair, the exquisite choice, and on and on.

"Lester," I said, "this may sound random, but do you know anything about guns?"

"Of course," he said, patting his side to indicate he had one on him. "You can never be too careful in this industry."

Because I trusted him, I put my gym bag on his desk and opened it. "What can you tell me about this one?" I asked as I cautiously picked up Mel's gun by the barrel and handed it to Lester. "In all my years, I've never shot a gun. Is this one even loaded?"

Lester looked at me curiously but was excited to show off his expertise. "It's a Smith & Wesson 442. It's dated but extremely accurate and easy to conceal. In a pinch, it's definitely dependable. Most importantly, in your case, the safety is currently on, and yes, it's fully loaded." He handed it back to me. "You know, David, you really should get a license to carry and practice at a range before taking that out anywhere. What do you even need it for?"

"An old friend gave it to me as a retirement present, and I'm still trying to figure out why. I didn't know if it was meant for protection or if he was trying to symbolize something. The fact you called it 'dated' makes me think it was just a joke."

I put the gun and the stupendous one-carat diamond earrings in my gym bag and thanked him for his help.

Back at headquarters, I browsed through my pamphlets. Unfortunately, there didn't appear to be anything about possibly witnessing a murder. There was a section about personal safety, but rules about gun licensing or how to shoot a pistol were not included. I read that the best way to stay safe and out of harm's way as a PI is to not get on a bad guy's bad side. I thought about what Mully said about Andy Wong having my name in his house and worried I was already on Wong's wrong side.

That was enough pamphlet work for the day. I needed to learn everything I could about Mel Weinberg. I searched his name online and discovered pinpointing his enemy would be a challenge. Who wasn't his enemy? This guy was suspected in multiple murder cases, and he'd been arrested a half-dozen times for everything from battery and threatening an officer to aggravated assault and grand theft.

I opened my gym bag and locked the gun in my bottom desk drawer. I pulled out Mel's leather notebook and found a bunch of names and phone numbers but nothing identifying their significance. It seemed like a makeshift address book with no rhyme or reason to the order.

As I flipped through, a ragged piece of paper and business card fell out. The card was for an insurance agent, but I was more interested in the paper. Written in pencil and with smudges all over was a list of all the different ways Mel would harm someone and the corresponding prices for committing said harm. I wondered if there was any way to misinterpret what I was looking at, but Mel had stick-figure drawings next to each line to depict the harm. Plus, on top of the page, he had written, *Price for Pain: Mel Weinberg's going rates*. The guy literally had a menu of his offerings. I was sure there was a lawyer or two who would have loved to submit this document into evidence.

I put down the notebook and skimmed through his wallet. Behind a frequent eater's card at a local all-you-can-eat buffet were two torn scraps of paper. One was to the locker Mel's stuff was in, and the other had a row of numbers on one side. I guessed it was a phone number but whose? I turned the paper over and gasped out loud, a sound I'm not sure I could make again if I tried. Written in lowercase letters was the name *tony santori*. I was surprised Mel would so clearly advertise this number as Santori's, but then I remembered his Price for Pain menu. Discretion was not something Mel excelled at.

I returned the scrap and looked at the insurance card. Based on its crispness, my guess was Mel obtained it recently. But why? There was only one way to find out. I gave Ricky Schwartz a call.

"This is Ricky Schwartz, and I'm your man. No matter the insurance, I've got a plan."

Being a former salesman myself, I figured the best way to get information from Ricky was to make him think I was a potential customer. "Hi, Mr. Schwartz."

"No Mr. Schwartzes here; my friends call me Ricky. Now what can I do? Your problem easy or tricky?"

Oh, I liked this guy. He was driving a train right through Bullshit City, and I was more than happy to hop aboard.

"Hopefully easy if I can work with you, Ricky. My buddy Mel Weinberg was bragging about the policy you just gave him and told me I should get the same one. Is it still available?"

"Oh, you mean the quarter-million ten-year policy benefiting his wife? Yeah, I can get that one for you, but for a few bucks more, you get double the coverage. You'd need to take a physical like Mel did—but come on, speaking among friends here, if your boy could pass it, anybody can. The doctor was kind of surprised. For a guy who smoked so much and exercised so little, Mel's heart was as strong as someone half his age. Genetics are a crazy thing."

"That sure is the truth. Hey, Ricky, since we're speaking among friends, how does the insurance provider deal with suicide?"

"All insurance providers have a clause in their policies that states if a policyholder commits suicide within three years of the policy start date, the beneficiary will not be paid. So don't kill yourself anytime soon," he said with a laugh.

"Good advice, Ricky, thanks. Let me chat this through with my wife, and I'll be back in touch."

I hung up before overzealous Ricky realized he'd never asked my name or for any contact information and therefore would have no way to follow up with me.

―

"You bitch!"

That wasn't quite the welcome Sarah Cutler expected to hear from her husband on Valentine's Day. Come to think of it, there it was in the late afternoon, and those were the only words she'd heard from him all day. Yes, their marriage was a sham, but still, he could have had the decency to make a "happy Valentine's Day" call, send a "Have a great day" text, heck, even a "Thanks for birthing my child" email would have been appreciated.

The two had had a quick minute alone in a back hallway of the Waldorf after Sarah's final rally of the day and before a cocktail dinner for her biggest donors. Kent always accompanied her at these types of events. They had to keep the image of a happily married couple, at least until the election. Kent was lowkey and always willing to play the game for the cameras but not that night.

"Good to see you too," Sarah responded. "Happy Valentine's Day."

"Oh, cut the crap, Sarah. I know politics is dirty, but today you crossed the line." He grabbed her by the wrist and pulled her in close, his voice down to a whisper. "You asked our son to cover up a murder. I don't know why, and frankly, I don't care. You put your political ambitions before your family today, and I will not stand for it."

"Kent, I don't know what you're talking about."

"Bullshit. I talked to Skip today, and he told me Lance had him hide evidence and rule a man's death a suicide before being able to investigate. I know our son, and he would never do something like that on his own. There's only one person with the power to make him choose bad over good, and that's you. And guess what? If Skip confided in me about this, you can be sure he's already talked to other people. You've ruined Lance's good name. You flushed our son's career down the toilet, and I will not sit by and let you get away with it. I'll smile for the cameras tonight, but Sarah, you have forty-eight hours to come clean, or else I'm exposing you as the ruthless menace you are."

He let go of her wrist and furiously stormed away, opting to spend as little extra time with his wife as possible.

Tony Santori was still fuming hours later with Vince at his side when Jermaine returned to the office. It helped having the head of security be the size of a refrigerator; it was usually easy for Jermaine to get any information he wanted. He told Tony what he'd found out so far:

- Many people had entered and exited the steam room that morning, but no one came forward as a witness.
- The bag left at the front desk for Mel was given to him, but it wasn't in locker 232 as had been instructed. Instead, it was found on the other end of the row of lockers. The only person who might have known why was Henry Jackson from the front desk.
- Henry's shift ended, but Jermaine called him back, and he was currently waiting in the Doom Room.

"That's good work, Jermaine," Tony said. "Now let's go find out what Henry has to say for himself."

Tony, Vince, and Jermaine left the office and entered the

Doom Room. Imagine a conference room, only there's no table, no chairs, and no windows. It was four black walls, a black floor, and a black ceiling. A collection of lesser-ranking members of Santori's squad stood guard inside, their presence more of an intimidation factor than anything else. Sitting on the lone chair directly in the middle of the room was Henry, his legs visibly shaking as he tried to calm his nerves.

Tony entered the room, closed the door, and walked right up to Henry, bending down so their faces were inches apart.

"Henry, do you know who I am?"

"Yes, sir," Henry responded quickly. "You're Mr. Santori."

"Damn right," Tony said.

He grabbed his pistol and slapped Henry across the face with it, knocking the grown man to the floor and sending one of his teeth flying to the other side of the room. As the blood rushed from Henry's mouth, Tony slowly walked over to the tooth, looked back at Henry, then stomped on it for good measure.

Henry pulled himself up and sat back on the chair.

"Now, Henry," Tony began, "it is my understanding you were given a bag and delivery instructions this morning. Is that correct?"

"Yes, Mr. Santori, that is correct."

"Then tell me, Henry, why is it the bag you delivered was found in a different locker?"

"Oh, I can explain that, Mr. Santori. The gentleman you're referring to—I believe he went by Mike Paselli—did not appear to reflect the class and dignity often associated with the WCC. I didn't like the looks of him, and I was worried he'd cause trouble for the club, so I gave him the other locker so I could keep an eye on him."

"Oh, I see. And did you keep an eye on him?"

"He stayed in the locker room for a while. Not doing anything, just kind of staring into space. Then he got up and left, and I didn't see him again until the medics wheeled him past me on a stretcher. I thought I was doing good for the club, Mr. Santori. I'm sorry if that was the wrong decision."

"I understand, Henry. I do," Tony said as he gave Henry a gentle pat on the cheek.

Tony asked Jermaine to get Henry some water and a cloth to stop the bleeding. Jermaine left, only to reappear seconds later with the items as well as a chair. Tony took the chair and sat down in front of Henry.

"You know, Henry, I remember seeing your name on the wall as employee of the year a few times. You must be good at what you do."

"Thank you, Mr. Santori."

"Oh, and I heard you are a father. I'm sure Terri and Hanna are adorable."

Hearing Tony Santori recite his daughters' names horrified Henry. It horrified Vince as well. He'd seen this tactic used in countless interrogations by the FBI. The agency calls it R&R—relax and reveal. When a suspect is more comfortable, they tend to let their guard down and share more information than they otherwise might want to. Vince was impressed with Tony's delivery, but he also knew this conversation would not have a happy ending.

"Henry, I confess I've never borrowed a locker here at the club. How does one go about doing that?"

"Well, Mr. Santori, that person would come to me or my colleagues and ask for a locker. We have them fill out a slip with their name and contact information. Then we write the locker number down and give them a key and part of the slip. They must return both the slip and the key when they leave; otherwise, there is a fine."

"I see. That's interesting, Henry. So it sounds like it's in a person's best interest to keep their slip with them and not lose it, correct?"

"Yes, sir. It's a two-hundred-dollar fine if you don't return the slip. I know it's old-fashioned, but management likes it that way."

"I understand. What I don't understand is this—and I'm hoping you can help me out. My associate Jermaine did a sweep of the men's locker room a few minutes ago and found the bag that you gave to Mike Paselli this morning. The problem is the bag didn't have his slip in it. In fact, it didn't have any identification in it. No wallet. No money. Just a pair of clothes. So, Henry, I ask you—and I suggest you think carefully before you answer this question—where are those missing items?"

The room was silent as Tony got up and slowly paced beside Henry. Then he pulled out his pistol again, sat down, and held it two inches from Henry's forehead.

"Henry," Tony continued, "would Terri and Hanna want you to be silent right now? You have my word that no physical harm will come to your daughters if you tell me who cleaned out that locker. But you need to tell me now."

Henry looked at the gun and knew his life was over. In the face of death, he had to protect his loved ones. Tears rolled down his face, and he continued looking at the end of the pistol in front of him.

"It was David Blazen. He did it."

"Who is David Blazen?" Tony asked.

"He's been a member of this club for years. He told me he was a detective and that I should call him Detective Blaze. He was investigating the steam room death, so I gave him a key to the locker. I don't know what he took from the bag, but he had his hands in it."

Tony silently got up, walked behind Henry, and massaged his shoulders for a moment. "Thank you, Henry. You did good."

Tony instructed Jermaine and the other men to escort Henry

to the room across the hall. There they took Henry's phone, bound his hands behind his back, and told him they needed to verify his story. They said they'd be back once everything was cleared up, and he'd be free to go.

Tony remained in the Doom Room. "Didn't I already hear the name Detective Blaze today?"

"Yeah, he was the one who exposed Andy Wong's operation," Vince said.

Jermaine and the others returned.

"I don't like this Detective Blaze," Tony said. "He's messing around in places he doesn't belong. Kill him before he learns too much."

Vince had taken an oath years ago to protect the lives and maintain the safety of the citizens he served. Over the past six years, he'd seen lives lost and people stripped of their possessions, but it was all in the battle of scum versus scum, evil killing evil, so Vince could justify it. He figured Tony would likely kill Henry; that seemed unavoidable, for he knew too much. But this Blaze guy, did he really need to die too? *He's just getting his rocks off pretending to be a detective. Is he actually causing any harm?*

Vince wanted to protect the detective, but he himself was close to totally exposing the Santoris. He needed more time to confidently bring the entire enterprise down. He needed to know more about some war-tribunal meeting he'd overheard Tony refer to, so he couldn't raise too many red flags by defending Blaze. Vince eventually came up with a solution that could work for everyone—and keep Blaze alive, at least for the moment.

"Boss, I have an idea," Vince said. "Right now, we don't know anything about what happened to Mel in the steam room. All we know is he was there, and then he died. What if this Blaze guy knows something?"

"Good point," Tony said. "Let's find him, torture him for the info, and then we kill him."

"Respectfully, boss, I'd suggest waiting on the killing-him

thing. We know he had his hands in Mel's bag. What if he took something important and already passed it off to someone else? Maybe he was working for Feldman and the Deli Boys. Hell, maybe he's the killer. Or maybe he's working for the police, and he's already given evidence he found to them, and they're perched outside waiting for us to react."

Tony was getting agitated by the uncertainty. "What do you suggest, Vince?"

"The way I see it, there's only one way to get this Blaze guy closer and find out what he knows."

"I know," a frustrated Tony said. "I already said we should torture the snitch."

"No, Tony," Vince said. "Don't kill him. Hire him."

"What?"

"That's right. Hire him. The guy is a detective. Hire the asshole and pay him to do our dirty work. Let Blaze find your killer. If he refuses, kill him. If he can't find the murderer, kill him. And if he does find the murderer—"

"Kill them both," Tony said with a menacing grin.

"I'd give him some space for now," Vince went on. "Have Jermaine put a tail on Blaze so we can follow him from afar, but I think we should wait a day or two before letting him know we're on to him."

"Fine," Tony said. "Now enough of this talk. It's Valentine's Day, and it's dinnertime. I've got the back room at Matalli's, and Momma Matalli is making her homemade lasagna. Nothing like lasagna to celebrate the anniversary of the Saint Valentine's Day Massacre."

Vince left the room first. He had to figure out a way to notify his outside team about David Blazen and the need for around-the-clock protection. He didn't see Tony signal for Jermaine and two of his guys to stay behind.

With Vince out of the room, Jermaine turned to Tony. "What about the locker guy in the other room?"

"Do you have his phone?" Tony asked. Jermaine handed it to Tony, who scrolled through the contacts. Within seconds, he found what he was looking for. "Okay, here's what we're going to do. Grab the explosives from the storage closet and stuff the backseat of Henry's car with them. Set them to go off right at ten thirty. I'm going to set the alarm on his phone for ten twenty-eight."

"For what?" Jermaine asked.

"For this dead man to be my messenger. I don't care what the fuck Vince said about giving this Blaze guy some space. I want him to know I'm on to him."

I looked at the clock and realized I'd have to break for dinner soon. I wanted to try to connect with Mel's wife, Amber, and fortunately she answered on the first ring.

"Hi, Amber, my name is Detective Blaze," I said, wondering if she'd been informed of Mel's passing.

"You must be calling about Mel's death."

That answered that question. "I'm sorry for your loss, Amber. How are you doing?"

"You know, I knew Melvin spent time with bad people, and I knew he'd done bad things, but I never thought he would take his own life. I could see him dying from a heart attack but not suicide."

"We rarely see it coming," I said, trying to comfort and learn more information at the same time.

"There was so much ugliness about Melvin's life, but behind all of that was a man with a kind and gentle heart. I saw it eight years ago when we first met. I was a nurse at Presbyterian St.

Luke's Hospital, and Mel came into the ER on a stretcher, beaten up pretty badly. We started talking, and quickly we began opening up to one another. When he was released a few weeks later, I invited him over, and a relationship began to develop. Three years later, we were married at City Hall."

"That's sweet, Amber."

"What's sweet is how Mel treated our girl, Summer. He found his fragile side the moment she was born. He'd spoil her rotten, but it wasn't long before he was back gambling and collecting unpaid debts. The majority of his time was spent on the streets or in cheap motels. I watched our marriage fall apart but made no demands. Once he went back to gambling, he was out of our lives, except for when he'd occasionally leave a wrapped present for Summer outside our house."

"When was the last time you saw him?"

"I don't even remember. Early on, we were inseparable, but once he reentered his dark phase, we saw him less and less. We were out at dinner three years ago, and he broke it to me that he didn't feel comfortable being around me or Summer anymore. He said if word got out he had a family, we'd be in terrible danger. He said he loved our little girl and didn't want her to grow up in fear. That's the kind of guy Mel was, and that's how I'll always remember him."

"That's a great memory, Amber."

Her train of thought broke. "I'm sorry, Detective, I have no idea who you even are, and here I am sharing my world with you. What was it you called about?"

"Of course, silly me. First off, I truly wanted to call and see how you're doing." Before I could go further, she began to cry.

"How am I doing? I'm scared. I'm scared for me and for Summer. I know Melvin said he wanted to look out for us, but from what I know of his lifestyle, he had debts that needed to be paid. And with him now unable to repay them, I'm worried the people he owed will start investigating and find out about me and Summer. Forget that—I'm more than worried. I'm scared out of my mind."

"Thanks for your honesty, Amber. Now let me be honest with you. My name is in fact David Blazen, and I'm here to help you out." I figured it best not to share my knowledge of the mystery man in the steam room, but I needed some information. "Who informed you that Melvin died?"

"You know, it was this kind woman Betty from the West Coast Club. They were very nice about it all, and she even said since he died on their property, the WCC would cover all costs associated with his death and burial."

"Wait, the club offered to pay for everything?"

"Yeah, I was a little surprised, particularly because I have no idea what Melvin was doing at the West Coast Club in the first place. But this woman was so kind. She said that funerals are costly and stressful, and suicides are even more difficult to cope with. She said the WCC wanted me to focus on mourning the loss of my husband, and they would take care of everything else."

"Everything else?"

"Yeah, I just need to meet with someone from the club tomorrow afternoon to go over some specifics."

"That is very generous of the club," I said, surprised.

"It is. To be honest, though, I'm still scared—not just for me but for Summer. Apparently when she got home from school with her babysitter, our door was unlocked, but we always lock it on our way out. There was a black car sitting outside our house with the motor running and two men staring at our house."

"Did you call the police?"

"No."

"That's it, Amber, I've heard enough. I would like to represent you. I need you to call your work and say your husband died and you'll need a few days off. Keep Summer out of school as well. I'm going to have a car pick you up tonight and bring you to my house. You'll be safe here."

"That's very generous of you, Mr. Blazen, but I can't pay for this."

"Don't worry about payment. Let's just keep you safe. Is the black car still outside your house?"

Amber paused to look. "Yes."

"Do you have an alley behind your house?"

"Yeah, we do."

"Okay, great. I'll have a car pick you up in the alley at nine-thirty. Stay out of view of the parked car and leave your lights on. We don't want anyone to know you're not at home. If I don't see you tonight, we'll see each other in the morning. In the meantime, my partner, Mary, will be here waiting to take care of anything you need."

"Thank you, Mr. Blazen, thank you so much."

"It's my pleasure."

I sat back in my chair and realized I had far more questions than answers. Why did Mel get a new insurance policy? If this was a murder, which it seemed like it was, why was it being covered up? How did the other guy in the steam room know Mel would be there? Was Mel the target, or was this a random case of being in the wrong place at the wrong time? If this was someone just looking to kill someone else, why did they choose Mel and not me? And what does Tony Santori have to do with all of this? Oh, and how would I tell Mary we were having a stranger and her four-year-old as houseguests—on Valentine's Day no less?

Those questions rattled around in my head until finally I heard a knock on the door. It was Mary. "Time to get ready for dinner, dear," she called. "We wouldn't want to forget our romantic Valentine dinner."

No, we wouldn't want to forget that.

7

As I changed for dinner, I told myself I needed to make this evening special for Mary. How to do that while also breaking news that I had to visit the club to photograph the crime scene and that Amber and Summer would be staying at our house, I wasn't exactly sure. I finished knotting my tie and realized she still wasn't ready, so I hustled to headquarters.

I texted Jeffrey and asked if he could pick up Amber and Summer and bring them to my house. Then I wrote him, Marc, and Wilt—otherwise known as Team Blaze: *Important meeting tomorrow morning at headquarters. Need everyone there at 8:30. Don't be late. And Happy Valentine's Day!*

I was determined to make the evening one Mary wouldn't forget, so as soon as we left the house, I tried to make the night about her. On our drive downtown, we enjoyed the sweet sound of Tom Petty on the radio as we basked in the beauty of nighttime in Chicago. The moon broke through the clouds and cast a radiant light on the glowing city skyline. The scenery was picturesque, and it felt like one of those nights where nothing could go wrong.

We got to our table, and Mary handed me the drinks menu.

"No alcohol for me tonight," I said. "I know it's Valentine's

Day, but I have to do a tiny bit of work after dinner. I know it's not ideal, but it won't take long."

"Work? David, you're retired. Plus, I was planning a surprise for you," she said as she suggestively looked down at her dress.

"I'm just doing some new friends a favor. It will be fast; don't worry. Now let's just enjoy our evening."

Gibson's has a great Valentine's Day couples' package that we ordered, and as we waited for the appetizer, Mary said she had something important to tell me.

"David, one of the most embarrassing moments in my life happened this morning when I went to pick up our dry cleaning."

"What happened?" I asked, legitimately curious.

"Well, I went to pick up your clothes that I dropped off at the Chins' last week. There were three other customers inside when I opened the door, so I figured I'd wait my turn. Before I could even say hi to Beverly, she screamed at me, 'Uh-uh, not today. You and your clothes not welcome here. Get out!' I asked her what she meant, and she said your detective work disrupted their community. People are furious. David, what did you do to them?"

"What did I do to them? I thought I helped them by exposing a crime syndicate wreaking havoc in the area."

"Well, apparently Beverly doesn't think so. I was speechless. All I could do was turn around and run out as fast as I could. She embarrassed me in front of our neighbors, David. Beverly Chin embarrassed me. What are you going to do about that? And where are we going to take our dry cleaning?"

"Mary, I'm sorry you had to deal with that. I think it was just a big misunderstanding. I'll go visit the Chins myself and try to clear things up."

Our shrimp cocktail arrived, and my reassurances appeared to help Mary, who moved on to critiquing other women's wardrobes. I feigned interest in her review of some woman's dress, but in my head, I was trying to understand why the Chins were upset. Then it hit me. Andy Wong! He must have had some sort of deal going on with the Chins. He had my name at his house, and now he had my clothes. He was going to take me to the cleaners—literally and figuratively.

In an effort to make Mary feel better, I decided it was as good a time as ever to break out my surprise. Just as I reached into my pocket to pull out the earrings, I felt a hand on my shoulder. I turned to find my former client Jerry Meade grinning from ear to ear.

"Jerry, long time no see! How are you, my man?"

I got up to give him the old high-school hug. I'd seen him at the gym over the years, but he had a strict routine there and was intentional about not talking with anyone. It must have been at least ten years since we actually exchanged words—I used to provide him with end-of-the-year gifts for his clients—and as the preeminent plumber in the Chicago area, it'd been inspiring to watch his business grow over the years.

"Things are great, David. Allow me to introduce you to my better half, Annette," he said as his attractive companion graciously smiled a calming, delightful smile. "And who is this knockdown model keeping you company?"

Jerry was always a sweet talker. I introduced him and Annette to Mary.

"Well, we don't want to interrupt you any more than we already have, but let's find a time to get the four of us together some time soon."

"Will do, Jerry. Great seeing you."

After they left, Mary asked where she'd seen him before.

"He's the Plumbco on the Go guy," I told her.

"Oh, that's right. His face is all over the place," she said.

"I remember one year we made him toy trucks that said, 'In a rush so you can flush.' That was one of the best slogans they ever had. Then we had the Plumbco logo on one side and Jerry's face on the other. But enough about Jerry. I don't want to talk about his face, Mary. I want to talk about yours."

"What, do I have cocktail sauce on my chin?" she said as she quickly grabbed her napkin.

"No, dear, your face is perfect. All of you is perfect. You have been so incredible these past few months, and I haven't thanked you enough for that. I really am sorry about what happened at the Chins today, but hopefully this can help you look past it."

I handed her the earrings box as well as a note I had hastily written two hours earlier.

> *Roses are red, violets are blue,*
> *Thank you, my angel, for all that you do.*
> *Since I retired, I've been a pain in the ass*
> *But our love endured, and it's because of your class.*
> *This PI stuff is truly meant for good fun*
> *Between you and it, though, you're number one.*
> *So relax, my sweet goddess, you should have no fears,*
> *Let's see how these diamonds look adorning your ears.*

"A goddess?" she asked with a giant smile and a tear rolling down her face. "Thank you, David." She opened the box and gazed at the earrings. "They're beautiful."

"Not as beautiful as you."

Mary got up and came around the table to give me a kiss. Our steaks arrived just as she returned to her seat. We enjoyed our meal, my goddess grinning giddily like we were newlyweds on our honeymoon.

"I actually have a surprise for you too," she told me as she finished her sautéed spinach.

"Oh, yeah, what's that?"

"I booked a ten-day trip for us in Mexico! Two weeks from

today, we'll be lying on the white sandy beaches of Tulum with margaritas in our hands and our worries behind us."

"Wow, that's great, Mary," I said with a fake grin.

I was worried my work wouldn't allow for that much time off, but this was not the time to discuss it. I had other news Mary was not going to like.

"Speaking of surprises, I actually have one more," I said as the waiter told us our chocolate mousse was on the house and would be out shortly. "We're going to have houseguests tonight."

"Houseguests? We never have houseguests."

"Did I ever tell you of my friend Mel?"

"No. Am I going to meet him tonight?"

"I sure hope not," I said under my breath. "No, Mel can't make it, but his wife and daughter need to stay with us for a day or two. They're the friends I said I'm doing a favor for."

"David, what the hell? It's Valentine's Day. First you tell me you must work late tonight, and now you're saying we're going to have strangers in our house. What's next?"

"I think that's it. It hopefully won't be a big inconvenience."

"Of course it will be an inconvenience, David. What were you thinking?"

"I know this is unexpected. The truth is Mel died, and I'm just trying to help. I told them all about you, and they're really excited to meet you. Actually, I told them you were a goddess."

"Don't give me that goddess shit and take back these damn earrings too," she said as she stood up and threw my stupendous gift right back at me. "David, you have officially ruined this night. I'm grabbing an Uber and going home."

"But what about the chocolate mousse?"

"To hell with the chocolate mousse," she said loudly, bringing the entire restaurant to a silence. "And to hell with you too. I know you skipped out on your shrink appointment today. Thanks for nothing, David."

She took her napkin and threw it at my face as she turned, walked away, got her coat, and left into the dark night.

Well, maybe not my best Valentine's dinner ever.

I found the waiter and paid for the bill. Then I darted out to the car to drive to the WCC, happy to have the romantic part of the evening behind me.

At 9:45 p.m., two of Tony Santori's men entered the room where Henry Jackson remained and assured him if he did as he was told, his family would live long and happy lives. Henry noticed they didn't say anything about his life. Henry was taken to his car, where he was given his phone and his instructions. He was supposed to head south from the WCC, hop on Wacker Drive, and drive through downtown before heading home. As soon as the alarm on his phone went off, he was supposed to call Detective Blaze, whom Tony Santori had conveniently put on Henry's speed dial. Henry was supposed to tell Blaze that Mr. Santori wanted to see him immediately. Henry was not supposed to make any other calls or try anything suspicious. Tony's men would be driving behind him and would not hesitate to shoot if he did not follow the plan.

As I drove to the WCC, I thought of everything I knew about Mel. The story is that Mel committed suicide, but if he did that, why the recent insurance policy? Fast-talking Ricky Schwartz told me Mel's heart was fine, so it couldn't have been a heart attack. I thought back to what I'd seen in the steam room and became more confident the figure I glimpsed was in fact the murderer. Whoever that person was, they were intelligent enough to know how to get away with murder, plus they had enough power to cover the whole thing up. I wasn't sure which of those realizations worried me more.

I checked in at the front desk and did a quick sweep of the lobby, trying to grasp where security's different cameras were in case one of them had captured the murderer entering the building. I went to the locker room, which was completely deserted, with one random exception. Robby Randall and I were in the same class in fourth grade, but he moved away a few years later, and we didn't keep in touch. I knew he was back in Chicago, but it had been years since we spoke, yet there he was. I heard through the grapevine his wife was in a tragic car accident and passed away around New Year's. It made sense he would be alone at the gym on what was supposed to be the most romantic night of the year.

I knew I was there to check out the crime scene, but I wanted to say hi and pass on my condolences. The crime scene could wait five more minutes.

We talked about the good old days and what our kids were doing. It turned out Robby's nephew Bryan was the night manager at the WCC. Bryan had broken up with his girlfriend from Stanford a few days earlier, and Robby promised his sister he'd look out for her boy on Valentine's Day.

"That's why I'm here so late," Robby said. "Well, that and I've got nothing else to do."

"I hear that." I didn't say anything about being at the club in a detective capacity, opting to imply I, too, had nothing better to do. "How long has Bryan worked here?"

"Almost a year. The WCC is lucky to have him. He finished top in his MBA class at Stanford and has a true gift as a leader. He's going to go far."

"Sounds like a great guy," I told him. "Is he around? I'd love to meet him."

"We're going to grab drinks and celebrate our loneliness after he gets off work at eleven. Why don't you join us?"

At first, I was just being cordial, but a conversation with a club manager could introduce a wealth of new information for my case. I had told Mary this errand wouldn't take long, but based on her performance at dinner, I didn't think she'd be staying up for me. Might as well see what I could learn from Bryan.

"That sounds great, Robby. Where are we going?"

"Meet us at Billy's Bar at 11:15 p.m."

"Sounds good. See you then."

Robby walked out of the locker room just as Jeffrey texted to say Amber and Summer were dropped off safely and he saw them make it into the house. *Good. My goddess let them in.* With that reassurance, I breathed a sigh of relief and sat on a bench to think. There I was in the men's locker room, the same place where Mel had taken some of his last breaths a mere twelve hours before, the place where Mel's killer probably walked—determined, focused, ready to kill. Was this guy a hired assassin? Did he kill people for a living? Whatever the reason, he clearly was a man on a mission. Now it was up to me to figure out how he did it.

Tony Santori finished his meal and made the rounds at Matalli's, making sure he had plenty of witnesses who could confirm he was there late into the evening. While Tony socialized, Vince snuck out of the restaurant to call the FBI. He confirmed his code name and was directed to the special unit on the case.

"I don't have much time, so please just listen," he told them. "I need you to research a David Blazen. He says he's a detective and goes by the name Blaze. I think he can be a key asset to us, but Santori doesn't trust him. He wanted his boys to kill Blaze today for getting too close to Mel Weinberg, the guy who died at the WCC. That death also is strange. The Chicago police are calling it a suicide, but who kills themselves in a steam room? Someone's covering up something. I don't know if this Blaze guy was involved or just in the wrong place at the wrong time, but either way, Santori has his eye on him. And as you know, if Tony Santori has his eye on someone, their time left on this earth is limited.

"I convinced Tony to hold off on the execution for now and instead suggested we hire Blaze to find out if Mel was murdered and if so, who killed him. That may have bought Blaze a couple of days, but I don't know anything about this guy. He could be working for anyone. Have the international team try to dig up any info as well. Who knows? He may be connected to the Russians. Get digging but do it conspicuously. I don't want to spook this guy and lose him. For all we know, he could be the missing link to bringing down the entire Santori crime syndicate."

"Got it, Vince. We're on it."

I needed to enter the mind of a murderer. I stood up and imagined myself as a killer. My brow furrowed as I sneered my most menacing sneer, my right hand in my pocket, pretending to hold the murder weapon. *If I was going to kill Mel in the steam room, how would I do it?* There was only one way to get to the steam room, and that was from the locker room. I pulled out my phone to record every step from the lockers to the steam room. I'd made that walk thousands of times, but I was determined to capture every angle and make sure I didn't miss anything.

I crept toward the steam room. If this were a TV show, this was when the dramatic music would cut in and slowly grow louder. I felt I was on the verge of a major breakthrough. My phone was out in front of me, capturing the view as I went, when suddenly the phone rang, nearly giving me a heart attack of my own. I juggled the phone and almost dropped it. *For the love of God, who is calling me at this time of night?* I didn't recognize the number, so I let it go to voicemail.

I bent over with my hands on my knees and tried to catch my breath. It was only then I realized how on edge I was, primarily because my brain and body had been working overtime the past few days. That morning was supposed to be a time to rejuvenate and reenergize, not find myself witness to a murder. I didn't put this much time into work when I actually had work to do. Sure, I went to conferences that lasted all day and schmoozed with clients late into the night, but that was just sales. If I blew a conference off or didn't click with a customer, it wasn't life or death. This was. A man had literally lost his life fourteen feet away from me, and it was up to me to figure out how and why.

I stood up straight and said those words again, this time out loud. "It's up to me."

A tingle shot up my spine. *You're damn right, Blaze. It's up to you.*

That brief encouragement gave me the energy to finish recording the walk and peek in on the scene of the crime. I didn't know what I was expecting to see—it wasn't like Mel was going to be lying there on the floor or the murderer hiding out drinking a cocktail where he committed the crime.

Still, I needed to be thorough.

The steam room was turned off, and it looked like any other nondescript room covered in square white tiles. I snapped a couple of pictures, then checked the time. The gym was closing in five minutes, and I needed to ride my adrenaline through my nightcap with Bryan and Robby.

Henry followed his instructions perfectly. At 10:28, he called Blaze, but there was no answer. He began to leave a message, but at 10:30, an explosion shook the city. A couple getting in their car, a homeless man, and Henry Jackson were burned to ashes.

I made it out of the building just before eleven and went to the car when out of the corner of my eye I saw a group of men in the next row of parking spaces heading toward the club. Did they not know it was about to close? I got ready to holler that they were too late when I looked a little closer. The group consisted of five men, and right in the middle was none other than Tony Santori. I wouldn't have recognized him if Jeffrey hadn't pointed him out at Stafani's two nights before, but I was sure it was him. What I wasn't sure about was why it seemed like he was staring at me. Yes, I was a little overdressed for leaving a health club, but I should have been a nobody to him. What was he looking at?

I kept my eyes on him as I walked to the car, and his gaze remained locked on me for what felt like forever but likely was only a few seconds. Maybe I was just tired, but in that brief moment, it felt like we were connected, not like two people just looking at one another but as if each of us was staring beyond the other's eyes and into the depths of their souls.

I had to push the interaction aside as I drove to Billy's Bar.

My strategy for this get-together was to have Bryan talk, me listen, and keep Robby out of the way. I walked into a nearly deserted bar and spotted uncle and nephew tucked away in a far corner. I slipped the bartender a hundred dollars with my business card and requested he forget the gin in my gin and tonics and double up on whatever my friends in the back corner requested. He gave me a nod and handed me my drink.

Let the party begin.

"There's the dynamic duo," I shouted as I approached their table, raising my glass to them both. "Who says you need a date to have fun on Valentine's Day? We've got all we need right here!"

I wrapped my arm around Robby and raised my glass to Bryan. "You must be the genius your uncle told me about."

Bryan looked at Robby.

"This is David, the guy I mentioned. He and I went to school together a long time ago. We ran into each other at the club and figured we'd reconnect."

"Any friend of my uncle's is a friend of mine," Bryan said, raising his glass back to me. "I'm Bryan, Bryan with a Y."

"I'm David. David with a D," I countered.

We all laughed as we got to know each other. It quickly became clear Bryan did not lack confidence in himself. Within minutes, he told me about being tops in his class and why he was the obvious choice to be named most likely to succeed. His narcissism would suit me well. The waitress came and interrupted Bryan's ode to himself to ask if we wanted another round.

"Another Johnny Walker Black for me and my nephew," Robby said.

"You know what? Scrap that order," I told the waitress. "Tonight's on me, gentlemen. Make those Johnny Walker Blues, and I'll take another gin and tonic."

The waitress smirked, which told me she got the memo from the bartender that this was an active investigation. For good measure, I called out across the room, "Hey, bartender, make it a good pour this time!"

Bryan and Robby couldn't help but laugh. We talked for a while before I turned the spotlight back on my target.

"So, Bryan, how did you get started at the West Coast Club?"

"Well, naturally, I had a lot of offers," he began. "I've always had a passion for physical fitness and athletics, and with the club being so large and so financially strong, it seemed like a great first opportunity that could then be a stepping stone for an even more lucrative career. After all, the GM at the club now makes over three hundred K, and his skill set is nothing compared to mine. I want to be making that much by the time I'm thirty. As of tomorrow, I'll have seven years to get there."

"Oh, is your birthday tomorrow?"

"Actually, it's today," Robby interrupted. "Look, it's past midnight. Happy birthday, Bryan!"

"Another reason to celebrate," I said. "Waitress, another round for the birthday boy if you please." I turned back to Bryan. "So tell me about this skill set of yours."

"Well," he began, "our GM right now is nice and has been at the club since it opened, but—and I hope you don't take this personally—he's old. He's not good at adapting to change, particularly when it comes to technology. A project that takes him six hours, for example, can be done by me in less than six minutes."

"Really?" I asked, genuinely interested as both David Blazen and Detective Blaze.

Bryan jumped on my interest. "Really," he said, bursting with pride as he pulled a leather-bound tablet out of his backpack. "It's all right here. I built my own app for the club that allows me to access anything from the 322,000-square-foot complex right here, from membership information to feeds from all eighty-seven of the club's cameras."

"I told you he was smart," interjected Robby, who was starting to stumble over his words and sway in his seat.

I nodded at Robby. "That's impressive, Bryan. How do you protect all that secure information?"

"Come on, David. How do you protect anything online? It's all password-protected."

As he said this, he logged into the tablet, not worrying about being discreet. I almost spit out my drink as I watched this cocky kid type "I'mNumber1$" to unlock the tablet. He started giving me a tour of all the apps on there, telling me what was for entertainment, what was for news, and so on.

I noticed a poker app I've occasionally used and decided it

was time to go in for the kill. "Waitress, can we have one more for the birthday boy?" I called across the room. From there, I turned to Bryan. "You play poker?"

"All the time."

"Me too. I tried playing on my tablet recently, but it said I needed to update my password. My kids and even grandkids have told me I need to be more secure about my password. I always just use my first and last name as a password for anything."

"Oh, Mr. Blazen, don't make that mistake again. The trick," he said, interrupted by a hiccup, "is to do something that only you'll remember. Like me. I always put a dollar sign at the end of all my passwords."

"Stoppp alllllll dis talk about techno, techno, techno talk," Robby said as put his head on the table.

He was officially of no use to me, and I feared he would become an obstacle instead. I texted my brother and asked him to drive Robby home.

"Go home, Robby. Get some rest. I'll make sure Bryan gets home safely."

"Thanks, Bavid Dazen. No. Blavid Crazen. Bravid . . . whoever you are."

I took Robby under his shoulder and walked him outside, where my Uber order was waiting. Knowing Bryan had even more alcohol in him than Robby, I figured I didn't have much time left. I returned to the table, where Bryan was scrolling on social media, looking at pictures of his old girlfriend. He quickly faded from cocky to sappy, complaining about how she said he cared too much about himself to make room for her in his life. His words were starting to slur, and he was swaying to the same imaginary music his uncle heard.

"Who says that?" he asked rhetorically. "I had plenty of room for her."

"Don't let it weigh you down," I said reassuringly, although clearly his ex was right. "Besides, I bet she didn't know as much about password safety as you."

"David, the dumbass could never remember her password. If her life depended on it, I bet she'd still forget it."

The beat of the music in his head was picking up, and I was nervous he'd sway right out of his seat.

"I always told her to create passwords that she could easily come up with. Like me. For my most important passwords, I always do something I can remember. I start with my first name, but the trick is to spell it backward. Then I add the year I was born. Those are two things I'll never forget. Then, just for good measure, I add a secret symbol at the end, just so I can't get hacked."

Check, please.

"That's smart of you, Bryan. And forget about her. I'm sure you'll be better off. Listen, it's getting late. I need to use the facilities. Then why don't you come and stay at my place tonight? My partner, Mary, would love to meet you, and we have some fun houseguests staying with us."

"That'd be great. I don't want to be alone tonight."

I left Bryan scrolling through his ex's photos while I quickly ran to pay the bill and visit the bathroom. There I made a frantic call to my neighbors' son, Patrick, whose curly red hair and freckles made him look like he was fourteen and not a twenty-year-old in college. Patrick was a geek, plain and simple, but I knew he was back living with his parents and that I needed his help. Over the years, he'd done a variety of odd jobs for me, and the money he received always went toward some new tech gadget. This was the oddest job I had yet, but I was pretty sure it was right up his alley.

"Hello, Patrick, it's David Blazen from next door."

"What? What's wrong? Who died?"

"Patrick, everything's fine. Take a breath. I have a chore for you."

"Mr. Blazen, it's one-thirty in the morning. Call me in the afternoon and I'll knock it out for you."

"Patrick, listen to me. I need this chore done now, and I'll pay you twenty-five hundred dollars for it."

"Holy crap, that's a lot of money. What do I have to do?"

"I need you to copy an app off a tablet for me. I'm hoping it's not too hard, but like I said, I'll pay you well for it. I'm heading home now. Meet me in my backyard in forty-five minutes."

"There's some more info I need to know—"

"I'll go over it all when I see you. Go splash some water on your face. It's going to be a long night. Oh, and I almost forgot—it needs to be done by 7 a.m."

I hung up as I heard Patrick say, "This is frickin' insane."

I left the bathroom and found Bryan standing up, his nose to the wall in a total daze. I needed to get him in the car and continue my interrogation before he was totally useless. His tablet that was so important was left on his stool at the table. I picked it up with one hand and used my other to usher the kid to my car. Once there, I tried grilling him as quickly as I could, this time with a louder, more authoritative tone to help keep him awake.

"Bryan, what goes on behind those mystery stairs at the club? You know, the ones that are guarded?"

"Man, I've never been up there, but there are some scary folks who occupy that space. I try to steer clear from them whenever possible."

"What about all those cameras that you mentioned? Are you able to see upstairs on any of them?"

"Nah, the cameras are angled away there, I guess on purpose for someone. Oh, except for camera twenty-seven."

"Twenty-seven? What's so special about that one? Bryan? Bryan?"

My valuable informant was passed out in the backseat. I spent the rest of the time driving figuring out my next steps. Time was going to be tight.

Once I got home, I left Bryan snoring in the backseat, grabbed the tablet, and ran to the backyard, where Patrick was sprawled out on one of our lawn chairs.

"What in the world could be so important you'd pull me out of bed and fork over twenty-five hundred dollars?" he asked.

"Just listen, Patrick, time is of the essence. I need an app copied off this tablet that is connected to the West Coast Club. There's a lot of video footage from eighty-seven different cameras at the health club that I need to look through."

"Stop right there, Mr. Blazen." Patrick got up, his hands in the air. "I'm not helping you spy on anyone or helping with any perverted fetishes. If you're looking for porn, I'm happy to direct you to some different websites. There's this one where all the women are—"

"Patrick, shut up and sit down. I'm not spying on anyone. There was a murder there, and I want to see if I can find the killer on the club's surveillance cameras. But time is of the utmost importance."

"Okay, then let's get going. I won't bore you with the technical details, but know there will be some limitations in what I can get. What times are we looking for?"

"I want to see everyone who entered the club between six and noon this morning—sorry, yesterday morning. On Valentine's Day."

"Okay. Now given our time constraints, I'm not going to be able to get footage from every camera. Which ones do you need?"

I never asked Bryan how the cameras were numbered. I went

out on a limb and guessed they went chronologically, beginning at the club's entrance. "Let's go with camera three, camera seven, definitely camera twenty-seven, and then just start picking randomly and get as much footage as you can."

"Got it," he said as I handed him the tablet. "What's the password?"

I had to think back to what Bryan had told me and what I saw. I knew how to get into the tablet, but what did Bryan say about the app? His first name spelled backward, then the year he was born, and the special symbol. If he turned twenty-three today, that meant he was born in 1996. Okay, perfect.

"To access the app, the password is Nayrb1996$, and to unlock the tablet, the password is I'mNumber1$."

"Really? What a douchebag."

"That's fair. Will this douchebag know if the app or tablet was accessed?"

"No, unless for some reason they think they've been hacked, and they go back and check. Most people don't think of that, though."

"Okay, well, either way, please make sure you put the tablet back under that cushion here before 7:15 a.m. I'll give you a check in the morning."

We said our goodnights, and I went back to the front of the house, where I helped a knocked-out Bryan through the front door and up the stairs to my daughter's old bedroom.

It was now after 2 a.m. What was supposed to be a relaxing day instead turned into one of the longest of my life. I made my way to the bedroom and emptied my pockets, desperate for a few hours of sleep. I noticed a voicemail on my phone. *Don't do it, David. Just leave it for the morning.* I walked away from my phone, only to turn back around, knowing my curiosity would keep me awake. I pushed play and heard a frenetic voice. It took me a second to recognize it as my pal Henry from the club.

"I'm so sorry, Mr. Blazen, I tried to keep your secret. I was so scared, and they threatened my family, and I just didn't know what to do. I told him you are a detective and all, and now he wants to see you. Tony Santori wants to see you. Mr. Blazen, I'm so sorry. I've got kids, and I had to protect them from that monster. I'm so scared of what he and his men are capab—"

The thunderous blast that came next would undoubtedly haunt me for the rest of my life. The message continued, boom after boom after boom, one explosion after another. Now I knew why Santori stared me down at the club. He knew exactly who I was.

I tried falling asleep, but every time I closed my eyes, I pictured Henry making that phone call. I imagined his children waking up to find out their dad was gone. I thought of Tony Santori and all the horrible things he might do to me. Finally, I fell asleep, but my dreams were no safe haven.

I dreamed of a celebrated lynching held in a town square before hundreds of criminals, mobsters, and gangsters. These men and women represented the worst of humanity. And in the middle of it all, standing on a wooden platform, was me, a noose wrapped around my neck and a wooden placard draped over my chest. The crowd began to cheer. The floor dropped from under me, and there was jubilation as I hung, lifeless and limp. The rope holding the placard fell from my shoulders as the piece of wood plummeted toward the ground. It bounced a couple of times before landing face up, much like a tombstone. There, marking my ultimate demise and failure, rested the placard, worn and battered with five letters burned into it: BLAZE.

8

The phone call came before the sun on the morning of Thursday, February 15, as the FBI special task force to apprehend Tony Santori had questions for Vince, questions he himself couldn't fully answer. Special Agent Clifford Stanley was in charge, and he wanted to know everything he could about the explosion that rocked Wacker Drive late the previous night. While Vince could confirm Santori was behind it, he was as stunned as anyone by its magnitude. He knew Tony would kill Henry Jackson, but why such a big show? His only guess was Tony was trying to deliver a message to Solomon Feldman and the Deli Boys for invading his turf and taking down Mel Weinberg.

"Listen, Cliff, I'll let you know if I can get more info about the explosion, but I need to get going. I have a feeling today will be a long day being with Tony."

"That's fine, but before you go, we have a little info on that David Blazen. No record anywhere of him being a detective. He is a self-made businessman who dropped out of Wright Junior College. I'll be honest, it's hard to find much else out about this guy. He's a frickin' dinosaur."

"What do you mean?" Vince asked.

"He has no social media presence. People today tell us more about themselves and their character on Facebook and TikTok than any of our FBI computers, but he's got nothing. All we can tell from his internet activity is that he turns to AOL for his news. To be fair, he's in his seventies."

"His seventies? Why the hell is he gallivanting around saying he's a detective?"

"I don't know. I've got the Edison boys scheduled to take down the whole grid around his house just after seven this morning, so hopefully we'll get to the bottom of this quickly. The FBI director was not happy to hear about an explosion potentially connected to the primary target of our task force. Director Mangold wants answers, and he wants them quickly. We'll see if this Blaze guy can help us out."

Vince hung up as the severity of his situation sunk in. Not only was his case at or near the top of the mind for FBI Director Thomas Mangold, but the fact that the Edison boys were being deployed for a code 7 indicated this might have been the biggest case on the FBI's plate right then. The Edison boys were legends within the FBI, and this was the first time Vince worked a case where they got involved. The team used power outages to set up surveillance and plant bugs in a subject's house, and they never failed an operation.

When a person's power goes out, their focus is on getting the internet back up and keeping the frozen vegetables cold, not who the people fixing the power are. The Edison boys shut down the power at their subject's house, then wait for them to call the electric company. Once the call comes in, trucks are deployed around the neighborhood, but the Edison boys only enter the subject's house. They are in and out in less than five minutes, giving the residents peace of mind and the FBI unfiltered access to the subject's daily life.

Things were escalating quickly, and as Vince got ready for what he figured would be a long day, he kept asking himself two questions: What does David Blazen know about the death in the steam room, and what the hell was Tony thinking setting off an explosion on Wacker Drive?

"Get the fuck outta here."

That's how an annoyed Tony Santori started his morning as he shooed his honey away. Tony was pissed off, and, worse, Tony was pissed off at Tony. It had been eight hours since he'd sent Henry Jackson to his grave, and Tony knew he overdid it. Yes, he had to make the locker room attendant disappear, and yes, he wanted to send a message to Feldman and the Deli Boys, but it didn't have to be so over the top. Fortunately, he had an alibi for the time of the explosion, but he knew he needed to not let his emotions get the best of him again. Knowing that and acting on it are two different things, as Jermaine found out after knocking on Tony's bedroom door.

"Who is it?" Tony barked.

"It's me, boss," Jermaine said. "We have a problem."

"I'm tired of all these goddamn problems. Get your ass in here. What the fuck is it this time?"

"It's that Detective Blaze, boss. We're not able to get eyes on his house at all. He lives in one of those quiet North Shore neighborhoods with the white picket fences and neatly cut lawns. If the same car circled twice, everyone would know it, and I bet the cops would be there to investigate. There's no way we can station a car outside his place."

"Jermaine, all I'm hearing is a bunch of excuses. Can you get the job done or not?"

"I'll take care of it, boss. We're working on other ways to bug his house, but until then, I've got guys stationed nearby who will tail him whenever he leaves. You can trust me, boss. I won't let you down."

"Good. I want to know what he knows, and don't forget, I want a face-to-face with him, and I want it today."

I woke up at 5:50 a.m. absolutely exhausted, my body drained, yet my mind was already racing. A week before, I was getting too much sleep because I had nothing to wake up for. Now that I was an active detective, I wasn't getting enough sleep because I had too much to wake up for.

I quietly got out of bed and tiptoed to headquarters in my briefs and white T-shirt. I didn't want to make any noises and wake Mary or our houseguests, particularly since the last thing I wanted was to wake Bryan up early and cut short the time Patrick had to collect video evidence from the club.

I opened the news and saw the top headline: *Downtown Chicago explosion kills 4.*

No, that can't be. I clicked on the story and was devastated to see Henry's smiling face staring back at me. *It just can't be.* I didn't want to read any more. This man, a man I considered a friend, was dead because of me. If I hadn't forced him to give me that locker key, Henry might still be alive. His children might still have their father, and those three other people who died could still be here as well. My commitment to seek justice had just gotten four people killed.

This was now bigger than me.

I had valuable evidence in my hand. My phone had Henry telling me who his murderer was or at least who orchestrated his murder. I needed to share it with the police. It was time to call them so professionals who knew what they were doing could take things from here. I had the 9 and 1 dialed but then dropped my phone in fear. *Hold on, I saw yesterday that the Chicago Police Department had no problem hiding things in its investigation of* the steam room death. What if they want to hide this too? Would the CPD take me out for reporting what happened? Shit, what if Tony Santori knows that I know? Would he come after me? If I can't go to the police, then I'll have to keep going with this case myself—well, with my team. I can trust them. Now that I think about it, there's one other person I can trust.

I fished through my wallet until I found the business card I wanted.

"This is Lexington," the *NorthShore News* editor said as he answered the phone.

"Tom, this is Detective Blaze. Sorry for calling so early, but I've got a story for you. I'm investigating a crime, a big one. Wheels are still in motion, but I wanted to give you the scoop so you'd be ready when it's time to run the story. Don't do anything with it yet; otherwise, you might hinder my investigation."

"Okay, Blaze, but why me? And why now?"

"Tom, I've been impressed with your news coverage, particularly when most media outlets are using scandalous headlines just to get a few extra clicks. You seem to care about sharing the news—the *actual* news—and I appreciate that."

"Well, thanks, Blaze, that means a lot. So what's the deal with this case?"

"Did you hear about the explosion on Wacker last night?"

"I was just reading about it now. What a tragic accident."

"Tom, it wasn't an accident. I've got proof. I need you to record this audio."

"Okay, give me a sec," Tom said. "All right, I'm ready."

I hit play and shared the audio of Henry's last words and his ultimate demise. When it was over, Tom confirmed he had it recorded. I went on to tell him about Mel and the steam room, finding the gun and his other info in the locker, and even about the mystery stairs at the WCC. When I reiterated that Tony Santori wanted to see me, Tom cut me off.

"Whatever you do, stay away from Tony Santori," he said. "That is a man you do not want to get on the wrong side of."

"I'm not sure I can avoid him, Tom, but thanks for the tip. I've got to run. There's lots to do today."

"Blaze, I beg you, please stay away from him. If you can't, at least make sure you get your family out of the house. If Tony Santori will blow up a car in the middle of downtown Chicago, he'll have no problem destroying a house on the North Shore."

"Thanks, Tom, I'll do that. Oh, one last thing. If you don't hear from me within twenty-four hours, consider Detective Blaze dead and print everything I just told you."

"Okay, David. Be careful. Don't do anything you'll regret later."

I hung up with Tom and leaned back in my chair, trying to picture all the pieces to this blood-soaked puzzle I'd become a part of. There was Mel and what happened in the steam room. There was Henry and his beautiful life cut short. There was Tony Santori. And then there was me. How did all the pieces fit together?

I reached for Mel's notebook and sifted through the pages, wondering if there was any clue inside to hint at why he'd been murdered. I unlocked my bottom drawer and carefully pulled out the dead man's gun. *All the great TV detectives have guns and badges—maybe I should take this pistol for myself and carry it around, partially for intimidation and partially for protection. The problem is I think I may be more intimidated by it than anyone else. What did Lexington just say?* "Don't do anything you'll regret later." *This feels like one of those times.*

I put the gun back and locked it up.

I looked at the clock and realized it was already seven. I texted Patrick to see if he was done but didn't get a response. Maybe he finished early, dropped the tablet off outside, and was back asleep. I wished I'd grabbed some pants before leaving the bedroom as briefs and a T-shirt were not preferred attire for Chicago winters, but they'd have to do. Not wanting to open the creaky door to the front closet, I grabbed the only coat hanging in the hallway—Mary's Burberry trench coat.

I made it outside and checked the cushion, but there was no tablet in sight. It was 7:05 a.m., so technically Patrick still had ten minutes. I texted him again. No response. I gave him a call, and his phone went straight to voicemail. *That twit really is going to make me wait until the last second, isn't he?* I started pacing, my bare legs frigid as Mary's coat barely made it past my underwear. I got ready to call Patrick again when suddenly the yard went dark. The flood light outside our back door was no longer on, and neither were the string lights over the patio. I peeked over the fence and saw all the street lights were out. *The whole neighborhood's power must be out.*

I couldn't worry about that, though. I needed the damn tablet, and I needed it now. I texted Patrick again and again and again but still nothing. I'd just have to get it myself. I did a quick thirty-second stretch, then climbed over our shared fence, despite Mary's jacket limiting my mobility.

Once over, I stared at my neighbors' house. I'd lived next door to Margie, Will, and Patrick Burch for thirty years, yet I'd never stepped foot inside their home. Based on the closed curtains, it looked like there was one bedroom downstairs and one upstairs. Were Margie and Will the type of people who had Patrick sleep downstairs so he wouldn't disrupt them in the morning when he left for school, or did he sleep upstairs so they could see him on his way out the door?

My phone buzzed. *Finally!* But it wasn't Patrick. It was a text from Mary.

David, why is there a strange man walking around our house in nothing but a pair of basketball shorts? Where the hell are you?

How could I answer those questions? I couldn't say I was trying to break into our neighbors' house without a heck of a lot more information, so I opted to just answer the first one.

Oh, that's Bryan, the night manager from the WCC. I ran into him yesterday. He was lonely and needed a place to crash.

There was no immediate response from Mary, so I turned back to Patrick's house. *Where's he sleeping? First floor or second floor? First floor or second floor?* I didn't have a ladder, so I hoped the first-floor room was his. I tiptoed over to the window and gave a soft knock. Nothing. I knocked harder. Still nothing, so I found a stick to smack against the window. I had it to my side, ready to swing it like a tennis racket, when suddenly the curtains flew open. A bewildered Will and Margie stared back at me, stick in my hand and damn near naked in little more than Mary's coat. I looked at them, frozen, unable to move. Finally, Will broke the trance and cracked open the window.

"David, what are you doing?"

I fumbled my words, not sure if I should answer literally or existentially. Fortunately, I heard Patrick's voice as he entered the room.

"Oh, Mr. Blazen, thanks for coming over and letting us know the power was out," he said as he walked toward the window. "We could have easily overslept without the electric clocks working. Thanks for being a great neighbor."

His parents looked at Patrick. They looked at me. They looked at one another. Apparently, that answer was good enough because they headed back toward their bed. Patrick rushed to the open window and slid the iPad to me.

"We have a problem," he whispered to me. "I'll text you soon."

He closed the window and the curtains, leaving me alone in their yard, this time with what I came for. I walked out the Burch's gate toward the front instead of tempting fate by trying to hop the fence again. Once around the house, I saw a dozen electric company trucks lined up and down the street, including one in front of my house. With no way to sneak the iPad inside, I tossed it in the backseat of my car.

As I approached my own front yard, I saw and heard one of the workers talking with Mary. "We're sorry for the inconvenience, ma'am, but we found the source of the problem. You can get on with your day, and everything should be back up and running in a matter of minutes."

Mary thanked him profusely. He got back in his truck just as I made it to Mary.

"What happened?" I asked.

"What happened?" she shouted back. "What happened was we could have been killed, David! There was some neighborhood blackout, and apparently there were risks of explosions on certain parts of the grid, and our house was one of those spots. I could have been blown to smithereens, David, while you were—"

Just then, Mary noticed my outfit. Her eyes moved down my body, then up again, mouth open in astonishment the whole time.

"While you were doing what, exactly?" she asked.

Just then, a little girl in pajamas, a winter hat, and mittens came and pulled at my—er, Mary's—trench coat. "Hey, mister. Did you see all those men in helmets? They said there was a problem with the power and made us all rush outside. It was really scary."

"You must be Summer," I said, kneeling down and opting to once again move on from Mary's question. "I'm sorry it was scary. You must have been very brave."

Bryan approached me, still wearing his hoops shorts and a puffy winter coat. "I'm Bryan. What am I doing here?"

There was something comical about us all meeting one

another outside in the cold, but opting to not attract too much attention from the neighbors, I suggested we move the party inside and get to know each other over a hot breakfast. As the group walked in, my phone buzzed with a text from Patrick.

"You all head in. I'll be there in just a minute," I said.

Mary, still annoyed, rolled her eyes and took everyone inside as I read Patrick's message: *Mr. Blazen, I got bad news, more bad news, good news, and lucrative news. What do you want first?*

I don't have time for games, just tell me, I wrote back.

Bad news = I fell asleep, he texted.

Another text from him. *More bad news = I only got footage from cameras 3 and 27.*

Another text. *Good news = I got more footage than you asked for from those cameras since they recorded all night.*

And his last text: *Lucrative news (at least for you) = I'll only charge you $1,250 for my services.*

That little shit.

Fine, I texted back. *Come over at 10:30 and I'll give you the money. Meet at the cushion drop off.*

Lieutenant Lance Cutler sat at his kitchen table, a bowl of cereal in front of him and the TV on in the background. He liked having the morning news on, if nothing else than to see how the local media spun the day's main stories. He hadn't checked the morning police report yet, so he was surprised to hear about an explosion that killed four people on Wacker Drive. When he heard the reporter say the driver of the car that exploded was a West Coast Club employee, he nearly choked on his cereal.

Lance put his spoon down as the reporter talked about forty-two-year-old Henry Jackson, who was survived by his wife and two children. Henry's image appeared on the screen as the reporter said Jackson was a mainstay at the club for years. Experts were still reviewing the scene of the crime, but initial reports made it sound like the explosion was intentional.

"Why anyone would want to hurt this sweet father of two, we still don't know," the reporter said. "Back to you in the studio."

Lance was stunned. Yesterday he'd covered up what appeared to be a murder at the WCC as a favor to his mother. She said doing so would protect the city, but less than twenty-four hours later, a WCC employee was executed in his own car, and that murder led to the deaths of three more people. Was that a coincidence? Lance didn't think so.

In a rage, he got up, grabbed his bowl of cereal, and threw it at the wall, the ceramic pieces shattering to the floor as soggy cereal and milk cascaded down the wall.

"This is all my fault!" Lance screamed to no one in particular. "Those deaths are on me! Henry's kids will grow up without a father because of me!"

He sunk down to the floor, covered his eyes with his palms, and began to cry.

Lance was one of the best cops in the city, the squeaky-clean son of Sarah, the presumed new mayor of Chicago, and Kent Cutler, a quiet yet successful attorney. Despite the vanilla reputation, this was not the first time he'd looked the other way on a crime, but it was the first time someone died as a result.

"I took an oath to defend this city," he whispered to himself, "and I just failed."

His trance was interrupted by his buzzing phone. It was a text message from Skip, his best friend, the officer he assigned to cover up whatever happened at the West Coast Club: *We need to talk.*

I made it back inside and promptly hung up Mary's trench coat, vowing never to wear it again. I quickly tossed on some of my own clothes and made it to the kitchen to find Mary heating up bacon in the microwave and Amber scrambling eggs on one side of the stove and making French toast on the other. Bryan was in search of coffee and some Tylenol, while Summer stood on a stool and tried to squeeze juice out of an orange. I felt like I had entered the scene of a sitcom. Yes, we had just met, but somehow we felt like family.

We all sat down at the table, and Mary seemed to genuinely enjoy having this random group together. Bryan told us about his broken love life and how much he appreciated not being alone on his birthday. Summer got out of her seat and asked me in a whisper if we had any candles. I directed her to a kitchen drawer, where she found a purple candle, brought it to the table, and stabbed it into Bryan's English muffin.

"Happy birthday!" she shouted. We all laughed as we sang "Happy Birthday" to our new friend.

After the song, Amber shared stories about Mel. Mary invited the group to stay as long as they wanted, not even looking in my direction to seek acknowledgment or approval. Just then, the doorbell rang.

The ringing drew me away from our morning meal. I opened to find Wilt, ready to hear my plans for the day. I had forgotten all about my emergency meeting, but with the Mel situation and Andy Wong out for me, I knew I needed to brief the team, even if that just meant updating Wilt.

I started to escort Wilt to headquarters, but before we made it out of the room, Bryan said he needed to get going. He thanked Mary for her hospitality and Amber for the delicious food. Then he picked Summer up and gave her a huge hug. He walked over to me, still holding the little girl, and asked if I knew where his tablet was.

"I don't remember you coming in with a tablet, Bryan. Are you sure you had it with you?"

I invited Wilt to grab some food while Bryan and I went outside to look for the tablet. I went over to the car and "discovered" it resting on the backseat, where I had tossed it just a few minutes earlier.

"Here it is. It must have fallen out of your bag last night."

"I would have been dead if I lost this thing, so thank you."

"Well, we're all glad that didn't happen," Mary said as she came outside to give him a hug.

He ordered a ride, and we waved him off. Back inside, I asked Mary to play with Summer while I talked with Wilt and Amber. She happily picked up the little girl and said it would be no trouble as she twirled Summer in the air around the living room while we went to headquarters.

I asked Amber if she knew Mel recently purchased a new insurance plan that would set her and Summer up for years to come. Her tears told me this was a surprise, though I omitted the part about her not getting anything if his death was ruled a suicide. My only chance at helping them see their $250,000 was to snag a copy of the autopsy report. For that, the team and I would have to do some digging.

While Amber went on telling us more about how incredible Mel was, Jeffrey entered the room and apologized for their lateness. *There we go, Team Blaze is starting to show up!*

Amber's compliments abruptly switched from Mel to Betty from the WCC. "That lady has been a saint," Amber said. "She's been so thoughtful through this entire process, from moving the remains out of sight quickly to covering the funeral. She even called me this morning to say Mel's body was moved to a crematorium and that as soon as I come in this afternoon to sign some papers, they'll be able to cremate his sweet soul."

Wilt, Jeffrey, and I shared confused looks.

"Why the rush?" Wilt finally asked.

"Honestly, we never talked about his end-of-life wishes, but Betty said this would be substantially cheaper and easier, and I'm fine with that. She and everyone at the WCC have been so accommodating and considerate; they're even covering all the expenses."

"That's very considerate," Wilt said as he pulled out two tissues, one for Amber and one for himself.

"So no autopsy. I wonder why," I said. "And why is the WCC so willing to pay for everything? I want to come with you this afternoon; maybe I can ask Betty then. Why don't you go be with Summer? I need to catch my team up on a few things, but I'll see you this afternoon."

"Thank you for everything, Mr. Blazen. I really appreciate it."

"It's my pleasure. Oh, one last thing," I said as she opened the door. "Do you know where Mel is to be cremated?"

"Oh, yeah. Holy Mother of Baby Jesus Crematorium."

Trying to rehash everything that happened since I'd last spoken with Wilt and Jeffrey was going to be too complicated and too time-intensive. Besides, right then my concern was that someone was trying to burn our only evidence—namely Mel. Without an autopsy, there'd be no way to prove he was murdered. If there was no proof, not only would Amber and Summer get nothing, but a killer would get away, and I could not stand for that.

"Wilt, I've got an important job for you," I said.

"Name it, boss. I'm on it."

"I need you to go down to the My Jesus of Lady Crem—"

Wilt cut me off. "Now hold on, Blaze. Let's call things by their real names. I believe it was Holy Mother of Baby Jesus Crematorium."

"Wilt, I appreciate your commitment to accuracy, but to save time and help out these three aging detectives, let's just call it Ashville for short."

"Ha, I get it."

"Wilt, stay focused. I need you to go down to Ashville and find out how they burn bodies and what times they do their cremations." I reached into the top desk drawer and pulled out a wad of cash. "And, Wilt, whatever you do, don't let them burn Mel. You're not on a budget, so do whatever's necessary. I want that body alive. I mean, I want that body to remain a body."

"Got it, boss. I'm the only able-bodied body who can keep this body a body."

He grabbed the cash and rushed out the door, leaving Jeffrey and me still working our way through his tongue twister.

"David, what can I do?" Jeffrey finally asked.

I handed him Mel's notebook and the scrap papers from inside, each filled with cryptic names, notes, and numbers.

"I got these papers yesterday from Mel's locker. Contrary to the picture Amber just painted, this guy was a lowlife, and from what I can tell, there were plenty of people who would want him dead. I can't make heads or tails of these. Why don't you work with Marc and see what, if anything, you can find?"

Sarah Cutler let her father down the day she was born. He wanted a son, but he was stuck with Sarah instead. She was his only child, and he was both strict and stern with her from an early age. He never went easy, whether it was a game of checkers or a father-daughter game of basketball in the driveway. He taught her to swim by tossing her in a swimming pool. He taught her to catch a baseball by hitting line drives at her head. She hated him growing up, but he made her who she was today. Strong. Relentless. Determined to win.

Sarah was hard on her son, Lance, like her dad was on her. She wasn't exactly sorry she pulled him into her situation—that would mean admitting she was wrong. Besides, she had to figure out how to handle Solomon Feldman and Tony Santori both potentially wanting to kill her.

Sarah turned off her bedroom lights and sat alone in the dark on one side of her king-size bed, thinking back to when she was four and her dad taught her a lesson in composure. He made young Sarah crawl into his full-size sleeping bag with her eyes closed. He zipped the bag, taped all but one corner of the top up, wrapped the excess part of the bag around his daughter, and then spun the bundle in circles. Inside the sleeping bag, she quickly became dizzy, confused, and afraid. She called out for help, but there was no response. She couldn't see any light, couldn't find a way out. She was trapped. She screamed for her dad, who finally spoke up.

"Sarah, no matter how bad things seem around you, there is always a way out. You just need to find it."

This sick lesson in parenting had nearly cost Sarah her life, but she found the opening in the top of the bag and pried off the tape, escaping the sleeping bag while gasping for air.

Right now, Sarah's world was closing in on her, and she didn't know what to do.

"There's always a way out," she said to herself. "I just need to find it."

"Skip, we've got to come clean about yesterday," Lance said before Skip could get a word in. "Did you see the news? Those deaths are on us!"

"Whoa, buddy, hold your horses. Good morning to you too."

"Is it, Skip? Is it a good morning? We killed those people, those four innocent people."

"Lance, now listen. First of all, we didn't kill anyone. I saw one of the guys worked at the WCC, but that could just be a coincidence. There's no reason to believe the two cases are connected."

"That's bullshit, Skip, and you know it. It's only a matter of time before someone figures out they're related, and as soon as they do, they'll find out what we did. Why did I listen to my mom yesterday? I should have just said no to the coverup."

"Come on, Lance, you know why you said yes. She's family, and we do whatever is necessary for family. Besides, your mom is going to run this great city, for God sakes; she wouldn't lead us astray."

That got Lance thinking. Skip was right that there wasn't a clear memory of when Sarah outrightly deceived her son or led him down the wrong path. But still. Why would she ask him to do something that so clearly jeopardized his career? Lance got so deep in thought that he lost track of what Skip was saying on the other end of the call.

"Lance, are you there?" Skip shouted, jarring Lance out of his own head. "Did you hear what I said?"

"Sorry, Skip, what was that?"

"I said we can easily make our suicide story stick. There's just one small catch."

"What's that?"

"Yesterday there was this old guy at the club who called himself Detective Blaze. He was asking me a lot of questions about how the steam room death was being handled, and I'm worried he may dig deeper. I don't think he saw the syringe, but I'm worried he may suspect it wasn't a suicide."

"What did you do with the syringe?"

"I still have it. I'll drop it at your house later today. I'm not too worried, though. Someone is pushing the body through the system, and it will be cremated today with no autopsy, so there won't be any proof to challenge our story."

"Wait, what?"

"Yeah, someone is trying to tie up any loose ends—maybe your mom, I don't know. But now the only loose end left is this

Blaze guy. The department doesn't have any info on him, but he gave me his card. It shouldn't take much to get what he knows out of him."

Lance was still dumbfounded. Could his mother really be covering this whole thing up? Yes, she taught him to stop at nothing to win, but her actions were not only reckless and illegal; they were costing lives. Maybe Detective Blaze really did know more and could shed light on what the hell Sarah Cutler was doing.

"Okay, Skip, give me Blaze's number. I'll track him down and let you know what I find out."

"You sure, Lance? Can I trust you?"

"Of course you can trust me, Skip. And don't worry about Blaze. I'll take care of him."

9

Patrick was prompt and apologetic for sleeping through the bulk of his assignment. I accepted his apology and asked for the thumb drive with the video he downloaded. He gave it to me but warily, seemingly concerned about my true intentions. I tried to ease his fears by explaining the killer had to have entered the club before 10:55 a.m. and left after 11 a.m. The plan was for my team to sift through the footage and identify the murderer.

"How are you going to do that?" Patrick asked. "What program are you going to use?"

"The program is called our eyes, Patrick," I said as I rolled my own. "We're going to use our eyes and watch the video. We'll see what time each person entered and then cross-reference it to when they left. From there, we'll have a narrowed-down suspect pool."

I appreciated Patrick's work, but I didn't have time for boneheaded questions or to catch him up on how real detectives work.

"Mr. Blazen, that's going to be virtually impossible to do."

My tolerance for this kid was waning. "Why, Patrick? Why is it impossible?"

"Well, it's not impossible, but there were hundreds of people who arrived before eleven, and it will take hours and hours to try to match each person's face to when they arrived and when they left."

Dammit, the kid was right. Had I just wasted valuable time and $1,250?

"So what do you suggest?"

"Well, fortunately, camera three is near the entry, but it doesn't appear to be a main entry camera. It's weird; it looks like it's tucked away in a corner, but it's positioned in a way to get a perfect head-on view of every person entering the club. The videos are high definition, and we should be able to use facial recognition to identify each person."

My blank stare paused Patrick's monologue.

"Facial recognition is what's on your phone right now. You know how you unlock it simply by looking at it? The phone uses facial recognition to know you're you and that it's okay to access what's on the phone."

"Of course," I said, trying to cover up my ignorance.

"Anyway, as soon as I realized facial recognition could be used, I knew I could write some code to match a person's face from when they walk into a building to when they walk out. With that, you should be able to easily reduce your suspect pool and know who was in the club at the time of the murder."

"That sounds great, Patrick, but how much will it cost?"

"Well, you have given me all types of odd jobs since I was a little boy, and while this one might be the oddest, it's also the most exciting, so I won't charge anything. Give me the green light, and I'll have a list of names for you tomorrow."

I hugged the kid. "Patrick, that's really great work. You've got the green light."

"Mr. Blazen, can I ask you one other question?"

"Go for it, but I'm in a bit of a rush. Lots of detective work today."

"Can I work for you? Maybe as your tech guy? Please, Mr. Blazen, can I be a detective too?"

"Sure, kid, welcome to the team."

I stuck out my hand to shake his, but he went for a fist bump. I switched to bump fists, but he tried a handshake. With my left hand, I patted him on the shoulder.

"We'll work on that," I said with a laugh to my new junior detective. "I've got to run."

Patrick recreated our awkward handshake with himself as I walked to the garage. The kid was a dweeb and nearly five decades younger than the rest of us, but he was right. His technical savvy could be an asset down the road.

I got back home, and my phone buzzed with a text from Wilt. *Ashville is a strange place*, he'd written, *and it doesn't smell too good. Mel won't be burned until his wife signs off.*

Amber and I are going to the club this afternoon to understand this whole rush-the-cremation thing, I wrote back. *Stay there until you hear from me. Anyone else awaiting the fire?*

Six or seven dead souls.

Keep track of those and any new arrivals. I'll be in touch later.

I wanted to get to the bottom of this assumed-suicide story, so I gave my doctor a call. Bill Cardorf and I went back forty-plus years, and I thought of him more as my friend than the guy who physically and mentally kept me on the straight and narrow. We'd played cards together and seen movies together and talked over just about everything under the sun.

Well, almost everything.

"Hey, Bill, random question for you," I said after he'd answered. "Is it possible for someone to kill themselves in a steam room?"

Bill was silent. "Well, technically, a person can kill themselves anywhere," he finally said, "so I'm guessing you mean can a person intentionally sit in a steam room until they're not able to breathe. Is that correct?"

"Yes, exactly."

"Is it possible? Yes. Is it probable? No. Imagine you want to die and set yourself on fire. If you change your mind, there's nothing you can do. You're toast. But trying to kill yourself in a steam room would take an incredibly long time, and with a door always accessible, chances are you'd eventually give in and escape. I can't imagine any person withstanding that pain for the necessary amount of time until death. I could get into all the specifics about carbon monoxide poisoning if you want."

"No, we're good. Here's another. If you were to murder a person by injection, how would you go about doing it?"

"Okay, Blaze, you're not going to catch me offering advice on that one. Lethal injections are legal in a lot of states. Just go online and you can find a whole host of recipes for end-of-life termination, but it's important to realize taking someone's life, no matter the reason, is a big deal. Executioners have self-medicated for centuries to calm their nerves and numb their senses before dropping the guillotine, pulling the noose, or flipping the switch."

"Got it, Bill."

"I do have to say these questions are making me uncomfortable, David. Besides, I've got to get back to my patient."

"Just one more quick question. If someone was poisoned by injection, how long does the poison stay in the bloodstream?"

"Once the heart stops, the poison stays still. It could survive years, maybe decades even, as the body decays."

"What about cremation?" I whispered. "Will the poison survive if the body is cremated?"

"No, David. No, it will not." He hung up before I could ask anything else.

I now had it on almost official authority that the probability of Mel killing himself was slim. That means unless someone had drugged him earlier, our mystery steam room companion was the one who poisoned him. Maybe the killer knew the poison would show up on an autopsy, which would explain the rush to cremate.

It was all starting to make sense and yet not make any sense at all.

I needed to get out of the house and try to think this steam room situation through. I figured I'd be productive and get my shirts from the cleaners at the same time. A few blocks from home, I noticed a car behind me with two men in matching suits, buzzed brown hair, sunglasses, and earpieces. Were they cops? Federal agents? *Holy crap, they must be the FBI. I bet they're following someone!* I didn't want to get in the way of other crime stoppers, so I quickly turned at the first traffic light. Hmm, so did they. I switched lanes so they could pass, but they switched as well. Weird. I switched again, and they did the same.

Wait a minute! These agents are tailing someone—me! To confirm my suspicion, I took a sharp right turn at the next intersection, then made three more right turns. Every turn I made was replicated by my FBI followers. I felt incredibly important to have a following and thought about all the exciting places I could take them, only to be embarrassed when I realized my next stop was the dry cleaners. Oh, well. Even good detectives need their shirts cleaned.

I got to the cleaners and decided to have some fun with my tail. I parked in the tight alley behind the cleaners, thinking my followers had to come along and reveal themselves or wait for me to exit before they continued their assignment.

I pulled in the alley and saw Beverly, the woman who had embarrassed Mary, being manhandled by an Asian man twice her size. Businessman David Blazen might have intentionally looked the other way, but Detective Blaze saw the abuse and sprang into action. I hopped out of the car with the ignition still running and shouted, "This is Detective Blaze. Get your hands off that woman!"

The tall, muscular Asian man looked at Beverly, then at me.

"Gladly," he said as he pushed Beverly into the wall.

Rather than walk away, he charged at me instead. I hadn't learned about self-defense yet in my pamphlet reading, but I had watched *The Karate Kid* with my grandkids a couple of times. Before I could remember what came after waxing on and waxing off, my attacker got me with a flying kick to the chest, sending me airborne into the side of a nearby garbage dumpster.

"That's assault and battery," I said as I staggered back to my feet.

Before I could get another word in, he delivered a roundhouse kick to the face, then started treating my kidneys like a punching bag. Right jab. Left jab. Right jab. Left jab. The hits kept coming as he screamed at me in a language I didn't recognize, although I did distinctly hear him reference Andy Wong.

The punches stopped, only for him to push me back into the brick wall. My attacker slowly approached me, a maniacal grin on his face. He put one hand around my neck and lifted me up off the ground, the smile on his face growing wider by the second.

This bastard was going to kill me.

I closed my eyes and watched my life pass before me. I saw the faces of my ten grandchildren. I saw Mary, crying at my funeral. Would she acknowledge my weeklong career as a detective? Dammit, why didn't she just come and pick up the shirts? *Wait, I can't have my last thought of her be one of anger.* Just then, I heard a distinctly American voice.

"Put him down now, or I'll pull the trigger!"

I opened my eyes to discover one of the FBI twins, a gun pointed squarely at the back of my attacker's head. The other agent stood to his right, his gun also drawn. Three Chicago police officers were running past my car and toward us, guns out with screams of "Nobody move" and "You're under arrest!"

My attacker put me down and was immediately handcuffed

and taken away. I leaned forward, my hands on my knees like I'd just ran a marathon, gasping for breath.

One of the FBI guys met my gaze. "You okay?" he asked.

Still panting and catching my breath, blood dripping from my nose, I pointed up at the *Chins' Cleaners* sign. "I just wanted my shirts back."

What made Vince such a valuable tool for the FBI and an effective undercover agent was his ability to display one emotion externally while feeling something completely different. Part of that skill came naturally, but most was developed during his early years at the academy, where he was trained and tested in the art of deceit. Passing a lie detector test became child's play for him. Of the eighty-eight other students—many of whom went on to be heroes in the military or serve as Green Berets—Vince was the best at displaying whatever emotion a situation called for. That was how he was able to appear shocked as he internally laughed at the irony of Jermaine, Santori's top security guy, calling to tell him the FBI was following Blaze.

"That's right, Vince. And they made no attempt at hiding it," Jermaine said. "From the moment I started following him, they were basically on his bumper."

"I wonder why they care about him," Vince said, feigning curiosity as he stood over his next shot at the pool table inside Tony's office.

"I don't know. Are you even sure this guy is worth our time? All I saw was a confused old man who probably knows more about bran muffins than steam room secrets."

"What do you mean?"

"I just watched him get lost and literally drive in a circle, and then he went to pick up his dry cleaning. That's it. It couldn't have been more of a boring morning."

"You sure all he picked up was his clothes? Did he meet anyone?"

"I don't think anything else happened. He went into an alley behind the place, and I couldn't follow without blowing my cover. I'm sitting a block away from the cleaners now waiting for him to come out the other side of the alley."

"Just stick with him. If the FBI is following him, there must be a reason."

"Will do, Vince. With them on his tail, I can't get a tracking device on his car, but I'll stay close by until the opportunity presents itself. Oh, he's coming out of the alley right now. Gotta run."

Vince had barely hung up the phone before Tony inquired about the call.

"Who is the FBI following?" Tony said as he paced across the room.

"Blaze," Vince said. "For some reason, the FBI is tailing him, and it's preventing Jermaine from putting the tracker on his car or telling him of his urgent appointment with you."

While Vince was an expert at hiding his emotions, Tony was not. The FBI's interest in Blaze stopped him in his tracks. That was an unexpected curveball, and as Tony had demonstrated the previous night with Henry Jackson, he did not do well with curveballs. Tony grabbed the pool cue from Vince's hands and snapped it in two over his leg.

"Fuck the FBI," he shouted as he threw half of the stick across the room. "And fuck Detective Blaze too," he added, the other half following suit. "I don't care what Jermaine said. I want Blaze here before the end of the day!"

"Got it, boss."

"And, Vince?"

"Yes, boss?"

"We need to talk later."

Vince nodded his head in agreement before turning to leave

the room. On the outside, he appeared calm and composed, but hearing that ominous warning not only made Vince nervous.

It made him scared.

My coat was covered in blood, dirt, and dumpster residue. My shirt was torn. My face was bloodied. My right eye was swollen shut. Mary took one look at me as I walked in the door and said I had to quit immediately. I didn't get a chance to tell her the story—or that I still hadn't gotten my damn shirts back—because the story didn't matter. This wasn't what retired life was supposed to look like.

Amber rushed over with a wet paper towel to wipe the dried blood and a pack of frozen peas for my eye. Her look of fear matched Mary's look of bafflement. The two women stood no more than three feet apart from one another, staring at me. Just then, Summer burst between them holding a green piece of plastic in her hand.

"Mr. David! Mr. David! I won Candyland three times in a row! I won! I won! I won!"

You couldn't help but smile at her victory dance.

"That's why I'm doing this," I said to Mary. "I want that girl to feel safe."

"How does getting beat up make her safe?" Mary asked.

Before I could answer, Amber wrapped her arms around me. Mary simply mouthed, "We'll talk later."

Amber and I were scheduled to be at the WCC shortly, but I needed a chance to decompress. Amber called Betty to say we'd be there in a bit. Meanwhile, I gave Summer a kiss on the forehead, then went to headquarters to clear my head. I sat down, leaned back, put the frozen peas over my bad eye, and closed my good one, desperate for a few minutes of calm and quiet. Seven seconds later, my phone rang. I answered exhaustedly, my eyes still closed.

"Detective Blaze, this is Lieutenant Lance Cutler of the Chicago Police Department. We need to talk."

My good eye shot open.

"I know you know something about the steam room incident yesterday, and I'm guessing you've realized it's somehow connected to the explosion last night on Wacker Drive."

"Okay," I said, not sure how to respond or how he knew so much about what I knew.

"I have information that I need to share with you, information that will ruin a lot of people's careers, but we need to talk in person."

"Why me? Why not just take it to the police?" I said, momentarily forgetting he was the police.

"When can we meet?" he asked.

"I'll be at the West Coast Club later this afternoon."

"Okay, I'll find you. And, Detective Blaze?"

"Yes?"

"Be safe. And trust no one."

He hung up, leaving me alone with my thoughts.

I put the frozen bag of peas down on the desk and considered skimming my pamphlets when the bag of peas fell to the floor. I reached to grab them and noticed a screw lying under the desk. Confused, I grabbed it and tried to figure out its home. There were no screws missing from anything on my desk, and nothing on my bookshelf seemed out of place. I considered asking Mary if she'd seen anything missing a screw, but she'd probably say the only thing in the house with a loose screw was me.

Just then, I found it. Across the room, the grate covering the air vent was missing a screw. *Now how did that come out?* I started toward the vent but stopped as I noticed a small camera peering at me from a gap in the grate. Someone had broken into headquarters, and they were watching me. But who were they?

I let out an audible gasp, realizing it must have been the FBI. I'd bet they did it during that power outage that morning. I wasn't sure if I should be honored or horrified, but either way, I was appreciative. I'd have been dead if it weren't for the FBI's help at the cleaners. I welcomed their surveillance, but as tempted as I was to wave hello to the camera, I decided it might be better if they didn't know I knew they were watching.

I scribbled a note for Mary informing her of the surveillance. My guess was if the FBI put cameras in, they also tapped my phones and could hear what I said in the house. Before I folded the note, I wrote the three words Lance said that continued to repeat in my head: *Trust no one.*

Out in the kitchen, I gave Mary a hug and slipped her the note. She read it, then gave me her patented "what in the world are you talking about?" look.

I whispered in her ear, "Trust me."

"You just told me to trust no one," she said.

Touché.

"Trust no one but our inner circle," I told her as I took back the note.

Amber and Summer were playing cards in the living room when I asked Amber if she was ready to go. My right eye was still swollen, but I could at least see out of it again.

I handed Amber the note and playfully tickled Summer. While the little girl was giggling outstretched on the floor, her mom reached into Summer's backpack and grabbed a pink kitty cat phone. She hugged her daughter, then slipped me the phone.

"Use this for anything you don't want the FBI to hear," she whispered.

I turned back to Mary and gave her a long embrace.

"We've got to run. If you hear from Team Blaze, let them know about this pink phone and the FBI."

She smiled, kissed my least bruised cheek, and whispered in my ear, "Just come home in one piece—and breathing, please."

Marc had gotten so caught up with work that he hadn't been able to check in on how David's psychiatrist appointment went. He was worried David didn't get any prescription at the appointment since David called for an emergency Team Blaze meeting, a meeting Marc figured wasn't that important.

Still concerned, he texted Mary. He didn't know if she had told the rest of Team Blaze about the possible delusional visionary perception and suicide risk, but he included Jeffrey and Wilt on the thread anyway.

Marc: *Hey gang, how's David doing?*

Jeffrey: *I haven't talked to him in a few hours, but he has a project for me and you. We're supposed to look through the dead guy's notebook and see if we can find any clues about his murder.*

Marc: *Dead guy? Murder!? What the hell are you talking about?*

Wilt: *I'm with Mel now.*

Marc: *Who's Mel?*

Wilt: *The dead schmuck from the steam room.*

Marc: *Steam room? Wait. How can you be with him if he's dead?*

Wilt: *Haven't you heard of Holy Mother of Baby Jesus Crematorium?*

Marc: *Of course I haven't heard of Mother of Baby Jesus Crematorium. Why are you there?*

Wilt: *Holy Mother. And it's complicated, but to put it simply, I'm here to prevent a fire.*

Mary: *Hi Marc, sorry for the delay. I just lost a game of Monopoly Junior to that sweet Summer. Goodness she is a cutie. I hope the boys caught you up on everything.*

Marc: *Who is Summer?*

Mary: *She's the daughter of Mel, the guy who died in the steam room. David is fine. He's still recovering from his near-death experience at the dry cleaners, but he and Amber just left for the WCC.*

Marc: *Okay, now I know this is one big joke. Near-death experience at the cleaners?*

Wilt: *Anyone know if Blaze will give us health insurance and if so if it covers black lung?*

Jeffrey: *I think that's just for coal miners.*

Mary: *I have a message from David. The FBI is following him and bugged his phone and planted cameras and microphones around our house. He has a different phone that he'll text you from, and he wants all communications with him to go through that phone. Don't use his usual number. Oh and he wanted me to tell you to trust no one.*

Marc: *Okay guys, very funny. All I was trying to do was check in on a friend, but if you don't want to take this seriously, be my guest.*

Wilt: *This is as serious as it gets, Marc. Blaze is for real.*

Jeffrey: *Amen.*

Wilt: *I gotta run. I think someone's about to get burned.*

Marc: *Mary, is this really happening?*

Mary: *Yes Marc, it really is.*

Marc: *Holy shit.*

Wilt: *God dammit, Marc, it's Holy Mother!*

10

As CEO, Betty was the face of the West Coast Club, but she was also the frontwoman for Tony Santori since long before he'd arrived in Chicago. Betty pulled the strings to make it possible for Santori to have a secret operation within such a notable health club. She was a master at balancing the legitimate presence of the club with the underworld dealings of the Santori family.

Betty grew up on the hard streets of Pittsburgh. Her father, Moe Harris, taught her the intricacies of creating a real business while at the same time picking clients' pockets clean. Moe said to always look for "win, win, win" scenarios—wins for the client, wins for the community, and wins for yourself. He orchestrated the nation's second-largest Ponzi scheme to that point, and had he not died in prison years ago, he would have been proud to see what his little girl had built. The WCC was the place to be for many of Chicago's wealthiest and high-profile figures, and those individuals were promised privacy in exchange for exorbitant member fees.

Tony Santori had his private run of the club thanks to significant under-the-table investments by his family back when the club was first proposed. At that point, the Santoris dreamed of one day expanding their reign beyond New Jersey and felt Chicago would be a natural location to set up shop. Years later, that was exactly what happened. The WCC was a win for the wealthy and a win for the guilty. As for Betty, her win came every January when the Santoris slipped her a five-million-dollar thank-you gift for all she'd done to keep their affairs private.

Tony's annual gift to Betty afforded him total control of the place. If he wanted something done to the club, he talked to her. If he needed the place closed occasionally so he could have a private meeting, he just had to say the word to Betty, and she'd make it happen. She helped design his whole part of the club, even to the point of picking out the flooring in his windowless torture room.

Betty was surprised Mel Weinberg's wife, Amber, was so late for their appointment, and she was confused why David Blazen was attending the meeting. Nevertheless, she waited, her eyes on one of the club's hidden cameras to see when Amber's car would enter the parking lot.

Lance Cutler slouched in his seat, his eyes barely able to see over the steering wheel. Surveillance was never Lance's favorite assignment, yet there he was, hiding out in the WCC parking lot, waiting for Detective Blaze. Lance didn't know how much Blaze knew about the steam room and his mother's involvement, but right then, Blaze felt like one of the few people he could trust. And so he waited. And thought. He thought about his mom's mantra of doing whatever it took to win. He thought about his fellow cops helping cover up yesterday's incident. And he thought about how this was not the first time he and his fellow officers in blue colored outside legal lines.

After an hour, Lance spotted Blaze's Lexus enter the WCC parking lot. Unfortunately, he saw the detective had company, both in and out of the car. Lance recognized the guys immediately behind Blaze as feds. He wondered why the FBI cared about Blaze, but if they were following him, they were probably listening to him too. That meant they likely heard Lance's call that afternoon and knew he knew something about the steam room.

Lance had to postpone his meetup with Blaze and get out of there before being spotted. Then, he noticed another car enter the parking lot behind the FBI, one he knew all too well. Lance quickly slouched back out of view as he saw his partner, Skip, park his unmarked car just a few spaces from Detective Blaze.

What the hell is he doing here? Lance wondered as he hurried out of the lot. He frantically called the only person who might be able to assist him.

"Kent here."

"Hi, Dad," Lance said. "I need your help."

"Name it."

"Are you still close with Mayor Paulson? I know you guys used to golf together before he took office."

"Good old Bump-and-Run Mitch? Of course! I haven't talked to him in a while. You know he was diagnosed with cancer, right? He's been holed up in the hospital and out of the spotlight for months, but we used to hit the links once or twice a month up through last summer. Son, did I ever tell you how he got his nickname? We were out at—"

"Maybe some other time, Dad. Can you set up a meeting with him and me ASAP?"

"I guess so. Do you want me to come with?"

"That'd be great. Want to pick me up from home in two hours? There's a chance I might be followed, so why don't you park two blocks from our place? I'll be at the end of the alley. I'm sure this sounds weird, but it's literally a matter of life and death."

"Son, I know more than you think. All I can say is I'm proud of you."

"Thanks, Dad. See you soon."

Skip never wanted to bug his partner's phone. He wanted to trust Lance. After all, the two had grown up together and shared hundreds of secrets. Sadly, it was some of those secrets that led to the bug.

Lance was held in the highest regard for his work on the force, but Skip knew the truth about his friend being a member of the Hungry 7, a group of cops who for years put their financial interests ahead of the good of the city. Skip knew about it because he, too, was a member, and thanks to their greed, he built up an extravagant lifestyle filled with fancy cars, a big house, and all the things you typically couldn't afford on an officer's salary.

A few months ago, Lance told Skip he was done with being dirty. He was ready to do good and abolish the Hungry 7. Two days later, Lance brought it up again. Skip wanted to support his partner's newfound self-righteousness, but he wasn't ready to give up his lavish lifestyle. He was worried about what Lance might do, so he'd bugged his phone. Nothing came of that "time to do good" talk until today, when Lance sounded ready to confess all of his sins. If Lance confessed, Skip knew he'd go down with him. So when he overheard his friend—his partner—betray him and tell this Detective Blaze he had information, Skip knew it was time to take matters into his own hands.

He heard Lance tell Blaze he'd find him at the WCC, so Skip hoped he'd find his partner before Blaze did. Unfortunately, with the FBI closely tailing Blaze, Skip couldn't risk getting any closer. But he also couldn't risk what would happen if Lance shared all he knew with Detective Blaze.

Skip scrolled through pictures on his phone of him and his partner. There they were water skiing. There was Lance as the best man at Skip's wedding, picking his buddy up and giving him a bear hug at the reception. And there they were as kids, two tween sluggers posing next to each other on the baseball diamond just like the Bash Brothers from the Oakland A's, the towering home run hitters who crushed their way to a World Series title and into the hearts of Lance and Skip.

The Bash Brothers were flawed, though, and so were Lance and Skip. A tear rolled down Skip's cheek as he looked at the picture.

"I love you, buddy," he said as he closed his eyes and made a call he'd never thought he'd make.

"Hey, I got a job for you," he said. "It's fifty K."

"Who's the target?"

Skip took a long breath, then opened his eyes. Gone was the compassion he felt scrolling down memory lane just moments ago. In its place was a glare of self-interest and self-preservation. After all, like Lance's mom had taught them all those years ago, you do whatever it takes to win.

"I said, who's the target?"

"Lance Cutler."

It was 3:25 p.m. as Amber and I got out of the car and walked toward the WCC entrance. Betty opened the club door, arms outstretched, ready to embrace Amber and offer condolences as she led us inside. But how did she know we were there? We were an hour and a half past when she and Amber were to meet. Unless she was waiting at the door the whole time, which wasn't likely, then someone had tipped her off, which meant she, too, was mixed up in this whole thing.

"Amber, this was a mistake," I said as I grabbed her by the arm.

I turned to lead us out of the lobby, but standing in the way was big Jermaine, who towered over me and blocked the club entrance.

"Detective Blaze, I need you to come with me," he said.

"I'm sorry, this sweet lady and I are actually late for a meeting," I said, pulling Amber closer and backtracking toward Betty.

Jermaine stepped toward us and whispered in my ear, "Now you listen to me. I'm not here for the dame. All Mr. Santori wants is you. Let go of her arm and come with me, or my knee will crush your balls so hard the pain will last a lifetime."

I didn't know how long my lifetime would last given the day's events. My face still stung, and my ribs ached, but just the thought of Jermaine introducing his knee to my boys made me shudder. I let go of Amber, who was briskly led away by Betty. I quickly looked around the lobby, but my FBI protection was nowhere to be seen. Jermaine directed me toward the secret stairs I so longed to climb, only right then, I had no interest in seeing what—or rather who—was waiting atop them.

We made it to the door at the bottom of the stairs. The last time I'd seen this door, it was Jermaine who kept me from going in. Now he was the one literally opening the door for me. At least he tried. He kept fumbling with the keypad code, and I saw his agitation.

"49651," I instinctively said.

Jermaine typed in the code, then looked bewildered at me as the door unlocked.

"How the hell did you do that?" he wondered.

I shrugged as he led me in. I took one step up the stairs and thought of Henry and whether he made this same walk before meeting his untimely death. Before my detective career began, I'd had given anything to go up these stairs. Now that I was there, I'd give anything to turn right back around and leave.

I arrived at the top for my date with destiny and saw a hallway with a series of doors. Jermaine opened one and led me into a room of emptiness—nothing but black walls and a black ceiling. He grabbed a chair from the hallway and brought it to me.

"Here," he said. "Sit."

I took the chair and put it down in the middle of the room, facing the door. The legs had been sawed down so the seat was no more than twelve inches off the ground. This must have been one of Santori's intimidation tactics, making someone feel small while being reprimanded. I did as I was told, my ass barely off the ground and my knees inches from my chin. I stared at the doorway, where Jermaine stood guard.

"What do you think about the Bulls this year?" I asked, trying to forge a bond.

"What do you think about bingo at the fuckin' old people's home?" he responded.

Maybe basketball's not his thing. Before I could try a new conversation starter, a different guy walked in, introduced himself as Vince, and asked if I'd like some water.

"I'll pass," I responded confidently.

"Suit yourself," he said. "Mr. Santori will be in."

He and Jermaine walked out and closed the door.

Mr. Santori will be in? Will be in when? In a few minutes? Later tonight? After killing all my loved ones? I was new to these criminal confrontations, but some clarity would have been appreciated, particularly since I passed on the water because I really needed to pee. At seventy with an enlarged prostate, holding it in for long periods of time was just something I didn't like to do. I looked around the room, hoping there was a bathroom sign, but alas, there was nothing. Literally nothing. There was no clock, no tables, and the walls were windowless. It was just me in there, and I needed to go. There I sat in a toddler-sized chair, tapping my foot on the ground and my hands on my knees, trying to think of anything besides my bladder.

I must have waited forty-five minutes, and any bravado I might have had vanished. It was hard to portray confidence with your legs squeezed together and your hands in your crotch.

Finally, the door opened. Tony Santori looked like he was ten feet tall, his arms folded across his chest, a pink pocket square barely peeking out over his arms. His chin was square and his face haggard, like it was carved out of stone, but the cracks remained. The light from behind him cast a long shadow into the room, stopping inches from my feet. Before he could say a word, I impulsively raised my right hand and blurted out the only thing on my mind.

"May I please be excused?"

I must have been eight years old the last time I said that. Santori's menacing stare switched to puzzlement. He turned to Jermaine and Vince behind him.

"What did this fucker just say? Did he just ask to be excused?"

Jermaine started laughing at me, but Vince came to my rescue.

"I think he needs to take a leak," Vince said.

Tony Santori looked back at me, the restless seventy-year-old fidgeting in my tiny chair. Thankfully, he put me out of my misery in a good way.

"Jermaine, take him to the john," he said.

Jermaine kept laughing as he led me to a bathroom down the hallway, and I could hear cries of "Are you kidding me?" and "This guy!" from Vince and Tony. My refrigerator-sized escort pulled himself together and leaned in as we got to the bathroom.

"Hey, you asked about the Bulls. They desperately need a new point guard. Now make it fast and keep this door unlocked."

I may have embarrassed the hell out of myself, but Jermaine had opened up to me. I chose not to check either of my phones while relieving myself, for now that my bladder was under control, my full focus needed to be on Santori.

Jermaine walked me back to the windowless room, where I returned to my tiny chair as the sinister Santori stood ten feet away, casually leaning against the far wall and whistling a slow tune. Vince and Jermaine stood on each side of the doorframe, staring straight ahead as we all listened to Tony.

The whistling stopped, and Tony stared at me. Those eyes could burn a hole through metal. He slowly walked to the other side of the room, his eyes never leaving me. He made it to the other wall, then slowly turned and walked back, his gaze still stuck on me.

"So you're the famous David Blazen, lowlife detective," he finally said.

I wasn't sure what proper etiquette was for dealing with someone like Santori. *Do I acknowledge his statement, congratulate him for being correct, be offended at his insult, or just stay quiet?* I opted for quiet.

"Detective Blaze," he slowly said, beginning a new lap in front of me. "I like you," he said as he made it to the other side.

Oh, thank God, I thought to myself.

"But that doesn't mean I won't kill you."

Shit.

Tony signaled to Jermaine for a chair, and within seconds, he was back with a full-sized seat for the boss. Even while sitting, Santori towered over me. He seemed to relax a bit as he leaned back in his chair.

"Unfortunately, there was a murder here at the club yesterday."

"Don't you mean a suicide?" I asked.

"You and I both know no one kills themselves in a fuckin' steam room. I know who did it, and I need you to prove it."

"I'm sorry, what? You know who the murderer is? But how?"

"Who else could it be? It had to be that son of a bitch Feldman."

There was silence for an uncomfortably long time. I recognized my place and waited to speak until I was spoken to. Santori eventually continued.

"Vince, give him the bag."

Vince came up from behind me and tossed a WCC fanny pack in my lap.

"Consider yourself hired. In that bag is fifty Gs. That's your first payment. Find me the killer who trespassed and murdered right here on my property, and I'll give you another fifty."

"I thought you said you know who did it."

"I know who's responsible. What I need to know is which one of Feldman's deli fuckers walked into my club and killed Mel Weinberg. I expect an update from you in forty-eight hours."

"Mr. Santori, I appreciate your confidence in me, but you know I haven't been a detective for all that long. I'm sure there are more experienced PIs who could help you."

From the doorway, I heard Jermaine suck his teeth. "Be careful," he said. "No one says no to the boss and lives to talk about it."

Santori leaned forward in his chair as if he didn't hear my refrain. "Find Mel's murderer and bring the bastard to me," he said. He stood up, straightened his coat, and began for the door. "Otherwise, you'll owe me two hundred grand." As he got to the door, he turned back. "Oh, yeah, and I'll kill you like that wiseass Henry Jackson."

Tony Santori closed the door and left the room.

Wilt had never been inside a crematorium but quickly discovered *Ashville* was a perfect name for the place. He was greeted by a cloud of smoke when he first arrived, and everywhere he looked there was dust and ash—on the floor, on the shelves, everything was covered with it. A small pile of gray sand sat in the far corner, and Wilt admittedly did not know if it was garbage for a dustpan or someone's remains.

He was relieved to discover Wilbur Writhers had never cremated a Jew before, and Writhers was young, new to the cremation industry, and incredibly gullible, as "Rabbi" Wilt quickly found out. Wilt explained the custom of having a rabbi accompany the body until it was turned to ash. He also kept handing Wilbur money, a custom he said dated back to Moses, who gave his followers and friends coins on his way up to Mount Sinai.

Wilbur liked the solitude of his chosen occupation, but if he could find a way to specialize in Jewish cremations, he thought he could make some serious money. He appreciated the lessons the rabbi taught him, and he was happy to share insights on his own profession in return. He told the rabbi about the temperature of the fire and how turning a body to dust is a bit of an inexact science. He also confessed that although he'd cremated about a dozen bodies so far in his young career, he hadn't been able to bring himself to watch the final moments.

"How can that be?" Wilt asked.

"It's a bit embarrassing," Wilbur said.

"There's no need to be embarrassed. You'd be amazed by some of the things I've seen during my rabbinic career. So how do you cremate someone if you don't look?"

"I have all the bodies here covered while they're waiting to be cremated. When I get an order to complete the task, I find where the body is supposed to be and pull down the sheet to check the face and make sure it is in fact the right body. Then I pull the sheet back up and take the body to the conveyor belt attached to the incinerator."

"And then what?"

"Then I say my own little prayer, close my eyes, and lift up the sheet. I turn around, walk to the other side of the room, and push the button to turn it on."

"That's not embarrassing, Wilbur; that sounds ingenious. Why put yourself through the misery of watching someone's body be turned to powder? I think you should be proud of what you do."

"Thanks, Rabbi."

"What are the zip-top bags stuffed with sand on that shelf over there? Is that how you transport the ashes?"

"Well, it is. They come to us in a body bag and leave in a lunch bag. Those bags are different, though. Those are our lost souls."

"Lost souls? Are you making judgments on people after they die, Wilbur? God will not look fondly on that."

"Oh no, nothing like that, Rabbi. The lost souls are just collections of extra ashes that spray out of the incinerator, don't fit in an individual's designated container, or somehow just end up on the floor. It's our own little attempt to keep the mood light, you know, since we deal with death all day."

"And everyone leaves in a zip-top? Does every bag weigh the same, or does it depend on how heavy the person was?"

"Like the flame, it's an inexact science, but once someone is cremated, there is no way to identify them again."

The crematorium phone rang.

"Holy Mother of Baby Jesus Crematorium, this is Wilbur speaking. Oh, really? That's good news. Okay, thanks for the info. Email me the copies, and I'll get everything set up."

Wilbur hung up the phone and turned to Wilt. "Good news, Rabbi. The paperwork is all signed. Mel's soul will be given to God at quarter to seven tonight. I have to go get a few things in order, but I'll be back shortly. Feel free to make yourself at home—just not permanently."

Wilbur laughed at his own joke as he walked out of the room, leaving Wilt alone with Mel and only a few hours to figure out a new plan.

Vince and Jermaine remained with me after Santori's departure. I wasn't sure if I was free to go and briefly considered repeating my "May I please be excused?" line, but humor didn't feel like the right play after having my life threatened. I sat looking at Vince, looking at Jermaine, then looking at the floor. I hoped one of them would say something, but after two minutes of silence, it was clear I'd need to make the first move.

"So who's Feldman?" I asked.

Jermaine looked at Vince, and Vince nodded approvingly.

"Solomon Feldman is the one man standing in the way of Mr. Santori controlling this city," Jermaine said. "He and his Deli Boys are a gang that gives good guys like us a bad name."

Wait, did Jermaine just call himself a good guy? This coming from the man who threatened everlasting pain to my nether regions.

"How so?" I asked.

"Feldman stands for everything we don't. He's been Chicago's top roller since before Mr. Santori arrived, and the majority of his gang's money comes from illegal drugs, prostitution, and hired killings. Straight up, the dude is a bad man. I'm sure he had no problem taking down those two."

"What two?"

"The guy in the steam room and the one on Wacker. Two murders in a day would be nothing for Sol."

Tony just admitted to killing Henry, but I didn't want to stop Jermaine from talking, so I played along. He gave me some fascinating background info. He told me how he was head of security for Tony's Chicago operation and that both he and Vince had been with the Santori family for the past six years. He also said that unlike those Jewish boys, the Santori family was heavily involved in the community and donated considerably to a variety of charitable organizations. He also said I better not let Mr. Santori down.

"I've got no plans of failing him," I said as I patted my new fanny pack. "Thanks for that helpful information, Jermaine. Am I free to go?"

"Of course. Move quickly, Detective Blaze. Mr. Santori is not a patient man. Oh, and one more thing. Be careful with Feldman. That man would do anything to keep his grasp on the city."

"Hell no, I'm not killing no cop! Especially for only fifty grand."

Solomon Feldman was appalled by the suggestion he would take down one of Chicago's finest for such a bargain price. Yes, he and his men owned the contract-killing business in this city, but killing a cop was a big deal. And that warranted a big price.

"Tell him we need double, maybe even triple the cost to even consider that."

Eli Cohen had figured this would be Sol's reaction. Eli came to the United States from Israel, where he'd spent a decade in the army, and quickly made his way up the Deli Boys ranks. When he came to the States, someone who knew someone got him connected with the Deli Boys, and it became clear Sol appreciated his strategic mindset. It didn't take long for Eli to become Sol's top dog, with most of the organization's major decisions running through him. At face value, Eli agreed that taking down a cop for so little was bad business. But Eli saw the larger picture and the potential of a much larger payout.

"Boss, I understand, but this offer came from a cop, and if we take the job to kill Lieutenant Lance Cutler—"

"Wait . . . Cutler?" Feldman interrupted. "Is he related to that two-timing Sarah, who promised to deliver a breathing Mel Weinberg to me?"

"He's her only son," Eli said, glad Feldman picked up on his hint. "Now just think. What if we took the job but didn't kill him? We could hide him away for a while, make it look like he was kidnapped. She'd be so distraught she'd give anything to get her son back."

"She'd owe me," Sol said with an emerging grin. "She'd owe me big."

"Exactly."

"That's why I keep you around, Eli. Take the job, and I want you to be the one to get the Cutler cop. Take him up to Wisconsin to the family lake house and hide away there until you hear from me."

Having just received my first $100,000 assignment and my first death threat seconds apart, I needed to think. The FBI wasn't in the WCC, but I was sure they were close by, and I needed some time without them on my back, so I grabbed my pink phone, called Jeffrey, and asked if he could drive me around for a bit.

He picked me up in the underground lot to help me evade the FBI.

"Where to?" he asked.

"Just drive."

There were thirteen text messages on my pink phone, but Wilt's all-caps alert, *Our evidence burns in 2 hours,* was the most pressing. That meant Betty got Amber to sign the papers, and it also meant any hope of Amber receiving the insurance money would burn to ash at 6:45 p.m. I quickly called Wilt to figure out what other options we had.

"Wilt, thanks for the heads-up. What are we going to do?"

"Don't worry, David, I've got it all under control," Wilt said, coughing after every three words. "Did you ever meet my uncle Isaak?"

"Um, I'm not sure. What do you mean you have it under control?"

"I've got a plan. Without an autopsy, we have no case, right?"

"That's right."

"And without a body, we have no autopsy."

"Of course, Wilt. What's your point?"

"Well, how much do you need?"

"What?"

"How much of Mel do you need? Just an arm? His heart? You don't need his head, do you?"

"Wilt, are you out of your mind?"

"Just tell me what you need, David." His coughing worsened. "And do it in the next forty-five minutes." He hung up the phone.

I wasn't sure what Wilt had in mind, but I didn't have a better solution. I thought back to what I witnessed in the steam room. The mystery man entered the steam room and stood in front of Mel. With his left hand, he covered Mel's mouth and with his right swung down to jab him. That meant a couple of things. One, the killer was assuredly right-handed. After all, you wouldn't fire a pistol or use a syringe with your off hand. Two, I saw Mel's left arm flop up and then down, which I presume meant the arm was the point of impact. And based on what Dr. Cardorf had told me, the poison should still be in that left arm.

I frantically called Wilt back to deliver the news. "The left arm, Wilt, that's what I need. And it can't hurt to get the left shoulder too."

"It certainly won't hurt Mel." He chuckled.

"Wilt, dare I ask? How are you going to make this happen?"

"David, this guy Wilbur who works here believes anything I say. He thinks I'm a rabbi and has been fascinated to learn about all the Jewish customs related to cremation."

"Such as?"

"Well, for our current purposes, I told him I need forty-five minutes to myself with no one else in the crematorium to offer my final blessings to the deceased. He said he'd grab a bite to eat during that time."

"That's good work, Wilt, but don't you think he'll notice when part of his dead man is missing?"

"Nope, he's too squeamish to look before he turns on the fire."

"Will there be enough ashes that he won't be suspicious?"

"David, there are ashes all over this filthy place. I probably have enough ashes stuck to my shoes to take the place of a grown man. Robbing Peter to pay Paul isn't a problem here. A little less Mel won't be a problem either."

"Okay, Wilt, but how are you going to get the arm and shoulder?"

"My uncle Isaak is on his way over now. He's ninety-six and almost completely deaf, but for fifty-five years, he was the best Kosher butcher in his neighborhood."

It took me a few seconds to wrap my head around what Wilt was saying. "Wilt, this plan is so crazy it just might work. What do you need from me?"

"I need someone to meet us here with some giant zip-top bags who can then take the goods."

"I'll make it happen, Wilt. 'The goods' will be in good hands."

Lance couldn't believe he was turning his back on his police family. Hell, he was turning his back on his own family, too, at least his mom. But he could not continue going on looking the other way, particularly when he knew his actions, or rather his inactions, directly led to the deaths of four innocent civilians.

"This is the right thing to do," he repeated to himself as he parked in his driveway and darted up the front stairs. He checked the mailbox and found the syringe in a zip-top bag.

Moments after he'd entered the house, the doorbell rang.

Lance froze. He didn't know whether to duck and hide or dart out the back door, but he had no idea who he would be hiding or running from.

Lance put the syringe in his pocket and tiptoed to the front door. He peeked through the eyehole to find a man of average build in an oversized beige trench coat staring back through the hole.

"Lieutenant Cutler, my name is Eli Cohen, and I'm here to save your life." Eli stood back and opened his trench coat. "I am unarmed. I am simply a messenger."

Lance didn't know an Eli Cohen, but the guy was convincing, plus he didn't have any weapons, which made it easier to trust him. He quickly opened the door and ushered Eli inside.

"What do you mean you're here to save my life?"

"Somebody wants to kill you," Eli said.

"You know I'm a police officer, right? I'm sure there are countless criminals who want to see me dead."

"No, Lance, you don't understand. A hit has been put out on you. Someone was willing to pay to have you killed."

"How do you know that?"

"Because I'm part of the team hired to kill you. Don't worry, though, I'm not going to."

"Wait, what? Someone paid you to kill me, but you're not going to kill me?"

"Yes. I'll give you the full story later, but right now, we've got to get you out of here. I've got a place where we can hide out until it's safe to bring you back."

"How do I know you're not just taking me to kill me somewhere else?"

"No offense, Lance, but I spent a decade in the Israeli Army. If I wanted you dead, you'd be dead already."

"Okay, that's fair. Can I pack some stuff before we go?"

"No, we need to leave immediately. Leave your car here.

I'll drive. Oh, and leave your cell phone. I don't want us to be tracked."

"I don't know, Eli, I just met you. Why should I trust you?"

"Because someone you trust with your life is trying to end it."

"What do you mean?"

"Your partner put a hit out on you."

"No way," Lance said. "Skip wouldn't do that."

Eli opened an app on his phone and played a recording of Skip putting in the order. Lance was speechless. Skip was like a brother. How could he stab him in the back now or, rather, pay someone to stab him in the back?

"I know this is hard to hear, Lance, but we really need to move. Come on."

Eli put his arm over Lance's shoulders, partly to console him but more so to direct him out of the house and toward the car. Before Lance could even get buckled, Eli made a U-turn and beelined toward Feldman's Wisconsin safe house as quickly as possible.

I had four missed calls and two text messages from Marc, all telling me to check in with him immediately. To that point, I was disappointed with his lack of commitment to Team Blaze, but with Wilt taking care of "the goods," Patrick focused on the security cameras, and Jeffrey driving me around, I knew I had to give Marc another chance.

"Hey, buddy, long time no talk," I said. "I wondered if you forgot about me."

"David, originally I was worried about you, but Mary, Jeffrey, and Wilt caught me up on what you've been up to. You've been a busy detective. And you're sure you're okay? I mean, mentally okay?"

"Marc, my friend, I have never been better."

"Okay, I trust you. Speaking of trust, have I got news for you."

"What's that?"

"Jeffrey dropped that book of Mel's off with me a few hours ago, and I got right to work on it. I probably called fifty numbers, and at least half immediately hung up as soon as I said I was calling about Mel. That dude was not liked. Anyway, I got used to the rejection, but then I stumbled on something. Or, rather, someone. I left a message for this guy named Carter, and he called me back moments after hearing I was interested in talking about Mel."

"Marc, it's been a long day. Can this story move along? Why do I care about Carter? I've never heard of the guy."

"Just wait. Mel was a hired hand for Tony Santori, right?"

"Yeah. So what?"

"Well, Mel was low on the totem pole. I'm not sure he ever actually dealt directly with Santori. Carter was Mel's go-between."

"Okay, now you've got me interested. Go on."

"Carter was the one who gave Mel the orders to kill Charlie Myers, you know, that nightclub owner who also was the nephew of Solomon Feldman."

"Feldman . . . I heard that name today. He's enemies with Santori. So Santori was the one who ordered Charlie Myers to be killed?"

"No. That's where it gets even crazier. According to Carter, it was Feldman who put out the hit on his own nephew."

"What? Why?"

"To escalate the turf war between him and Santori. Also, apparently Myers had a gambling issue that was starting to cost Feldman."

"Why is Carter telling you all this?"

"Once Myers was killed, Carter went into hiding. He figured shit was going to hit the fan between Feldman and Santori and didn't want to get stuck in the crosshairs. He thought his best chance at survival was to pretend he was dead. That's why he broke off all communications with Mel. Then when he heard that Mel died, he figured he was next. He's on the run and thought he could trade his secrets for protection."

"Marc, this is incredible. Are you with him now?"

"No, I'm going to go pick him up later tonight and hide him out at my house. I'm not crazy about having a criminal here, but I figured knowing where he is at all times was best. What do you think?"

"Yes, I definitely agree. Let me think about how we can protect him and use this info to our advantage."

"Anything else I can do? I took a few vacation days from work, so I'm all yours."

"I do have a favor to ask. Do you still have that freezer in the basement?"

"Yeah, it's where my wife keeps the leftovers. Four years of leftovers."

"Is there enough room to fit an arm and a shoulder in there?"

"I guess so. Why? Did Mary go crazy at the store again?"

"No, I mean a literal arm and shoulder."

"I guess. But I don't understand."

"You probably don't want to know the rest. Before going to get Carter, grab some big zip-top bags and meet Wilt at Holy Mother of Baby Jesus Crematorium."

"A crematorium and zip-top bags? What the hell is going on, David?"

"Just tell Wilt you're there for 'the goods,' and he'll explain the rest. And, Marc, great job with Carter."

I hung up with Marc, overjoyed the team was back together. I just hoped his wife wasn't planning on having leftovers that night.

11

Special Agent Cliff Stanley had spent the past six years of his life leading the FBI task force assigned to the Santori family. He was a veteran of the war in Afghanistan and helped Vince infiltrate one of the nation's most notorious criminal families. Then this Detective Blaze appeared.

Special Agent Stanley was the one who begrudgingly assigned a tail to Blaze. He didn't want to waste valuable resources on a senior citizen, but Blaze had done more in a day than the FBI had in years. His phone call with Lieutenant Lance Cutler all but confirmed the FBI's suspicion about dirty cops within the Chicago Police Department, and it also implied a connection between the death in the West Coast Club steam room and the murderous explosion on Wacker Drive. Plus there was the Chinese bootlegging ring he'd uncovered earlier in the week.

The man may be in his seventies, Stanley thought, *but he's good at what he does.*

At the moment, though, he was missing.

"Sir, it's been almost three hours since Blaze entered the West Coast Club, and we haven't heard or seen anything from him," a tech analyst said. "Should we be worried?"

"No," Agent Stanley said confidently. "Santori wouldn't kill

Blaze in his own house. Honestly, I bet Blaze isn't even there anymore."

"Well, where is he, and what is he doing?" the analyst asked.

"Those are the million-dollar questions," Agent Stanley said.

Seconds later, a call was made to Blaze's phone, which went straight to voicemail.

"Hey, Mr. Blazen, it's Patrick," the message began. "Listen, I found something good. We got the lead we've been looking for thanks to the WCC cameras. Give me a call as soon as you can. Oh, and, Mr. Blazen, this detective stuff is fun."

The FBI tech team had advanced technology to track Blaze's phone's location. He had indeed left the WCC and was currently driving through one of the city's northern suburbs.

"Just keep an eye on him," Stanley said as he stared at the large monitor with the map of Chicago and a red dot representing Blaze heading north away from downtown. "What are you doing, Blaze? What are you doing?"

Lance's world was collapsing around him. In the span of a day, his mother asked him to cover up a murder, which led to four innocent people dying, and his best friend hired a hitman to kill him. Now he was in the passenger seat of a total stranger's car driving to some secret hideout. Eli seemed like a nice enough guy, though at that point, Lance wasn't sure he should trust his ability to trust anyone. The fact that Eli was allegedly trying to save his life did give him a leg up on Sarah and Skip, though.

Traffic was always slow at this time of day as commuters fled the city after a long day's work. Eli could tell Lance was in a fragile state, and he genuinely felt sorry for the guy. With nothing but time, Eli thought it might help Lance to talk through his current situation.

"So why does a cop put out a hit on another cop?" Eli asked.

Lance worked so hard to keep his dark past hidden, but he couldn't hide anymore. He had to tell someone, and Eli was as good a person as anyone, if not better, since Lance owed him for saving his life.

"Skip and I were friends growing up and have always been close," Lance began. "What started all of this, though, was my selfishness a few years ago. A crime was committed, and someone paid me to look the other way. I said it would only be a one-time thing, but the money was good. Real good. One thing led to another, and within months, I was addicted. After a few months, the money was pouring in, and life was great. Then Skip discovered my secret. He said he wanted in on the action, or else he'd expose me."

"I see," Eli said.

"I figured it was better to share the wealth with my best friend than have him double-cross me. We didn't hide our newfound wealth, and some of the other cops noticed. Before I knew it, there were seven of us who routinely took bribes to overlook certain illegal activities. It got so bad that we even created phony crimes and pinned them on enemies of our financers just to keep the money flowing."

"So what happened?"

"It took me way too long, but I finally came to my senses. I told Skip I wanted to come clean, but he didn't want to. Apparently he decided I could no longer be trusted."

The two sat in their own silence. For ten minutes, Lance stared ahead, embarrassed by his selfishness but relieved to finally share his secret with someone. Eli, meanwhile, was inspired. He, too, had horrible secrets he'd kept to himself for years, and the stress was debilitating. His jet-black hair showed far more signs of gray these days, and his blood pressure was consistently at a concerning level. Lance seemed to relax by sharing his dark past. Eli wondered if the same could happen for him.

"Thank you for being so open," Eli said. "I also have a dark past that's weighed on me for years."

"Oh yeah?" Lance said, intrigued.

"I told you I was in the Israeli Army, and for ten years, I defended my country against those who spoke ill of us or our religion. But the decade of constantly being ready to fight and kill took its toll, and by the time I got out, I was emotionally scarred. I was angry and vengeful, and that made me make some bad decisions, decisions I regret to this day."

"Been there, done that."

"When I came to Chicago," Eli continued, "I got connected with this guy named Solomon Feldman. I don't know if you've come across him during your time on the force."

"Come across him? Every cop in Chicago knows Solomon Feldman."

"Ah, so you know all about him and his ruthlessness."

"Yes, I know it well."

"I normally wouldn't lay this out for a cop—no offense—but I quickly rose through the Deli Boys ranks and became Sol's most trusted team member. I quickly lost count of the number of times he had me or one of the boys do something so sinister, and I just went along with it."

Traffic opened up and the two were silent, lost in their own heads as they stared out the front window. A sign said Wisconsin was just a few miles ahead.

"Eli," Lance said finally. "Thank you."

"For what?"

"One, for saving my life. But two, for letting me get that off my chest. I've been holding those secrets for so long, and right now, I feel more at peace than I ever have, despite the fact my best friend wants me dead."

"It was my pleasure. And thank you for doing the same. Who would have guessed an Israeli soldier working for Chicago's most notorious thug and a Chicago police officer would have so much in common?"

Lance smiled. "What a small world."

Kent's tone walked the line between calm and frantic as he called his longtime friend and current mayor of Chicago to apologize for blowing off their meeting.

"It was getting so late, I wondered if I'd made up your request to meet," Mayor Paulson said.

"I'm sorry, Mitch. I had every intention of being there by now, but Lance is missing."

"Missing?"

"He was a little paranoid when we talked on the phone earlier, and he wanted me to pick him up a couple of blocks from his house. I waited where he said for almost an hour, but then when he didn't show, I drove to the house. His car was in the driveway, and the door was locked, but he wasn't there."

"Are you sure?" Mayor Paulson asked.

"Yeah, I have a spare key to the house, so I let myself in to look around. It was like he had been there but then left in a hurry. There was a broken bowl on the floor; maybe he threw it at an attacker. And his phone was still there. Lance would never leave his phone by choice."

"That is concerning, Kent. But if he was attacked, why would he lock the door on his way out?"

"I'm not sure, Mitch; this is all very strange. I need to call Sarah and let her know, but I wanted to make sure you knew I wasn't trying to stand you up."

"Thanks for letting me know. When one of Chicago's finest goes missing, it's a big deal. I'll go straight to the FBI director and tell him I want his best on the case. We'll find Lance and bring him home to you."

The ability to compartmentalize is one of a politician's greatest skills, and right then, Sarah Cutler was doing her best to keep her crumbling world organized and in control. In the span of seventy-two hours, she made enemies of the two biggest crime bosses in the city, forced her son to risk his distinguished career to cover up a murder, and was threatened to be exposed by her husband. And through it all, her popularity as the potential next mayor of Chicago continued to rise. If she could just keep things together for a few more weeks, the most powerful seat in the city would belong to her.

To help continue her campaign's momentum, Sarah agreed to an exclusive one-on-one TV interview with Matt Vanner, host of *Views with Vanner*. Sarah thought Vanner was a bore, but the public loved his show, and Sarah knew to go where the voters were. As a viewer, she didn't like that the conversations with Vanner always came across as scripted, but as a politician, she appreciated being able to submit the approved questions ahead of time so she could practice her responses. Her campaign team confirmed the questions were delivered to Vanner and that he approved them all. *This should be a cake walk*, Sarah thought as her stylist put the finishing touches on her hair and makeup.

"Ten minutes, everyone. Ten minutes to showtime."

Just then, Sarah's phone rang with a call from Kent, perhaps the last person she wanted to talk with right then. Against her better judgment, she picked up the phone.

"Kent, can I call you back in a bit? I'm about to go on air with—"

"Sarah, listen to me. Lance is missing. No one knows where he is."

"That's preposterous, Kent. I'm sure he's just—"

"No, Sarah, he's not. Whatever you were going to say, he's not doing it. Someone has taken our son, and you and I know that it's got something to do with what you made him do."

"Now hold on a second. Just because—"

"I don't want to hear any excuses. Our son is missing, and it's all your fault!"

Matt Vanner hated his show. He hated the premise, he hated the structure, he even hated the name. *Views with Vanner* made it sound like he got to offer up his opinions on hot-button topics, but the reality was he was a glorified spokesman. All his guests submitted questions ahead of time with the understanding that Vanner would not go off script. He was more of a publicist than a journalist, and he hated it. He had dreams of emulating the legends of TV journalism, of doing high-profile investigative pieces that could bring about real change and hold guilty parties responsible for their misdeeds. Instead, there he was, a thirty-five-year-old mouthpiece with his own show but not his own voice.

Tonight had all the makings of another boring *Views with Vanner*. The Cutler campaign submitted their approved questions, and it was a laundry list of Sarah Cutler's main talking points: her plan to build on Mayor Paulson's school revitalization, her push for a more sustainable Chicago, and of course, her promises to improve safety throughout the city.

"Boring, boring, and boring," Vanner said as he sat back in his office, his feet on his desk and a crumpled piece of paper in his hands. He balled the piece of paper up and tossed it toward the mini Chicago Bulls basketball hoop stuck to the wall two feet above the garbage can. The shot went wide.

As the paper hit the ground, the door opened, and a familiar voice said, "Thank goodness you don't get paid by the basket."

Vanner looked up to find Tom Lexington standing in his doorway.

"Lex, how are you?" Vanner said as he got up to greet his former boss.

Vanner's first job out of college was as an evening crime reporter at the *NorthShore News*. Tom Lexington was the one who encouraged him to try broadcast journalism instead of newspaper reporting. He was a mentor to Vanner, but the two hadn't spoken in more than a year.

"What are you doing here?" Vanner asked.

"You ready to make some headlines, kid? 'Cause I've got a story for you."

"Always, boss, but I've got to finish getting ready for the show tonight. Can we talk after?"

"No, it's about your show tonight. You've got Sarah Cutler on, right?"

"Yeah."

Tom proceeded to tell Vanner everything he'd learned from Blaze. Vanner quickly jotted down notes, too focused on the details to process the magnitude of what he was hearing. When Tom finished, Matt stared at his notes.

"Lex, how do you know all this?"

"I've got an in with a Detective Blaze. You probably haven't heard of him, but he's a difference maker. He single-handedly busted a crime syndicate selling stolen clothes and purses earlier this week. But you can't tell anyone that part. Please don't mention his name on the air. I gave him my word I wouldn't tell a soul."

"So why are you telling me?"

"Because Sarah Cutler is dirty, and the public needs to know it. Who better to show that to the world than you? You reveal Sarah for who she is, and the national networks will come calling in no time."

"I don't know, Lex. I'm not sure if I can do that."

"Bullshit, Matt, you were born to do it. Do you want to spend your career doing these horseshit interviews where you don't even get to ask your own questions, or do you want to make a difference? Do you want to be a journalist people want to hear from, or do you want to keep doing this fluff you're doing now? I believe in you, Matt. I always knew you were destined for greatness."

Tom gave his former reporter a hug and snuck out to grab a seat in the audience, leaving Matt to himself to stew over what he'd just learned.

"Three minutes, everyone. Three minutes to showtime."

Annette snuggled on the couch with her husband and a bowl of popcorn to watch Sarah on TV when her phone rang. It was her oldest son informing her of Mel's passing and that the funeral was scheduled for the next day. The conversation lasted no more than a minute.

"Everything okay?" Jerry asked.

"Yeah," Annette replied matter-of-factly. "Mel's dead. The funeral's tomorrow."

"Want to talk about it?"

"Nope. I want to hear what my friend and our next mayor has to say."

I walked in the front door just as Mary finished clearing the dinner table. Summer was already in bed, and Amber was putting away the leftover food. Mary came over and gave me a hug, thanking me for returning in one piece—and breathing. Amber pulled out a plate to warm up some food for me, then also came to embrace me.

"Mr. Blazen, I was so worried when I couldn't find you at the club," she said. "But Betty, she told me everything would be alright, and she was right. That woman is a saint, I tell you. She had everything waiting for me when I walked into her office. The cremation just needed a couple of signatures for approval, and somehow, in the midst of all her actual work, she found a way to plan Mel's funeral. For tomorrow! She even called Mel's boys to tell them."

"Wait, the funeral is tomorrow?" I asked.

"Yep, at 2 p.m. I know you said not to sign anything, Mr. Blazen, but with everything she did to help, I just couldn't say no. I'm sorry."

"No need to apologize, Amber. You did what you thought was right."

I looked at my clock and saw it was exactly 7 p.m. Based on what I'd learned from Wilt, Mel—or at least most of him—had been turned into ash by then. And as I jotted down the funeral time in my notebook, I feared my to-do list for the next day was quickly going to surpass my to-done list from today.

"Thanks for understanding," she said. Looking at the clock herself, she asked if we'd mind watching *Views with Vanner.* "I love that show," Amber said. "That Vanner is a cutie."

The three of us sat on the couch, the two of them listening to the show's introduction as I lost myself in my head, my frozen peas back on my eye as I thought about all that had happened and how draining life as a detective could be.

"Ladies and gentlemen, here's your host, Matt Vanner."

The studio lights went on, and Matt Vanner came walking out from behind a curtain, waving to the audience. Included in the crowd was MGBC's Norman Yellin, one of the station's top executives, who candidly did not like Matt Vanner or his show. He'd had numerous conversations about canceling it, but for some reason, viewers kept watching. He was in attendance that night to see how Vanner handled the presumptive next mayor of Chicago.

"Thank you all for coming tonight," Vanner said as he walked to his desk. "Our guest tonight needs no introduction, so let's get right to it. Please give a warm welcome to the current frontrunner of Chicago's mayoral race, Mrs. Sarah Cutler."

Sarah walked out to a raucous ovation. She pushed what Kent said about Lance aside. It was time for Candidate Cutler to shine. Time to compartmentalize. She waved to the crowd and shook Matt Vanner's hand as he invited her to take a seat.

"Mrs. Cutler, thank you so much for taking the time to talk with me tonight."

"It's my pleasure, Matt. I have the highest regard for you and your in-depth questioning of your guests. I hope I'm up to the challenge."

"Me too, Mrs. Cutler, me too. Let's jump in. My first question is why do you think so many people have been drawn to your campaign?"

Sarah had practiced answering this question dozens of times. "Well, Matt, I'm glad you asked that. There are so many people to thank for this, but it all starts with the beautiful people of Chicago. They've been with me since day one, and to each one of you out there, I thank you. I think people have been inspired by what I'm trying to do. Mayor Paulson put Chicago in a great place during his time in office, but he would be the first to tell you that crime remains a major problem in our city. That's why I've vowed to make Chicago safer, and I think that's resonated with the public. Everyone wants to live in a safe city. Why, Matt, just today I got a letter from a little girl who said when she grows up, she wants to be like me and fight for what's right. That warms your heart, doesn't it, Matt? It certainly warms mine."

This was how the bulk of the interview went. Vanner teed up talking points for Sarah, and she delivered on every one of them. The show was nearing its end when a chant of "safer with Sarah" rang out from the crowd. Matt grappled with his ethical dilemma. He'd agreed to the campaign-submitted questions, but he also had inside dirt on this candidate, information that would blow open the mayoral race. Should he do what was safe or do what was in the best interest of the public—and himself?

Watching Sarah smile and wave to the audience, he took a scrap of paper out of his pocket and placed it on his desk. He knew what he had to do.

"Safer with Sarah indeed," Matt Vanner said. "Speaking of protecting our city, Mrs. Cutler, have you ever heard of the West Coast Club?"

"I have," a confused Sarah said. "I've had several lunch meetings there and even lifted a weight or two." She flexed one arm to a few chuckles from the crowd.

"Did you know it was the scene of a crime yesterday?"

"Mr. Vanner, I'm not sure where you're going with this. As a mayoral candidate, I do have access to a variety of confidential information, but I don't think this is relevant to our conversation."

"Actually, Mrs. Cutler, I think it is. When a murder takes place at such a public place, I think it's important for the public to hear what the candidate running on promises of a safer city has to say about it."

"Mr. Vanner, clearly you've been misinformed. There was no murder. There was a suicide, which is always an unfortunate thing to have happen. But I'd like to get back to my vision for further strengthening Chicago's schools."

"With all due respect, I think the public has heard plenty about your school plans. I have a few more questions about yesterday's West Coast Club incident. Did you know your son and a fellow officer named Fred Skepper led the investigation? Or that the man who died was on the payroll of Tony Santori? You know of the Santori family, yes?"

"Yes, I know of the Santoris."

"And did you know your son ruled the cause of death a suicide without a proper investigation? There were no photographs, no information given to the media, and I'm told there was even no autopsy. Why would that be?"

"Mr. Vanner," an agitated and offended Sarah said, "you've heard the phrase 'I'm not my brother's keeper.' Well, I'm not my son's keeper. I know that Lance is a decorated police officer who's proudly served this great city, but what he chooses to do or not do professionally has nothing to do with me. I have no say in how he does or doesn't investigate a case. Lance Cutler is his own man, and I do not speak for him. These allegations you're throwing out about him, you'll have to take them up with him."

"That's a great idea, Mrs. Cutler. In fact, I'd like to speak with everyone involved in this suspicious activity at the WCC yesterday. On behalf of *Views with Vanner*, I personally invite Lieutenant Lance Cutler, Officer Fred Skepper, Detective Blaze, and Tony Santori to come on and help the City of Chicago understand what happened yesterday. And, Mrs. Cutler, I'd love to have you join them so we can go in depth on the state of our city and how we can make it safer for everyone. That's all the time we have for tonight. Mrs. Cutler, thank you for being here. I hope you'll join us again soon so we can continue this conversation about truly making Chicago a safer city. Goodnight, everyone."

Matt Vanner stood and bowed after the greatest interview of his life. He went to shake Sarah's hand as the audience burst into applause, no one louder than Norman Yellin. The executive was stunned by Vanner's performance and had visions of this version of Matt Vanner taking not just the show but the entire station to new heights.

Sarah, dumbfounded, didn't know what had just happened other than that this so-called journalist broke his agreement. And where did he get all that information? Sarah wanted to give him a piece of her mind, but recognizing there were still audience members—and potential voters—in the room, she refrained. She stood up, shook his hand, and smiled.

"That was certainly interesting, Matt," she said behind clenched teeth.

"That was only the beginning, Mrs. Cutler," he replied with a grin.

"What the fuck?"

Tony Santori did not get caught off guard often, but he was not expecting to hear his name come up while watching the Cutler broad on TV. And he certainly was not expecting an invitation to appear on TV himself.

"Who does that jackass think I am, Robert De-fuckin'-niro? I'm not going on TV."

"Boss, this could be really bad," an equally surprised Vince said.

"No shit, Sherlock. Let's talk through this with the boys tomorrow. And, Vince, after our council meeting in the morning, let's you and me go take a drive."

"You got it, boss."

"What the fuck?"

Tom Lexington had specifically told Vanner not to name his source of the information, and what did he do? He not only named Blaze, but he invited him on to the show. David had trusted Tom with confidential info, and now Vanner revealed that info to the world.

"I hope David shared that with someone else besides me," Tom said to himself.

"What the fuck?"

Mary rarely swore, but after hearing Matt Vanner say my

name, she kept looking back and forth between me and the TV screen. "Did he really just say your name?"

She wouldn't admit it, but there was a growing part of Mary that was fascinated by this new career of mine. Adventure. Drama. Now notoriety. Mary turned and took the ice pack from my eye. She gave me a long kiss on the lips, one meant for a man of mystery, not a retired businessman.

"What the fuck?"

Now backstage and alone for a minute, Sarah allowed herself to be furious. Her campaign would have Vanner's head in the morning, but now she needed to make a different call.

"Why, hello, Madam Mayor," a cocky Skip said. "That was quite an interesting interview."

"Cut the crap, Skip. Where's Lance?" an agitated Sarah responded.

"I don't know what you're talking about. I haven't talked to Lance since this morning. Besides, after the bus you just threw him under, you're probably the last person he wants to talk to. Nice going, Madam Mayor."

"Stop calling me 'Madam Mayor.' I haven't won anything yet."

"You're damn right, and after tonight's performance, maybe you never will."

"What's that supposed to mean, Skip?"

"You just blamed your son for a crime you and I both know was your idea. And when the city finds that out, well, let's just say your time as mayor will be over before it begins."

"Skip, you son of a bitch."

"Meet me for breakfast out in Hinsdale, and we'll talk. Goodnight, Madam Mayor."

"What the fuck?"

Sol Feldman thought Sarah would go on air that night asking the public for help finding her son. Instead, she wouldn't even defend his honor against a weak TV host. Here Sol was thinking he could use Lance as leverage against Sarah, but he'd thought wrong. He figured a mother would do anything for her son, but he misjudged Sarah and the depths she would sink to in order to win.

A Cutler victory would guarantee Sol continued control of the city. But with Sarah turning on her own son, Sol feared Lance would do the same. What if he revealed dirt about his mother as a way of defending his own name? What if there was no such thing as loyalty in the Cutler family?

With Lance alive, he was a threat, both to Sarah and Sol. Feldman texted Eli that the plan had changed. He was sending someone to the safe house tomorrow to make Lance permanently disappear. He then made a rare confession.

We were wrong, Eli, Sol wrote. *Lance Cutler has to die.*

12

Eli woke up Friday confused by Sol's text message. Why did Lance have to die? What changed since they'd last spoken?

Still in bed, Eli checked the news and was bombarded with stories about Lance and his mother. The Chicago media bashed Sarah for her comments on Vanner's show. One headline read, *Mayor Mom? Maybe Not. Cutler Throws Son Under Bus on TV.* Another asked, *If Cutler Won't Stand Up for Son, Who Will She Stand Up For?* Eli read on to learn how Sarah Cutler refused to defend her son and his record as a police officer amid cries of murder and foul play.

And it wasn't just local news. National news organizations jumped at the chance to share clickbait headlines like *Chicago Mayor Candidate Bizarrely Blames Son for Murder* and *This Woman Definitely Won't Win Mom of the Year.* The most surreal headlines came from the tabloids, which tended to operate without rules or a desire to stick to the truth. One tabloid said Sarah murdered someone who wouldn't vote for her, while another introduced a seductive love triangle among Sarah, Tony Santori, and a mysterious Detective Blaze.

Eli had obviously heard of Santori, but Detective Blaze was a new name to him. He tried searching online for the detective and found him mentioned in a wide range of contexts. One story said he was an undercover spy for the Turkish government. Another said he was no detective at all, just a former businessman masquerading as a crime solver.

Eli looked at close to a dozen articles about the previous night's events, each with its own unique angle on what happened. The one constant was a single sentence he found in each story: Lieutenant Lance Cutler was unavailable for comment. Eli was one of only three people on earth who knew why he was unavailable; another was Lance, and the other one had just said Lance had to die. Eli was in a bind. He had enjoyed yesterday's conversations and genuinely liked Lance. On the other hand, he understood Sol's dilemma and knew his boss lost the leverage he hoped to have over Sarah Cutler.

"Too bad," Eli muttered to himself as he put down the phone to get ready for the day. "In a different situation, I think we could have been friends."

Sol Feldman didn't need a friend right then. What he needed was a killer. It would be easiest if Eli could just do the job, but Sol didn't want to stain Eli's hands and run the risk of him getting caught. Contract killing is an expertise anyway, and Sol always preferred to hire out rather than ask one of his Deli Boys to do a job. The average person may think it is just pulling a trigger, but contract killing required the three Ps: planning, precision, and picking up the pieces. A good hit left no evidence and no witnesses.

As Sol waited for the sun to rise, he thought through his options. Good hitmen were hard to find. The young ones lacked patience, and many learned how to shoot on the internet or, worse, in video games, which meant they tended to lack real-life accuracy and precision. All the other good people Sol could think of were dead, an unfortunate risk of the contract-killing profession.

Sol recalled an interesting duo he once used years ago. They were a pair of older Orthodox Jews—two guys who surely didn't look like assassins—who spoke very little but completed the job cleanly and on time. He didn't have many other options, so he texted the pair to see if they were interested.

Good morning boys, Feldman texted. *I've got a job for you, but it's in Wisconsin and needs to be done today. Want it?*

Within seconds, he got a response: *Send us the info. Shalom.*

The two Jews didn't want to take the job, particularly on a Friday, knowing sundown brought Shabbat. But when Sol Feldman gave you a job opportunity, you didn't say no. They knew they weren't getting any younger, and if they turned Feldman down, he'd likely never come to them again.

The two men didn't like Feldman, but Feldman owned Chicago, and being on his good side could do wonders for them and their community. They called themselves *general contractors*, but really they were hitmen, and when they were not praying, their services were available to anyone willing to pay. They did not think of themselves as killers—they viewed their profession as ridding the world of poisonous souls. And they were fundraisers. They'd made good money over the years and gave 30 percent of it to the synagogue, whose rabbi looked the other way because of its benefits to the congregation.

The two were not related, but they lived life as brothers. Both remembered the exact day destiny had brought them together. It was a Friday morning more than fifty years ago when they were young boys helping their mothers prepare for the Sabbath meal. They met at the live chicken store, where they were introduced to Yitzhak, the chicken butcher. They watched as he took two chickens, cut off their heads, and handed the bodies to the boys' parents, who would cook and serve the chickens for dinner that night.

Both were fascinated by how Yitzhak calmly yet calculatedly killed the animals. Each was given a part-time job between Bible studies and learned from their new mentor—and role model—the art of killing mercifully. Yitzhak often said that other people slaughter, "but we do not slaughter. Not here. Not now. Not ever." He often shared that the chickens arrived in the store happy and left the same way. That way, their lives had purpose. The boys never forgot that, and now as older men, they continued to follow that creed.

Beyond their distaste for Feldman, the men were nervous about the timing of this job. Yes, the sun was just on its way up, but February in Chicago meant early sundown, and tonight was to be a special sabbath as each man's entire family—including kids and grandchildren—was scheduled to break bread together and welcome Shabbat. Having all those people under one roof was going to be a feat to be sure, but one did what was necessary to support one's family. Taking this job meant they would need to drive two hours north into Wisconsin, kill a disgraced law officer, clean the whole thing up, and make it back well before sunset to help with the evening's feast. They would perform their morning prayer, then get on the road and hopefully beat rush-hour traffic out of the city.

The men thanked God for giving them this responsibility and for looking out for them, their family, and their community. When their prayer was done, they looked each other in the eye and recited their own creed, one inspired by their first encounter so many decades ago: "It is time we take another soul's life, time to continue our holy endeavor. Remember, though, we shall not slaughter, not here, not now, not ever."

I woke up Friday morning with the same nagging question I went to sleep with the night before: how did Vanner get all that information? Santori wouldn't leak anything, and Lance wouldn't use that format to expose himself or his mom. I hadn't met Feldman yet, but I couldn't imagine he had that much intel into what happened. And my team hadn't been brought up to speed yet on everything I saw. That only left me, and I sure didn't tell Vanner.

Then the realization hit me.

It was me—well, indirectly me. I'd been telling everything I knew to *NorthShore News* editor Tom Lexington, and he must have fed that info to Vanner. I ran to my office and did a quick online search to find that, in fact, the two used to work together at the newspaper. That bastard betrayed my trust and the ethics of his profession!

I grabbed my pink phone and headed to the bathroom. In my sweep of the house, I hadn't found any cameras or recorders there or in the bedroom, which assured me the FBI was allowing Mary and me at least a bit of privacy. I was pissed Lexington double-crossed me, but I also realized last night's fiasco could ultimately benefit my investigation. I figured he'd try to show remorse, which was good because I had a favor tailor-made for him. I needed someone who could document extensive information and who was able to lie, and he'd now shown he excelled at both.

Tom answered the call after the first ring as if he was expecting to hear from me, even though I was calling from an unknown number. He immediately apologized and blamed Vanner for his overzealousness.

"Your name was never supposed to be revealed," he sympathetically said. "I'm sure Tony Santori and Fred Skepper aren't too happy either. But Blaze, I had to expose Sarah to the larger public, and I've got to tell you, people are eating up this story.

Our overnight website traffic jumped 273 percent thanks to our story on the interview and our poll on whether Lance is a villain or a victim. You should check it out and vote. We're getting thousands of submissions."

"I'm happy for you, Tom, but I've got bigger stories on my mind. Are you interested?"

"What could be bigger than a missing cop and an embarrassing interview by his mayoral frontrunner mom?"

"Are you interested?"

"Of course. I'm always interested."

"Tom, you proved you would compromise your integrity for what you assume to be the greater good." I was met with silence. "Well, I have a man named Carter currently staying at the house of one of my associates. This man was the boss of the steam room victim, and the city's top crime families as well as the Chicago Police Department would love to get their hands on him. He has hundreds of stories to tell and is willing to disclose locations, victim names, and the perpetrator's names for more than eighty murders. He'll only do this in exchange for safe passage out of the country. If I turn him over to the police, he'll clam up, and if I let him go and he's spotted, he'll be dead in minutes."

"Blaze, I can't harbor a criminal and then get him out of the country. I'd be a bigger criminal than he is."

"That's why I've chosen you, Tom. Lie to him. Lie to him for the greater good, just like you lied to me. Say you'll give him new identification and documentation in exchange for the stories."

"But then what do I do with him?"

"I'm still working on that. What I need, though, is those stories on record—just don't publish them until we're ready"

"I don't know, Blaze. Lying to a criminal is a lot different than lying to you, no offense."

"Tom, remember how excited you just were about your internet poll? Imagine what your traffic will look like with this exclusive. Carter's information will bring closure to hundreds of people and potentially protect thousands more in the future. This investigative work could earn you a Pulitzer. Heck, you might even be sainted."

I don't know if it was the Pulitzer or the sainthood that convinced him, but either way, Tom Lexington was in on my plan.

Eli was out grabbing donuts for himself and Lance when his phone rang. It was Sol, who got straight to business.

"Okay, here's what's going to happen. At some point before noon, there's going to be a knock on the door at the house. Outside will be two older Orthodox Jews who are lost and looking for directions. Let them in and offer to help. Introduce them to Lance, and they'll introduce him to two bullets in the forehead. They'll take care of the body. Once they leave, get your ass back to Chicago. Got it?"

"Understood. I'll be back to the house in a few minutes and will keep Lance there until the men arrive."

"Thanks, Eli. I'm glad I can count on you."

Lance awoke, unsure if he'd ever had as good a night's sleep. Telling his story to Eli relieved so much stress off his shoulders, and without his phone or laptop, he had nothing to distract him but his own thoughts. He still couldn't believe Skip wanted to kill him, but that made him even more excited to get back and expose the crimes and coverups going on within his own department. He would suffer, but his conscience would be clear, and right then, that felt like a worthwhile trade-off.

His thoughts were interrupted by the sound of the front door opening. Lance got dressed and walked out to the main room, where Eli was setting up donuts and coffee. Lance thanked his host, and the two sat down for a morning meal—Lance knowing it was his first meal with a clear mind and Eli knowing it would be Lance's last. The two men made small talk about sports and life in Chicago, but the conversation quickly turned serious as Lance once again thanked Eli for saving his life and listening to his plight.

"I still can't believe Skip would put a hit out on me," Lance said. "After all we've been through, I wish he would have just talked to me."

"It is sad," Eli said. "You would think friendship and loyalty were more important than money." Inside, Eli cringed, knowing Lance would be dead in a few hours because of money.

"I know we just met, but you showed me you're a better friend than Skip ever was," Lance continued. "Thank you for saving my life and letting me open up last night."

Lance's words took Eli aback. He thought they were friends? It was clear the conversation in the car was therapeutic for Lance, and Eli wondered if he would rid his own demons by opening up the way Lance did. What was the worst that could happen? It's not like he'd tell anyone; he'd be dead in a couple of hours.

"It was my pleasure," Eli said. "You know, Lance, our talk last night clearly helped ease your nerves a bit. Would you mind if I gave it a try by telling you part of my past?"

"Sure. Tell me anything."

"I've never told anyone this story before, but I spent ten years in the army in Israel, and during that time, I never killed another person."

"Wow, that's admirable."

"It is, and it isn't. Allow me to explain. One day during my service, I was on patrol when I heard a Syrian soldier had robbed an Israeli food stand. The soldier was running, and he apparently was close to my post. I spotted him and chased him down a narrow alley. He was just about to escape through a building's back door, but I grabbed him and tossed him to the ground. Fruit and bread fell from his grasp as he sat upright against the wall, my gun aimed directly at his face. He said he did not care about conflict between our two countries but was forced to join the fight. He explained the only reason he took the food was to feed his wife, his two daughters, and his newborn twins at home. He asked me to spare his life, and I did. I put my gun down, reached my hand out, and helped him to his feet. Together we grabbed the food, and I told him to disappear before someone else spotted him."

"That was incredibly generous of you."

"That's what I thought, until the next day. It was 10:43 a.m., and I was in the same village patrolling alongside three other special assignment soldiers. Out of nowhere, I heard rapid-fire shots ring out from behind me. My three comrades instantly fell to their deaths. I turned around to find the same Syrian soldier holding a machine gun. We stared into each other's eyes as he fired a bullet straight through my gut." Eli pulled up his shirt to reveal a scar. "Every day, this scar reminds me that I killed three people—if not more—by not killing one."

Eli hid his face in his hands. Lance got up from the table to console his new friend. He handed Eli a napkin and put his hand on the man's shoulder.

"Believe it or not," Lance said, "I've got a very similar story."

"You didn't serve, did you?" Eli asked, wiping the tears off his face.

"No, but Chicago can be like a warzone. This happened my first year on the police force. One morning, I was on the South Side, and we got a report of an active shooter at a small supermarket. There were about a dozen customers in the store, and our special hostage situation team was set up outside, with one of our negotiators using a loudspeaker to try to calm the perpetrator down. My job was to guard the alley behind the store in case the shooter tried to slip out the back. There I stood, steps away from the door, ready for the criminal to barge out. Then from behind I heard, 'Hey, cop.'

"I turned around to find a Hispanic man holding a gun to the head of a woman, who frantically pleaded for her life. I pulled my pistol and told him to let the woman go. 'No way. Not until you call off the SWAT. That's my brother in there,' he said. He walked closer toward me, refusing to put down his gun or let the woman go. 'I will shoot,' I said.

"Eli, I had an open shot, but I froze. Just then, we heard hundreds of rounds of bullets as screams and shattered glass echoed for blocks. I turned back to the door, and as I did, the man screamed for his brother. He threw the women aside, pushed me into the wall, and charged in the back door. I turned to see if the woman was okay, but as I did, I heard another ring of gunfire and two words no cop ever wants to hear. 'Officers down! Officers down!'

"I charged through the back door and found the initial shooter dead. I looked out the front of the now windowless store, and my heart sank. Five police officers lay motionless in the store's parking lot, while a good twenty others formed a circle around someone lying in a pool of blood, their guns all pointed. I ran to the circle to find the man I just saw in the alley, now barely alive. He saw me there, smiled, and said, 'You.' I knelt in his blood, and with his last breath, he whispered three words in my ear, three words that haunt me to this day."

The cabin was silent. Lance's eyes were closed, the memory clearly still painful. Eli sat motionless.

After two minutes of silence, Eli finally broke. "What did he say, Lance? What did the man say to you?"

"Eli, I've never told anyone."

More silence. After another minute, Lance opened his eyes and looked directly at Eli.

"The man lifted his head perhaps an inch out of his own blood, looked me right in the eye, and said, 'You fucking coward.'"

Sarah needed some time out of the limelight, a challenge since every media outlet she could think of was waiting outside her condo door in hopes of scoring a quote from her about her son and the debacle that was last night's interview. It had been almost forty-eight hours since anyone had seen Lance, and as each hour passed, interest in the story grew stronger. Sarah was just as curious as the rest of the world where her son was. She'd tried calling his cell phone, but there was no answer. She hoped her unexplained meeting with Skip would reveal Lance's current location.

Sarah had her limo driver, Oscar, rush out of the garage, taking the media trucks with him as he gave them a roundabout tour of the city—Sarah, meanwhile, walked outside dressed in jeans, a Cubs hoodie, a poofy winter coat, aviator sunglasses, and a blue baseball cap. She found a taxi nearby and took it twenty miles west of downtown to the diner where Skip said to meet. Sarah arrived first and grabbed a booth in the back corner, ordered a cup of coffee, and waited, opting to stay in her sunglasses and hat. She was hoping most people mistook her for a millennial as opposed to the next mayor of Chicago.

Skip arrived twenty minutes late with a strut in his step and a grin on his face. "Good morning, Madam Mayor," he said as he sat down.

"Screw you, Skip. Where's Lance?"

"I'm sorry," Skip said.

He reached into his pocket and passed a folded newspaper across the table. Sarah opened it to find a picture of herself flexing on TV last night with the headline, *Safer with Sarah? Yeah, right!*

"I'm sorry you almost blew your whole campaign last night," he added.

"I know, I know, it was stupid. My communications team is working on a whole new social media push now to offset the damage that pompous Matt Vanner caused last night."

"That's a waste of time and resources. Only three scenarios can come from this."

"Since when did you become a political strategist?"

"It doesn't take a genius to see this. The first scenario is you drop out of the race, hanging your head in shame as you announce that you've decided to focus on repairing the harm caused to your family."

"Hell, no!"

"I didn't think so. The second scenario is Lance appears and lies on your behalf, but we both know that after what you did last night, it's unlikely he'd do that."

"That's true. What's the third option?"

"The third is the messiest, but I think it will guarantee you a victory."

"I'm listening."

Skip leaned in close. "If Lance never reappears," he whispered, "you'll have sympathy on your side."

"Fred Skepper, are you suggesting I have my own son killed?" she whispered back. "Have you gone mad?"

"Just hear me out," Skip continued. "I know it sounds bad, but think about it. Yes, you turned your back on him yesterday, but voters will forget that when they hear of his unfortunate passing. They'll see you as a grieving mom broken by the very crime that's riddled this city for years and that you're fighting against. They'll think you'll fight harder than ever to clean up this city in honor of Lance and so no other mother must endure what you're going through. You'll win in a landslide."

Sarah sat silently. She hated Skip for even suggesting they kill Lance. But he had a point. Sympathy is hard to come by as a political candidate, but if you can get it, it can be a golden ticket toward victory. Did she love the idea of being mayor more than her own son? Honestly, she didn't know.

"Hypothetically, how would we make the third scenario even happen?" she whispered across the table.

"I'm glad you asked because the wheels are already in motion."

"Wait, what if I don't want that?"

"It's too late. Lance's fate is no longer in your hands. You're being handed a lifeline. I suggest you get ready to take it."

Skip got up, put on his coat, and gave Sarah the same smile he had when he first sat down. "Enjoy your day, Madam Mayor."

I knew today would be less productive than the past few since Mel's funeral was that afternoon, and I promised Amber I'd attend. The sign of a good leader is knowing how to delegate, so I spent much of the morning back in headquarters, trying to catch up on messages and wrap my head around where we were and what, if anything, I could pass off to the team to work on while I celebrated Mel Weinberg's life and death.

Since my team was instructed to primarily use my pink phone for communications, that became the phone I checked more often. I hadn't even realized I missed any calls on the black one until I noticed a voicemail. I listened to Patrick say he'd found something interesting on the WCC cameras and realized the FBI now knew I had access to the club's cameras. For a kid who was supposed to be a genius, Patrick could sure be a dumbass sometimes. Still, I was curious what he'd found. I texted him to say I'd come over at 7 a.m. the next day.

I went through the team roster to figure out who was working on what and who may have capacity to take on the day's major projects. Patrick was on camera duty, Marc was hiding out with Carter, and Jeffrey was on call for any necessary driving. That left Wilt. Wilt had been a surprise all-star for Team Blaze so far and was quickly moving up the ranks of most reliable associates. I needed someone I could count on, and Wilt proved he was that guy.

I went to the bathroom to secretly call him from the pink phone. Dependable as ever, he answered on the first ring.

"Hey, Wilt, job well done last night at the crematorium. I still can't believe you pulled off what you did, but thanks to you, this case is not done yet."

"Just doing my job, Blaze. Happy to help. What's up for today?"

"I'm going to be tied up for most of the afternoon with Mel's funeral."

"Most of Mel's funeral, you mean. Remember, not all of him will be there."

"Correct, Wilt. Most of the afternoon will be spent at most of Mel's funeral. Anyway, I've got a job I could really use your help with, but it may be tricky."

"Trickier than amputating part of a body and stealing it before it's burned to ash?"

"Fair point. Maybe not that tricky. I need you to set up a meeting for me with Solomon Feldman. He runs a group called the Deli Boys out of Morry's Deli on the South Side. Don't tell him this, but I think he either killed Mel or hired the person who killed Mel, and I need to understand why."

"On it, Blaze. Anything else?"

"That's it, Wilt. Keep up the good work."

Vince was instructed to meet Tony in the underground basement of the WCC ten minutes after their morning meeting concluded. All of Vince's training in undercover work and espionage prepared him for this moment, but he was still nervous. Tony didn't like leaving "the compound," as he referred to the WCC, and rarely did he opt to drive. But as the two men sunk into the front seats of a nondescript sedan, Vince could tell something about this excursion was different. He subtly peeked in the backseat to make sure there were no bombs or wires he could potentially be strangled with; fortunately, there was nothing. The two left the club and drove west in silence for close to twenty minutes.

"Boss, can I ask where we're going?" Vince finally said.

"We'll be there in forty-five minutes," Tony replied.

He turned on some jazz music, leaned back with one hand on the wheel, and began to whistle. Vince didn't know where they were going. All he knew was for them to be going that far out of town, Tony either wanted to show him something incredibly secretive or go somewhere so isolated that no one would find Vince's dead body.

Another thirty minutes passed. Tony turned off the radio and looked at Vince.

"How long have we worked together, Vince?"

"Six years, boss. The best six years of my life."

"And have we ever kept secrets from one another, Vince?"

"No, boss, not one."

"Well, that's not entirely true," Tony said, taking his gaze off the road to look Vince in the eye.

Shit, Vince thought, *my cover's been blown!*

The car stayed silent for a full minute as the tension grew. Finally, Tony continued.

"Vince, I've been keeping a secret from you."

"You have, boss?"

"Yes, and as my most-trusted soldier, you deserve to know."

Vince's mind was racing. *Does he know about me? Is he giving up the business?*

"Every ten years, Vince, there is a clandestine meeting featuring a handful of Italian families like my own. It's a tradition dating back more than one hundred years, and it gives the families a chance to reconnect and share accomplishments and concerns with one another."

"Like a big networking event?"

"Exactly." Tony took the next exit and drove another two miles until they were in front of a rundown abandoned bowling alley. "This year, we are hosting the meeting, and this is where it will be."

Tony went on to explain that each family would fly into Chicago discreetly. The top men from each family would be coming, as well as their own security detail. The East Coast families also agreed to offer an exclusive invite to Los Angeles's Torallini family, the most prominent criminals up and down the West Coast, to learn best practices from one another.

"That all sounds great, boss," Vince said, "but why are you telling me?"

"Because, Vince, the meeting is going to be part of a larger event to celebrate me and my accomplishments, and I want you to coordinate it all."

Tony went to the trunk of the car and pulled out a briefcase. Inside was a stack of papers he handed to Vince. On it was the list of families who would be in attendance for the meeting, as well as everyone on the Santori payroll that should be invited to the gala. This stack was what Vince had spent six years working for. Six years of lies, deceit, danger, and even death, and now, in

Vince's hands, were the documents that would bring down Tony Santori. Inside, he was jumping for joy, but ever the master of emotional deceit, Vince simply nodded.

"Thank you for trusting me, boss," he said. "You won't be disappointed."

The two Orthodox men hired to kill Lance Cutler did not beat rush-hour traffic as they had hoped, and their journey through Chicago and north to Wisconsin was going at a snail's pace. What was supposed to be a two-hour drive was now looking like it would take twice as long, and both men's nerves were on edge. By the time they made it to the Wisconsin state line, it was nearly 11 a.m.

Wisconsin may be a short drive from Chicago, but for these men, they might as well have been in a foreign country. They seldom were outside the Chicago area, and as each minute passed, they became more resentful that they had taken this job. They considered turning back and declining the task but only briefly, for they knew if they declined Sol Feldman's job, they'd be dead before sundown. And so they pressed on.

At eleven-thirty, they exited the highway and drove three miles into a deserted town called Brutte to get gas. Calling Brutte a town was being generous. The welcome sign to the town, written in permanent marker on an old train crossing sign, said, *Wellcum 2 brutte*. Brutte's history dated back to the late 1700s, fifty-plus years before Wisconsin officially became a state. Forrest Brutte fought on the front lines of the Revolutionary War, and afterward, he decided he deserved a town in his honor. So he moved out to present-day Wisconsin and made one.

There wasn't much to the town—an abandoned warehouse on one side and an equally abandoned church on the other. In between, a field of dead grass surrounded a decrepit two-pump gas station. That was Brutte.

Brutte was also home to the world's smallest motorcycle gang—or at least one of the smallest. To be a gang, you needed more than one member. Brutte's gang had two. Their XXXL leather jackets proudly showcased the name of their gang: The Bruttes. Forrest Brutte IX and Lucas Brutte were large in stature and short on patience, a poor trait to have in a town with nothing to do.

As the Jews pulled into the gas station, they saw The Bruttes sitting on their motorcycles outside the store entrance. Like the Jews, The Bruttes sported long beards, although theirs were orange, and Lucas's was braided. Excited to see other living people, The Bruttes hopped off their bikes and approached the old men's car, Forrest on the driver's side and Lucas on the passenger's.

"Howdy, fellas," Forrest said to the driver. "Welcome to Brutte. My name's Forrest, and this is my brother, Lucas. Pleased to meet you."

He stuck out his hand to the driver, who stared blankly out the front windshield, ignoring him.

"I said my name is Forrest. Pleased to meet you."

Still nothing. Forrest looked at the men's black suits and black hats. Then he looked at his own hand still outstretched.

"What, were you Mormons never taught basic manners?" he asked, his tone rising. "Shake my damn hand."

The driver, anxious about getting back home in time and frustrated after four hours behind the wheel, had no interest in talking with Forrest, let alone shaking his greasy hand. Still staring forward, he responded to Forrest's demand.

"Sir, we come here peacefully, but we have a job to do and need to move on quickly."

"You heard the Mormon, Lucas, fill 'em up," Forrest said, his hand still outstretched before the driver. "Now I get you're in a hurry, but I'm still waiting for my handshake. Besides, we get so few visitors here, we'd love to get to know you. After all, we've never met no Mormons before."

"Please," the other Jew said, "we really must get going. Allow us safe passage, and we will wish God's blessing on your beautiful town."

"Lucas, it sounds to me like they think they're better than us," an agitated Forrest said. "Is that what it is, Mormon? Do you think you're better than us?"

Silence.

The pump stopped, and Lucas closed the tank.

"That will be thirty-one dollars and seventy-five cents," Lucas said.

"Here," the passenger replied, sticking the cash out his window.

"Forrest, I think you're right," Lucas said as he reached to grab the money. "These assholes must think we're not as good as them. That's not very kind."

"Not very kind at all," Forrest said, pulling his hand back and bringing his face to the driver's level. Lucas did the same to stare at the passenger.

"I think we need to introduce y'all to Momma," Forrest said. "She doesn't take kindly to people disrespecting her boys." He grabbed the driver's arm. "And, mister, you've disrespected us."

The Jews locked eyes. The driver whispered, "*Shalosh, shtayiim, echad*." They pulled out their pistols, and each took down a Brutte brother with a single shot to the forehead.

Forrest Brutte IX hit the ground first, followed a second later by his brother, Lucas, his hand still clinging to the cash. The old men put their guns away, rolled up their windows, and continued their journey.

13

MGBC executive Norman Yellin was supposed to fly back to New York and network headquarters following the last night's *Views with Vanner* show, but with so much attention being paid to Sarah Cutler, he decided to stay in Chicago. Of more significance to him was that he may have just found a star in Vanner. He wasn't sure what had gotten into the host, but Vanner became a bona fide journalist before Yellin's eyes. Vanner had a newfound charisma. He had courage. And most importantly, he had control.

Yellin had worked in this business for decades alongside some of the best anchors in the history of broadcast news. The common trait the greats had was the ability to own the room and the broadcast. They were never caught off guard, and they steered the conversations in the direction they wanted to take it. That's what Vanner did last night, and Yellin suddenly had enormous respect for him.

Vanner openly invited a notorious crime boss to sit alongside the presumptive next mayor and not one but two police officers to talk about a mysterious murder. That by itself would get eyeballs. Throw in the fact that one of the cops was missing, *and* he was the son of the mayoral candidate, who basically trashed his reputation on live TV, and Yellin was staring at the potential for broadcast gold. Forget having those folks appear on a regular episode of Vanner's show—Yellin was thinking bigger. Questions about Lance Cutler's disappearance were spreading across the country, and Yellin thought he could pitch a primetime national broadcast. This had everything a TV executive could ask for: crime, murder, politics, family drama, and a whole lot of mystery.

Yellin called his fellow executives, and they agreed the show had potential. They wanted to wait a few more hours to see if Lance showed his face, but in the meantime, Yellin was to quietly check in with the key players and see if they'd participate. He was supposed to start working on the production lineup and logistics but keep everyone at the local station quiet about the project. If Lance didn't appear by 5 p.m., the network would announce the Sunday primetime national special would air two nights later on February 18.

Few people outside of superstar celebrities found a way to live life with a single name, but Hanford was one of them. For thirty-three years, he'd been a Wisconsin state trooper, patrolling the area just west of Milwaukee like it was his own backyard. His loved ones knew him as Francis, but he always felt his first name was not manly enough. And at five-foot-four and 125 pounds, he tried everything he could to appear as manly as possible. That was why he got into law enforcement in the first place. It was why he wore a cowboy hat wherever he went. And it was why he grew out his signature handlebar mustache that had faded from brown to white over the years.

Hanford began his career as a street cop in Milwaukee. He still called himself a street cop, except now the streets he oversaw were dirt roads off the beaten path of the nearby highway. His days followed a similar pattern, beginning by staking out the highway for early-morning speedsters and ending by driving the dirt roads to make sure everything remained status quo. At sixty-five, he was weeks away from calling it a career. All he wanted was to ride out the last couple of weeks in calm normalcy before calling it quits and moving north to a cabin he'd built off Lake Michigan.

Friday began like any other day, but when he started his local patrol and arrived in Brutte, he found things were anything but normal. He got to the Brutte brothers' gas station to find the two lying face up on the ground, victims of single gunshots to the head. Hanford wouldn't say he was friends with the Bruttes, but after spending so many years driving through the area, he felt he at least knew them. They even invited him to eat dinner with their momma a couple months ago, an invite he had to decline, though he was honored by the gesture. *Poor boys*, he thought to himself, *they never saw this coming.*

Hanford hadn't seen a murder in this area in decades, but you wouldn't know that by his calm demeanor. He meticulously looked for any clues on the bodies, but all he found was Lucas Brutte clinging to $31.75, which ruled out robbery as a possible motive. The bodies were warm, so Hanford knew the killers must still be close. He called to dispatch, requesting roadblocks on every road within a fifteen-mile radius of the town. He guessed there were two shooters in the car.

"Question anyone who looks suspicious," he said. "Oh, and they'll have a full tank of gas."

With the call out of the way, Hanford entered the gas station in hopes the boys might have security cameras that caught the murderers in the act. Instead, he found a stench like nothing he'd ever smelled before. He imagined raw pork left out in the sun for days then soaked in rotten eggs and decided even that would smell better than the inside of the gas station.

Hanford grasped for his shirt to cover his nose and quickly

discovered he was surrounded by death. There were bones everywhere, some human, some animal. There must have been hundreds of them, maybe over a thousand. There was a tic-tac-toe board made from bones on the floor and all-bone picture frames on the wall. In all the years he'd driven by the gas station, he never saw the shades opened, and now he knew why.

In the opposite corner sat a pile of bones at least four feet high. *These boys don't deserve sympathy*, Hanford thought. *They were monsters.* He had to get out of there.

He turned to leave—and that was when he saw the most horrid sight of all. Just to the right of the door sat a reclining chair. In it was a full body of bones, flesh still decaying off parts of the upper body and remnants of hair still stuck to the skull. Nailed to the chest plate was a wood plank with MOMMA carved into it. Underneath the word were two black hearts drawn in marker.

Hanford frantically ran outside with two disturbing thoughts. The first was when he turned down that dinner invite from the Bruttes, he unknowingly saved his own life. The second was that whoever shot down these Brutte brothers may not be criminals after all—they just might be heroes.

Sarah Cutler kept replaying her conversation with Skip in her mind. Did Skip really say Lance was going to disappear permanently? And was Sarah really going to do nothing about it?

She didn't recognize the number calling her phone, but thinking it might be about Lance, she answered it anyway.

"Hello, Mrs. Cutler, this is Norman Yellin. I'm a senior executive with MGBC."

"Oh, hi, Mr. Yellin. I'm always happy to talk with the media, especially MGBC, 'the network of truth,' or so you say."

"Relax, Mrs. Cutler, this isn't an interview, and you're not being recorded."

"Oh, well, in that case, what can I do for you?"

"Mrs. Cutler, we both know that last night's appearance on Vanner's show did not paint you in the best light."

"And your point?"

"I'd like to offer you a second chance with Matt Vanner."

"No way. I'm not getting back on stage with that pompous prick!"

"Just hear me out. As you undoubtedly remember, Vanner invited you and several other people to appear on TV to sort out this steam room murder."

"Suicide."

"Whatever. Between you and me, I don't care about that. What I care about is that your son, Lance, still appears to be missing. You haven't heard from him yet, have you?"

"No, not yet. What are you getting at, Mr. Yellin?"

"The network is planning a Sunday night national special focused on Lance and his illustrious career."

"You mean like a memorial? That makes it sound like he's dead."

"No, not at all. What we want is to show the public how important a person he is to the city of Chicago and how we need everyone's help to locate him. And we'd like you to be the evening's star figure."

"Me?"

"Yes, you, Mrs. Cutler. No one can sell the story of a man's success and conquests quite like his mother. We'll have millions of people from across the country tuning in to hear his story, and that will be millions of people who will be listening to you."

"Millions of people, you say?"

"Yes, millions, Mrs. Cutler. I know you're running for mayor right now but just think—maybe a run at governor could be in your future. Why not get your name and face out there now? Besides, there's no better way to win over an audience than by tugging at their emotions. These people will feel awful for you, and that might make many forget about last night's debacle, and it could lead those in Chicago right to the polls to vote for you. What do you say?"

Sarah knew Yellin was right. Yes, she felt horrible about the situation she'd put Lance in, and yes, she was worried her only son may not be alive much longer. But Skip did say the Lance situation was out of her control. This, however, was something she absolutely could control.

"I'm in," she said.

"Great. That's great news, Mrs. Cutler. Assuming no one hears from Lance in the next few hours, the station will announce the special this evening at five. In the meantime, may I ask a favor? We're still looking to get other participants for the show, and I'd love your help securing some of them."

"Sure. Who did you have in mind?"

"Your husband, for one. And also Mayor Mitch Paulson. I know his health is not great right now, but I wondered if he'd make an exception to appear on air given the severity of this situation."

"Kent will be no problem; consider him in already. I'll see what I can do about the mayor."

"That's great, Mrs. Cutler, thank you very much. I'll be back in touch later with more details."

"No, Mr. Yellin, thank you for this opportunity. I truly appreciate it."

Lance and Eli spent the rest of the morning sharing war stories. The more they spoke, the more Eli regretted that Lance had to die. Eli told Lance things he'd never told anyone before; after all, his secrets would be buried with Lance. What Eli hadn't expected was the relief that came by speaking about his innermost thoughts and feelings. Lance became a pseudo-therapist for Eli, and Eli felt awful that he would now have to watch his therapist die.

He checked his phone and was surprised to see it was already 12:30 p.m. Sol said the hitmen would have the job done by noon. Maybe Sol had some sort of awakening too? Maybe Lance didn't have to die after all? Eli texted Sol to confirm the job was still on.

Of course, Sol texted back. *It's not done yet?*

No sign of the old men, Eli wrote.

Sol wanted to text the two Orthodox Jews but knew they wouldn't respond. The Sabbath didn't start until sundown, but they chose not to use their phones beginning on Friday after their morning prayer.

What's a guy gotta do to get another guy killed these days? Feldman texted in exasperation. *Where the hell are they?*

They must have hit traffic, Eli wrote back. *All good. I'll keep the target here and keep you posted.*

Thanks Eli.

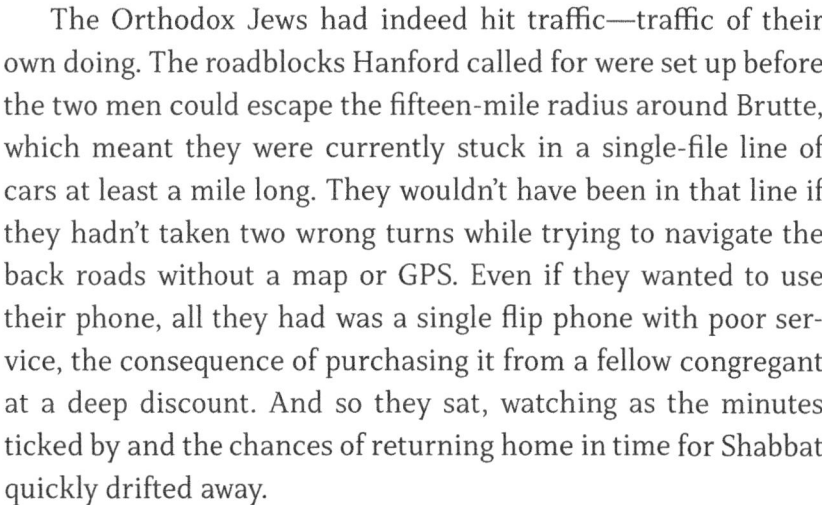

The Orthodox Jews had indeed hit traffic—traffic of their own doing. The roadblocks Hanford called for were set up before the two men could escape the fifteen-mile radius around Brutte, which meant they were currently stuck in a single-file line of cars at least a mile long. They wouldn't have been in that line if they hadn't taken two wrong turns while trying to navigate the back roads without a map or GPS. Even if they wanted to use their phone, all they had was a single flip phone with poor service, the consequence of purchasing it from a fellow congregant at a deep discount. And so they sat, watching as the minutes ticked by and the chances of returning home in time for Shabbat quickly drifted away.

When the two men finally made it to the front of the line, they were questioned and let through.

"No way you guys are who we're looking for," the officer

kindly said. "We're on the lookout for a couple of young thugs and are just trying to protect law-abiding, Bible-loving people like yourselves. Sorry for the holdup. *Shalom.*"

The men said *shalom* in return as they drove off, cautiously optimistic they might still get the hit done and return home in time for sundown.

After getting off the phone with Norman Yellin, Sarah was in full political mode. She knew having Kent by her side would help convey the image of worried parents, and the visual of a distraught mother and father asking for the public's help to find their only child would also bring in the sympathy vote. She then imagined having the frail yet revered current mayor of Chicago arm in arm with her and how that would help establish credibility among the voting public. She had no idea what Skip had up his sleeve for Lance, but she knew there was a golden opportunity sitting before her. And she was going to take it.

Sarah called Kent to confirm he still had not heard from Lance. She then told him about the TV special and asked that he come on with her to help plead for their son's safety. He begrudgingly agreed—for Lance's sake. Knowing she had him on her side, at least for the moment, Sarah pushed a little more, asking if he'd be willing to join her shortly for a meeting with Mayor Paulson. Sarah knew how close the two were, and she figured if Kent asked the ill mayor to appear on TV with them, there'd be a better chance he'd say yes.

Kent saw right through the plan, but again, for Lance, he said he'd do it.

The two arrived in separate cars at the hospital where Mayor Paulson was being treated. Their visit was unannounced, but they hoped their son's life and safety would be enough of a reason for the mayor to see them. Mayor Paulson was eating lunch in his bed as Kent entered the room first. The mayor smiled to see his old friend again, but the smile turned serious as he saw Sarah enter behind her husband.

"Hey, Mitch," Kent said as he walked over to shake his friend's hand.

"Good afternoon, Mr. Mayor," Sarah followed.

"This certainly is a surprise. How can I help you both?"

Sarah sprang into action. "Mr. Mayor, our son, Lance, is still missing, and no one has heard from him since Wednesday. We're worried he's in danger and were hoping you'd be willing to help us out."

"I see, Mrs. Cutler. Well, as your husband knows, I've already informed the head of the FBI about Lance's situation."

Sarah gave Kent a side-eyed look as she heard this news for the first time. "I hadn't realized that; thank you, Mr. Mayor. I'm sure that will be a big help."

"Now, if you don't mind, I'd like to get back to my lunch. Kent, want to call me with any updates later today?"

"Absolutely, Mitch. Thank you again."

"Actually, Mr. Mayor, there is one more thing," Sarah said. "MGBC is planning a Sunday night show pleading for anyone who knows anything about Lance's whereabouts to come forward. They are looking to have several guests on it, and Kent and I will obviously both be there. We, as well as the network, were hoping you'd participate as well."

"Mrs. Cutler, I'm in no condition to be on TV."

"We know that, Mitch," Kent said, cutting in. "It's just . . . this is for Lance, and we're trying to do everything we can to get him home safely. We think a few words from you could really go a long way."

Mayor Paulson looked into the eyes of his old friend. He glanced at Sarah, then returned his gaze to Kent. "If you think it will make a difference, I'll ask my doctors what I need to do to get out of here for a couple of hours. Assuming we haven't heard from Lance by then, I will come on and ask for help locating him."

"Oh, thank you, Mr. Mayor, thank you so much," Sarah said. "You won't regret this. Unfortunately, I need to jet. There is a funeral for that man who died at the West Coast Club a couple of days ago that I feel obligated to attend. After all, it was in Lance's jurisdiction. Thank you again, Mr. Mayor. Kent, I'll talk to you later."

Sarah walked out of the room. Mayor Paulson waited a full minute to make sure she was no longer in earshot.

"Kent, are you crazy?" he finally said. "You know if I come on TV it will look like I'm endorsing Sarah, right?"

"Believe me, Mitch, I know. Right now, though, I'll do anything to get my boy home safely. We'll worry about the political angle later."

Kent hugged his good friend and said goodbye.

It was time for me to get ready for the funeral. One of the decisions weighing on me had been when to let the FBI know I knew they'd been watching and listening to me. It was important to keep certain pieces of information hidden from them, but with everything going on, it would help to have everyone understand we were on the same page. As I began to change for the funeral, I got a call from Tom Lexington on my black phone.

"Hey, Tom, what's up?"

"Holy hell, Blaze, where did you find this guy?"

"What do you mean?"

"Carter. The stories he's spilling are unbelievable. I see why so many people would be interested in him. I just don't understand. Why did he come to you?"

It was fortuitous Tom called on my black phone instead of the pink one. This way, I could drop subtle hints to the FBI during the conversation.

"That story is for another day, Tom. What kind of information are you getting?"

"Blaze, it hasn't even been two hours, and this man has already told me about six different unsolved murders. Who died, who killed them, where the bodies are. I'm starting to expect him to tell me the victim's shoe size and favorite food soon. This is incredible!"

"I knew you were the right man for the job, Tom Lexington. If the FBI plays things right, they'll let you get a few more hours of interrogation in before swinging by to snag Carter and relieve you of your duties."

"The FBI? I hope no one comes for a while, Blaze; I may need another day with this guy. I'm running out now to get more batteries so my digital recorder doesn't die."

"That's great, Tom. I'm glad he's being so open. Has he told you anything about Mel Weinberg?"

"Not yet, but I'm sure we'll get there this afternoon."

"Okay, keep me posted. I'm heading to Mel's funeral shortly."

"Will do, Blaze. And, Blaze?"

"Yes, Tom?"

"Thanks for giving me another chance."

"When it comes to lying in the name of the greater good, there's no one greater than you, Tom."

Mary, Amber, Summer, and I entered Horowitz and Sons Funeral Home and found our way to the sanctuary, which already had nearly one hundred people inside waiting for the service. We took a seat in the third row, and I reminded Amber we were there to support her. The room reached capacity before the service began.

"Who knew Mel was so popular?" Mary said to Amber.

I didn't have the heart to tell them I believed most of the attendees were there to ensure Mel was in fact dead. And he was. Resting in a gold urn before all of us were the ashes of Mel Weinberg—well, most of Mel Weinberg.

The funeral slowed down my investigating, but it gave me an opportunity to sit back and think, something I really had not had a chance to do much of as a detective. Since I became Detective Blaze, my pace had been nonstop. This funeral gave me a chance to get lost in my thoughts, and as I listened to Rabbi Rabinowitz talk about Mel's legacy, the moment made me ponder my own.

At some point, hopefully many years from then, family and friends would be in a similar funeral home celebrating my life as I lay in a casket—hopefully in one piece. *What will they say about David Blazen? I'm sure they will say I was a successful businessman, a philanthropist, and, of course, a loving father and grandfather. But what about this new stage of my life? What will they say about my work as a detective? Will they even acknowledge it?*

Suddenly, something happened, something I could only describe as an out-of-body experience. I saw my spirit escape from my chest and float like a ghost above me. My arms shivered as a cold spell rippled down my body. What was happening? Was I dying, right then, right there? My spirit continued to rise, then slowly turned, and I saw my own smiling face staring back at me. *Oh my God, I am dying!* Then a voice spoke out of my spirit's mouth. I don't know if it was a god within me or the God referred to in different bibles, but as I heard the words "Hey, champ, you did good," that cold surge transformed into a warm embrace.

Mary squeezed my hand and brought my attention back to the funeral. Rabbi Rabinowitz carried on about Mel's devotion to making the world a better place.

That wasn't Mel's legacy. But it was going to be mine.

Cliff Stanley was also at the funeral, and he, too, was thinking about legacies. His FBI colleagues knew about his dedication to getting the job done, and for the past six years, that meant trying to bring down Tony Santori. Cliff was known as a man who would do anything to accomplish a mission, but few people knew the depths he'd go to.

It's hard to be at a funeral and not think about death, and as he walked along the room's perimeter, his mind went to the lives he'd cut short. Stanley was an explosives expert, candidly one of the best in the world. His first foray into blowing things up came roughly twenty years ago in the US Army, where he became a tactical genius with explosives.

Cliff didn't count the number of innocent people his explosives killed. It was callous, but it hardened him. What made him so effective was he accepted innocent lives could be lost in the name of justice.

As he gazed out at the funeral audience, he spotted Detective Blaze. He had never seen anything like this guy before. Stanley's team made more progress in the last two days thanks to Blaze than they had in the past two years. He wondered what made Blaze so effective, only to be interrupted by an all-caps five-word text message from Vince, his inside man with Santori: *We need to meet tonight!*

Eli checked his phone again. It was 4:30 p.m., and still no sign of the hitmen. *This must be a sign from up above*, he thought. *God must not want Lance to die yet.* Eli knew he sure didn't. This day had been an awakening for him, and it was thanks to Lance that he felt freer than he had in years.

Eli texted Sol that the old men still had not shown. He also mentioned that after spending the day talking with Lance, he didn't seem like that bad of a guy and that maybe there'd be a way to keep him alive after all. Sol received the message and was livid.

Of course he has to die! Sol texted back. *If he's alive, Cutler doesn't win, and if Cutler doesn't win, our control of the city weakens. Get your head in the game, Eli!*

Sorry boss, I just wondered if there was another way.

No other way. You better not have told that cop anything about the Boys.

Of course not. You can still trust me.

I better. I don't know where the hell those old Jews are, but they're running out of time. If they don't make it there before sundown, they won't do the job until after the Sabbath ends tomorrow night.

What should I do?

They'll need a place to stay. Give them some food and a bed and figure out how to keep everyone together tomorrow. Tell the cop they're my cousins or something. Just get the damn job done.

Don't worry, Sol. I'll take care of them.

Eli put his phone down to find Lance staring at him.

"Everything okay?" Lance asked.

"Lance, I have to tell you something," Eli said.

"Go for it."

"Well, you know how I said I was part of the team hired to kill you?"

"Yeah, pretty hard to forget that one."

"Well, at first, we were going to kill you. Skip hired Sol to do the job."

"I know, Eli, we've been through this already."

"Let me finish. Last night, there was a TV show with your mom, and she had an awful interview. Things got out of hand, and she was asked about some murder in a steam room that happened under your watch. Instead of defending you, she basically ruined your credibility to elevate her own."

"Wait, what? That woman has no—"

"There's more. Before the show, I convinced Sol that if we kidnapped you, we could use you as leverage when your mom becomes mayor and have the Deli Boys secure their grasp on the city. But when your mom turned on you, Sol realized you wouldn't have the value we thought you'd have, so he changed his mind again and wanted you killed."

"I'm getting lost here, Eli."

"Sol hired two contract killers to come up here and kill you. They were supposed to be here by noon, but obviously they've not arrived yet."

Seconds of silence passed. "Why are you telling me this?" Lance finally asked.

"Originally, I was fine going along with the plan, but as we've talked, I've learned more about you, and more importantly, I've learned more about myself. You have given me a gift of peace and calm like no other person ever has, and to be honest, I now consider you a friend. Unlike your former friend, I cannot sit by and watch you die."

"Well, thank you, Eli. But if someone is supposed to be coming to kill me, what are we going to do?"

"I'm still working on a plan. What I do know is these men are old Orthodox Jews and won't kill you after sundown. We may have to take them down ourselves, though, to find a way to escape."

"Now wait a minute, Eli. You told me you've never killed before. Let's not start now, particularly with two elderly men. Let today be a new day for us, one that doesn't require killing, crime, or violence."

"Well, what do you have in mind?"

"It seems to me that you should let them in, if they ever even get here. Be hospitable and escort them to their room. Then while they're here, we'll sneak out of the house. They can't kill us if we're not here."

"That's true. And if they fail their mission, I'm sure Sol will kill them anyway."

"That's the spirit," an enthusiastic Lance said. "No need for us to be murderers."

"But then what?"

"I'm not exactly sure, but I think I know someone who might be able to help us."

"Who?"

"Have you ever heard of Detective Blaze?"

After the funeral, I told Mary I had an evening work event to go to. She gave me a stern look, but I promised I would not be out late. I ordered an Uber for her, Amber, and Summer, then walked to my own car. Moments after I got in, the black phone rang. Before I could say hello, I was greeted with the distinct shout of the one and only Tony Santori.

"God dammit, Blaze, are you trying to screw me over?"

"Hello, Mr. Santori. I'm not sure what you mean."

"The fuck you do. One of my associates told me they saw you at Mel Weinberg's funeral. You already know the bastard is dead; you're supposed to be finding his killer. Do I need to remind you what's at stake?"

"Mr. Santori, I assure you I have not forgotten what you hired me for. You want me to identify Mel's killer, and I will do that."

"Figure out which one of Feldman's fuckers did it and bring him to me, Blaze, or I swear to God the next funeral you attend will be your own!"

Tony Santori hung up, and I prayed the FBI was picking up the clues I was leaving for them. Just in case, I'd be clear with them tomorrow that we were all on the same team.

The clock struck 5 p.m., and still no one had heard from Lance Cutler. Norman Yellin called his fellow MGBC executives and said he had Sarah and Kent Cutler confirmed, as well as Mayor Paulson, who had made no TV appearances in months. Fred Skepper was reluctant to participate, but he agreed after Yellin offered him a fifty-thousand-dollar participation fee. Tony Santori's people not so politely declined, but even without him, Yellin thought this special had all the makings of a ratings jackpot. He hadn't tried to contact Detective Blaze yet, but he wasn't too worried. No one would be tuning in for his opinion anyway.

The network bosses gave the broadcast a go. Fifty hours from then, the network would go live with a one-of-a-kind, ninety-minute special pleading for the safe return of Lance Cutler. Yellin shared the news with Vanner, whose first thoughts were about Emmy Awards and how this performance would be the one to catapult him into the national spotlight.

Sol Feldman was getting anxious. He hadn't wanted to take the job to kill Lance Cutler, and now the job had turned into an interstate debacle. He tried calling the Jewish assassins to figure out what the hell had happened, but he knew they wouldn't answer. His anxiousness turned to anger.

He hated the fact he hired unreliable old men. He hated Lance Cutler. And he began to hate Eli.

It was Eli who convinced him to take the job in the first place. And why the hell did he want to know if the cop's life could be spared? That was when Sol's anger turned to paranoia. What if Eli double-crossed him? What if his texts about the killers not showing up were a cover because he'd killed them and run off with the dirty cop?

The sheer idea of his closest confidant turning on him pushed Sol over the edge.

"Fuck them all!" he shouted to no one in particular. "I'm Solomon Abraham Feldman, and I'll show those sons of bitches why I own this city!"

Sol darted to his back storage area, grabbed a machine gun and some explosives, and tossed them in the trunk of his car.

"No one crosses Solomon Feldman and gets away with it," he shouted as he left the deli parking lot. "No one!"

The two old Jews lost the highway after Brutte and were forced to try to navigate Wisconsin's back roads. They lost count of how many wrong turns they'd made as they pulled their car over to the side of a dirt road at 5:07 p.m., still several miles from Feldman's lake house. Sundown was at 5:08 p.m. Jewish customs told them cars could not be driven during Shabbat, so they locked their doors and began the final stretch of their journey on foot. They had no luggage since they had figured to be home hours ago.

The sky was black by the time they slowly made their way up Feldman's driveway. Eli saw them approaching and had Lance hide in the back room where he'd slept. Feldman said the men wouldn't kill after sundown, but Eli figured there was no harm in being careful. With Lance hidden, he opened the door and greeted his new guests.

"*Shalom. Shalom*, my friends. My name is Eli, and you two look exhausted. Come. Please come in."

The old men put their frustration and fatigue aside. It was now Shabbat and time to celebrate God for giving this day of rest. The two men nodded appreciatively and entered the house. They glanced around the room, then whispered to Eli, "Where's the cop?"

"Oh, he's knocked out," Eli said. "I slipped him some Xanax, and he's been out like a light. No need to worry. Unfortunately, I don't have much to make a proper Sabbath meal."

Eli opened one bare cabinet after another. With no sign of food in the kitchen, he reached into his own bag and pulled out an apple, an orange, and some M&Ms.

"Sadly, this is all I have. But hey, at least it's kosher."

The two men grinned slightly. "Thank you, friend. This will do."

"You guys must be tired," Eli said. "Here, let me show you to your room; it's got the best view in the whole house."

He led the men upstairs and into the master bedroom with a sprawling view of the nearby lake.

"Thank you. This will be perfect. Thank you, Eli. You have been too kind."

"It's my pleasure. *Shabbat shalom.*"

Eli closed the door and calmly walked downstairs. He and Lance waited an hour before making their calculated departure. As they sat waiting in the kitchen, Eli looked at Lance.

"You sure this Detective Blaze is who we should go to?"

"Yes. If anyone can guide us on the correct path, it will be him."

Sol was still livid as he crossed the Wisconsin border, his mind racing with rage as he thought of Eli betraying him. The idea that his number two had double-crossed him made his stomach ache. He pushed the accelerator harder. His plan was to get to the house, barge in the front door, and take down Lance and the old men. Then he was going to sit Eli down and have a talk. If Eli could convince Sol of his allegiances, he'd let him live. If not, there would be four bodies Sol would need to dispose of.

Just then, Sol heard a pop. A pothole caused his front right tire to blow out, bringing his Cadillac to a grinding halt. Sol steered the car to the shoulder. He got out, saw his tire out of air, and his rage took over. He kicked the car as hard as he could, then began punching the passenger door as he screamed out in anger, "God dammit, how could this day get any worse?"

Sol's tantrum continued for another three minutes as he put dent after dent in the passenger door. It was only when a police car pulled up behind him that Sol began to calm down.

"Good evening, sir," the officer said as he exited the car. "What seems to be the trouble?"

'My tire popped on a fucking pothole back there, and now I'm stuck in God knows where at this time of night."

"Now, sir, there's no need for that kind of language."

"I'm sorry, Officer; it's just been a really long day."

"I know how that goes. Well, let me have your license and registration, and we'll get you a tow."

Sol handed the officer his license and waited as the cop called it in.

"Okay, Mr. Feldman, I see you have an Illinois license, but dispatch said you also have a place not far from here. You want me to give you a ride over there, and we'll get your car towed in the morning?"

Feldman knew the last place he could have a cop go was his hideaway occupied by a kidnapped cop and hired assassins. His trip for vengeance would have to wait.

"Thanks for the offer," Sol said, "but I think I need to head back to Chicago. I was going to grab a bite to eat and then turn around."

"Oh, I see," the officer said. "Well, how about this? You need some food, and I need a beer. I know a guy who can come out and get a new tire on for you within the hour. I'll give him a call, and while we wait, I'll take you to get the best sausage and cheese curds you've ever had."

The only thing Sol hated more than cheese curds was the

idea of eating with a cop, but he didn't see a way out. "That'd be great, Officer. Let me make a quick call, and then I'm good to go."

Sol turned away from the officer to call Eli. There was no answer. *That two-timing son of a bitch*, Sol thought. He frantically texted Eli, *Is it done?* He waited a minute, but there was no response. He would have to deal with Eli later. For the time being, he had a date with an officer.

"Sorry about that, sir," Sol said.

"No problem. Need anything from the car before we go?"

The only things Sol had in the car were the guns and explosives, all hidden under a blanket in the trunk. "Nope, I'm good, Officer. Thanks again for doing this."

"My pleasure. Oh, and no need to call me *Officer*. Everyone just calls me *Hanford*."

Cliff Stanley and Vince met on the top floor of a ten-story parking garage north of downtown. It was late in the evening as the two parked and walked to the side of the garage, peering out over the city skyline and Lake Michigan in the distance.

"What's up, Vince? Why are we out here freezing our tails off in the middle of the night?"

"Cliff, our patience has paid off. I know how we can take down Santori—and not just him but some of the worst crime bosses in the country."

"You've got me intrigued. What's the angle?"

"You know the war council I'd heard rumblings about? Every ten years, Santori and his family get together with other powerful criminal families to celebrate themselves and their accomplishments—our country's most heinous bastards all under one roof."

"Right?"

"It's a very hush-hush event for obvious reasons. Anyway, the get-together is apparently coming up next week, and it will be hosted at a bowling alley west of the city. And guess who Santori just trusted with not only the guest list but the coordination of the entire event?"

"You're kidding."

"Nope. Yours truly."

Cliff waited a minute to speak again, realizing the implications of what Vince said and carefully thinking through his own next words.

"Have you reported any of this information to Director Mangold?"

Vince, confused by the question, shook his head no.

"So how do you propose bringing them to justice?" Cliff asked.

The two stood there silently for a good five minutes, staring out at the night sky. Vince repeated the word *justice* to himself as he played out possible scenarios in his head. He envisioned different scenarios where teams of FBI agents stormed the party just as Tony raised a glass to his own accomplishments. It would be a total humiliation for Santori and would rattle his standing as so-called leader of the Italian families.

With each scenario, though, Vince kept seeing a problem. It would be a great look to arrest all of those criminals in one fell swoop and would make for a great photo in the next day's newspaper, but they'd all lawyer up right away. Then what? Their cases would drag through the legal system for months, maybe even years, and they'd go about continuing their dirty ways. And what about Santori? If he figured out Vince set him up, he'd have his head on a platter.

So much for justice.

"I don't know if we can bring them to justice, Cliff," Vince said, suddenly dejected. "Even if we arrest them, they'll pay someone off and be back on the street within hours."

Cliff had already come to that realization. "What if we go outside the legal system?" he whispered, even though he and Vince had the garage to themselves.

"What do you mean?"

Cliff remained silent for another minute. "Vince, I admire you, and I respect you for all you've done for our investigation, and I trust that you won't turn on me after hearing what I'm about to say."

"You know you can trust me, Cliff."

"As you know, I served in the military and spent time in Afghanistan. What you don't know is I was an explosives expert—still am to this day. Ever since I was discharged, I've built up a collection of historic bombs, weapons, and other destructive devices I've been able to get my hands on. I've got a rundown barn west of the city where I keep them. Well, it looks rundown from the outside. Inside are state-of-the-art blockades plated with three-inch-thick iron on the inside, just to protect the neighbors should anything go wrong."

"Cliff, why are you telling me this?"

"You said it yourself: The legal system is broken. For six years, we've tried to find a way to bring down Santori. You just handed us our best play yet, and even that won't bring him to justice. But what if we bring justice to him?" Cliff paused, then leaned in inches from Vince. "I've got the equipment and the knowhow, and we both have the desire," he whispered. "What if we blow the whole place up?"

Vince was silent. He stepped away to think, and the more he replayed Cliff's question, the more he thought it might make some sense. Killing people was awful, but was it wrong to kill certain people to protect others? That was what Vince asked himself as he walked around the top of the garage. Cliff stayed where he was, staring out at the skyline and giving Vince all the time he needed.

Five minutes later, Vince was back. "There's one problem with your plan."

"What's that?"

"If Santori goes boom, then Solomon Feldman secures an even greater grasp on the city. Rumor has it that he's in the pockets of Sarah Cutler, our presumptive next mayor, which means crime may run even more rampant with her in office and Santori out of the picture."

"So what do you propose?" Cliff asked.

"If we're going to deliver justice to these criminals, let's deliver justice to Feldman as well. We just need to figure out a way to get him to a meeting he'd never be invited to."

"That works for me. I'll figure some way to get him there."

"If you can get Feldman there, this Operation Boom will be a total apocalypse of evil."

There was silence between the two for a couple of minutes.

"Operation Boom," Cliff finally repeated. "It has a nice ring, or should I say *bang*, to it. I know a few other people who will be good for the job. I'll coordinate with them and set a meeting time for tomorrow night so we can all introduce ourselves and get on the same page."

"I'll be mostly out of pocket setting up the event for Tony but keep me posted on what you need from me."

"Right now, having your support is the best thing I could ask for." Cliff fist bumped Vince. "Boom, boom, bang, bang."

"Boom, boom, bang, bang."

I was abruptly awoken from a deep sleep that night with a hand firmly pressed against my mouth.

"Don't move and don't make a sound."

I squinted through the darkness to see a second man holding Mary's head down. "Lady, we're not here to hurt you or the detective," the second man said with a thick Israeli accent.

"That's right," the first one continued. "I'm not sure you're aware, but there are two FBI agents outside your house, and I'm guessing they have the place bugged. Now, we can't turn the lights on, but we'll introduce ourselves if you promise not to scream or make any sudden movements."

Mary nodded her head in agreement. The fact they called me *the detective* was a tell they needed something from me and likely would not hurt us. One man patted my side and told me to move to the middle of the bed. His partner did the same to Mary. Then they each lay beside us, four grownups squished against each other in a queen-sized bed. We must have looked ridiculous as we stared up at the ceiling, but I realized this was a smart move by our intruders so they could continue to whisper while preventing us from escaping.

"Detective Blaze, we haven't formally met in person, but my name is Lance Cutler. This is Eli Cohen, a close confidant of Solomon Feldman."

Lieutenant Cutler and Eli walked us through their past twenty-four hours, from why they were together to their respective awakenings and their escape from the old Jews in Wisconsin. Lance and Eli realized the wrongs of their past and wanted to now do good for the world.

"We are looking for guidance," Lance said, "and we've come to you for help."

"Me?" I clarified as I rubbed my eyes. "I guess I can help. Give me a minute to think."

In the past twenty-four hours, Lance Cutler's face had become one of the most recognizable in the country. Millions of people were looking for the guy, and I was practically spooning him in my bed.

"Lance, we clearly need to keep you out of sight, and my house won't work as a hiding spot. Eli, take him to a motel and check him in under a false name. Then you hightail it back to Wisconsin to deal with the hitmen. I can't approve of killing them, but you need to restrain them until we can figure out what their fate is. Do you have access to any handcuffs?"

"No, unfortunately I don't," Eli responded.

"No worries. Mary, give them ours."

Even in the dark I could see Mary blush as she turned to reach over Eli into her nightstand drawer, where she grabbed her pair of pink fuzzy handcuffs and my leopard-print ones.

"Thanks, hun," I said. "Now, Eli, once you detain them, get back to Chicago as quickly as you can before Feldman gets suspicious. Better yet, text him when you drop Lance off and say Lance is dead. We'll pray he believes you."

"That could work," Lance said.

"One more thing. I can't say I love the idea of sharing my bed with Mary and two other men, so if you need to get in touch with me, use this number. It goes to my pink phone, the one the FBI doesn't know about."

"You got it Blaze," Lance said. "Oh, and here's something for you." Lance reached into his pocket and handed me a zip-top bag with a syringe inside it. With that, he and Eli snuck out, leaving Mary and me alone, still squished side to side in the middle of our bed, staring up at the ceiling.

After a minute, Mary whispered, "Are they gone?"

"I think so."

"That was incredible."

I wasn't sure if Mary was referring to my authority and control or the fact she was in bed with three men. She turned her head and looked me in the eyes.

"This detective thing is for real, isn't it?"

"It sure seems like it."

She put her head on my shoulder.

"I think I can get used to having Detective Blaze around."

Eli did just as he was instructed, first stashing Lance at a rundown motel on the outskirts of downtown and then texting Feldman that the job was done. He apologized for the late notice but said things got "a bit complicated." Then he began the trek back north, contemplating how he'd detain the two Jews. Yes, they were older than him, but still, one against two was never good odds in a fight.

At 4:15 a.m., Eli spotted a diner just off the highway and decided to stop, not because he was hungry but because he figured he'd need some energy for the job ahead.

He walked into the Harvest Cow and grabbed a seat at the counter. There were only two tables with people at them, and it was hard to tell if those folks were early risers or late-night insomniacs. An overweight and underdressed waitress approached him with a pot half-filled with coffee. Her name was Marge, at least according to her upside-down name tag.

"Morning, stranger," she said energetically as if she already drank the other half of the pot. "What will it be?"

"Can I have two scrambled eggs, hash browns, and some toast?" Eli asked. "Oh, and some orange juice, please."

"You got it, mister. Back in a flash."

She moseyed off to the kitchen to drop off the order, then was back with the juice and a need to gossip. She yakked about the latest comings and goings in the nearby towns, like how so-and-so's cat got caught in a tree and how some lady gave her a new apple pie recipe she was dying to try. Eli couldn't care less, until she piqued his interest.

"Shame what happened to those boys."

"What boys?"

"You didn't hear? These two Vietnam vets, they called themselves the Brutte Brothers. Shot down outside their very own gas station just a few miles up the road. Everyone around here is talking about it. The police say they were the killing kind, but I don't believe it. They used to come in here all the time, sat right at that table with those boys over there now." She pointed to a group of three huddled up in a corner booth. "I didn't know much about the Bruttes, but they were always good tippers."

"That's too bad," Eli said.

"Yeah." She looked around the diner to make sure no one was watching, then leaned in closer to Eli as she topped off his coffee. "Want to know something even the cops don't know?"

Eli was starting to like upside-down Marge's gift of gab. "Sure."

She stood back up but kept her voice down. "That boy right there, Drake, sitting in the corner, he saw the whole thing."

"Really?" Eli was now legitimately curious about this back-road drama.

"Yep, he saw the car pull up and watched both Bruttes go down with single shots to the forehead."

"Why didn't he tell the police?"

Marge looked around again, then leaned forward. "Because they were fuckin' Jews."

Eli nearly choked on his juice. Marge gave him a few seconds before continuing.

"Those boys back there have their little KKK council meetings in here all the time. Drake said he didn't tell the cops because they fully intend to find those Jews and kill them themselves."

"That's crazy," Eli said, now trying to disguise his Israeli accent as best he could.

Marge stood and let the magnitude of what she said hang over them. She disappeared for a minute as Eli contemplated what he'd just heard. He was on his way to detain the same old men these white thugs wanted to kill, but he didn't know how to do so. Then he realized he didn't have to. Did he like the idea of colluding with the KKK? Of course not. Did it give him a way out of trying to restrain two career assassins by himself? Yes.

Marge came back with Eli's food in hand.

"Hey, Marge, do you mind bringing my food over and introducing me to those boys? I might just have a lead on where those old Jews are hiding out."

"Sure thing. Hey, I never caught your name anyway."

"Christopher," Eli said. "Christopher O'Brien."

Eli followed Marge over to the corner booth. Drake and the other two were busy on their phones and didn't notice their company until Marge placed Eli's plate on the table.

"What the hell, Marge?" Drake said. "We didn't order this shit."

"Boy, you better watch your mouth," she responded. "Besides, it ain't for you. It's for your new friend Chris over here."

Drake sized Eli up. "What are you selling?" he asked.

"I know where those old Jews are right now."

That was enough to get Drake and the others curious. They put their phones in their pockets and quickly invited Eli/Christopher O'Brien to join them.

―

At 4:30 a.m., Sol Feldman rolled over in bed, frustrated after driving to Wisconsin just to eat cheese curds with a police officer and then drive back to Chicago. With one eye open, he saw a text message waiting for him. As his eyes adjusted to the light, he read that Eli said the job was done and that the cop *cried like a little baby*.

Sol let out a sigh of relief. Lance was dead, Eli wasn't a traitor, and all was right with the world. He put the phone down, rolled over, and went back to sleep.

14

I woke up Saturday ready for a jam-packed day. I was scheduled to meet Solomon Feldman in the morning and Tony Santori in the afternoon, plus I promised myself I'd let the FBI know I was on to them. I thought an official broadcast from headquarters would do the trick. It was 6 a.m. I figured by nine I'd have a sufficient audience. Besides, I promised Patrick I'd check in with him at seven.

Saturday might have been the day of rest for many people but not Detective Blaze.

My face was still bruised from the beatdown I received behind the cleaners, but as I quickly inspected my wounds in the bathroom mirror, I knew I should wear the battle scars with pride. I turned on the shower radio as I washed off and shaved and was bombarded with speculation about Lance. Had he been kidnapped? Was he alive? Had he ditched his badge to become a monk and enter a monastery? I heard expert after expert spout out different hypotheses based on their decades of experience, and it quickly became clear they were experts in being full of crap. None of them knew a thing about Lance, particularly that my bedfellow from last night was just a few miles outside of downtown.

One of the talk-show hosts shared that MGBC was running a

ninety-minute special tomorrow night called *Looking for Lance*, where a collection of individuals would talk about the police officer's distinguished career and attempt to figure out what had happened to him and where he might be. Minutes later, Sarah Cutler, who was scheduled to be on the TV special, called into the radio show pleading for the safe return of her son. Within seconds, she seamlessly transitioned from Sarah the mom to Sarah the mayoral candidate, saying that whether her son was alive or not, he was a victim of the criminal activity that had run rampant in Chicago for too long. She said she was more committed than ever to helping solve the city's crime problem.

Then, as she choked up, she finished by saying, "I'm running for mayor so no mother ever has to experience what I'm going through right now—the agony of uncertainty, the potential loss of a child. Help me rid the city of this terrible plague and help me bring my boy home."

The woman was compelling, but I had to move on. I quickly got dressed and snuck out the back and over to Patrick's house. His room looked more like an eight-year-old's than a college kid's—glow-in-the-dark stars decorated the ceiling, posters of Bart Simpson and Pokemon adorned the walls, and bunk beds sat in the far corner. Patrick was too thrilled to show me what he'd discovered to be embarrassed by the decorations.

"Okay, Detective Blaze, do you remember when you asked me to copy all those feeds from the different cameras at the West Coast Club?"

Does this kid think I'm senile? "Yes, Patrick, I remember giving you that assignment three nights ago."

"Good. Then you also remember that I fell asleep recording camera twenty-seven. Now, at first, I wasn't sure why you wanted me to record that camera because it literally just points at a wall. I knew you must have a reason, though, and yesterday I figured it out."

He turned his computer monitor toward me.

"What am I looking at?"

"Okay, Detective Blaze, you want to keep quizzing me? That's fine. You wanted me to record this camera because of that picture on the wall—see it there, the famous one of the dogs playing poker?"

"Keep going," I said, legitimately lost at where Patrick was taking us.

"Look at the dog on the right. If you zoom in on his left paw, you can see a reflection of a door. From watching the extra footage I got, it's clear there are some bad men who hang out behind that door. And look at this—right around quarter to ten on Valentine's Day, three men exit from behind the door. The guy in the middle sure looks like Henry Jackson, that guy whose car blew up on Wacker Drive thirty minutes later. I couldn't get facial recognition to work on the reflection, but look for yourself. That's him, isn't it?"

I didn't need to look closer. Patrick was right. There was Henry, his arms held by two of Tony Santori's men.

"Patrick, this is really good work."

"Thanks, but I'm just getting started. Look at this. Later that night, those two other men arrived back at the club with four others and seemingly looked at every camera like they were trying to show they had an alibi or something. I got clear shots of them on camera three and identified the group."

Patrick pulled up a still photo of the six men. "I'll start with the biggest name. This guy is Tony Santori."

"Yeah, I know Tony," I interrupted. "And that guy next to him is Vince. I met him, and he seemed like the nicest of the group."

"That makes sense."

"Why?"

"Because Vince is a plant."

"Excuse me?"

"He's FBI. Must be real deep undercover. His real name is John Sedgwick."

"How did you figure that out?"

"The power of technology, Detective Blaze. I used some advanced facial recognition software and found a picture of John, or Vince as you call him, from an FBI class photo some fifteen or so years ago."

"Well, that's good to know. Patrick, I'm impressed."

I began to get up, but he pulled at my sleeve.

"But wait, the best is yet to come."

I was annoyed he pulled at my arm like a little kid, but I reminded myself that to a certain extent, he still was a kid. A kid doing some incredible detective work. I sat back down.

"Okay, shoot. What else you got?"

He clicked a few buttons, and a video popped up.

"Come over and watch this," he said.

"What am I looking at?"

"This is camera three, the same camera where we identified Santori and his guys. Only now, this is the feed from earlier in the morning on Valentine's Day. I've sped the playback up, but this shows everyone who entered the club between when it opened and 2 p.m."

Despite the speed, I recognized a few familiar faces. There was Mel Weinberg arriving early in the morning. There was Bryan, the manager who unintentionally gave me access to these cameras. There was Betty, who called me out on my snooping and arranged for Mel's funeral. There was Candice, the woman who wore the same outfit day after day.

"There's Henry," I said to Patrick. "Little did he know that would be his last morning on this earth. Oh, look, there's me walking in."

"By my count, there were 419 people who entered the club that morning," Patrick said. "I eliminated 285 of those because they left prior to when you said the murder occurred. Now I have to say, of all the remaining people, there is one clear candidate to be the murderer."

"Really? Who is that?"

"You," Patrick said, staring right at me. "You arrived in the morning, you were there at the time of the murder, and by your own admission, you were in the steam room with the victim. I've got to say, this detective thing is a pretty good cover." He stared at me for a few more seconds before breaking out in a giddy laugh. "I'm just kidding, boss."

I could have strangled the kid for his sense of humor, but I placated him with a quick grin. The kid had been coming through; the least I could do was pretend his joke was funny.

"Funny, Patrick. Can we continue?"

"Sure thing. Now, you maintain that the murderer was a white man about five-foot-ten, correct?"

"I think so."

"Okay, well, of the one hundred and thirty-four remaining people, eighty-seven are female, so we can cross them out. Thirteen of them are Black, and another eleven are elderly and not that tall, so we can eliminate them. That gets us down to twenty-three suspects. I isolated these individuals and put a haze over their bodies to mimic what you saw in the steam room. If you're ready, I can show you each one and see if we can narrow this list down even more."

I watched each person's movement through the haze and eliminated seven on the first watch and another five the second time around. Six of them just didn't feel right, and I had Patrick take them off the suspect list. That left us with five potential culprits. The problem was I didn't feel confident about those five either. Still, I had to give the kid credit.

"Patrick, this is impeccable detective work. Can you dig

deeper into each of these five and see if they have a criminal record or any connections to our victim?"

"You know I will, Detective Blaze. I will not let you down."

"Thanks, Patrick. Great job with all of this. I've gotta run, but keep me posted with what you find out."

I got up and was two steps from the door when Patrick said, "Oh, Detective Blaze, hold on; there's one more thing."

"How could there be anything else?"

"This one actually has me stumped. Take a look at this. There's one guy who appears in camera three leaving the building, but we don't have any record of him entering. It's like he appeared out of nowhere."

Patrick pulled up the video. The man had a jacket and backpack on and a baseball cap covering his head. He never looked at the camera, but I recognized him.

"That's the guy!" I shouted. "I think that's the killer we're looking for."

"But how do we look for a guy we can't actually identify?"

"You let me worry about that, Patrick. Now I really need to run, but Patrick, this was fantastic. You've made Team Blaze proud."

"Thanks, boss."

He held his fist out for a fist bump, and I gladly returned it. I wasn't sure I'd ever seen a wider smile on the kid's face in my life.

Norman Yellin woke up in a cold sweat. The previous night, the MGBC executive was on top of the world, thrilled his idea for a Sunday special was approved by the network's top brass, but now Yellin faced the reality of his situation. In thirty-six hours, his brainchild *Looking for Lance* would go live, and he had no idea how he was going to fill the ninety minutes he'd pushed for.

His lineup featured a grieving mom who would undoubtedly try to turn the broadcast into a rally for her mayoral campaign. He had the missing cop's close friend and the current mayor, who hadn't been seen by the public in months. And he had an inexperienced host who was supposed to keep the whole broadcast flowing smoothly.

Yellin was so impressed with how Matt Vanner had handled his last interview with Sarah Cutler, but a good night's sleep reminded him that up until then, Vanner was stale and boring. Yellin worried he let one performance cloud his judgment of Vanner and his abilities to coordinate a complicated live telecast. He'd feel more comfortable if there was a cohost to sit alongside Vanner, just in case things got messy or the conversation needed to be steered in a certain direction. But who?

Yellin thought through the other broadcasters from the station, but he worried about the competition between Vanner and any of his colleagues. Vanner was used to running his own show, and Yellin didn't know how he would take having a co-driver along for the ride. For this to work, he'd need someone Vanner was comfortable working with, even if they came from outside the network.

Yellin opened his laptop and pulled up Vanner's bio. At the bottom, he saw Vanner credited his success as a journalist to his mentor and role model, his first boss named Tom Lexington. Yellin didn't recognize the name, but after some quick research, he discovered Vanner began his career as a newspaper reporter, and Lexington was his boss. Today, Lexington was editor of the *NorthShore News*. Yellin read more about Lexington and some of the work he'd done over the years. He seemed like a dedicated journalist who cared for his craft and sharing the truth with the public. He didn't have TV experience, but Yellin found a video of him speaking, and he had a good voice. Besides, Yellin didn't need a TV star. All he needed was someone who could keep Vanner in line.

Yellin found Lexington's number and gave him a call to pitch the idea. Not only was Lexington interested, but he said he had previously unreported information about some major crimes in Chicago, including some that fell under Lance Cutler's jurisdiction. The info he had would be shocking to the public and could be great information to talk through with Sarah Cutler. He promised it would make for quality television. Yellin couldn't believe his good fortune and said he'd email a contract over to Lexington right away.

Yellin put down the phone and looked in the mirror. "Norman Yellin," he said to himself, "this broadcast may be the best thing you've ever put on television."

I snuck back into the house after meeting with Patrick. I had less than an hour before my FBI broadcast and needed to let everything I'd just learned sink in. I still hadn't figured out what I was going to tell the FBI and what I wasn't, so I retreated to the bathroom, where I knew I'd have privacy from my surveillance team. On the way, I heard a beep on my black phone. It was an email from Betty, the CEO at the WCC, with the subject line: *Steam Room*.

Intrigued, I opened a message sent to all club members.

As you all know, there was an unfortunate incident at the club on February 14. We've heard all sorts of speculation about what happened, but here is what we can say. An elderly man suffered cardiac arrest from spending too much time in the steam room. As the signage says outside the door, excessive time in that space can be unhealthy, and in this man's instance, that was the case. We are sorry for his loss, but we will use it as a reminder to all patrons to be mindful of how long you spend in the steam room. Beginning today, you will see signs inside and outside of the room reminding you to limit your time in the steam room to ten minutes at most.

Thank you for your cooperation.
Betty, West Coast Club CEO

It was weird the WCC was so emphatically stressing a murder was not committed, but I cast aside the email for the moment. I needed to turn my attention to the FBI, who would be able to assist with some of my investigative work but could easily get in the way of other parts. I started making a mental list of everything I wasn't going to tell them: my knowledge that Feldman ordered the hit on his nephew, that Vince was undercover, any info about Eli, and that Lance was not only alive but also my snuggle buddy. I had some ideas of how the FBI could help me, but for that, I needed to make one last call, this time on my tapped phone.

"Hello, Bryan, this is David Blazen. How are you doing?"

"Blazen, you jackass, you didn't tell me you were a detective. Your name is all over after that *Views with Vanner* show. That bastard Vanner, he seems like a real piece of work the way he turned on Sarah Cutler like that."

"I don't know him, Bryan, and I wasn't expecting to hear my name on TV either. Listen, do you remember when we were out at the bar celebrating your birthday? You showed me that fancy app you created with all the cameras inside the West Coast Club. I'm investigating what happened in the steam room, and I could really use a look at footage from some of those."

"Forget the steam room," Bryan said, clearly following a WCC script. "The guy died of a heart attack. Move along. Nothing to see there."

"I know that's what you have to say, Bryan, but if I could get a quick look at the tape from just a couple of the cameras—"

"I'm going to stop you right there, Mr. Fancy Detective Who Gets His Name Called Out on Late-Night Television. I appreciate what you and Mary did for me, but I'm upset you didn't tell me you were a detective. You want that footage? Get a warrant."

Bryan hung up, leaving me hoping the FBI picked up on the conversation and would do just as Bryan said.

Hanford the state trooper was a sucker for routine, but what happened yesterday was anything but that. He was shocked by the murder of the Brutte Brothers, but nothing could prepare him for the sights and smells he'd discovered inside their gas station. He hoped he'd ride these last few weeks of his career out quietly and then trade in his badge and gun for a beer and a fishing pole. He'd given out thousands of tickets and likely saved hundreds of lives by preventing people driving under the influence from harming themselves or others, but his discovery yesterday in Brutte would likely be what he was remembered for, and he didn't know how he felt about that.

Feeling both sentimental and a bit dismayed, Hanford left his home and headed for the Harvest Cow, his go-to place for a hearty breakfast every Saturday morning. There was nothing overly memorable about the diner's food, but he enjoyed chatting with Marge, who was often a bundle of useless information. Marge had a gift for gab, and Hanford always loved that she intentionally wore her name tag upside down. She thought it made her more approachable and helped strangers ease their way into conversations with her. Hanford had never seen anyone Marge couldn't talk to. If you wanted peace and quiet, the Harvest Cow and Marge's counter was not where you wanted to go.

Two inches of snow had fallen overnight, casting a beautiful white backdrop against the otherwise barren Harvest Cow. Hanford walked inside and stomped the snow off his boots as he gave Marge a quick hello. She smiled, then turned and shouted to the cook for Hanford's usual.

"Morning, Hanford," she said as she poured him a cup of coffee, "or should I say 'Hero Hanford.' You've been the talk of the town around here after what happened yesterday."

"Hey, Marge. No need to gossip about me today. What's new?"

"Just another Saturday," she said as she grabbed a plate with scrambled eggs, bacon, and toast.

"That's it? No gossip? That's not like you. Why so quiet? Come to think of it—" Hanford cut himself off as he gazed around the diner. "Everything in here is quiet. Where are the boys?" he asked, motioning toward the corner and an empty booth.

"I don't know what you're talking about, Hanford. Oh, but you know what is new? You know my boy Harlan? He just got a new job at the grocery store down the street. He's going to be a bagger, and, Hanford, I'm just so proud of him."

"That's nice," Hanford said, noticing how quickly she changed the subject. "I didn't ask you about your boy, though. I want to know about those boys, the ones who pretend they're in the KKK and are always in here. Where are they now?"

"KKK? Hanford, you must have spent too much time in the sun. You're talking crazy. Is that bacon crispy enough for you?"

"Marge. I know we're friends, but I'm also an officer of the law. I could arrest you for withholding information. Now what the hell's going on?"

"Fine. They're out chasing Jews. You happy?"

Hanford put his fork down and stared at her. He knew the

boys fantasized about being in the Ku Klux Klan, but the only thing he'd ever been able to cite them for was public vulgarity. They were a lot of talk but no action. At least until now.

"What do you mean chasing Jews?"

Marge reached into her apron and pulled out a crumpled piece of paper with scribbled handwriting.

"This guy named Christopher O'Brien stopped by early this morning, and he and the boys were talking about the murder of the Bruttes and that they were killed by two Jews."

"Why do they think that? We haven't found any evidence—"

"Are you telling the story right now, or am I?"

"Sorry, Marge, go ahead."

"Anyway, one of the boys said these two Jews took down the Bruttes with single shots to the forehead. This O'Brien guy told the boys he knew where the Jews were hiding out."

"And then what?"

"One of the boys made a couple calls. Each time he said, 'It's go time. Bring the big ones.'"

"Where did they go?"

"I'm not sure."

"Marge?"

"I swear, Hanford, I don't have an address; all I have is a name. It's on the other side of that paper."

Hanford turned it over and did a double take. "Feldman?"

"O'Brien said the Jews were hiding out at this guy Feldman's lake house not too far from here."

"That can't be. I was with Feldman last night."

"Really? Did he say anything about some Jews?"

"Marge, I've got to run. Thanks for the info."

"Hanford, what's going on? Don't do anything stupid."

"I'm worried it's too late for that."

As Hanford left the Harvest Cow, he called dispatch. "This is State Trooper Hanford. I need backup at 2221 Water Front Row.

It's the residence of one Solomon Feldman. I'll be there in fifteen minutes. No one goes in before me. And get me some snipers. I don't know what we're going to find, but I have a feeling it won't be pretty."

"Ladies and gentlemen of the Federal Bureau of Investigation, my name is Detective Blaze, and I come in peace."

I paused after that line to give the FBI a minute to alert anyone who needed to know that I was about to deliver an important message. I stood alone in front of my office desk as if I were addressing a crowd of thousands, wearing my gray Zegna suit, ready to officially bring two crime-fighting organizations together.

"Of course, you already know my name and probably more about me than I can imagine. As I'm sure you're aware, I am not a detective by training. I have perhaps overexaggerated the extent of my investigative education, and I admit that in fact I am an official nothing when it comes to crime solving. That being said, I think you will admit that in a short amount of time, my team and I have made great strides. This speech is to confirm for you that the FBI and Team Blaze are on the same side, and our goals are identical. Before I go any further, I'd like to formally thank you for the protection you all have provided me thus far. It's good to know there are still good guys in the world.

"Now, I don't need to tell you that crime has gotten out of control in this city, but thanks to Team Blaze, we are on the verge of exposing the culprit of a major crime. To close the case, though, we could use a little FBI assistance. For the last few days, I have been gathering information on the West Coast Club steam room murder, and yes, it was a murder. Tony Santori is under the belief that Solomon Feldman was involved and has hired me to prove just that. I have a meeting with Feldman later today, and based on what I've heard about him and his rivalry with Santori, I wouldn't be surprised if he thinks Santori was responsible. Between me and you, I don't think either family had anything to do with it.

"I mentioned I could use some FBI help. You should have recently heard a phone call between me and a man named Bryan, who is the night manager of the WCC. He has access to footage from every camera in that club—of which there are many—and said he would not turn it over without a warrant. If you could present him with that warrant and confiscate the video, I would appreciate it. That video will provide a lot of useful information, but I'm hoping it will also solve a riddle that's puzzling me. That riddle is how someone can leave a place they've never entered. I'll explain later.

"Once you have the footage, please visit the home of my good friend Marc—I'm sure you already have his address. Ask Marc for 'the goods' from the basement freezer and tell him Blaze invited you. I will warn you that 'the goods' are in fact partial remains of Mel Weinberg, the steam room victim. Team Blaze is confident there is a coverup going on, and fortunately we were able to secure enough of Mel for a formal autopsy to be performed.

"Also, as a treat for you, hiding out at Marc's house is a man named Carter. Arrest him but please don't mention my name. He was Mel Weinberg's boss and Tony Santori's primary hitman—he should be able to give you plenty of interesting information.

"In conclusion, I know some of my ways may be unconventional, but I request that for now, you allow my team and me to continue as we have. We're not hampered by many of the legal restraints you are, and as you've seen, we get results. As a thank-you, I will have an associate send you a recording that proves Tony Santori was involved with that horrible explosion on Wacker Drive three nights ago. Please know that is not even the tip of the iceberg in terms of what you'll get from Team Blaze.

"At the end of my investigation, you will receive documentation that solves hundreds of unsolved cases from across Chicago over the years. These findings will do more than simply earn you special accommodations from your higher-ups. It is my belief they will bring a number of criminals to justice and give hundreds of victims' families closure. That is my goal as Detective Blaze. I fight evil in this world. I know you do the same.

"Thank you again for supporting Team Blaze and please know that if there is ever anything we can do for you, we are at your service. Detective Blaze, signing off."

Special Agent Cliff Stanley and three of his FBI associates were in the truck outside Blaze's house and heard every word of the speech. When it was over, they all turned to Stanley.

"So, boss, what are we going to do?"

Cliff Stanley stared out the front windshield of the van, mentally balancing his job as an FBI agent with his new role as leader of Operation Boom. Blaze had just provided a lot of pertinent info the FBI could use, but what Stanley zeroed in on were those lines about fighting evil and bringing the bad guys to justice. It felt like those words were directed solely at him. Blaze may have started out as a pawn to get to Santori, but at that moment, Stanley realized Blaze could be a valuable addition to the Boom team.

"Boss?" one of Stanley's colleagues repeated.

"Let's take him at his word for now," Stanley finally said. "I want to introduce myself and see if we can truly trust him, but for now, we'll play Blaze's game. Go get a warrant and the footage. Then pick up 'the goods.' So far, Detective Blaze hasn't led us astray. Let's hope he keeps it that way."

15

The fresh snow gleamed in Wisconsin's morning sunlight as Hanford sped from the Harvest Cow to Feldman's home. The soft powder blanketed the ground and nestled against the bare trees, making for a truly picturesque setting, momentarily distracting Hanford from what he thought he was about to see. He'd already glimpsed two freshly dead bodies and the horror that was inside the Bruttes' gas station yesterday. Now he readied himself for two more deaths—these Jews who rid the world of the Bruttes and were now to be condemned by the KKK.

I just wanted to retire in peace, Hanford thought.

Peace would have to wait, though, as Hanford was brought back to reality by the sounds of sirens close behind him. *The cavalry is coming*, he thought as they turned onto Water Front Row. Hanford's was the first car to park in the driveway; a dozen squad cars flanked close behind. He didn't get out immediately like the rest of the officers, who jumped out and sheltered behind their cars, guns aimed toward the house. Hanford sat motionless, stunned by the contrasting beauty and horror in front of him.

He finally turned off the car and slowly got out, gazing at a white wonderland. The house was sandwiched between two rows of pine trees, each glistening with the fresh snow. Behind the house was a frozen lake, also covered with snow. And in front of the house, spread across the front yard, lay twelve white mounds, each draped in hooded cloaks with red blood stains soaking through. In the corner of the wraparound porch stood two old men, each holding a Bible in one hand and a pistol pointed at Hanford in the other. Hanford could not believe those two had taken down a dozen KKK boys by themselves.

"Officer, we mean you no harm," one of the men said. "We do not wish to hurt you. Please, have your men turn off their sirens and stand down while you join us up here. Allow us to tell you our story, and we promise you will walk away from here safely."

Hanford did not feel he had many choices, so he motioned for the officers to stand down. The sirens were turned off, casting an eerie silence over the area. Hanford slowly made his way up the steps, hands in the air, prepared to do as these old men commanded. One grabbed a large wicker chair, brushed off the snow, and brought it to the corner of the deck. Its size blocked the two chairs across from it where the men sat, preventing any snipers from having a clear shot.

Hanford sat in the large chair, put his cowboy hat on one knee, and stared out at the lake. If it weren't for the twelve dead bodies and the two pistols still aimed at him, this could have been very calming.

With his back to his backup, Hanford asked the men for their names. The two men put their guns and Bibles on the table between them.

"Sir, we can skip introductions," one said with a thick Israeli accent. "Formalities like that are for the future, and our future is over. As you've seen, we've rid the world of twelve hateful souls this morning, souls scarred with bigotry and hatred that had no place on this earth. They were not the first we've killed, but they will be the last."

"We have no regrets," the other Jew said. "Any life we've

taken was a life that was a threat to others. We are not killers. We are savers."

"Is that why you killed the Brutte brothers yesterday?" Hanford asked.

"Ah yes, those two were unjust and not deserving of God's praise. We did not want to bring them harm, but we believed it was our duty."

"And it is my duty to tell you we have laws for a reason," Hanford said. "You two have made a mess for me to deal with. All I wanted was to coast into my retirement, not deal with vigilantes. Now you may have a fighter's chance in court if you claim self-defense, but you've just admitted to an officer of the law that you've committed at least fourteen murders in the past twenty-four hours. I'm not sure self-defense will protect you from that fact."

"We understand that, sir," the first Jew said, "and we have no intention of seeing a judge or being tried. You see, we, too, are retiring, and this can't be an accident that we're meeting you today. We've always believed God had a plan for us, and now we see that you are part of that plan."

"What do you mean?" Hanford asked.

"We can tell you are a believer in justice and doing what is right."

"Yes. So what?"

"Yesterday, we were hired to kill someone, but he got away. As he escaped, we heard him and an associate say that a Detective Blaze could help guide them on their correct path."

"Detective Blaze? Never heard of him," Hanford said.

"We have. A few days ago, our rabbi shared a story the detective wrote about looking out for others. It is our belief that we now need to look out for him."

The Jew picked up his Bible and reached to hand it to Hanford.

"This Bible has been our guide, but it is of no more use to us. As we said, it is time for us to retire. Please see to it that Detective Blaze receives it."

The two men stood as Hanford looked at the book.

"What do you mean it has no more use to you?"

The two did not respond. Hanford looked up to see the men again pointing their guns at him. They weren't going to shoot him, but the snipers didn't know that. The snow-covered silence was disturbed as the sounds of gunshots rang out. The two men fell to their deaths as Hanford sat startled, his arms clinging to the Bible against his chest.

Eli arrived at Morry's Deli Saturday morning wishing he were anywhere else in the world. Albania, Africa—hell, even Antarctica would have been better, and that was just the As. The former soldier was a different man than the last time he'd set foot in Solomon Feldman's headquarters—for better and for worse.

Eli was ready for a new life, one that didn't involve working for criminals, but before he could run off and start anew, he had loose ends to tie up. Unfortunately, Feldman was involved with all of them. First off, Eli had to make sure Feldman was convinced Lance was dead. Secondly, while nestled up in Detective Blaze's bed, he heard Blaze say he was going to meet with Feldman today. Eli had just met the guy, but he felt he owed him a debt and wanted to make sure the detective left his meeting with Feldman in one piece. Lastly, Eli was curious how the whole Lance situation would turn out. The two bonded, and Eli now felt a connection to the police officer, who he hoped would be able to live a life with less guilt.

Eli didn't even make it in the front door before coming face to face with Feldman, who was hanging out in front of the deli. Eli put on a brave face as he approached the door and his boss. Feldman saw him and gave him a little head nod.

"We good, Eli?" he asked.

"Yeah, boss. We're good."

"Good."

The two men walked inside, one pleased he was rid of Lance Cutler forever, the other knowing the truth that the Chicago police officer was alive and well.

Lance Cutler discovered there is only so much to do when you're alone in a hotel room. After counting the number of stripes in the wallpaper followed by a scintillating round of counting shower tiles on the wall, Lance needed something to pass the time. He turned on the television and found his own picture staring back at him. Surprised but more confused, he turned up the volume.

"It's now been seventy-two hours since disgraced Chicago Police officer Lance Cutler has been seen or heard from. Hopes for his safe return are beginning to dwindle, but all hope is not lost."

Disgraced? Eli had told Lance that Sarah Cutler did not paint him in the best light when she was on TV, but disgraced? He flipped the channel to another local station, and they, too, were talking about him. He even turned to a sports channel, and the story was about how the Chicago Bulls were going to wear warm-up shirts with Lance's face under the line *Have you seen him?* for their next game. He eventually switched to MGBC, where there were two tickers on the side of the screen, one counting up with the amount of time since anyone had heard from Lance and one counting down to a show called *Looking for Lance*.

"Looking for Lance? I'm right here," he said to himself.

The show went to commercial, and once again Lance saw his own face on the screen as the network promoted its Sunday special.

"A beloved son. A defender of the law. That is Lance Cutler.

But who else is this mystery man? And more importantly, where has he gone? Join us tomorrow night for our ninety-minute special, *Looking for Lance*. Hear from his parents and those who know him best as the world tries to solve the riddle of his disappearance."

Lance was speechless. He was stunned to hear about this TV special, although he was not surprised to hear his mom was involved.

"She's probably trying to turn this whole situation into a plug for her campaign," he muttered. "What a bitch."

Lance got up and paced around the bed in his dark room. Were there really so many people interested in his whereabouts?

Lance texted Blaze and asked if he'd heard about this TV special. No immediate response. *He must still be sleeping after last night's odd disruption.* Lance knew he was supposed to stay out of sight, but he had to talk to someone. With Blaze not answering and Eli likely still dealing with the Deli Boys, he called the one other person he felt he could trust and who would keep his secret.

"Dad, is that you?"

"Oh, Lance, thank God you're alive. Where are you?"

"Dad, I can't tell you. Are you alone, or is Mom close by?"

"I don't know where the hell that devil is, and I don't care. Oh, Lance, you've had us all so worried."

"I know, Dad, and I'm sorry. I never meant to hurt you—I never meant to hurt anyone. I've made so many mistakes, but I've been given a chance to rectify it all, and, Dad, I'm taking it."

"Lance, I'm so proud of you. Everyone will be so happy to know you're alive and safe."

"Dad, you can't tell anyone you've heard from me. If certain people find out, they will do everything they can to locate me and kill me. Right now I'm working with a Detective Blaze, who is protecting me and working to ensure my safety. He's a good guy, and

I trust him, something I can't say about most people, including Mom."

"That woman is the scum of the earth."

"You can't tell her we've been in touch. And what's with this *Looking for Lance* show?"

"I told you we were all worried. To be honest, I think your mom is going to try to turn the whole thing into a campaign rally, but now that I know you're okay, there's no way I'll go on and support her."

"That's good, Dad. The last thing this city needs is her in control. I've got to run, but please know I love you. I'll call again when I can."

"I love you too, son. Be safe."

Two FBI agents were all business as they knocked on Marc's front door. His wife answered, confused by the well-dressed company.

"Hello, ma'am. Do you know a Detective Blaze?"

"Detective Blaze? Oh, you mean David Blazen. He and my husband have been friends for decades. Talk about a sad situation—calling himself a detective now that he's retired. My husband has been playing along, but I think David needs help. Why do you ask?"

"Ma'am, we just wanted to make sure we had the right house. We have a warrant to inspect your basement freezer."

"A warrant? For what?"

The officers ignored the question and nudged their way into the house.

"Who are you anyway?"

"Ma'am, we're with the Federal Bureau of Investigation," the agents said as they walked downstairs. "Please open the freezer."

"Okay, but I don't know what you expect to find. All that's there," she said as she unclasped the lid, "is my award-winning…"

That sentence was never finished. Marc's wife saw the bags of Mel Weinberg's remains and screamed. The officers took the bags and thanked her for her cooperation. They walked up the stairs with Mel's shoulder and arm, leaving a startled woman alone in her basement, frozen in fear.

Sarah Cutler was pleased with her radio performance earlier in the morning and felt herself becoming comfortable adopting the "poor mom" persona. Her campaign saw an influx in donations when word first got out of Lance's disappearance, but as the subsequent hours turned into days, the financial support skyrocketed. People were embracing Sarah as a victim far more than they did when she was just a woman trying to combat crime. Sarah had no idea what Skip had in mind for Lance, and she knew she would need time to grieve for her son at some point. But that time was not now. She had a primetime special to prepare for.

Sarah knew that Matt Vanner would start the show armed with questions about the steam room incident and the subsequent investigation—or lack thereof—into Mel Weinberg's death. She had to minimize what she knew about the investigation while not making the same mistake she did the last time she was on with Vanner. She would explain that she never meant for her comments to sound like a judgment of her son. In fact, she meant she would never question the actions or decisions Lance made, so if there was a question about a certain investigation, it would need to be discussed with him.

When pressed about her claims of a suicide, Sarah would say that the information she was given indicated Weinberg did in fact take his own life. On further analysis by the Chicago Police

Department and under the leadership of her dear son, Lance—she'd be sure to pause and tear up at mention of his name—the motive for Mel's death was not as clear, she'd say. All that was known, and as had already been shared by the West Coast Club, was that Mel Weinberg, an overweight gentleman, went into the steam room and was in there too long. She'd use that line as a segue to some sort of lighthearted humor about the importance of healthy eating, not to disgrace Mel but to make her more approachable to undecided voters.

If the topic of the quick funeral came up, Sarah would say she didn't know the reasoning behind it but assumed the reputable West Coast Club was simply looking out for the victim's family and wanted to move the process along so they could begin their period of mourning—"Something I'm afraid I'll have to do, too, soon," she'd say. With that, she'd squeeze Kent's hand tight and turn her attention to Mayor Paulson.

"Even our current city leader will admit that it's our job—I'm sorry, his job—to look out for the well-being of his constituents," Sarah said to the mirror.

She liked that line a lot, a playful dig at the old regime and yet another way to personalize her to the wider audience. *This show might just be what seals this election*, she thought. *And who knows? Maybe that TV exec was right. Maybe this could be the beginning of a push for governor.*

With my speech to the FBI out of the way, I was ready to confront Sol Feldman. As I put my shoes on, I was interrupted by a call to my black phone from an unknown number. Was the FBI calling me out on my lecture? There was only one way to find out.

"Hello?"

"Hello, is this Mr. Blaze or, rather, Detective Blazen?"

"It's Mr. Blazen or Detective Blaze. Close, though. Who is this?"

"Hello, Detective Blaze, my name is Norman Yellin, and I work at MGBC television. I'm sure you've heard about our *Looking for Lance* special that's airing tomorrow night."

"I have, Mr. Yellin. Listen, I have a very busy day ahead of me. Is there something I can do to help you?"

"There is, Detective Blaze. Tomorrow night's lineup is coming together, but I'll be honest—we're still a little thin. We have the current mayor and the presumptive future mayor, who will be begging for the safe return of her son. We have Vanner and a journalist named Tom Lexington cohosting the event. But we need more. I'm trying everything. I got in touch with Tony Santori's people to follow up on Vanner's personal invitation about appearing on TV."

"Tony Santori is going to be on the show? What else do you need?"

"Frankly, I needed him to say yes. Instead, his people told me to go fuck myself."

"That sounds like Santori."

"Anyway, I'm following up on the rest of Vanner's invites from Thursday's show, which is why I'm calling you. Vanner made it seem like you could provide some perspective on the steam room incident at the West Coast Club and that there may be some connection between that case and the disappearance of Lance Cutler."

"Mr. Yellin, I can confirm that I am investigating the case."

"Then, Detective Blaze, please come on the show. Not only will you be helping me, but you'll be helping yourself as well."

"How's that, Mr. Yellin?"

"Detective Blaze, this show will be broadcast live across the country. I don't know how well your business is doing now, but imagine what your reach could be if people all over the United States heard about you. This could be an incredible opportunity."

I wanted to play hardball, even though Yellin had me once he said *opportunity*.

"I don't know, Mr. Yellin. I have a very busy schedule these next few days—although it would be nice to share a stage with Tom Lexington. He and I go back. Also, I could use this as a venue to reveal some previously unreported details about my investigation. When do you need to know my answer?"

"Detective Blaze, I don't mean to pressure you, but I need an answer right now. I'm not a man to beg, but I can tell you the network is prepared to offer you sixty thousand dollars for your appearance."

I was ready to do the broadcast for free, but sixty thousand? If they wanted to give me that kind of cash, I'd gladly take it off their hands.

"Okay, Mr. Yellin, you've got yourself a deal."

"That's great, Detective Blaze. I appreciate it. I'll be in touch with more details. Just know that there will be no script for this show. There will be suggested topics to discuss and questions from the audience, but this will be more of a freewheeling conversation that hopefully will lead to the safe return of Lance Cutler."

"That sounds good, Mr. Yellin. Thanks for the opportunity."

"You've made the right choice, Detective Blaze. I don't want to oversell it, but if we do things right, this just might be the broadcast of the century."

It wasn't even 10 a.m., but Kent Cutler needed a drink to celebrate. He broke out a bottle of champagne and poured himself a glass. He wanted to shout out to the world that his boy was safe, but he would follow Lance's wishes and not tell a soul. He also no longer would participate in tomorrow night's special. The only reason he'd agreed to it in the first place was to find his boy, but now that he knew Lance was safe, the show was not necessary. Besides, the last thing he wanted was to help enable Sarah to use her son's disappearance as a political ploy. As soon as this election was behind them, Kent was going to file for divorce.

He grabbed his phone to call Sarah and tell her he wouldn't do the show, but then he had an idea. He'd stood by for too long and watched Sarah be vindictive for her own gain. Kent decided he could be vindictive too. Why tell Sarah now and give her time to prepare? Why not spring it on her at the last minute? Better yet, why not have Mayor Paulson back out as well? This idea brought an even bigger smile to Kent's face as he refilled his glass. He grabbed his phone again and called the mayor.

Kent was surprised to hear Mitch Paulson answer his own phone, particularly in his declining state.

"Hey, Kent, what's up?" the mayor said, his tone energetic.

"Mitch, is that you? I haven't heard you sound like that in months."

"Kent, let me tell you, in preparation for tomorrow's show, the doctors have been . . . let's just say livening me up a bit. I'll be honest, I don't know what they're giving me or if it's even legal, but whatever it is, I don't want it to stop. I know I was against doing this show, but if it means I get to feel this good, then, dammit, I may just go out and support your wife for mayor."

"About that, Mitch. I know I said I would do the show because I was worried about Lance. Well, don't tell anyone, but let's just say I'm not as worried anymore and have every intention of backing out."

"Wait, have you heard from Lance?"

"I can't say anything. Just know that I'm drinking a glass of champagne right now."

"Kent, my boy, it's never good to drink alone. Grab that bottle and bring it over. I haven't had a drink of anything in months."

"You got it, Mitch. Oh, and just so you know, I'm not going to tell Sarah or the network that I'm backing out until later tomorrow. And I think you should back out too. You can easily blame it on your health. But don't tell them until an hour before the show."

"Sounds good to me. I know I just said I'd back Sarah for mayor, but you know I can't stand that bitch, and I apologize for using that term to describe your wife."

"Don't apologize. She is a bitch. And she's going to be in for a surprise tomorrow."

"I'm so glad to hear you're not worried about Lance. I hope you can tell me more when you're ready."

"Of course, but right now, you can't tell a soul."

"You have my word, old friend."

Between the revelations at Patrick's, my own speech to the FBI, and now my sixty-thousand-dollar TV appearance, I felt like I'd already put in a full day's work. I saw Lance's text and wrote that maybe we could have him crash the broadcast and have him reveal the truth about his mother. I said I'd be back in touch later in the day.

I didn't know what the dress code for my meeting with Feldman should be, but I figured it'd be best to show I meant business, so I kept my Zegna suit on. I knew I'd be overdressed for a deli, but at least I'd stand out professionally. Besides, if he killed me, I'd already be dressed for my funeral.

I opened the garage to back out, but as I shifted into reverse, I saw a man in a suit standing in my way, his hand held up before him.

"Detective Blaze," he said authoritatively. "I need you to get out of the car."

I knew that speech was too much! The FBI finally had it with me and is bringing me in. Well, it was fun while it lasted, I thought. I got out of the car and held my hands in the air as I slowly walked toward the man.

"Put your arms down, Detective Blaze. I don't want to arrest you; I want to shake your hand."

Surprised, I followed instructions.

"Detective Blaze, I'm Special Agent Clifford Stanley from the Federal Bureau of Investigation. Come, walk with me."

When the FBI wants you to go for a walk, you go for a walk. Special Agent Stanley and I walked down the driveway. As we approached the sidewalk, he pointed to a car across the street and said his colleagues would wait there while we went for our stroll. He then motioned toward the FBI van that had been outside my house for days.

"You've gotten yourself mixed up with some pretty high-profile criminals, and we want to keep you protected," he began. "My team will continue to watch over you and Mary until this whole thing is sorted out."

"What whole thing is that, Special Agent Stanley?"

"In time, Detective Blaze, in time. By the way, do you like to be called Detective Blaze, or can I call you David? You can call me Cliff," he said as we began to walk up the street. Before I could answer his question, Cliff continued. "Now, David, this may sound strange, but as we walk, I'd like to ask that you keep looking forward."

Cliff took out his earpiece and unplugged it from its cord. "This conversation is not being recorded, but my boys back there are expert lip readers, and I'd rather they not know everything we're about to talk about."

Cliff Stanley seemed overly paranoid to me, but maybe that was just what FBI special agents were like. If the FBI tells you to walk looking forward, you walk looking forward.

Cliff began to give me his life story. He started listing off his credentials like he was sharing his résumé with me. Wait a minute—was he sharing his résumé? Was that what he didn't want his colleagues to know? Was this FBI agent trying to join the Blaze organization? Team Blaze was making good progress on the investigations, but I was sure the FBI had better benefits.

This background talk went on for fifteen minutes. We were in the middle of our second lap around my gated community when Cliff began talking about his time in the military. At that point, I had to cut him off.

"Cliff, thank you for your service, but I'm going to have to cut our stroll short. I'm not actively hiring right now, and I really have a busy day and need to get moving."

Without flinching, Cliff kept walking. "Trust me, David, you and I need to have this conversation. Frankly, it is in both of our best interests."

I didn't see how his military background was going to help me in my upcoming talks with Feldman and Santori, but I kept walking nonetheless.

"As I was saying, my background is in explosives. I spent years in Afghanistan and have the horror stories to show for it. But you know what? You're right. That's enough about me. I want to talk about you, the impressive and inspiring Detective Blaze. Based on your tip this morning, my team retrieved the remaining remains of Mel Weinberg. An autopsy will be performed later this afternoon. We also brought Carter into custody. He was yelling about some sort of immunity thanks to Detective Blaze, but we said we'd never heard of a detective by that name." Cliff winked with a devilish grin. "I'm not sure what we'll do with him yet, but I'm positive he'll be an asset. A second team secured a warrant and retrieved the camera footage from Bryan, the night manager. We have a team of techs who will sift through it all this afternoon.

"I have to be honest, David, while I appreciate your diligence in trying to solve this steam room case, the killer is not our top priority. The FBI's interest is Tony Santori. My team has been focused on the Santori family network for six years, and thanks to you and your team, we're closer to him than ever before. FBI director Thomas Mangold has been supervising the entire operation, and his singular goal is to bring Santori to justice."

We were back in front of my house, and Cliff motioned to his team that we were going to circle the neighborhood again.

"David, we are aware you have had a private audience with Tony Santori, and we understand from what you've said that you were hired to find the steam room killer. Now, as I said, we don't care about the murder as much as we want to know who's been covering it up and what role Santori played. It looks like it's all a part of this turf war between him and Solomon Feldman that has been intensifying lately, but now with the disappearance of that police officer Lance Cutler, it might be more complicated, particularly if his mom, Sarah Cutler, is involved. If you ask me, it seems like this is all a ticking time bomb that's ready to explode. Ah, but there I go getting ahead of myself again. Sorry about that. Let's talk about you. We've done our digging into you and your background. Why did you decide to become a detective, particularly at your advanced age?"

"Well, Cliff, the short answer is I didn't like the direction humanity was heading and wanted to do something about it."

"What's the long answer?"

"Same as the short, just with more words. I've lived a fruitful life, have successful children and adorable grandchildren, and I was a good businessman. But since retiring, I needed a new purpose. I wanted to make a difference. I didn't care if Detective Blaze ever got famous. All I've wanted is for him to be effective. I know I'm in the late innings of my life, and I'm looking to drop down a bunt or a single to help move the runners along. I want to make a small contribution to my fellow man. I was not expecting to be entrenched in this 'ticking time bomb' as you called it, but my new career is moving fast, and I like to think it's because I'm helping."

"Well, you're certainly good at what you do," Stanley said. "So let's get back to Santori. You've met the guy. How much damage do you think he's caused?"

"Damage?"

"You know, how many lives have been lost or negatively impacted by him and his men?"

"Honestly, Cliff, I have no idea, though I do know he's killed at least four people in the last couple of days."

"Ah, yes, that Wacker Drive explosion. You said you have proof Santori was involved, but even if you do, it doesn't matter."

"Why's that?"

"Have you ever heard of the law firm of Pearlman, Pearlman, and Muffy?" Cliff asked.

"Yeah, Donald Pearlman. Hotshot lawyer who can get anybody off, right?"

"That's the one. The bigger the crime and publicity, the likelier it is that Pearlman's client is ruled not guilty."

"I never realized he had a relative who worked with him."

"He doesn't. His ego is so big he decided to use his name twice. And I think Muffy was his cat. Anyway, Pearlman is Santori's attorney, which means even if we had an open-and-shut case against Santori, Pearlman would almost assuredly find a way to get the charges dropped."

As we walked past my house, a voice from the FBI van called out, "Boss!" It was one of the FBI agents. "I know you didn't want to be disturbed, but you need to hear this."

Cliff asked me to wait one moment as he took a phone from his colleague. I only heard one side of the conversation, but it didn't sound good.

"This is Stanley. What? How many? Are you sure? Okay, keep this under wraps. I'll call you back in twenty minutes." Cliff was visibly upset as he handed the phone back.

"Everything okay?" I asked.

"No, but it can wait," Cliff said as we continued our walk. "Now, David, let's cut to the chase. The work you and your team have done is remarkable, and again, on behalf of the FBI, I want to thank you. We're going to respect your wishes and let you carry on your investigations as you'd like. We'll continue to monitor your calls and provide protection in whatever way you'd like. But there's something else you need to know. In your meeting with Santori, you met a man named Vince."

"Oh, you mean John Sedgwick?"

I caught Cliff off guard with that one. "Sedgwick has been undercover for six years, and Santori has no idea. How did you figure it out?"

Team Blaze got a boost in credibility with that. I chose not to answer and instead simply smiled as I continued to look forward.

"Anyway, Vince—or John—is one of ours. He informed me last night that there will be a confidential and highly secretive meeting Wednesday with the Santori family and a few other similarly powerful families from across the country. This type of meeting happens once every ten years, and John—actually, let's keep calling him Vince if you don't mind—is coordinating it. More than a dozen of the biggest criminals in the country will be together in one room. This is a dream scenario for us."

"It sounds like it. How many agents are you going to need to storm that meeting?"

"Well, that's where it gets interesting." Cliff looked back to make sure his agents were distracted and not trying to follow the conversation. "I just mentioned Pearlman's success rate. Well, each one of these families has its own Donald Pearlman. If we invade the meeting, they'll all be released and back on the streets in a matter of hours."

Cliff waited a good thirty seconds before continuing.

"Blaze, when you told me why you wanted to be a detective, you said you wanted to make a difference, to leave a legacy. That's what I've always wanted to do too. I joined the FBI because I wanted to bring the most notorious criminals to justice, and for six years, I've dreamed of delivering justice to Tony Santori. Well, Blaze, on Wednesday, Santori is going to get his justice, and so is everyone else at that meeting."

"I thought you just said you can't arrest them. How are you going to bring them to justice?"

Cliff stared ahead of him, letting the silent suspense soak over us for a minute. Then, still looking forward, he answered, "I'm going to blow them all up."

I knew I wasn't supposed to make any sudden movements or reactions, so I tried my hardest to keep walking like we were talking about the weather or last night's basketball game. But this was insane! An FBI agent just told me he was going to blow people up! Now, admittedly, I had not finished reading all my detective pamphlets, but I was pretty sure the remaining ones didn't say anything about it being okay to use bombs to get the bad guys. That seemed like an obvious unwritten rule.

"Why are you telling me?" I finally asked.

Cliff, still as calm and casual as before, kept looking forward. "Because I need your help."

"Me? Why me?"

"One, I need someone who still believes in justice, and you clearly have shown that. But more importantly, I need to get Solomon Feldman at that meeting, and I think you're the one who can do it."

"Feldman? What does he have to do with this?"

"If we're going to take down a bunch of bad guys here in Chicago, we might as well take down Feldman too. Besides, you know that phone call I just got? Apparently twelve people are lying dead in a Wisconsin field outside of Feldman's summer home. Think that's a coincidence? I don't. Feldman's scum, and we're going to take him down too."

"Cliff, you're saying *we* a whole lot here. What makes you think I can get Feldman there? I've never even met the guy."

"You told us in your speech that you're meeting with him later today. I've seen you in action; you'll figure something out. Now, you're a civilian; I can't force you to get involved with this. When you talk about leaving a legacy, though, what better legacy is there than bringing down the country's most powerful villains? You said you want to lay down a bunt or a single, but David, I'm talking about hitting a walk-off grand slam to win the World Series."

I lost count of how many times we'd circled the neighborhood, but we'd been going for at least an hour. We both walked in silence for several minutes. Then, with my house back in sight, Cliff continued.

"Obviously, everything we've talked about here is strictly confidential. No one on my team except for Vince knows anything about Operation Boom. If you want in, we're having a meeting at 9 p.m. If you go out your back door and through your neighbor's yard, we'll have a car waiting in the alley on the other side of the street."

"I'll have to think about all this, Cliff," I said as we walked up my driveway and to the car.

Before he turned his earpiece back on, Cliff looked me in the eye, seemingly for the first time all morning.

"Detective Blaze, you do what you think is right," he said as he shook my hand. "If you decide Operation Boom isn't for you, I won't hold it against you." He paused. "But I also won't let you stand in our way."

16

What are you supposed to do after an FBI agent tells you he's going to blow a bunch of people up? You can't call the police, or the FBI for that matter, can you? They would think I was some nut job. That made me think—was I a nut job? Did that whole conversation really happen? I had so many questions, but I wanted to get away from my house before someone else got in my way.

I left my gated community and drove a few minutes to a local donut shop. I didn't like donuts, but the shop had a parking lot that overlooked a nice pond, and it was a great place to sit and think. The FBI car that tailed me must have thought I was making a stop for them, because the agents hopped out and went inside for a snack. If I wanted, I could have lost them, but frankly, I didn't mind them. Besides, I was on my way to meet Solomon Feldman—a little backup was probably a good idea.

I pulled out my black phone and saw I had one missed call. Then I looked at my pink phone and was surprised to see that Marc, Wilt, and Patrick had all left messages during my seventy-minute morning stroll. Not knowing whose was most important, I listened to them all.

Tony Santori left a two-minute-long message on my black

phone. If I removed all the vulgarity, the message essentially said, "See you today at two; I expect an update on the case."

"And remember," Santori said at the close of his message, "if you're late for your meeting with Tony, you will be fucked."

Marc left the first message on my pink phone. He wanted to know how well I knew Tom Lexington because he didn't have a good feeling about the guy. I'd only known Lexington a few days, and he'd already screwed me over. I'd known Marc for sixty-plus years, and his instinct about people was rarely off. No one else knew I'd be sharing the TV stage with Lexington and Vanner, but I'd have to keep Marc's concern in mind.

Patrick's voice was the next one I heard. The kid did some phenomenal detective work that morning, but it was still grating to hear his nerdy voice, particularly over the phone.

"Hey, boss, this is Patrick, your next-door neighbor and detective apprentice," he began.

Does he really think I don't know who he is?

"Listen, Blaze," his message continued, "this morning was a lot of fun. It's great to feel a part of a team and be respected for my knowledge and abilities. My parents still treat me like a little kid, but Detective Blaze, I'm not a kid anymore."

Where the hell was this message going?

"Anyway, that's why I'm calling. I completely forgot to tell you that there's this girl Kelly in my broadcasting class, and I really like her. I'm thinking about asking her out on a date, but boss, I'm nervous. This may come as a surprise to you, but I've never been on a date before, and I don't want to screw it up. I've never even kissed a girl. I'd ask my parents for advice, but I know that would be useless. Do you think you can give me a few pointers? Call me. Thanks. Oh, by the way, I narrowed the suspect list down to three. Thanks, boss."

I deleted Patrick's message as quickly as possible. I wasn't sure which horrified me more, the fact that he was turning to me for advice on women or the image of him making out with a girl on his bunk bed under the glow-in-the-dark stars. I was also a little annoyed that Kelly had distracted him from giving me important investigation information, though I still wasn't convinced any of Patrick's suspects was our steam room killer.

It was time to meet Solomon Feldman. I checked my rearview mirror and saw one FBI agent looking at his phone and the other wiping powdered sugar off his mouth.

"All right, boys," I said to the mirror. "It's go time."

Cliff Stanley still had to assemble a team for Operation Boom. He and Vince were in, and he hoped Blaze was too. But three people were not enough. When it came to explosives, Cliff knew there was one person he had to get involved. He needed his good-luck charm; the man who was alongside Cliff every step of the way in Afghanistan, assembling and disassembling explosives of all shapes and sizes; the man who was born for this type of mission.

He needed Dan Baum.

Cliff hadn't talked to Dan in years, but he knew his friend still lived in the Chicago area. He gave Dan a call to sell him on Operation Boom.

"Cliff, are you out of your damn mind?" Dan responded. "How on God's green earth do you think you can pull off such an attack?"

"If you're asking about logistics," Cliff clarified, "does that mean you support the idea in principle?"

"I'm asking about logistics because I'm the logistics guy! It doesn't matter what I believe if we can't make it happen. So what's your plan?"

"Well, Dan, you remember that old barn I've got?"

"Remember it? I helped you fix it up, Cliff, complete with

those super-thick exterior walls. You said you were going to turn it into some mini rifle range, which I never understood. You never were the type who liked to fire anything."

"Buddy, I hate to say it, but I lied to you."

"Figures. Get on with it."

"For many years, I've used that barn as a hideaway for explosives I've gotten my hands on. After all we saw and did in Afghanistan, I figured it would be good to build up my own collection just in case."

"Just in case of what?"

"I didn't know at the time. Now I do. I was collecting them for this exact mission."

"How many bombs are we talking about?"

"Dan, I've got my own museum of all types of explosives. You name it, and I've probably got it. C4. Suicide vests. Grenades—fourteen different types of them. Collecting has become a hobby of mine."

"How many do you have altogether?"

"I've never counted but at least a hundred."

"And they all work?"

"That's what I need your help with. Well, that and the actual execution of Operation Boom."

"Is that really what we're calling this mission?"

"It is. And when you say *we*, does that mean you're in?"

Dan was silent.

"Dan?" Cliff pressed.

"Cliff, I'm thinking. For this to work, we're going to need a team of experts. And these explosives need to be top of the line. Do you have a team?"

"I'm building it now, Dan. I knew I couldn't have one without you. Now that you're in, I'll keep building it out."

"And the explosives?"

"Come check them out for yourself. I'm off today. I can meet you at the barn in a couple hours."

"Okay, Cliff, I'll be there at one."

"That's great, Dan, it really is. It will be great working together again."

"I haven't committed to anything yet, Cliff. I need to see the explosives first."

I'd been to a few delicatessens in my lifetime, but Morry's Deli just might have been the largest I'd seen. When you walked in, there was a buffet counter on your right serving up the classics—pastrami on rye bread, potato pancakes, and matzoh ball soup. To your left was open cafeteria-like seating for guests to verbally spread the gossip and nonsense of the day.

On any other day, I'd settle in for some corned beef and kugel, but I had business to take care of, and I was absolutely terrified to take care of it. I'd heard the warnings about Solomon Feldman, and now it was time to see if they were true. My first goal as I entered the deli was to exit the deli on my feet and not on a gurney. My next goal was to see what information I could get from Feldman.

Judging by the eight large men noshing on potato pancakes near a roped-off back area hidden by a black curtain, I'd found Solomon Feldman's headquarters. Those stout men with their bottom shirt buttons popping open must have been his Deli Boys.

As I approached the men, they instinctively put their plates and food down and stood in a line, hands behind their backs and legs straight like soldiers, blocking me from the rope that already blocked me from entering. Any of these men could have broken me with his bare hands, but I had to stay calm. I tried to peek around them, but they leaned in my way. I quickly tried to look the other way, but they were too fast. I got up on my tiptoes to look over them, but again, they followed suit. It was like my own game of follow the leader.

Before I could get them to do anything else, a voice from behind the Boys said, "That's enough." Out walked Eli, who gave me a faint wink. "Who are you, and what do you want?" he said, not wanting to show he already knew the answer.

"My name is Detective Blaze, and I am here to talk with Solomon Feldman."

"Solomon Feldman has no interest in seeing you," Eli said. "I suggest that you leave."

"How do you know that?" I asked. "You didn't even ask him."

"I don't need to, Detective Blaze."

"That's pretty rude, mister. Now, I really need to talk with Mr. Feldman, and I'd appreciate it if you checked if he's available."

"Have it your way."

Eli disappeared into the dark behind the rope. Twenty seconds later, he returned, a smirk on his face.

"Just as I said, Mr. Feldman does not want to talk and suggested you leave. Now scram!"

"Mr. Feldman should know I have been retained and well compensated by none other than Tony Santori to find who killed the man in the steam room at the West Coast Club. I have to ask Mr. Feldman a few questions about his whereabouts."

Eli disappeared again, only to reappear thirty seconds later.

"Mr. Feldman is not suggesting you leave anymore—he's demanding it. Now go, Detective Blaze."

I didn't know how much of this was a show by Eli and how much was real, but I knew I couldn't keep pushing. I turned for the front door, somewhat fearful the Deli Boys would come after me. I made it halfway when I decided to try one last Hail Mary, a concept that seemed sacrilegious in a Jewish deli.

I turned and found Eli's eyes as I shouted, "Please tell Mr. Feldman that his boy Carter sends his love."

The entire deli turned to look at me. I hadn't meant for that to be heard by everyone, but it sure made for a dramatic effect as the whole place went silent. Eli once again went to the back. No one spoke a word as the tension continued to grow throughout the restaurant. Doing my best to break the ice and calm my own nerves, I asked an older gentleman at a table near me if he recommended corned beef or pastrami.

"Go for the corned beef," he said.

I nodded in approval. Before I could ask him anything else, Eli returned.

"Detective Blaze, Mr. Feldman will see you now."

The Deli Boys stepped aside, and Eli undid the velvet rope and pulled back the curtain for me. I feigned confidence as I entered a dimly lit hallway filled with framed posters of the greatest Jews in sports—Sid Luckman, Bo Belinsky, Hank Greenberg, and Sandy Koufax. Eli opened the third door on the left and led me inside.

"Carter is dead, you lying piece of shit," Feldman yelled before I could even close the door. "I could kill you right here for disrespecting the dead like that."

If he thought that was disrespectful, imagine what he'd think of what we did to Mel's dead body! Now, most people would cower in fear at an accusation like that, particularly coming from perhaps the city's most feared villain. I knew I had information on Feldman, though, and if I could just appear confident, I could steer the conversation how I wanted.

"Hello, Mr. Feldman, it's nice to meet you too."

"I don't like you, Detective Blaze."

"That's your right, Mr. Feldman; I've never asked for anyone's approval. But as I told your associates, I've been hired by Tony Santori to investigate the murder in the WCC steam room, and

I have a few questions for you about your whereabouts and allegiances."

"If you're connected with that piece of shit, then I really don't like you."

"Again, Mr. Feldman, your likes and dislikes are not my concern. You currently are a suspect in a murder, and I have a few questions I need to ask."

"I didn't kill Mel Weinberg. There. Have any more questions?"

"I do, Mr. Feldman."

"Well, just know I didn't kill him, although I'll admit I wanted to," he said, nodding with a smirk to Eli. "That bastard killed my nephew Charlie Myers."

I was worried I wouldn't get straight answers from Feldman while Eli was with us. I needed more privacy, even if that meant separating myself from Eli.

"Mr. Feldman," I said, "as you probably know, there are two FBI officers outside who followed me here. I do not work for the FBI, and you have my word that I am not wired or carrying a weapon of any kind. I just want to get some information, but some of my questions are a little more personal in nature. Is there somewhere private we can talk?"

Feldman looked at Eli in bewilderment. Eli shrugged, legitimately unsure what the hell I was doing.

"I don't know what game you're playing, Detective Blaze," Feldman said, "but I'll play along. Come with me."

The two of us walked back into the hallway and turned left, with Feldman leading me farther away from the main cafeteria. He opened the next door on the right.

"In here," he said.

I walked into what turned out to be a storage closet and found two folding chairs three feet apart and facing each other. I sat on the one in front of a wall filled with mayonnaise jars, and Feldman sat on the other, a backdrop of boxes and cleaning supplies behind him. This was not an ideal space to confront one of the most notorious bad guys in the country, but then again, did such an ideal place exist?

"Okay, Blaze, what are we doing here?"

"As I said, Tony Santori hired me to identify who killed Mel Weinberg in the West Coast Club steam room."

"I already told you I didn't do it, and I can assure you my men were nowhere near that place on the day in question."

"Mr. Feldman, do you even know what day we're talking about?"

"It doesn't matter. I know we weren't involved. Here, I'll put my money where my mouth is. I'll double what Santori is paying for you to find the killer. I guarantee it was Santori who orchestrated it, and now he's playing you." Feldman got up and turned his back to me. "Just like he played me and prevented me from getting justice for the man who murdered my nephew."

"About that. Mr. Feldman, the reason I asked for privacy is that I have it on good authority that it was actually *you* who put the hit out on your own nephew."

Feldman turned and looked straight in my eyes.

"Do you really have the nerve to sit there and accuse me, Solomon Feldman, of ordering my own nephew to be murdered?"

"Did you?"

Feldman kept his eyes locked with mine as he sat back down. The two of us stared at each other for ten more seconds.

"Detective Blaze, I take back what I said earlier. I think I might like you after all. You've got some guts. I'll give you that."

"Did you have your nephew Charlie Myers murdered?"

"Yes, yes, I did."

Feldman leaned forward, his elbows on his knees as he stared at the ground.

"I didn't want to, but that stupid kid went too far."

Feldman began to choke up. Was the city's biggest crime leader about to cry in front of me?

"Charlie was a good boy," he said, still staring at the ground, "but he liked to gamble. He started accumulating some large debts and kept using my name to get out of them. When my name wasn't enough, he began feeding confidential information about me and my organization instead, and I couldn't have that knowledge getting in the wrong hands."

Tears rolled down both of Feldman's cheeks. He looked up at me, and his eyes were bloodshot.

"I tried talking to him, but he wouldn't listen," Feldman said. "Originally, I was going to have him roughed up a bit, but then I heard he used my name again for some debt to Santori, and I had to take matters into my own hands. I knew Santori used Carter a lot to clean up messes, so I reached out to Carter myself. Carter said Santori was paying him to rough up Charlie for some overdue debts, and I said I'd pay him extra to make sure Charlie never breathed again. He said he'd have his guy Mel take care of it."

"So then did you kill Mel?"

"I was going to, but Santori got to Mel before I could."

"And what about Carter?"

"I assumed he was dead because he never came to collect the money for taking out Charlie. In my line of business, Detective Blaze, there's only one reason someone doesn't collect money for a job, and that's because they're not alive to get it." Feldman wiped the tears from his face and sat up, leaning back against his chair. "So is Carter in fact alive?"

"Mr. Feldman, I'm asking the questions here. Now, I also am aware that the night before the steam room incident, you sat in this very deli with our presumed future mayor, Sarah Cutler. What was that meeting about?"

Feldman was dumbfounded. "How the hell do you know about that meeting?"

I thought how thankful I was to have Uber-driving Jeffrey as my brother to share that info with me.

"You're confirming that a meeting took place, correct?"

"Yeah, so what? She initiated it."

"What did she want?"

"I've supported her financially for years, and she wanted to talk with one of her biggest donors."

"About what?"

"She asked me not to retaliate against Santori for murdering my nephew until after the election. She said if I'd do that, she'd deliver Mel Weinberg to me to dispose of in any way I wanted."

"Why would she do that?"

"I don't know. I can't speak for that woman. I can speak for myself, though, and I want to know how you know all of this."

"I'm not done, Mr. Feldman. Let's talk about Lance Cutler."

Feldman threw his hands up in the air. "Are you some mind reader or something? How could you possibly know about Lance Cutler?"

"Is it true that you accepted a job to kill Lieutenant Cutler, the man the entire world is currently looking for?"

"I shouldn't answer that, but I'm guessing you already know the answer. Yeah, I took the job, but I didn't want to. Even after I took it, we weren't going to kill him. We were just going to hide him for a while."

"Why would you do that?"

"We were going to use him as leverage for when Sarah Cutler became mayor. Knowing the whereabouts of her kidnapped son would have serious benefits for me and my associates."

"But you just said you were already backing her financially. Why did you need more leverage?"

"Detective Blaze, you can never have too much leverage."

Boy, did I know it. I had the city's top criminal eating out of the palm of my hand and confessing to a host of crimes. I wanted to see how much more I could get out of him and get a sense of if he knew what happened with Lance. The fact that Eli was still breathing likely meant Feldman didn't know what really took place, but I figured there was no harm in getting confirmation.

Or so I thought.

"So what happened to Lieutenant Cutler?" I asked.

"We were going to keep him alive, but once Sarah bombed on TV, we knew we'd lost our advantage. I wanted to just be done with the job and move on, so that's what we did."

"Are you saying Lance Cutler is dead?"

That was one question too many.

"You've got some nerve, Detective Blaze. Is Lance Cutler dead? You're the one who's going to be dead in a second."

Feldman stood up and picked me up by the neck as my confidence vanished. He looked me right in the eyes, a puzzled look on his face.

"I don't know anymore if I like you or not, but I need to know I can trust you. I can't have you going off and telling anyone what I did to Charlie or, for that matter, anything else I've said today. Can I trust you?"

It was admittedly hard to nod when a grown man was holding you off the ground by your neck, but I tried. It wasn't enough for Feldman.

"I said, can I trust you?" he repeated, his face getting redder by the second.

I was beginning to get lightheaded. I tried to say, "Yes, you can trust me," but before I could get it out, Feldman threw me backward into the wall of mayonnaise. I fell to the ground as the jars came crashing down, covering me in the eggy, creamy, caloric mess. Feldman walked over to me, kneeled down, and put his pistol deep in my mouth.

"If I can't trust you, I can't have you alive. It was nice knowing you, Detective Blaze."

I didn't want to die smothered in mayonnaise. I hated mayonnaise. I closed my eyes and wondered if my last microsecond on the planet would be spent seeing my brain fly past my eyes, only to realize that with the gun in my mouth, my brain would go flying out the back of my head. *That's a relief.* I closed my eyes just as I heard Feldman pull the trigger.

Silence.

After a few seconds, I opened my eyes to find Feldman still kneeling over me, the gun still in my mouth.

"Next time, Mr. Detective, I'll use bullets."

Oh, thank God.

Feldman pulled his gun out and stood over me. He looked at my pathetic self on the ground, doused in a bath of creamy white goo, and smirked. He reached his hand out and grabbed mine, pulling me up to my feet.

"I like you, Blaze, I do," he said. "I'm sure we're now on the same page about everything said here."

I had no need to tell anyone about Charlie Myers. As for the other stuff, I'd keep it to myself—for the time being.

"We're on the same page, Feldman, but in return, I'd like a favor."

"You're something else, Detective Blaze, you really are," he said with a grin. "Sure, what do you want?"

"I'll get back to you. Just know that I'll need help with something down the road."

It was hard to look or feel confident when dripping from head to toe in mayonnaise, but I apparently did enough to earn Feldman's respect.

"You got it, Blaze. Now get the hell out of here."

He opened the door and watched as I took the long, slow walk down the hallway, plops of mayonnaise falling to the ground with every step. I opened the black curtain to the main cafeteria, and there were the Deli Boys, who took one look at me, glanced at each other, and broke out in laughter. I looked like a fool, but this was a victory. Not only did I get valuable information, but I'd earned Solomon Feldman's trust as well as a favor. I would walk out with my head held high, even as clumps of mayonnaise dripped down my face.

Passing by the Deli Boys, I locked eyes with Eli, who exhaled after seeing I'd survived my one-on-one encounter. I made my way through the cafeteria tables toward the door. On the way, I passed by the same man who just a few minutes earlier raved about the restaurant's corned beef.

"Hey, mister," he said. "You didn't tell me you wanted to put mayonnaise on your sandwich. In that case, definitely go with the pastrami."

"Thanks," I said sarcastically as I slopped my way toward the door, leaving a trail of mayonnaise behind me.

Mary heard the doorbell ring and darted to the front door. She opened it to find an older man several inches shorter than her with an impressive mustache and a cowboy hat that added an extra foot or so to his diminutive height.

"Can I help you?" she said.

"Good afternoon, ma'am, is this the home of Detective Blaze?"

"It is. And who are you?"

"Ma'am, my name is Hanford, and I am a Wisconsin state trooper. Is Mr. Blaze home?"

"Not now. Is he expecting you?"

"He's not, but I need to give him something."

"To be honest, I'm not sure how long he'll be. Can you give it to me?"

Hanford reached into his coat pocket and pulled out a battered leather Bible. He looked at it for a second, then handed it to Mary.

"What's he supposed to do with this?"

"I don't know, ma'am. All I know is two old men gave it to me right before they died and said that they were looking out for Detective Blaze."

"Looking out for him? Did they even know him?"

"I don't know, ma'am."

"And you said just before they died? What happened?"

"My snipers took them out after they killed fourteen men in the last twenty-four hours."

Mary gasped. "Fourteen people?"

"That's right, ma'am, although I'll tell you they thought they were good people. To be fair, twelve of the men they killed were in the KKK, and the other two apparently were cannibals. How these old men knew that, I don't know. But they were convinced they were doing good. They called themselves *savers*, not *killers*."

"My word. And what does this have to do with Detective Blaze?"

"I don't know, ma'am. You now know as much as I do. Hopefully, your Detective Blaze can figure it out."

With that, Hanford tipped his hat to Mary and turned back to his car to make the drive back to his Wisconsin home.

Mary, meanwhile, remained in the doorway, processing all Hanford had said. As she stood there, she opened the Bible to the first page, where a short message was scribbled in pen.

It must be done.

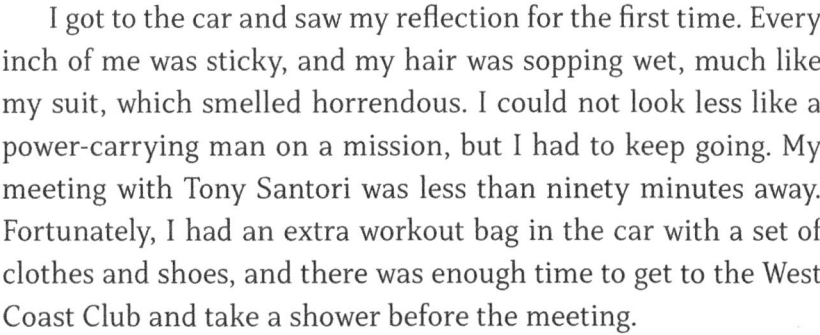

I got to the car and saw my reflection for the first time. Every inch of me was sticky, and my hair was sopping wet, much like my suit, which smelled horrendous. I could not look less like a power-carrying man on a mission, but I had to keep going. My meeting with Tony Santori was less than ninety minutes away. Fortunately, I had an extra workout bag in the car with a set of clothes and shoes, and there was enough time to get to the West Coast Club and take a shower before the meeting.

I got into the car and immediately stuck to the seat. It didn't take long for the smell to overwhelm the inside, forcing me to drive with the windows open on a chilly February afternoon.

I wanted to keep everything about Operation Boom to myself, but I had to tell someone about what had just happened. I missed two calls from Mary but didn't feel she'd appreciate hearing about my latest near-death experience.

I left the deli and drove to the WCC, giving Marc a call along the way. He let me run through the whole mayonnaise story, but it was clear he had other things on his mind.

"David, that sounds pretty crazy, but you and I need to talk about Tom Lexington."

"Sure thing. What's up?"

"Well, David, you tasked Tom and me with getting as many stories out of Carter as possible, and we've done that. The gruesome details he's shared would make for some sick psycho films. But as a valued member of Team Blaze, I also feel it's my responsibility to snoop around whenever possible. And, David, snoop I did."

"Okay. What did you find?"

"While Tom went to the bathroom, I went onto his computer where he was taking notes and found a contract between him and MGBC television. He's going to cohost this *Looking for Lance* special they're airing tomorrow."

"Yeah, I'm going to be on it too."

"Oh, yeah? Are they paying you a hundred and sixty grand?"

"No, I'm only getting sixty."

"That's not bad, David, but let's talk about that later. Lexington is getting paid one hundred and sixty thousand dollars, and it specifically says in the contract that he'll disclose previously unreported information about the steam room victim from a key individual who had a working relationship with him."

"You think that individual is Carter?"

"It's got to be."

I knew from my previous interactions that Lexington always put himself first, but I couldn't believe he planned to take the stories I helped him get and disclose them for his own gain. What a jackass. I could officially no longer trust him.

What a funny thing trust is.

Lance Cutler and Eli instilled their trust in me. Hell, Cliff Stanley trusted me with a secret that would land him in jail for the rest of his life if I disclosed his Boom intentions. I thought Cliff was insane when he first shared his plan with me, but as I thought about it more, I wondered if he was on to something.

Take Adolf Hitler, for example. If I lived during the prime of his reign, and I got a tip about where he would be and had the opportunity to kill him in cold blood and save countless lives, wouldn't it have been my moral obligation to my fellow man to end that bastard's life? Yes, murder was bad, but did preventing more murder make it okay? Forget Hitler; the same question applied to any villain. Joseph Stalin. Benito Mussolini. If I discovered John Wilkes Booth planned to shoot Abraham Lincoln, would it have been right to pull my own gun on him before he entered Ford's Theatre?

Those were all philosophical questions of the past, but they were the same question Cliff posed to me. Was committing a crime—scratch that—was committing *murder* to prevent more crime and murder justifiable?

"David, are you still there?" Marc asked, bringing me back to reality.

"Sorry about that, Marc. Yeah, I'm here, but I'm pulling up to the West Coast Club and need to get going."

"What about Lexington?"

"I'll try to think of something. Gotta run."

I hung up with Marc as I parked the car. I'd have to think more about that philosophical debate, but first I had to get rid of all my mayonnaise. I unstuck myself from the seat and grabbed my extra workout bag from the trunk. When I walked into the club, the front desk attendant noticed my smell before noticing me. I checked in, and as the kid behind the desk covered his nose in disgust, he informed me that Betty, the CEO of the WCC, needed to speak with me immediately. I checked my watch; I had a little less than an hour before needing to meet with Santori. Rather than waste my precious time, I told the attendant I'd check in with Betty on the way out.

In the locker room, I gladly stripped out of my mayonnaise-covered suit. I tossed my stuff in a locker, grabbed a towel, and made my way to the steam room. I thought the steam would feel good after my latest near-death experience, but I also figured it'd be good to revisit the scene of the crime, particularly since Patrick narrowed down the suspect field.

I walked in and was relieved to see I had the room to myself. The last time I inspected the steam room, I sat where I was on the day of the crime, but I remembered one of my pamphlets saying the best detectives look for clues others may have missed. I took a few minutes to move around the room, sitting in different seats and searching for new perspectives. I sat where Mel was seated. I stood on top of the seats to look down on the room. I even lay down on the floor in the center of the room, scanning to see if I'd missed anything before. I really thought I'd find a key clue there, but alas, there was nothing.

Dejected, I stood up and made my way out to take a shower and prepare for my meeting with Santori, my head hung as I pushed the door open. And that's when I found it! Hidden behind the long towel rack just outside the steam room was a small maintenance door, camouflaged so well that I'd walked past it thousands of times and never noticed it before. The rack was on wheels, so it would have been easy for Mel's killer to move if he had been hiding in there. Where the door led to, I wasn't sure, but what I did know was it opened up new avenues for the killer to enter or exit the club.

That just might have been the break I'd been looking for.

I was getting closer to pinpointing the person I'd spent my whole career searching for, but as I stood in the shower, I realized what happened in the steam room was no longer the top thing on my mind. It wasn't even in the top five. I was still shaky from my encounter with Feldman and the feeling of having a pistol in my mouth. I was anxious about Tom Lexington disclosing everything I'd told him on national television. I was still dumbfounded by Cliff and his plans for Operation Boom. And I was unsure what in the world to say to Tony Santori in our upcoming meeting.

Tony wanted an update, and while I was getting closer to identifying the killer, I wasn't ready to tell him that.

I dried off and changed into my T-shirt, shorts, and sneakers usually reserved for exercise. I felt ridiculous wearing a shirt that said *Basketball is life* for my meeting with Santori, particularly because I could care less about basketball—it was a party favor from some friends' kid's *bar mitzvah*—but it made for a good exercise shirt. Besides, it was better than the mayonnaise-covered alternative.

I left the locker room and made my way to the hidden staircase, which was again guarded by Jermaine. The man I first described as Mr. Refrigerator looked me up and down, then stared at my shirt. I was ready for the jokes to come, but instead, he stuck his hand out for a fist bump.

"Damn straight, Blaze. Hoops is life. You play?"

"Nah, I'm just a fan," I said, praying Jermaine wouldn't ask me about any specific teams or players. "It's a beautiful game, isn't it?"

"Hell, yeah. Basketball was my ticket out of the hood and got me where I am today."

"Yeah? How's that?"

"Man, a hundred pounds ago, I used to have a killer crossover. Nobody could stop me. Once when I was in high school,

I was hooping on a court just down the block from here, and I crossed the shit out of a Bulls player who was trying to get some play in during the offseason. I had the ball in my right hand," Jermaine said, mimicking the scene he described. "I was going right, going right. Then just like that, I crossed to my left, then back to my right. Booyah. The Bulls guy tripped over himself on that double move and fell as I stepped back and drained the shot, nothing but net. He got up, shook my hand, and just walked off the court."

"Wow, Jermaine. I had no idea."

"I had college coaches offering me scholarships left and right to come play for them."

"What happened?"

"I tore my knee up two weeks later and never played again. I wanted to stay close to the game, so I cozied up to some of the top prospects around town and said I'd work security for them. For fifteen years, I did that. I looked out for some of Chicago's best ballers. Some went on to college; two made it all the way to the NBA."

"Then how did you get connected with Santori?"

"I was at a club one night about six years ago holding it down with one of my former hoopers who was back in town. Drinks were flowing, and everyone was having a good time until some drunk came and started harassing my man, saying he cost him thousands of dollars on a missed bet. The drunk guy began to get physical, which meant I had to step in. I tried to stay civil, but once he started going after me, let's just say I had to put him in his place. Mr. Santori happened to be at the same club and watched the whole thing. He came right up to me afterward and said he'd pay me triple whatever I was getting paid to work exclusively for him. And I've been with him ever since. But it all goes back to basketball. I'm going to have to get myself one of those shirts."

"Listen, Jermaine, I'd love to stay and talk, but I've got to get up there to meet with Tony."

"Oh, yeah, no problem." Jermaine opened the door and escorted me up to Tony's office. Outside Tony's door, Jermaine stuck his fist out for another bump. "To hoops," he said.

"To hoops."

Tony Santori was alone in his office as I walked in at precisely 2 p.m., saving myself much vulgarity. He looked at my outfit the same way Jermaine did, and I wondered if I'd get another fist bump or an inspirational story. Sadly, neither was the case.

"Is that how you dress for an important meeting with Tony Santori? Tony's not your trainer. Are you trying to disrespect Tony?" Tony asked me.

"No, Mr. Santori, no disrespect at all. In fact, I'm wearing this in a way to respect you. It's kind of a long story; you may get a laugh out of it."

"Okay, funny man. Make me laugh."

"Well, I went to see Solomon Feldman at his deli earlier, and . . . well, we had an altercation."

"You had an altercation with Solomon Feldman? And you lived to tell about it?"

"Yeah, he didn't like my line of questioning and threw me into a stack of shelves covered with mayonnaise jars."

"Wait, shelves with jars of mayonnaise?"

"Yeah, he tossed me into them, and they shattered all over me, dousing me in white goo."

I clearly had Tony's attention. "You're kidding," he said. "Let me guess. Did he stick his gun in your mouth and pull the trigger?"

"How did you know?"

Tony leaned back in his chair and let out a roaring laugh from deep in his belly.

"How did you know?" I repeated.

It took Tony another few seconds to gather himself. "That's one of the oldest tricks in the book. It's a classic humiliation tactic meant to attack all your senses. I've done it a dozen or so times myself but never with mayonnaise. I've only ever used eggs or tomatoes. The boys on the West Coast mostly use apple sauce."

I stood there in silence, not sure how to respond as Santori continued to picture my encounter with Feldman.

"If he used mayonnaise, that son of a bitch must have used fake glass for the jars." He looked me up and down again. "There's no way a geezer like you would have survived being thrown into real glass."

I'd figured my superior conditioning was the reason I withstood the blow from Feldman, but as I thought about it, I realized I'd never found a shard of glass as I brushed myself off. There wasn't any blood or cuts. That son of a bitch had worked me, big time!

"Mayonnaise," Santori said as he grinned and straightened himself up in his chair. "I'll have to remember that. So, Blaze, give me some updates. Have you figured out which of Feldman's fuckers came into my house and killed Mel Weinberg?"

"I'm closing in on the assailant. As I said, I was at Feldman's deli earlier, and I've just come across some new information I think will lead me even closer to IDing the killer."

"That's good, Blaze, that's good. I'm ready to teach that fucker a lesson. But I need you to speed things up. Did you hear that fuckin' Vanner guy on TV bring up the murder in his interview with Sarah Cutler two nights ago?"

"I did. That was surprising."

"Not as surprising as hearing Tony's name mentioned soon after. Apparently, Vanner's people had the nerve to call and ask Tony to appear on some special they're doing tomorrow for that missing cop."

It was still jarring to hear Tony refer to himself as Tony, though it brought an added sense of authority with it.

"So what did you say to them?" I asked, already knowing the answer from my conversation with MGBC's Norman Yellin.

"My associates said fuck no."

"That makes sense. They called me, too, about that show. I thought about declining at first, but the money was too good to pass up for this lowly detective."

"Why do they care about a lowlife detective?"

I thought about correcting Tony's description of me but decided to let it pass.

"They think I can provide insight into the cop's disappearance."

Tony stood from his chair, clearly not comfortable with the conversation's direction.

"And can you?"

"Can I what?" I asked, realizing I, too, was getting uncomfortable.

Tony walked toward me and brought his face within inches of mine.

"Can you provide insight into the cop's disappearance?"

I realized that if I told the truth, I might see my life flash before my eyes for the second time that day. Best to play to Santori's ego.

"Of course not," I said. "I'm just in it for the cash."

"Let me tell you something, fuckface. You're not going on TV tomorrow."

"I'm not?"

"No, Blaze. You know why?"

I guessed this was a rhetorical question, so I continued staring into Santori's dark eyes.

"Because I fuckin' own you, and you do what I say. You took my money, and in my world, that's the same as signing a contract. Your life belongs to me, Blaze, and I say no TV. You set foot in that TV show, and I'll kill you."

I almost began to explain that you don't set foot *in* a TV show, but fortunately I held my tongue.

"I fucking own you, Blaze, you hear me? Do I make myself clear?"

"Loud and clear, Mr. Santori. You own Detective Blaze."

"And don't you forget it."

"I want to follow your instructions, but I also want to remind you that to find the steam room murderer, I have to go where the clues take me. Those clues may take me to that TV show, but you have my word that if I do go on, it will only be to boost your credibility and prove your innocence."

"You're playing with fire, Blaze."

"Don't worry, Mr. Santori. I'll be careful."

"You better. And remember—"

"You fuckin' own me."

"That's right. Now get the fuck outta here."

He didn't need to tell me twice. I opened the door and left Santori's private space as quickly as I could.

I hustled down Santori's stairs and into the WCC lobby, almost to the front door, when I heard someone calling my name.

"Mr. Blazen! Mr. Blazen!"

I turned around to see the front attendant running toward me.

"Remember, Betty needed to see you."

I had completely forgotten. The last thing I wanted was to spend one more minute in that club, particularly if she was going to chastise me again. I left the lobby and walked toward Betty's office. Her door was open as I got there, but before I could knock, I heard Betty demandingly shout, "Get in here, Mr. Blazen."

Betty and I had known each other for years, and we'd always been cordial, at least until she called me a pervert. This tone, though, was different than I'd ever heard, like she was performing for someone. I walked in and found Betty standing behind her desk.

"Sit," she ordered, pointing to a chair in front of her desk.

I found her eyes as I walked to the chair, and she subtly shook her head as if she didn't want me to speak. Maybe she was performing for someone, someone who had bugged her office.

"Now listen, Mr. Blazen. You have been a member here for many years, and we appreciate your ongoing support. I know I don't need to remind you of our previous conversation, do I?"

I shook my head no.

"Well, there are concerns at the club that you are continuing to overstep your bounds. I'm afraid this is your last warning. If we need to discuss this again, I will be forced to cancel your membership. Do I make myself clear?"

I nodded yes.

"Good. That's all, Mr. Blazen. Thank you for your time."

She reached out her hand to shake mine. I was hurt and insulted by this performance, but I shook her hand nonetheless. As I did, I felt a sheet of paper slide between her palm and mine. I took it and carefully slid it in my pants pocket. As I started to turn away, Betty gave me a quick wink.

I left Betty's office with my right hand in my pocket, safely guarding the note. I needed some time to think, time to myself or at least away from the FBI. I texted Jeffrey to ask if he could pick me up from the club so I could get the FBI off my tail.

Be there in 20 minutes, he wrote back.

Great, thanks. Meet me in the underground parking lot. Oh, and bring me a sweatshirt and pants.

I found my way to an elevator and went down to the basement. I walked around the lot for a couple of minutes, trying to figure out if there were any blind spots out of view of all security cameras. I found a pillar in the northwest corner to stand behind, and once sure no one was around, I pulled the note out from my pocket and read it to myself.

Tomorrow, 9 a.m. Lakeside Cafe. We need to talk.

The handwriting looked vaguely familiar, and as I put the note back in my pocket, I couldn't help but smile. I may have been a lowlife detective in Tony Santori's eyes, but I was pretty sure I had just solved the steam room mystery.

17

I shivered in my T-shirt and shorts as I stood in the basement parking lot, waiting for Jeffrey and his getaway car. I had missed a call from Mary as well as from MGBC's Norman Yellin, who left a message saying to dress like a detective for tomorrow's broadcast, arrive ninety minutes early to go over last-minute logistics, and make sure not to demean Sarah Cutler.

In the past three hours, I'd gone toe to toe with the two baddest men in Chicago, had my life threatened twice, had a gun shoved down my throat, was doused in mayonnaise, and was now being told to be nice to Sarah Cutler, a woman I knew was dirty. Screw Sarah Cutler. Forget that—screw Norman Yellin. I still couldn't believe he offered Lexington so much more money than me, particularly after my team did all the work.

And screw Lexington too. Based on what Marc had discovered, it sounded like Lexington wanted to steal the spotlight tomorrow night and make the *Looking for Lance* show a chance to cash in on my investigative work. There were too many moving parts between my work for Santori and my own team's investigations that could fall apart if Lexington shared the wrong information. The only way I could see keeping him quiet was to keep him off the air altogether.

Jeffrey pulled up and gave me sweats and a winter coat.

"Okay, David, where are we going?" he asked.

"Just drive. I've got a lot on my mind, namely what to do with two-timing Tom Lexington."

"Marc told me all about it," Jeffrey said. "He said Lexington got all kinds of info from Carter. Names. Locations. Payment amounts. Do you think he'd really give that info up on air?"

"I haven't known Lexington long, but what I do know is he will do whatever he thinks is in his own best interest. So yes, I'm sure he's planning on sharing that information. The only way I can figure keeping him quiet is to keep him off the air."

"How are you going to do that?"

"That's what we need to figure out."

We sat in silence, formulating makeshift plans in our heads. I wasn't paying attention to where Jeffrey was driving until I noticed we were on Lakeshore Drive, north of downtown. I looked out at Lake Michigan, the waves calmly rolling in toward the snow-covered shore.

"Hey Jeffrey, pull over there. Let's go walking on the lakefront."

"David, it's thirty degrees outside."

"Put a hat and gloves on, then. Come on, it will help me think."

Jeffrey got off at the next exit and parked along the lakefront. We walked south, back toward the city skyline, just two brothers sharing a moment and strategizing an important mission.

"So we have to keep Lexington away from the studio?" he asked.

"I think so."

"What if you talk to him? Would he listen if you explained why it's important he not share that info?"

"I don't think he'll listen to anything but cash, and I'm not interested in paying him a hundred grand from my pockets."

"Yeah, me neither. Can we blackmail him?"

"We could, if only I had some dirt on him."

We kept walking as the whistling winter wind filled the silence between us. All of a sudden, the pieces came together in my mind.

"That's it!"

"What?"

"Blackmail."

"You said you don't have any dirt."

"I don't, but he doesn't have to know that. We can pretend to blackmail him."

"Pretend?"

"Yep," I said with renewed energy. "Oh, this is going to be good. We're going to scare him shitless to keep him quiet, and if it works, it just might be my best selling performance of all time. We'll make him look like an idiot on national television, which will also humiliate the network executives—they deserve it for giving him all that money. They'll wish they never offered him the gig in the first place. But for it to work, it's going to take a full team effort. You, me, Marc, Wilt, Patrick, and some special guests."

"I thought you wanted to keep Lexington off the air."

"This idea will be even better, but we've got a lot to do and not a lot of time. Can you get the car? I have a quick call to make."

As soon as I was sure he was out of ear's reach, I pulled out the pink phone and called Eli. The phone rang five or six times before he answered.

"Blaze, is that you?" Eli asked.

"Yes, it's me. Are you still at the deli?"

"Yeah, I had to sneak outside to answer the phone. Listen, Blaze, I don't know what you and Feldman talked about, but whatever you did, you earned some serious respect from him, even if you ended up covered in mayo. He said you had real *chutzpah*."

"That's great, Eli, but that's not why I'm calling. I need to talk with Feldman again. Can you make sure he stays around for a bit? I'll be there in twenty minutes with one of my associates."

"Yeah, I can, but he might not be happy to see you again so soon."

"Trust me. A man named Tom Lexington is going to share some of Feldman's darkest secrets with millions of people on live television tomorrow unless I stop him."

"Okay, Blaze. I'll make sure Feldman's here. Now I should go."

"Wait, Eli, before you do. I have a meeting about a different project tonight, and I'd really like you to come with me."

"A different project?"

"Well, it's sort of connected. It's called Operation Boom."

"That sounds ominous."

"I can fill you in later. Meet at my house tonight at quarter to nine—and not in the bedroom this time."

"What about the FBI outside your place?"

"Oh, good point. There's an alley across the street from my neighbor's house. There will be a car there picking me up. If you beat me, the driver's name is Cliff. I'll tell him you're coming."

Jeffrey pulled up beside me and rolled down his window. "Where to?" he asked.

"Morry's Deli."

MGBC's Norman Yellin started the production meeting with a rhetorical question: "Are you ready to make history?"

The junior production assistants looked at each other, unsure what Yellin was referring to. They knew they were working on a major Sunday special, but history? That seemed a little overboard. They were also wondering why Sarah Cutler, the presumptive future mayor, was sitting in on the meeting.

"That's right, ladies and gentlemen, we have the chance to make history with our show tomorrow night. The world is wondering where Lance Cutler is, and we have the potential to answer the question. We've got ninety minutes to make it happen, and we've got to make sure we capitalize on each of those minutes. So let's talk through the rundown."

Sarah Cutler coughed into her fist, not so subtly trying to get Yellin's attention.

"Ah, yes, forgive me everyone. Allow me to introduce Sarah Cutler, Lance Cutler's mother. Since this broadcast is all about her son and she will be one of our primary guests, she insisted on joining our meeting to understand the show's structure."

"Thank you, Norman," Sarah said. "I also want to make sure we don't have any surprises like the last time I was on TV at this network."

"That's right," Yellin said. "No surprises here. So let's get to it. Right now, here's our confirmed guest list for the show tomorrow: Mrs. Cutler—"

"You can call me Sarah," she interrupted.

"Yes, sorry about that. We have Sarah; her husband, Kent; Mayor Paulson; Officer Fred Skepper—"

"Skip is going to be on?" Sarah interrupted.

"Yes. As you know, Skepper—or Skip, as you referred to him—is one of Lance's longest and closest friends. He is also a police officer in your son's precinct, and I believe he was the first responding officer to the West Coast Club steam room incident. Having a fellow officer on the show will not only speak to your son's character, but he could provide insight into what the Chicago Police Department is doing to locate Lance, as well as offer a perspective on how law enforcement handles missing persons cases. Is that going to be a problem?"

"No, not at all," a flustered Sarah said. "I'm just a little surprised, that's all."

"Don't be surprised so many people want to help find your son, Sarah," Norman said, attempting to console her while also trying to regain control of the meeting. "Our goal is to find him, and we'll do whatever we can to do that during these ninety minutes, okay? May I continue?"

"Yes, I'm sorry, Norman," Sarah said. "Please, go ahead."

"In addition to Skepper, we have a Detective Blaze confirmed. I don't know that he's going to add much to the show, but Vanner mentioned him by name on the last show, so we figured no harm in bringing him on."

"Vanner also mentioned Tony Santori," one of the producers added. "Is he going to be on? That would certainly draw some ratings."

"Yes, it would," Yellin said, "but no, unfortunately Mr. Santori declined our invitation. That's who we've got so far, and we've got Vanner lined up to cohost the show with a former mentor of his named Tom Lexington, but that's it. I think we'll be able to have some interesting conversations, but we don't have enough to fill ninety minutes. As you all know, content is king in this business, and we need more content. Who can we add?"

Yellin's question was met with silence.

"Come on, people, let's brainstorm. There are no stupid ideas right now, so start throwing some out. What can we do to fill ninety minutes?"

"How about a musician?" an assistant said.

"That's good," Yellin said. "We can have some pianist or guitar player open the broadcast with a somber ballad. I like it. What else?"

"A psychic?" one of the producers suggested.

"Hmm," Yellin said, "I've never believed in that mumbo jumbo, but that's a possibility. What are you thinking? They can visualize where Lance is located?"

"Yeah," the producer said. "Maybe we could have the psychic come on early in the show, and if the location they say is nearby, we could send a crew out there and, if we're lucky, find Lance Cutler on camera before the end of the broadcast."

"That's a big if," Yellin said, "but sure, let's go for it. These are good, people; keep going."

"What about a mime?" a different assistant suggested.

Everyone in the meeting turned and stared at him.

"Why would we get a mime?" Yellin said.

"You know, to break up the show," the assistant said, "so it's not just everyone sitting and talking. We could have the mime depict the feelings Lance Cutler has right now as the world looks for him."

Everyone continued to stare, including Yellin.

"I take back what I said about there being no stupid ideas. Moving on. I'm liking where most of your heads are right now. Take that momentum and go find us a psychic and a musician and keep thinking about other people who could bring a little more flair to the show. Sarah, thank you for joining us for this meeting. There's no need for you to stick around. I'll give you a call if we have any questions or major changes in plans."

"Thank you for that consideration. And please remember what we talked about, Norman. Obviously, my son's safe return is our top priority—"

"Say no more, Sarah. Yes, Lance is our focus." Norman turned to everyone else in the room. "But ladies and gentlemen—and this is off the record—we must make sure Sarah is presented in a positive light. After all, she is going to be our next mayor."

Norman nodded at Sarah as the production staff looked at one another, confused.

"Okay, everyone, get to work. Meet me back here in two hours."

Jeffrey and I spent the car ride talking through all the steps it would take to effectively censor Tom Lexington, making it impossible for him to reveal any of the confidential information he wanted to disclose on air.

When we got to the deli, Solomon Feldman was at a back table with Eli, who awkwardly introduced himself to Jeffrey and me as we approached.

"What can we do for you gentlemen?"

"I need to speak with Mr. Feldman," I said, looking at Feldman, not Eli.

"My friends call me Sol," he said with a smile as he stood to shake my hand. "Can you guys give us a minute?"

I nodded at Jeffrey that it was okay for him to go off with Eli. Once they were gone, I turned to Feldman, who motioned for me to sit across the table from him.

"Thanks Sol," I said, acknowledging our new friendship.

"You've got some nerve coming back here so soon, Blaze," he said as I sat down. "What the hell do you want?"

"I need that favor, Sol, but it's a favor to protect you. Do you know a man named Tom Lexington?"

"No, who is he?"

"He works at a local newspaper, but that's not why you should care about him."

"Okay. Why should I care about him?"

"Unfortunately," I whispered as I leaned in over the table, "he knows you ordered the hit on your nephew Charlie Myers, and he's planning on sharing that info on TV tomorrow during that *Looking for Lance* broadcast."

Sol jumped up in a rage and flipped our table over, narrowly missing clocking me in the face with its side.

"That piece of shit," Sol shouted, drawing the attention of the few patrons still eating in the cafeteria, as well as Eli and Jeffrey. "How does he know?"

I motioned for Sol to calm down and take a seat as Eli ran

toward us. I told Eli we were okay as I picked up the table and sat back down, with Sol continuing to stand and stare at me.

"Right now, that's not what matters. We need to focus on keeping him quiet, and I have an idea."

Sol sat down, his eyes never leaving mine. "You want me to kill him?"

"What? No! But you get to pretend to."

"Pretend?"

"That's right. If you don't mind, I'd like to bring my associate Jeffrey and your man Eli back so the four of us can discuss the plan. Each of them will need to play a role in its execution."

Sol thought for a few seconds. Then he smirked and signaled for Eli and Jeffrey to join us. Over the next fifteen minutes, I talked through the logistics. Once everyone understood their responsibilities, the four of us stood to shake hands. I thanked Sol for his assistance as I turned to leave.

"You better hope this plan works, Blaze. Otherwise, I'm going to reintroduce you to my pistol, and this time I won't be so forgiving."

"Fingers crossed." I smiled as I crossed my fingers.

"In all seriousness, Blaze, thanks for looking out for me."

"You can always count on me to do the right thing, Sol. Don't ever forget it."

"I won't. Now get going. Besides, Eli and I need to find some more mayonnaise."

Jermaine banged on Tony Santori's office door, then bent over with his hands on his knees to catch his breath after taking the stairs two at a time.

"What?" Tony snidely responded.

"Boss, it's me. We've got a problem."

"If one more person tells me we've got a problem, I swear I'll blow their brains out on the spot. Get in here. What's wrong?"

Jermaine walked in the room, still breathing heavily. "Boss, I was just in the lobby, and through the windows I saw the FBI snooping around the outside of the club."

"FBI? What the hell are they doing here?"

"I don't know, boss. I've definitely seen their cars here before. You think they're looking for you?"

"Fuck if I know," Santori shouted as he got up and began to pace.

"You don't think it has to do with that guy we blew up downtown, do you?"

The office went silent. Jermaine wasn't sure if he should have mentioned Henry Jackson's murder, but at that point, he was more worried about his own safety than Santori's. After all, it was Jermaine who'd put the explosives in Henry's car.

Santori stopped pacing. "Fuck, I bet you're right. I've been so focused on Wednesday's family dinner and getting that fuckin' Feldman back for the steam room hit that I forgot all about that."

"Do you think they found something?"

"Dammit, Jermaine, why are you asking me? I don't know what the fuck they've found." Santori stopped his pace in front of a mirror. "I was afraid this day would come. I just didn't think it'd be so soon."

"What day?"

"The day when I say goodbye to Chicago. If the FBI is on to me, then it's time for me to leave. I'll retire at the top of my game and disappear to some foreign country. They won't bring me down if they can't find me."

"How can you leave, boss? What about everything you've been building here?"

"We'll still have an operation in place. I'll have Enzo come back, and he and Vince can lead things while I'm gone."

"Where are you gonna go?"

"I don't know, I've always wanted to get back to the Caribbean. Maybe I'll take an extended vacation there—somewhere where the authorities don't have jurisdiction."

"But boss, what about the big dinner on Wednesday?"

Santori was silent, still staring in the mirror as he pondered Jermaine's question. A maniacal grin slowly formed on his face.

"That's it! Instead of that dinner being a gathering to share info, I'll have it be an ode to me and my successes as I walk off into the sunset."

"Like a retirement party?" Jermaine clarified. "That's a great idea, boss, a great idea."

"An ode to Tony," Santori said as he sat back down, pleased with himself and his new idea. "If this is going to be a celebration, then we need more people. We need this to be a blast like nothing the city's ever seen."

He grabbed a sheet of paper and began to write down additions to Wednesday's invite list. It wasn't until Tony was eight names in that he realized Jermaine was still standing there, his gaze on the floor.

"Jermaine, why the fuck are you still here?"

"Well, boss, I was just wondering," he said, still focused on the ground in front of him. "If you go off to the Caribbean, and Vince and Enzo are running things here, what happens to me?"

"Oh, for fuck's sake, Jermaine, I don't have all the answers. I'm sure some hoopster from the hood will take you back as his security guy. Now leave me alone. Tony's got to plan out this celebration of Tony."

Jermaine didn't want to go back to that old life. Santori had introduced him to this new world—a world where he thought he was valued and appreciated, but suddenly, that world was falling apart. He turned and left the room, his eyes never leaving the ground.

Jeffrey was practically giddy as we got back in the car and began the drive north to my house.

"David, that was incredible how you walked right in like you owned the place," he said, talking so fast he made that sentence sound like one long word. "And then how he called you his friend and just so naturally followed your lead. David, that guy is the most feared man in this city, and he was listening to *you*. How the hell did you do that?"

I cracked a smile at Jeffrey's new fandom. "I guess when you're a good detective, people respect you. Even bad guys."

"Apparently," Jeffrey said. "Just imagine what you could have done if you started this whole detective thing earlier. I get it now, all your kooky behavior these past few days and weeks. It's all led you to this, hasn't it?"

Jeffrey didn't wait for an answer, which was good because I tuned his question out. We were back on Lake Shore Drive, cruising north between the lake and the city skyline. The skyscrapers popped out of the ground like beanstalks, casting a mesmerizing backdrop. The picturesque view, our lofty plan, and the reality of my past few hours had me feeling philosophical.

"Jeffrey," I finally said, interrupting his fourth or fifth verbal recreation of the deli scene, "what am I doing?"

"What do you mean? You're going home."

"I know that, but how did I get here?"

"I drove you, remember?"

"No, Jeffrey, I mean existentially, how did I get here? How did I become this person who has a crime lord like Feldman calling me his friend? How did I become the one with all the information? Why am I always in the right place at the right time? I was the one at the shopping mall who stopped those thieves. I was the one in the steam room. Why am I the one who keeps piecing everything together? Mel Weinberg and his shady activities. The explosion on Wacker Drive. Sarah Cutler and her connection with

Feldman. And don't even get me started on everything with Tony Santori. Why the hell hasn't he killed me? Better yet, why haven't any of the people who could have killed me in the past couple of days finished the job? Why do I keep on surviving? Why? Why is all of this happening to me?"

The car was silent. After a minute, Jeffrey turned to me.

"You know, surviving is better than the alternative."

"I know. I'm not complaining about that. I just mean—this is going to sound weird, but I think I might have a greater purpose."

"Greater than what?"

"Just follow along. A little while back, I was a retired businessman looking for something to do to keep my mind fresh. I was a people-watcher. Now suddenly I've become the guy trusted by Solomon Feldman and Tony Santori—and, oh yeah, the FBI; let's not forget about them. That can't all just be one big coincidence, can it?"

Jeffrey was becoming more fascinated. "I don't know, David. What do you think?"

I paused to carefully plan out my response. "Don't laugh," I whispered as I pointed my finger upward, "but I wonder if I'm on a mission from God."

"David, you've never been that religious. Don't you think God would choose someone more devoted to their beliefs?"

"I don't know. I'm starting to wonder if a script is written by a higher power the day we're born with our predetermined destiny."

"And your destiny is to be a crime-solving detective? Why wouldn't he just give you superpowers to save Metropolis?"

I ignored Jeffrey's sarcasm as I let my idea weigh over us. After three long minutes, he broke the silence.

"Well, whatever your destiny is, I hope this higher power doesn't want to see you in person anytime soon."

We looked at each other for a second, then let out two long, hearty laughs that eased some of my stress.

"I agree," I said as I pulled out my pink phone. "Now that's enough philosophy. We've got work to do."

I called Marc and asked him to invite Lexington to join me for lunch tomorrow before the broadcast and asked Jeffrey to pick up Lexington from home. After that, I spent the rest of the drive texting Wilt and Patrick to let them know our plan and the roles each of them would play.

Cliff Stanley was finishing setting up seating at his barn for the night's initial Operation Boom meeting when his phone buzzed.

"Blaze gave us the shake, boss," one of his agents said. "His car is still here at the West Coast Club, but we've scouted the perimeter and peeked inside, and we're pretty sure he's not here anymore. What do you want us to do?"

Cliff chuckled at the idea of this seventy-something-year-old giving his men the slip—again.

"Hold on." Cliff called the truck stationed in front of Blaze's residence. "Any sign of the detective?"

"Not yet. Wait, hold on a minute. Yep, there he is. Looks like his brother, Jeffrey, is dropping him off in the driveway right now."

Cliff chuckled again. "Got it." He hung up and called the first agent back. "Yep, you got played by a senior citizen," he said with a laugh. "He's back home, so no need for you to stay. Leave his car there. I'm sure there's a reason he left it."

"Okay, people," Norman Yellin said, sitting down at the same conference table he'd stood at two hours earlier, "what do we have?"

"I found a local guitarist who will do the show for free," an assistant said. "He specializes in acoustic love songs."

"Great," Yellin said. "Get him booked. Who's next?"

"How about Sherwin Kite?" a segment producer asked.

"Who?"

"Sherwin Kite. He's a psychic who won one of those TV talent shows a couple of months ago for identifying what different audience members had in their purses and pockets. He's doing a show in Chicago next week."

"Get him," Yellin said. "If he won, he's got to have a knack for the camera. Who else do we have?"

"Gerald Scherer is in town, and we can get him for under twenty-five grand," a producer piped in.

The room was silent as everyone looked at each other. Yellin finally took the bait.

"Who the hell is Gerald Scherer?"

"He just published his autobiography, *Don't Yank My Chain: My Life As a Hostage Negotiator*," the assistant said, "and it's already a bestseller."

"That's good for him," Yellin said, "but why do we need a hostage negotiator?"

"Well, unless Lance Cutler is dead, it certainly seems like he was kidnapped. And if he was kidnapped, eventually there will be a ransom request, and his kidnappers will need to be negotiated with."

"I guess that makes sense. Sure, go for it."

"Mr. Yellin?" a young assistant piped in.

"Yes?"

"What if Lance Cutler is dead?"

The question hit at the elephant in the room. It had been more than four days since Lance's disappearance, and it was not unreasonable to think the reason no one had heard from him was because he was dead. Still, Yellin didn't want to go down that route.

"Ladies and gentlemen," he said, "our goal is not necessarily to find Lance during our ninety minutes, although that would be incredible. Our top priority is putting together a memorable piece of television. We want unique perspectives and opinions that haven't been heard before, and we want to shed a light on who Lance Cutler is—or was—as a person. Our focus is quality television, that's it. From there, we'll let the chips fall where they may."

Sarah Cutler frantically knocked at Frank Skepper's front door. No answer. The sun had already set, and now a light snow was beginning to fall. She knocked again.

"Skip," she shouted, "open the damn door!"

Skip opened the door, confused and annoyed. "Madam Mayor, what the hell are you thinking? Get in here," he said, ushering her in as he did a quick check to make sure no one was looking. He closed the door and turned to Sarah. "How stupid are you?"

"Excuse you," Sarah shot back.

"Lower your voice," Skip whispered. "My kids just got to sleep. What are you thinking? The last thing we need is to be seen together, particularly with everyone still looking for Lance."

"That's why I'm here, Skip. I heard you're going on the TV special tomorrow."

"Yeah, so what?"

"Why would you go on?"

"The money, Sarah, pure and simple. Ninety minutes on TV and I'll make as much as I do in a year on the force."

"But Skip, the show is all about looking for Lance. You and I both know that's a lost cause. Isn't it?"

"That doesn't mean I can't still cash in on it. Look at you—you're only going on to appeal to voters."

"I beg your pardon. That's not the only reason. And you didn't answer my question. It's a lost cause looking for Lance, right?"

"Yes, it's a lost cause, but no one besides you and me ever has to know that. Now you need to get out of here. Stay calm on TV tomorrow, and no one will find out what we know."

"I don't like this, Skip."

"Well, Madam Mayor, you don't have a choice. Now go before my wife comes down."

Skip opened the door and sent Sarah into the cold night.

I got back home and was immediately confronted by Mary, who wanted to know where I'd been.

"Why didn't you answer my calls?" she asked. "And why are you getting presents from murderers?"

"Excuse me?"

"This," she said, tossing the Bible to me. "A Wisconsin state trooper stopped by to give it to you. He said it was from a couple of old men who killed a dozen KKK members and said they were protecting you by giving it to you. David, what the hell is going on?"

"I have no idea, Mary. Listen, I have a couple quick phone calls to make. Do you mind making dinner, and then we can talk?"

"David, are your phone calls more important than me?"

"Thanks for understanding," I said, clearly not listening as I darted off to the bathroom, leaving Mary standing stunned in the hallway.

Once I had privacy from the FBI, I called Lance, whom I hadn't spoken with since that morning.

"Blaze, I'm dying in here, I'm so bored," he said.

"Hang in there, Lance. I promise I haven't forgotten about you."

"Do you know how depressing it is to flip through the channels and see everyone talking about you? Blaze, I can't find anything to watch. Even the frickin' cooking channel was just talking about me during a mother-son cookie competition. I don't know if I can make it until tomorrow night before I need to get out of this hell hole."

"About that . . ."

"What?"

"I know we talked about you crashing the show to embarrass your mother and defend your name—"

"David, don't do this to me."

"I've learned more about this broadcast, the people involved, and the motives behind it, and I don't think it's a good idea to have you show up. It's going to turn into a celebratory event for Sarah, and she's going to ride it right into the mayor's office."

"But what about everything I'm going to say about her?"

"No one will hear it. All the focus will be on the fact you're alive and safe, and that will be the story."

"David, you promised me time on national television with my mother to show the country what kind of monster she is."

"And you still will, Lance, just not tomorrow night."

"Then when?"

"Sometime soon, I promise. Let me get past tomorrow night, and then we'll get it worked out."

"David, I don't know how much longer I can do this. I've got nothing to do. Can you at least bring me some magazines or crossword puzzles?"

"Sure, I'll swing them by tomorrow. Now I gotta run. Hang in there."

I hung up with Lance and checked for updates from the team. There was a text from Marc confirming Lexington was excited to have lunch with me tomorrow, but it would need to be late. He would be practicing with Vanner at the studio from 9 a.m. to 1 p.m., but he would be ready to be picked up around 2 p.m. for a late meal. I gave Jeffrey a quick call to confirm that timing.

"I'm on it, bro. Anything else?"

"Actually, yes, I've got something for you and Violet."

"Violet? Why does my wife need to be involved?"

"It will be easy, I promise. At 10 a.m., I need you to go over to Tom Lexington's house and knock on the door and talk with his wife. Oh, and wear a long black overcoat, gloves, and a hat."

"Okay. What about Violet?"

"I need her to take a cell phone video of you talking with Lexington's wife. Make sure she doesn't get any audio. I just want the video."

"What should I tell his wife?"

"Something that will get her visibly upset. Something like you work with Tom at the newspaper, and he agreed to watch your pit bull, Princess Peaches, next weekend while you're out of town. Throw in something ridiculous with it, like that the little princess eats at the dinner table, or she promises not to bite anyone this time."

"I won't even ask why, but okay, we can do that."

"Thanks, Jeffrey. Oh, and don't forget a tarp for the backseat."

I texted Wilt to pick up my car from the WCC and wrote Cliff to inform him Eli would be joining the Operation Boom meeting and that he might beat me to the pickup location.

That left me with the mysterious bible. I opened the book and saw the hand-written note. I quickly flipped through the rest of the book, looking for any other signs. Before getting too far, I was interrupted by a knock on the bathroom door.

"If you're not too busy in there, dinner's ready," Mary said.

I stood up, put my phone away, and put the Bible down, ready to give Mary my undivided attention. I opened the door to find her staring at me, tears in her eyes.

"David, I'm losing you. Come back to me."

I motioned for her to join me in the bathroom. She gave me a confused look as I showed her in and closed the door.

"David, what the hell is going on?"

"The FBI can't hear us here. Come, sit with me."

I stepped into the tub and turned to stick my hand out to Mary. She shook her head at the ridiculousness of sitting fully clothed in the empty tub before begrudgingly climbing in. My love sat opposite from me, our feet resting against each other's hips.

"Okay, Mary, what do you want to know?"

"Why didn't you answer any of the times I called today?"

I wanted to be truthful, but I also figured telling her I had a pistol in my mouth was not what she wanted to hear. Skirting the truth seemed to be best.

"I had a series of meetings today with Chicago's biggest crime bosses, and they weren't really meetings I could get out of."

"What did you need to talk with them about? And what's the deal with that Bible? David, what have you gotten yourself mixed up in? "

"It's complicated."

"That's not good enough, David. This detective nonsense was supposed to be a hobby. Now you're off living some other life, and you've left me behind." Tears ran down her face as she looked deep into my eyes. "Either let me in, or tell me there's no place for me."

"Of course there's a place for you, Mary, and it's right here," I said as I spread my arms out wide.

Mary pulled herself up and came toward me. She lay her head against my chest and wiped her tears on me.

"I want to tell you everything, but I need you to understand that once I start, you'll never look at me the same way again. And you'll also be privy to information that, in the wrong hands, could be incredibly dangerous."

Mary picked her head up and looked quizzically at me. "This detective stuff—"

"It's real, Mary, and I think it's what I was born to do."

Her quizzical look remained. We sat there in the tub, locked in a lovers' stare for who knows how long. It probably was only seconds, but in that time, our bond grew stronger than ever. She put her hand on my cheek.

"If this detective thing is what you're made to do, then let's make it what we're meant to do."

"Are you sure?"

She kissed my lips. "I'm sure."

I spent the next thirty minutes telling Mary everything—what happened to Mel, the Chicago Police Department coverups, the history of Feldman and Santori, the truth about Lance Cutler, the vision I had at the funeral, and most notably Operation Boom. She listened intently, stunned that so much had happened to me in such a short amount of time. As I talked, I felt some stress releasing from my shoulders, the sheer relief of not keeping so much information hidden from my love and best friend. When I finished, I looked inquisitively at her.

"So what do you think?"

Mary paused. "I think you would have been a hell of a detective if you'd started years ago."

I gave her a nod of appreciation. "But what do you think I should do?"

"You mean 'we,' right?"

"Yes, sorry. What do you think we should do?"

"Well, that Bible the state trooper delivered said, 'It must be done.' Who knows what kind of biblical message that means, but for now, let's say it means we must go to the Boom meeting tonight. From the little you've told me about it, I don't like it, but it sounds like there's still a lot you don't know. What's the harm in going and getting more information? We're talking about the FBI and other good guys, right? It's not like they're going to kill us if we don't do what they say."

"That's true," I said as I wrapped her in my arms. "You know, I've never felt closer to you than I do right now."

"That's because we're lying in a damn bathtub, David," she said with a grin. "Come on, we've got to get ready. What does one wear to an underground meeting anyway?"

"A sneaking-through-the-backyard-undetected outfit. And no heels."

The two of us ate and then changed, with Mary opting for a pair of black leather pants and a contoured black blazer that made her easily pass as one of Charlie's Angels. Holding hands, we snuck out the back door and entered a new chapter of our lives. We both knew that David and Mary as we had known them would never be the same again.

I wanted to go out into the alley behind our house, but a pool of slush made our back gate inaccessible. Instead, I walked us toward the shared fence between our house and Patrick's and asked if she wanted a boost. As I put my hands out, Mary smirked. She put both hands on the fence and almost effortlessly pushed herself up, swinging one leg over the fence and then the other like she was an Olympic gymnast. My jaw dropped.

"What?" she said, looking back. "You're not the only one with secrets. Besides, you already know how flexible I am."

She winked as I hopped over the fence. We'd barely left our property, and already I was seeing a different side of Mary. And I liked it.

We tiptoed across our neighbors' yard and made it halfway when we heard heavy breathing coming from near the back fence.

"Oh, shit," a young lady cried.

Mary and I both turned to find a startled Patrick and a coed adjusting their clothes on a back bench.

"Hey, boss," Patrick said nonchalantly.

"You know these people?" the girl asked Patrick.

"Oh, these aren't just people, sweetums. This is my boss, Detective Blaze. And you must be Mary, or do I call you Mrs. Boss?"

"Mary's fine, dear," Mary said. "And who is this lovely lady?"

"This is Kelly." Patrick put his arm around her. "My girlfriend."

"Congratulations to both of you," I said.

I wanted to ask Patrick why they were out here on such a cold night, but I remembered when I was his age being hot to trot, plus I thought of how much of a buzzkill his bunk beds must have been, and the whole situation made a little more sense. We all looked at each other uncomfortably for a few seconds. Patrick ultimately broke the ice.

"So, boss and Mary, what are you guys doing here?"

"Sorry, we didn't mean to interrupt you," I said. "We were trying to get out to the alley, and our yard was flooded, so we hoped to go through your backyard." Not wanting to give them a chance to further interrogate us, I changed the subject. "Kelly, you're in Patrick's broadcast class, right?"

"She's not just in my class; she's the smartest in the class," Patrick boasted. "Last summer, she did three internships at the same time just so she could learn as much about the broadcast industry as she could."

Kelly blushed.

"That's admirable," I said. "It's important to be focused on your goals. What do you want to do after graduating, Kelly?"

"I'm not quite sure yet," she said. "I just know I want to use my skills to make a difference."

"That is a great goal to have." I turned toward Patrick. "Don't let this one get away. You could learn a lot from her. Anyway, we'll let you two get back to whatever you were doing."

Kelly blushed again as we began to walk away.

"No problem, boss," he said. "Thanks for stopping by."

Mary and I hurried along to prevent any further conversation. Once we were outside the yard and a good distance from them, we broke out in uncontrollable laughter. We were still gathering ourselves as we held hands and crossed the street to Cliff Stanley's car. Cliff was outside, and he did not look happy.

"What the hell, Blaze?" he said as we got to the car. "This isn't a bring-a-guest meeting."

"Ah, you must have met Eli."

"Yeah, he's in the car already," he said.

"I see. Well, Cliff, allow me to introduce you to—"

"You must be Mary," he interrupted, reaching to shake Mary's hand. "My name is Cliff Stanley. It's a pleasure to meet you. David, can I talk with you for a second?"

I started to walk off to the side, then stopped. "Cliff, anything you want to say to me you can say in front of Mary." She squeezed my hand with affection.

"Does she know anything about tonight?"

"She knows everything I know. And if you want Detective Blaze involved, Mary comes with. We're a package deal."

Cliff put his hand on his forehead, then shook his head. "Fine, hop in. But this is not what I had in mind."

Mary and I slid into the backseat as Cliff got behind the wheel. He turned on the car and sped out of the alley, turning us away from our peaceful neighborhood and toward a future we could not yet fully comprehend.

18

Cliff, Eli, Mary, and I were silent as we approached our secret meeting place. From the outside, Cliff's hideout looked like an average, run-of-the-mill red barn, but it quickly became apparent that nothing about the night would be average. Cliff opened the barn door to a dimly lit, cavernous space that felt more like an exhibition hall than a barn. Dozens, perhaps hundreds, of crates marked with *explosive* and *danger* in different languages were neatly arranged in piles around the room, including a precarious pyramid to the left that extended up like a staircase to a dark loft space. Newspaper clippings and old military recruitment posters covered much of the interior walls.

It looked like this was once a stable for horses, but all the stables were removed except for one halfway down the right side of the barn. Mary and I walked over to the stall and were surprised to see a memorial commemorating the September 11 attacks on the United States. There were framed pictures of the Pentagon ablaze and Flight 93's crash site in rural Pennsylvania, as well as an eight-photo sequence of images that showed each of the World Trade Center Twin Towers being struck by airplanes and subsequently collapsing. Hanging above the pictures was a tattered American flag and a chalkboard with the number 2,996 written on it.

"David, Mary, over here," Cliff called.

We turned toward the far end of the barn to find Cliff standing on a makeshift stage of three crates, a half-circle of seven folding chairs in front of him. All but two of the seats were taken. We walked over and found a folding card table with a package of chocolate chip cookies, a pitcher of coffee, and a stack of paper cups. I grabbed a cookie and took a seat directly across from Cliff and next to a wheelchair occupied by a one-armed man whose legs were amputated below the knee. Beside Cliff was another chalkboard, this one with the words *Operation Boom Welcome Meeting* on it.

"Thank you all for coming and volunteering for this mission," Cliff said to the group. "We are on the cusp of history, folks. Fifty years from now, students will read about this gathering. They will learn your backstories, but more importantly, they will discover how you put the greater good before yourselves. You saw evil, and you stepped up to do something about it."

If Cliff hadn't gone into law enforcement, he would have been a damn good motivational speaker.

"You all will go down as the men and woman who fought back against crime and corruption," Cliff continued. "Operation Boom will rid this country of some of its most notorious criminals. When we succeed, the world will be a better place."

"Oh, cut the crap, Cliff," said the man in the wheelchair. "Get on with it."

"Sorry, Stubs." Cliff hopped off the stage and sat on its edge. "Each of you has a general idea of why we're here, but the high-level summary is that many of our country's dirtiest crime lords are coming together for dinner on Wednesday to talk shop and brag about their criminal accomplishments. This is a gathering that has taken place every ten years for generations—the Santoris, the Rossis, the Romanos, the Maramonas, and the Torralinis. But Wednesday will not be a celebration for those bastards. It will be a celebration for us. I'll get into the specifics of the operation in a bit, but for now, let's go around and introduce yourselves and explain why you are here. Please know this meeting is the most confidential of confidential. Anything said here will remain here and never be shared outside of these barn doors. So, please, speak freely. Vince, why don't you go first?"

Tony Santori's right-hand man stood up, and I whispered in Mary's ear that his real name was John Sedgwick and he was an undercover FBI agent.

"Thank you, Cliff," Vince said as he stood in front of his chair. "For the past six years, I have worked undercover to gain the confidence of the one and only Tony Santori. That work has paid off as Santori now trusts me with his most confidential information. Just today, he notified me that he will have his private plane gassed up and ready to go Wednesday night. He's planning on leaving the country immediately after the evening's get-together and has no plans of returning. He's also changed the agenda for the evening. Instead of being a party where they talk shop and exchange best practices, Tony fully intends for this gathering to be a celebration of him and all he's accomplished. He is a monster who constantly needs to feed his ego, and he views this as his final hurrah before flying off to paradise. My friends—and I say that term with sincerity—Operation Boom needs to succeed; otherwise, Tony Santori will disappear, and we may never hear from him again."

"We will succeed, Vince," Cliff said. "Thanks in large part to you."

"Thanks, Cliff. As for my specific role, as Tony's most trusted confidant, I oversee coordinating Wednesday's festivities, which will be held in an abandoned bowling alley. I've got the blueprints for the building, and I know everyone working the event as well as who was invited to attend. As chief coordinator, I'll be able to get you all into the venue and where you need to be."

"Thanks, Vince," Cliff said, beginning to turn to the next speaker.

"One more thing, Cliff," Vince said, turning to look at me specifically. "I know some of us have extensive training for this type of operation, and some of us don't. But I want each of you to know that you all have critical roles to play. I wholeheartedly agree with Cliff. Whether we live or die, we can all consider ourselves heroes."

Vince turned his gaze away from me and sat as Mary leaned toward me. "Vince seems very convincing."

"Yeah, but I'm not crazy about that 'die' part."

"Agreed."

Stubs was next to speak. It felt insensitive to call him that, but he embraced it.

"My name is Mike," he began, "but as Cliff already demonstrated, you can call me Stubs. I've known Cliff for more than twenty years. We served together in Afghanistan, and as you can see, much of me remains there. Cliff asked us to introduce ourselves, but for me to do that, I need to share some information that has never been made public. High-ranking government officials, both past and present, would be quick to deny the facts of what I say, partially because it would cause a financial crisis and total mistrust of the US government and negatively impact the psyche of the American people but also because nearly all, if not all, of them simply would not believe it. What I am about to say is 100 percent true." Stubs turned to Cliff. "Are you sure we can trust everyone?"

Cliff nodded his approval for Stubs to share his story. Stubs turned toward me as he began his tale.

"David, I saw you and Mary looking at Cliff's 9/11 memorial back there. Do you know the significance of that number on the chalkboard?"

"I do," I said, surprised by the question. "That number, 2,996, is how many people lost their lives that day."

"That's right," Stubs confirmed. "Think of all that changed that day. Those 2,996 people died—children lost their parents, husbands and wives lost their partners—and we as a country lost a sense of our own security. Sure, one of our greatest cities lost part of its iconic skyline, but those were just buildings. When those towers collapsed, a part of who we were as a nation collapsed with them. Do you remember life before 9/11? You used to go all the way to the gate at an airport to see someone off or welcome them back from a trip. September eleventh took that away from us. I always ask people I meet whether they knew someone who died on 9/11. What about you, David? Did you know anyone?"

"Fortunately, I didn't," I responded, "but one of my past employees lost her brother when the second tower came down."

"The next time you see that woman, please pass on my condolences and apologies."

"Apologies?" I asked.

"Yes." Stubs paused and looked around at the group. "We all know the unfortunate events of what happened that fateful day. But Cliff and I, as well as four of our most trusted brothers in combat, we knew what would happen ahead of time . . . and we didn't do anything about it."

We stared silently at Stubs.

"We were part of an elite team that got wind of the plan to take over airplanes and fly them into American landmarks. The threat seemed credible, but our superiors didn't take it seriously, particularly when we heard box cutters would be the weapon of choice. Stupid American ignorance. We were told to stand down and continue our established mission, which was to locate some sort of weapon of mass destruction that had the potential to take out an entire city. Word was the Taliban was eyeing Chicago, Dallas, or Minneapolis, and the fear was that if we went after this airplane threat, we might spook the Taliban and not be able to secure the WMD before they decimated one of our country's biggest cities."

Stubs paused as we all looked at him with fascination.

"The airplanes did plenty of decimating on their own. Our inaction cost 2,996 people their lives, and every day I live with regret about not taking matters into my own hands." Stubs turned toward Cliff. "If we had a meeting like this back then, we could have saved those people, as well as all the loved ones and friends who lost someone they cared for because we stood down."

Stubs hung his head in shame as the barn went silent. We all looked at the ground, not sure how to follow Stubs' tale. After thirty seconds, I looked at Cliff and raised my hand.

"Yes, David?"

"What happened next?"

Stubs wiped a tear from his eye and looked up at me. "Our bosses called us back to our base immediately after the attacks. We were told to ignore all previous instructions and that we'd be returning stateside in forty-eight hours. A mistake had been made, and the airplane takeovers were in fact the Taliban's big attack. But that 'mistake,' as they called it, changed the six of us, and we were never the same. We met in our barracks that night and formed a pact that from then on, we would do whatever was necessary to protect the greater good—rules and superiors be damned."

"Amen," Cliff said.

Stubs smiled at his longtime friend. "Anyway, the next morning, Cliff got wind of an additional planned attack by the Taliban—a major bomb that could level an entire city. They had the audacity to think they were going to sneak the bomb onto one of our military carriers returning to the US. Once we were over land, they were going to attempt to take over the aircraft and crash it in the heart of either Boston or Chicago, setting the bomb off right before impact—destroying the city as well as thousands, maybe millions, of people in the process. The Taliban had been transporting the bomb to get closer to our base, and allegedly they were now a mere couple of miles from us. We thought about telling our superiors, but we worried they'd tell us to stand down. We could not risk another catastrophic blow to our country and its people. So the six of us formed a plan.

"Cliff and I both have expertise in explosives, and we figured between the two of us, we could defuse the bomb and steal it before it could be used against us. But we didn't want to just take the bomb—we wanted to take the lives of men so evil they could even consider bringing such darkness to our country.

"We identified the house where the bomb was located and surrounded the exterior with bombs of our own. The thought was we'd defuse the bomb and take it, then set off the other explosives to ensure no survivors. At least, that was the plan."

Stubs hung his head again as silence filled the barn. Cliff took over where Stubs left off.

"Tim, a twenty-three-year-old firecracker of a soldier, took down two insurgents as we breached the building, and Carl, a twenty-six-year-old devoted husband and father, was right behind him. Their job was to take care of anyone inside the building while Stubs and I focused on the bomb. It was impressively crafted and would in fact have annihilated dozens of city blocks, but we were able to defuse it and remove it within minutes.

"Everything was going according to plan. Jackson and Bennett, our two other men, were stationed outside to guard the exterior. Jackson escorted us to a Humvee we parked a block away, where we were to store and secure the bomb. Just as we got to the car, we heard a cry from Bennett. Within seconds, all hell broke loose.

"A throng of insurgents entered the building from the other side and had our two boys inside pinned down and surrounded. Stubs and I were supposed to detonate the explosives once we were sure the six of us were safe, but when Bennett cried out, Stubs and Jackson went running back to help. I secured the bomb in the back of the car and was about to go help when I heard Stubs scream at me to detonate our explosives. I didn't want to push the button and accidentally blow up my own men, but it was clear we were outmanned. Seeing no other option, I did what I was told. Bomb after bomb went off as the house disintegrated before my very eyes."

Cliff paused and looked back at Stubs. "You want to finish?"

"Yeah," Stubs said. "I'll make it short. Nineteen people died in those early-morning hours, and you all are looking at the only two survivors. Well, one-and-a-half survivors." Stubs looked down where his legs ought to be. "We lost four good men that day, but we killed fifteen Taliban members and saved one of our country's most iconic cities, along with thousands of people, in the process."

"You two are heroes," I said. "But why haven't we ever heard of this story? Our entire nation owes you two an incredible debt."

"That's because it was never made public," Cliff said. "Stubs and I returned to the base with the bomb. We were questioned and told never to speak a word of what happened ever again."

"And we never did," Stubs said, "until now. But that vow Cliff and I made all those years ago remains. When Cliff told me about Operation Boom, I said I was in. What we're doing here is just like what we did all those years ago. People might die on Wednesday, but they will die to protect far more innocent lives. If we band together, no one can stop us. The eight here can do what the six of us did then. I may lack mobility now, but I still have ability. I may have lost my legs and an arm, but I still have my brain, and no one can ever take my heart. And right now, both are telling me that Operation Boom needs to happen. This is our destiny, people. This is our chance to become heroes."

Mary instinctively stood up and began a slow clap. "Thank

you two for your service and sacrifice," she said. "Truly, we are all indebted to you."

Cliff and Stubs nodded in appreciation. Then Cliff motioned toward the man on Stubs's other side to go next. I was grateful I didn't have to follow that incredible tale.

"My friends call me Reggie," the man said. "Unfortunately, given my career choice, there are few people who I can call friends. Vince here is one of them. He and I trained together in the FBI, specializing in counterintelligence."

Looking at Reggie and Vince, I never would have guessed they were in the same organization. Vince was built like an athlete; Reggie was built like a toothpick. He stood five-foot-ten but couldn't have weighed more than 120 pounds, and his pants bunched in the front as his belt wrapped one-and-a-half times around his tiny waist. Then there was the hair: thin, slicked-back, oily black hair that was likely meant to make him look mean but instead simply accentuated the fact he was balding.

"Vince's success with infiltrating the Santori family mirrors mine with the infamous Torralini family, the dirtiest family in all of California," Reggie continued. "Their legitimate enterprises often put them in the public spotlight, but do not think for a second there is anything legitimate about them. They are cold-blooded and ruthless, and they will destroy anyone or anything that stands in their way. What differs between them and the Santori family is the Santoris are led exclusively by Tony Santori. The Torralinis are led by five different adult family members, each of whose greed has them constantly trying to one-up their siblings to show they are the most important Torralini. On the flight here, I tried to calculate just how many people have been hurt by the family, but I lost track. In the past four years I've been with the family, I know of eighty-nine murders they've contracted. Add the family members who lost loved ones in those crimes to the list of people hurt by their child prostitution rings and drug-smuggling operations, and the number of victims quickly approaches the thousands. And that's only what I know of happening in the past four years. The family has owned the West Coast for decades.

"As a member of the FBI," Reggie continued, "I only thought there was one approach to justice. But when Vince told me about you all and Operation Boom, my eyes were opened to new possibilities. My role here is relatively simple—making sure the Torralinis are in place when the bombs go boom—but my respect for you all and appreciation for your courage know no end. Thank you all for being here and may God bless us all."

"Thanks for being here, Reggie," Cliff said. "Dan, why don't you go next?"

"Thanks, Cliff," a balding man with a pudgy belly said. "Two men here have already said they are explosives experts, but with all due respect, I am the bomb maven of the group, and I have the name to prove it. My name is Dan Baum, and I, too, served in the US Army with Cliff. Together we were tasked with assembling explosives for use. I never saw combat, and I never had the pleasure of meeting Mike—sorry, I mean Stubs," he said, turning toward Stubs in the wheelchair, "but it is an honor to be in your company."

Mary leaned over to me. "David, this is a dream team of FBI agents and military heroes. This thing is no joke." I nodded in agreement.

Baum continued. "I was the man the army turned to when determining what explosives were needed and understanding how they should be connected and where they should be placed. You could think of me as a bomb whisperer, I guess. Now, while I agree with the motives and goals for Operation Boom, I must say I'm against this operation. I agree that these mafioso mobsters you've been speaking of deserve their own special place in hell for what they've done, and I also recognize that our justice system best serves the criminals, especially the wealthy ones. I worry, though, that this plan will not work in the way we hope."

"Why do you say that?" I interjected. "We haven't even heard the plan yet."

"Cliff had me here earlier to look at some of the explosives, and without getting overly technical, everything in this barn is well past its expiration. Look at those artifacts behind Cliff."

We turned our attention to the crates behind Cliff, where there was a machine gun, a gold-plated grenade, and a dusty suicide vest.

"That grenade has a half inch of dust on it," Dave continued, "the suicide vest appears to have been used already, and that machine gun must be at least fifty years old."

"It's actually almost seventy years old," Cliff said, turning to pick up the weapon with pride. "This baby is an MG-42. The Germans used it during World War Two, and our boys quickly came to know it as the Buzz Saw. Hitler's men could put out twenty-five rounds per second with this beast."

"That's great, Cliff," Baum said, "but this is the twenty-first century. We shouldn't be fighting with weapons Hitler used."

"Oh, this isn't for us," Cliff said, putting the gun back on the crate. "This is part of a donation I'm making to the Smithsonian. These were the last pieces I needed to send off."

"Okay. Well, good, we're not using those exact weapons," Dan continued, "but still, the reality is everything in here is old, and we can't guarantee how they'll work in the field."

"Do you think they still work?" Reggie asked.

"Well, that's the thing," Dan responded. "With explosives, you only get one try. It's not like we can really take them out for a test drive. I assume Cliff will walk us through the plan shortly, and it may be the greatest plan in the world, but if the explosives don't work, the plan won't work. Getting them to work is on me, and as you can imagine, it's a very precise activity. One false move, one ill-timed trigger, and not only will our plan be revealed, but we could lose our lives—"

"Or limbs," Stubs interjected.

"Exactly," Dan said. "And even if the explosives do work, we're talking about executing an operation in less than one hundred hours, and we have so many other factors to consider. Cliff is our leader here, but he also needs to carry on with his daily FBI responsibilities. Combine that with needing to get all the explosives and people in the right place, and there simply are too many moving parts. All that being said, though, I fully support the mission and will follow the group's ultimate decision. Cliff told me there will be a vote tonight on whether to move forward with Operation Boom. There are eight of us here, so to avoid a stalemate, I am pulling my vote. Boom is inspirational in its goals—I just worry about pulling the whole thing together."

"Thank you for your honesty, Dan, but Boom will work," Cliff said, "and there will be no tie. Our decision to move forward must be unanimous. I'll go over my plans in just a few minutes, but let's get through the rest of the introductions. Next up is Eli, who I confess I just met earlier tonight, but from what I hear, he is a perfect addition to the group. Eli, please tell us about yourself."

Eli got up and looked around the circle. "Thank you for allowing me to join your group. I come with my own backstory, but it is not as moving, so I'll keep things brief. I grew up in Israel and spent many years in the military. I, too, live with the regret of my inaction over the years—over men who I should have killed who wound up murdering dozens of my fellow soldiers and friends.

"Since coming to the United States, I have become a trusted confidant of one Solomon Feldman. Over the years, he and his Deli Boys have torn families apart and been poster children for how not to be decent human beings. I went along with it for years, and I've hated myself for it. In the past few days, I've had an awakening of sorts. I can no longer live like I have, standing pat as I see injustice all around me. I've realized I need to stand up for what I believe in. I'm looking forward to hearing specifics from Cliff, but I assume my role will be to help get Feldman in position to succumb to the wrath of Operation Boom like the other men you all have spoken of, including Tony Santori, who is Feldman's biggest enemy. The two have fought over control of Chicago the past few years, and the tension between the two continues to rise. How we're going to get Feldman invited to a special Santori event, I have no idea, but I trust that Cliff or Detective Blaze has an idea.

"Allow me to close with this. I understand that what we are talking about here is murder, but it is murder to prevent mass murder, and I'm on board. Detective Blaze invited me to tonight's event, and I wasn't sure what I was getting myself into. Hearing your stories, though, I know I am in the right place."

Eli sat down, satisfied with his delivery, but Stubs was staring at him quizzically.

"Okay, next on the list—" Cliff began.

"Hold on, Cliff," Stubs interrupted. "I've got a few questions for Eli over here."

"Please, go right ahead," Eli responded.

"Cliff just admitted he hadn't met you before tonight. How do we know we can trust you?"

"That's a fair question, Stubs. If it's all right, I'd like to defer my answer to Detective Blaze, who I believe can vouch for me and speak on my behalf."

"I'm asking *you*, but fine, we'll hear from him in a minute. My second question is about this awakening of yours. What caused it? Why such a sudden change in attitude?"

"I don't mean to put you off, Stubs, but again, I will defer to Detective Blaze to explain the cause of my awakening."

Stubs turned his attention from Eli to me. "Well, this Detective Blaze must be some fuckin' miracle man if he can explain your awakening better than you can. Okay, Detective, dazzle us."

Everyone else's gaze turned to me. I appreciated Eli not breaking the news about Lance to the group, but that was not exactly the introduction I'd hoped for. I turned to Cliff, who leaned forward with an elbow on his knee and his hand on his chin, ready to hear my tale like everyone else. He clearly wasn't going to give me a proper intro, so it was up to me to share my value to Boom. I stood, brushed some cookie crumbs off my shirt, and told the story of how I'd become Detective Blaze.

"Good evening, everyone. My name is David, although, if you don't mind, I'd appreciate everyone just call me Blaze."

"Oh, you've got to be kidding me," Stubs said as he leaned back in his wheelchair.

"Shut up, Stubs," Cliff interrupted. "Let the man speak."

"Thanks, Cliff," I said. "Now, since we are all being honest and transparent here, I need to begin by admitting that I'm not actually a detective. As a retiree, I had a bit of free time—actually a lot of free time—so I became a self-appointed, uncertified private investigator who has a knack for being in the right place at the right time. By stretching some truths a bit, I have quickly gained the respect of certain members of the Chicago Police Department and the FBI." I turned to nod at Cliff. "I also have become a trusted resource for both Tony Santori and Solomon Feldman."

Over the next twenty minutes, I outlined my recent activities as Detective Blaze, from the murder of Henry Jackson to the ongoing investigation related to the WCC steam room murder. I shared how I came to know Eli and that in fact he was a reputable man. My claim that presumptive future Chicago mayor Sarah Cutler was involved in a coverup connected to the steam room got everyone's attention, as did my assertion that I had damning information about both Santori and Feldman from a trusted source whom both men believed was dead.

"Okay, I need to stop you right there," Dan said. "Are you telling us that in the course of less than a week, you—a retired salesman with no formal detective training—discovered dirt on a woman who appears destined to be mayor and found a way to not only gain the trust of the two most untrustworthy people in Chicago but also possess incriminating information about both of them?"

"Yes, Dan, that is exactly what I'm saying."

"Bullshit," Stubs shouted. "I call bullshit on this. Cliff, what the hell were you thinking? I thought this operation was legit. You know better than any of us that the only way something like this can work is if we can all trust one another." Stubs turned toward me. "I don't trust this son of a bitch. No way what this Blaze character says actually happened."

I turned and walked toward Stubs, kneeling in front of his wheelchair to look him in the eye rather than down at him.

"I will never disgrace a man who defended our country, Stubs, but I don't appreciate being called a liar."

"And I don't appreciate being lied to. Stop wasting our time and get the hell out of here."

"Okay, okay, everybody break it up." Cliff came over to stand between the two of us. "Blaze, go sit back down. Stubs, you know I wouldn't bring someone in here I didn't trust. It may sound unlikely to you, but I can confirm that everything Blaze has said is true. The FBI has been following him, and he has in fact become a confidant of both Santori and Feldman. I have found in the few days I've known him that he just may be one of the most trustworthy people I've come across in a long time. I trust him, and I'm honored to have him here."

"But what is he doing here?" Stubs asked. "It's not like he has explosives expertise, or is that on tomorrow's agenda for you?" he said, turning to me with a smirk.

"Stubs, I'll be honest with you," Cliff said. "Blaze just may be the most important person in this entire meeting. He's gathered more incriminating information on Santori in three days than the entire FBI has in three years. And that's in addition to the other cases and work he mentioned. You should believe him, Stubs. Scratch that—you should believe *in* him."

"I believe in him," Eli said, standing. "Blaze went face to face with Solomon Feldman earlier today and didn't blink. When most people would cower in fear, Blaze didn't flinch. I don't know how he did it, but he earned Feldman's respect, something few people can do."

I gave a gracious head nod to Eli.

"I also believe in him," Vince said, standing up as well. "What Eli just said Blaze did in earning Feldman's trust, I witnessed him do the same thing with Santori. It took me years to earn Santori's trust, and I trained with the FBI's best in the art of deceit. Blaze has a gift. For this operation to succeed, we need him on board."

I held my hand to my heart as I turned to thank Vince for the kind words. Stubs, still clearly irritated by me, turned his attention to Mary.

"Mary, is it? You've been awfully quiet. What do you have to say about all of this?"

All eyes turned to her. Mary looked at me, at the chalkboard, then back at me. "I'm here as David's partner, and I say that if this Operation Boom is going to happen, we should focus on the operation and not bickering about who's the most valuable team member."

"Hear, hear," Reggie shouted. "I'm with Mary. Let's get back to Boom."

Cliff, still standing in front of Stubs, looked down at his friend. "Are we good, Stubs?"

Stubs rolled his eyes. "Yeah, we're good."

"Good," Cliff said, walking back to his seat. "Blaze, did you have anything else you wanted to say?"

My ego was sky high, though I would have loved it if Mary would have bragged about me a little.

"Actually, yes, Cliff, there is one last thing. I am scheduled to appear on national television tomorrow on the *Looking for Lance* special. I will be sure to make no mention of this meeting or our intentions."

"You're damn right you won't," Stubs said.

"Shut up, Stubs," Cliff and Dan both said at the same time.

I sat down, content with the information I provided and not interested in getting in any more conflict with a decorated war hero.

"Okay, now that we know everyone," Cliff said, "let's get on with the plan."

For the next ten minutes, he railed against the justice system and how a person's guilt was often determined by the amount of money they could spend to be defended.

"If you've got money, you've got freedom," he said. "The bastards coming together on Wednesday have more money and power than any of us can imagine, and because of that, they all remain free, despite everything we know about their criminal histories. That all ends now."

Cliff dramatically flipped over his chalkboard to show a complex diagram of what looked like a blueprint to a building with circles, Xs, and triangles scattered all over the board. There were so many scribbles, codes, and diagrams that it looked to me like some complex mathematical equation, maybe geometry or trigonometry. Either way, I had no idea what the hell any of it meant. Everyone else in the group nodded their heads in agreement, with Dan asking questions about velocity and projectile angles and Stubs talking about chemical makeups of certain explosives.

This continued for another fifteen minutes before Cliff realized the conversation was over my and Mary's heads.

"Sorry about that, Blaze. I sometimes get tunnel vision when I'm zeroing in on a plan of attack," Cliff said. "Do you see any problems?"

"I see a problem," Vince cut in. "You didn't account for the added guests Santori now wants to invite. I don't have the full list yet—some of them may be innocent."

"Losing some innocent civilians is a price we may have to pay for this operation to succeed," Cliff said stoically.

"That may be," Vince said, "but in this diagram, you're not accounting for all the extra people and where they'll be when the building goes boom, let alone the extra explosives we'll need. And I don't know if I can go ahead with killing more innocent people, even if it is for the greater good. I think I may be starting to side with Baum—there are just too many hoops to jump through to make this whole thing work, and there's simply not enough time to get it all done."

Cliff did not take Vince's change of heart well.

"Are you kidding me, Vince?" he said. "What happened to that gung-ho spirit you had last night when we talked about this? You said it yourself that if we're ever going to take down Tony Santori before he flies off into the sunset, this is our chance. The logistics will work themselves out here. You've got to have faith."

"Okay, Cliff," Baum interjected, "I love you and all, but you didn't really just say the logistics will work themselves out, did you? We're talking about *bombs*, Cliff. And lives! Perhaps innocent lives. We can't be so nonchalant with the planning. We've got to be precise. We have to know where each and every person is going to be and how the explosives will be distributed around the facility. Without that precision, Operation Boom will quickly turn into Operation Bust."

"Do you really think innocent people will be there celebrating Tony Santori's professional successes?" Cliff countered. "Not a chance in hell. I bet Blaze here is the only innocent person Santori knows."

"I'm still not convinced Blaze is all that innocent," Stubs said, once again looking at me. "And besides, who the hell brings a date to a meeting like this?"

I started to stand, but Cliff motioned for me to hold my ground.

"Stubs," Cliff said, "if you insult Blaze one more time, I swear to God I will break your arm myself. We're a fucking team here. Let's start fucking acting like it."

I stood up, walked toward Stubs, and once again kneeled in front of him.

"Mike," I said, "I swear, I am not here to cause trouble. You and I are a lot alike. When you called out to Cliff to set those bombs off, you did so knowing you might be killed. But you did it anyway because you were focused on the bigger picture. That's all I'm doing here. I started this detective work as a pastime, but it's quickly become my life's work, and I feel that my purpose is to help this operation move forward. This is not about Detective Blaze or Dan Baum or any of us individually. It's about ridding the world of evil to prevent more pain and suffering. I'm on board. Are you?"

I reached out my hand to him. He looked at it for a few seconds before shaking it.

"Fair enough, Blaze. I'm in. And I'm sorry."

"Okay, now that we've all kissed and made up, can we get back to the plan?" Reggie asked.

"Vince," Cliff said, "do you know anyone from the expanded invite list?"

"I haven't seen it yet," Vince said. "I do know Santori's personal attorney, Donald Pearlman, was to be added."

"No way that son of a bitch is innocent," Stubs said. "You

know how many criminals he's kept on the streets because they had the cash to afford him?"

"Even if that's the case," Vince said, his voice rising in frustration, "there's still the issue of needing to choreograph where everyone will be. And don't forget we still need Blaze and Eli to get Feldman over to the bowling alley too. I just don't know how we can make it all work."

The group began arguing over one another until a piercing whistle came from my right. I turned to find Mary standing confidently, two fingers still in her mouth, her blazer and tight pants giving her a sexy, dominating look. In all the years I'd known her, I never knew she could whistle like that.

"Now that I've got everyone's attention," she said, "it's time for me to have a turn to speak. I may have come here as a guest of Blaze's, but I'm a member of this team."

"With all due respect, ma'am," Dan began, "what is it that *you* bring to the group?"

"First off, hun, don't you ever call me *ma'am* again," Mary said. "Now, as Cliff said at the top of this meeting, we all have our backstories. Mine did not seem relevant until just now when I heard exactly how I can help. You men who served in the military, you all have the brains and the brawn to execute this complex plan. You know where the bombs will go and what needs to happen, right?"

The group nodded in agreement.

"Well, Blaze and I have an ability to make people do what we want."

I had no idea where Mary was going with this, but I was oddly turned on by her authoritative control of the room.

"That's nice and all," Dan continued, "but we've already heard about Blaze's wizardry and getting in the good graces of Santori and Feldman. Who can *you* get to do what you want?"

Mary flashed a bit of a grin. "Donald Pearlman."

"Donald Pearlman?" Cliff said in bewilderment. "How do you know Donald Pearlman?"

"Yeah," I echoed. "How do you know Donald Pearlman?"

Mary turned and came toward me, putting her hands on my cheeks and leaning in to kiss my forehead.

"David, my dear, I love you, but I did have a life before I knew you." She patted my cheek before standing straight and turning back. "Gosh, it must have been thirty years ago when Donald used to visit me on a pretty regular basis."

"Visit you?" Baum asked.

"Yes. I was an exotic pole dancer back then."

"A what!" I shouted as I stood up. "You were a pole dancer?"

"An *exotic* pole dancer," Stubs said.

"Shut up, Stubs," I said, refusing to look back at him.

Was this really happening? There, in front of this group of male strangers, my love broke the news that she used to be an exotic dancer? If Mary didn't have everyone's attention before, she damn sure had it then.

"Back then the cops often came in and busted us for one thing or another. Whenever I was arrested and tossed in the slammer, Donald would bail me out and speak on my behalf to my parole officer."

"You were *in jail*?" I said, sitting back down to wrap my head around the second bombshell Mary had dropped in a minute. "You have a criminal record?"

"Well, technically, Mary as you know me now doesn't. Back then I went exclusively by my stage name, Muffy."

"And how many times was Muffy in jail? And for what?"

"David, dear," she said, looking down at me, "like I said, I love you, but right now, I need you to kindly shut up. I'm not sharing all of this to make you jealous."

"Well, why the hell are you telling it?" I asked.

"To show my gratitude to Donald. I repaid him over the

years with a few *favors*, shall we say. The favors continued for a while even after my debt was paid off."

"This just keeps getting better," I said as I threw up my hands.

"Shut up, David," Stubs said. "Let the lady speak."

"My point is that Donald Pearlman owes me, and he owes me a lot. I'm confident that I—sorry, *we*—can use that to our advantage. I'll arrange for Donny—I mean Donald—to get a bus to transport the extra guests Vince mentioned. Instead of taking them to the party, Donald will drive them somewhere else safe—or maybe straight to the police department. We'll have to figure that out. Like I said, you all worry about the explosives and getting everything where it needs to be, and Blaze and I will make sure the necessary people are in place."

I did a quick glance around the circle to find everyone still staring intently at Mary. I didn't know if they were focused on what she said or if they were imagining her stripping, but either way, I had to give it to her—her plan made sense. Being able to blackmail a man like Pearlman could really help Boom have an even greater impact.

I also began to wonder. Was this all part of God's plan? Did my relationship with Mary happen specifically for this purpose, for us to be able to use her history as a pole dancer to help make Boom happen? If so, God's got some sick sense of humor.

"Well, that was an unexpected twist, but thanks for sharing, Mary," Cliff said. "I think you're right. Splitting up the team to focus on what we're good at makes sense. Vince needs to be included in the logistics of where Santori will be, same with Reggie and Eli and their respective men. Dan, Stubs, and I will focus on the explosives, and I'll be in close contact with Blaze to understand the finer points of who will be where when the bombs go boom. Vince," Cliff continued, "are you still worried about the extra people?"

Vince looked at Mary, then at me. "You two really think you can handle this?"

Mary walked over and put her arm around my shoulder. "I think together, we can do anything," she said.

"Then I'm in," Vince said.

"Good. Then it's settled," Cliff continued. "Now you all are right: there's a lot of work to do and not a lot of time. Let's meet again on Monday night—same time, same place. Any other questions before we head out?"

The room was silent.

"Okay, everyone, have a good night, and I'll see you Monday," Cliff said. "To Boom," he shouted, raising one fist in the air.

"To Boom," we all echoed.

The group quickly dispersed.

As Mary took her arm off my shoulder, I glanced up at her. "I have one more question."

"Yes, dear?" she responded.

"How come you don't pole dance for me?" I whispered.

She bent down and put her lips to my ear. "Because we don't have a pole."

19

I awoke early Sunday and couldn't get back to sleep. I figured I'd use the time to gather my thoughts on Operation Boom and my additional responsibilities. I tiptoed out of the bedroom toward headquarters, where I sat at my desk and wrote a list of everything I was currently committed to do:

- Identify the steam room killer for Tony Santori
- Bring entertainment to Lance Cutler
- Make sure tonight's *Looking for Lance* special doesn't go according to plan
- Get Solomon Feldman to Wednesday night's dinner for Santori
- Buy a pole
- Blow up the bad guys on Wednesday

I was almost positive I'd confirm the steam room killer later that morning. After breakfast, I'd bring some magazines to Lance. I'd check in with Marc, Wilt, and Patrick to make sure they were all clear with their assignments for that night's show. That only left Wednesday's dinner—and Mary's pole, but that could wait for now.

Determining how to get everyone where they needed, particularly Feldman, would be a Herculean challenge by itself, but even if I was able to do that, there was an added element I hadn't considered. How would we justify Operation Boom to the public? If Boom went off, we would have committed mass murder, and the lives of dozens of people would be on our hands. The public would demand answers, not to mention the authorities, who would likely lock us up for the rest of our lives. I didn't want to die in prison, but I also had decided this was something that must be done. But how would I explain that? I didn't have some inspiring tale of bravery and sacrifice like Stubs. I could get people to do a lot of things, but I didn't know if even I could get the justice system and the general public to look past murdering a bunch of bad guys.

My phone buzzed with a text from Patrick.

Great news boss, it said. *My broadcast professor would love to have you come into class tomorrow and talk to us about your experience on the big show.*

The big show. That was it! I could put together my own show with a bunch of victims of Santori and Feldman—and of anyone else who would be at Wednesday's dinner—and broadcast it right after Boom went off. Then the public could see that our actions were justifiable or at least understandable.

How in the world I could put such a thing together and get it on the air, I had no idea, but I was sure Patrick could help. I called him to share the big news.

"Hey, Patrick, I'd love to talk to your class, but maybe another time," I began. "I have another assignment inspired by you that I think you can help with."

"I'm in. Just name it."

"And you're all set for tonight?"

"Yep, I'll head down to the studio early in the afternoon and find a way to get myself into the control booth for the broadcast."

"Remember, Patrick, I need you to figure out a way to override any time delay the station has in place. We also need to make sure that nothing can get beeped out, you know, like curse words or things like that."

"No sweat, boss. I doubt I even need to get into the control room for that. I just need to have my laptop, and I'll be able to hack into their system. It'll be like taking candy from a baby."

Norman Yellin woke up with the sun on what would be the biggest day of his life, anxious to read what was written previewing the night's *Looking for Lance* special. Still in his bathrobe, he opened his laptop to check out the local and national news sites. Excitement was building about this primetime drama playing out in real life, and several national columnists were hyping the show up as one of the biggest TV events of the year.

But that wasn't enough for Yellin.

This was supposed to be can't-miss television, right up there with Apollo XI landing on the moon. Yellin had sold his team on making history, and he sold his bosses on Super Bowl-like ratings. This couldn't just be *one* of the biggest TV events of the year—it had to be *the* biggest event of the year. Yellin decided the show needed more. It was too late to find any other guests for the broadcast, so he needed something else that would create attention, something that would bring the audiences he'd promised.

Yellin texted his son Josh to see if he was awake. *I am now* was the response. Norman called and told Josh his predicament. "Is our show trending on social media?" he wondered.

"Not really, Dad. There are a few news stories, oh, and there's a funny meme going around with people #LookingForLance in the most ridiculous places, like under a rock or on the moon. But that's about it."

"This is terrible. I need more eyeballs on the show tonight. I need something that will force people to tune in and watch."

"Why not bribe people? Give them some money to watch."

"Oh yeah, that would be great," Yellin said sarcastically. Then he thought about it and realized his son was a genius. "Wait a minute, that really would be great. What if we offer a cash prize if anyone can give credible information that helps us locate Lance Cutler?"

"That could work, but it'd have to be a big amount—like one million dollars."

"One million! You think I have that kind of money just lying around?"

"Isn't that what your sponsors are for?"

"Good point, kid. Okay, I can figure out those details. But we still have a problem. That money only works if someone knows where the lieutenant is. That doesn't get us the huge uptick in views we need."

"True. Wait, Dad, I've got it. Run a contest on social media."

"What kind of contest?"

"You could put out a post that announces the one-million dollar reward, and then say that as part of the reward, you'll also give out a hundred grand to one lucky viewer who shares the post on social media."

"Why would I do that?"

"Ugh, Dad, do I need to explain how social media works again? If people share your post, more people see it. They're able to amplify your message."

"Okay?"

"Asking someone to hit the share button on a post is not much of a commitment, especially if there's a chance they could walk away with a hundred grand. It will be a social media blitz."

"But how does that get me more viewers?"

"If Lance Cutler is located during the broadcast, you will read the name of the lucky winner on air, and they'll have to call in within five minutes to claim the prize; otherwise, it will go to the next name you select. It will force people to watch. How depressing would it be if you won a hundred thousand dollars but lost it because you didn't hear your name called?"

"Josh, that's brilliant, and then even if we don't find Lance—which, between me and you, is what I'm sure will happen—we'll still have a captive audience."

"Bingo."

"Thanks, kid. We just might surpass the moon landing with this one. Now I gotta run. I have to go find a sponsor with a million dollars to spare. Hell, maybe even multiple sponsors."

"Good luck, Dad. Go make history!"

My adrenaline was pumping as I opened the door to the Lakeside Café. I'd eaten breakfast there dozens of times but never with a killer—at least, not that I knew of. I told the hostess my name and that I was meeting someone, and she pointed to the back corner booth, where all I could see was the back of a man's head covered by a black knit hat. This was it—my chance to bring this steam room mystery to a close. I approached the table, and as I slid into the far seat, I was welcomed by a familiar face and an outstretched hand.

"Long time no see," the man said.

"Yeah, not since Valentine's Day," I said, shaking Jerry's hand.

"Want anything to eat?"

"Right now all I want to know is why a successful businessman like yourself, the face of Plumbco on the Go, murdered a thug like Mel Weinberg."

"Ah, so you had figured it out. Congratulations. I guess I could ask you why a successful businessman like yourself has become a detective, but you asked first, so I'll go. To truly understand my reasons, I need to give you a little background info."

"Do you mind if I take notes?"

"Yes, David, I do mind. I didn't request this meeting so I could formally confess. I just wanted to know if you had realized I was the killer. Now I'll answer your questions as a courtesy and off the record—consider it a thank-you for all you did for me over the years. Just realize that if you try to turn me in, there'd be no way to prove anything now that Mel's been cremated."

I smiled at Jerry's confidence.

"Now, when I saw you at dinner on Valentine's Day, I introduced you to my girlfriend, Annette. Smokin' body, am I right?"

"She is gorgeous, but let's stay on track."

"Right. Anyway, Annette has two adult children, and their father is—rather, was—Mel Weinberg. That man was a heartless human being who never gave a damn about Annette or the boys. The oldest was born after Mel raped Annette, and he continued to beat her for the next few years, including while she was pregnant with the younger one. She finally found the courage to leave him, and once she did, she committed her life to those boys, and it was like that for twenty years until she found me. We've been together for a decade now, and it's been incredible."

"That's great, Jerry, but what does that have to do with the actual murder?"

"Well, beyond my knowledge of plumbing, I am an electronics whiz. A few years back, I installed hidden cameras throughout our condo and tapped all the phones, including Annette's cell phone."

"Why?"

"Mostly because I could. Anyway, I was out of town at a plumbing conference a few nights ago, but when I checked the live feed from our condo, I was surprised to see Annette and Sarah Cutler together."

"Sarah Cutler, the woman running for mayor?"

"That's the one. They've become friendly, and between me and you, I was hoping I might get to see a little girly action, if you know what I mean."

"Jerry, focus!"

"Sorry. The next day, they talked on the phone for a while, and somehow Sarah found out Mel was going to be at the West Coast Club the following morning, and I decided to take advantage of that knowledge. I'd always wanted to get revenge on Mel for what he did to Annette, but I never was able to find him. I took the fact that he would be at the WCC as a sign that now was the time to get payback."

"Why was that a sign?"

"Well, David, as you may know, Annette and I live in the West Coast Club Condos near the WCC. What you may not know is that the plumbing systems for the two are connected, and it was my people who installed the pipes. I know every inch of the entire system, as well as all the maintenance access points necessary to monitor the massive amounts of water used and disposed of by the WCC.

"I got back in town and parked in the club's underground garage. I always carry plumbing supplies in my trunk—you never know when you'll get an emergency call for assistance and what supplies you'll need. I had a pack of syringes, which can be great plumbing tools in a pinch, though goodness, they take a while to get the job done. Anyway, I found my heaviest-duty liquids that are filled with various toxic chemicals and created a poisonous concoction. I filled a syringe with the mixture and put the rest back in the trunk to dispose of later. I left the syringe in the car and grabbed my backpack, which I'd had with me on the trip, and stuffed a pair of workout clothes, an extra pair of clothes, and a baseball cap inside it. Then I took the bag and went up to the club entrance, just like I do every day."

Jerry's story was getting more and more interesting.

"As you know, I have a precise regiment that I follow at the club for my workouts."

"Yes, Jerry, the whole club knows about your no-nonsense, no-talking routine."

"Hey, I view the gym as a place to exercise, not fraternize."

"To each his own. Anyway, as you were saying, you went to the entrance."

"Right. So I made my way up there and checked in at 8:42 a.m., just like I do every day. I went about doing my normal workout so nothing appeared odd to any club regulars or anyone who looked at security footage afterward. Then I went into the locker room, which was the perfect place to commit the crime since there aren't any cameras—except for my own."

"Wait a minute, you have cameras in the men's locker room?"

"Not usually, just on that day. See, once I made it to the locker room, I had to position this bad boy," he said, holding up a square camera that was no larger than a dime. "I assumed Mel was going to visit the steam room, so I tucked this into the bottom towel on the long rack next to the steam room. Once that was set, I had to discreetly pull the rack about eighteen inches from the wall. No one knows this, but there's a small maintenance door tucked behind the rack that is right next to the steam room entrance."

"Okay, that's pretty slick," I said, pretending I didn't know that door was there.

"I know. Anyway, after that, I stored the backpack in a locker and nonchalantly walked out at 10:15 a.m. like always. I made a point to stop in the lobby in front of the camera to tie my shoe. That way, if anyone reviewed the tapes, they'd see I left before the crime ever happened, thus ruling me out as a suspect."

"That was good thinking, but then how did you get back in?"

"This is when it gets good," he said with a sly grin as he sat upright. "I made it back to the car and drove home. I put the syringe in a plastic bag before placing it in my pocket as I left the car. I intentionally struck up a conversation with our doorman before heading toward the elevator so I had a clear alibi if anyone suspected me. Then when no one was looking, I snuck away from the elevator and toward our side maintenance door, where there is a tunnel that leads back to the WCC. Once there, I maneuvered around until I made it to that steam room maintenance door. I took the syringe out of my pocket and stripped naked, placing all my clothes in the plastic bag and hiding them in a dark corner nearby. Now I admit, there were a few flaws in my plan."

"Like hiding naked in a tunnel?"

"Yeah, that wasn't the greatest, but see, it was necessary for the plan to work. The camera I placed in the towels was connected to my smartwatch." Jerry held it up to show me. "As I was crouched naked with the syringe in my hand, I was watching for Mel to enter the steam room. I also used the watch to increase the amount of steam entering the room so Mel wouldn't see me when I entered. Once he walked in, I took off the watch and tossed it with my clothes. I quietly pushed the door open, entered the steam room, and stabbed the bastard. Then I dropped the syringe and left, grabbing the camera and a towel outside the steam room and pushing the door and towel rack back in place in the process."

"Wow. I've got to give you credit, Jerry; that was an elaborate plan. Now what were you saying about flaws?"

"Right. Well, for one thing, I hadn't planned for what I'd do if anyone else was in the steam room. You were actually there when this whole thing took place. With all the steam, I didn't think you'd seen me, but I had to be sure. I hid in one of the bathroom stalls until you left to work out. By your mannerisms, it seemed you hadn't realized anything happened, so I was fairly confident I was in the clear. Still, I heard you had reservations at Gibson's that night, so I figured I'd drop in just to make sure.

"Once you went to work out, I went to the locker where I'd previously stored my stuff, got dressed, and pulled the baseball cap low over my face, then exited the club out the front door. I tried to avoid the camera and intentionally looked forward the entire time so my face couldn't be seen. I figured that if some tracking system analyzed the footage to identify suspects, even if it recognized a figure who wasn't on camera entering the club, I'd be ruled out since I was already seen entering and exiting. Then I walked home, went through the tunnel again to grab my stuff, and then made my way back home. And that was that."

"Jerry, consider me impressed. So all of this was for revenge?"

"More than that, David. This was done so Mel couldn't do what he did to my Annette ever again. I heard he got married—probably raped that poor girl too—and had another kid. I just couldn't live with myself knowing he was alive and still able to hurt more people. His victims didn't deserve what he did to them, but that bastard sure deserved what he got."

"You said you dropped the syringe on the ground. Why did you leave it?"

"Well, for one thing, I already needed to hide the camera, and I didn't want to worry about holding on to other evidence. But two, I knew the steam would remove the fingerprints, and with no way to identify who held it, it would support the theory that Mel stabbed himself to commit suicide."

We sat in silence as Jerry sipped from a glass of orange juice. "I brought Annette to Gibson's that night just to make sure you had no idea what happened to Mel or the role I played in his death."

"At that point, I didn't know you were involved. But it was only a matter of time."

"Now it's time for me to ask the questions, Mr. Detective, but really, I've only got one. How did you know it was me?"

I briefly considered making up a fake explanation, but I figured Jerry wouldn't kill me if I told him the truth—at least not there in public. Besides, his knowing I knew what he did could come in handy. And so I began.

"Well, Jerry, like I said, your plan was well thought out, and you have in fact evaded the authorities. But there were some additional flaws in your execution."

"Like what?"

"Well, first off, as you said, I was at the scene of the crime when it happened. I couldn't tell it was you, but I was pretty certain I saw someone stab Mel. Secondly, you were right that security cameras clearly showed you entering and exiting the club at your usual times. However, when you left, you didn't have the backpack you were wearing when you arrived. Interestingly, the mystery man who was unaccounted for in the footage had the exact same backpack that you had when you walked in.

"Then there was the icing on the cake. You were correct that Mel Weinberg was cremated; however, you were wrong in assuming *all* of him was cremated."

"Excuse me?"

"My team was able to obtain part of Mel's remains before he was cremated, and an autopsy revealed the presence of multiple plumbing fluids, including one used exclusively by Plumbco on the Go."

Jerry's cockiness disappeared before my eyes as we sat in silence for ten seconds.

"Well, I'll be damned. You're certainly finding a way to keep active in your retirement. You could have been one hell of a detective. The world needs more crime solvers like you."

"Thanks, Jerry, though that compliment feels odd coming from a murderer."

"Yeah, about that . . . " There was a long pause as Jerry looked down at the table. He finally found my eyes. "What do we do from here?"

A few days earlier, I would have stood up and screamed that the WCC steam room murderer was there. This would have been my crowning achievement, the feather in my proverbial detective's hat. But the reality was I had bigger fish to fry. Santori wasn't going to be happy knowing Feldman had nothing to do with Mel's death. Besides, was what Jerry did any different than what Operation Boom was all about? Jerry saw an opportunity to prevent more harm to the world, and he took it. That was exactly what we were doing with Boom. He didn't need to know that, though.

"I'll tell you what, Jerry. For now, I'm going to forget that we ever had this conversation. I never told anyone on my team that you were my primary suspect, and I'm happy to keep that information between the two of us. I might, however, require your technological abilities in the coming days."

"You name it, David, and it's yours."

"Oh, by the way, I think this belongs to you."

I pulled the syringe Lance gave me from my pocket and tossed it to Jerry, who was stunned to see the murder weapon back in his own hands. I slid out of the booth and told him I'd be in touch.

Jerry, dumbfounded, simply shook his head.

"Well I'll be damned Blaze. You really would have been a hell of a detective."

Norman Yellin called one of the senior-most executives at the network to ask to find a sponsor willing to give $1 million—actually $1.1 million—as a reward.

"Yellin, I'm a bit disappointed this morning," the executive said before Norman could say hello. "I see there's some good media coverage for our show tonight, but you promised us the Super Bowl for ratings, and there's no way we're getting close to that. This is the problem with setting high expectations—it's easy to fall short. If you had told us we'd be having a good show—heck, even a great show—I'd be feeling fine this morning.

But Yellin, you sold me on record-breaking ratings, and we're not on pace to break any sort of records. What are you going to do about it?"

"Well, sir, this is actually part of a plan."

"A plan?"

"Yes, sir. I'd like to run a social media blitz campaign."

"A social media what? What the hell are you talking about?"

Norman repeated the plan his son just came up with, finishing with words he knew would resonate with the exec. "This contest can get the show in front of the always challenging younger demographic," he said.

There was silence on the other end of the call.

"Sir? Are you there?"

"Yellin, that's brilliant! That little ploy could get us millions of viewers with ease."

"That's the plan, sir."

"I had no idea you were so social-media savvy. Listen, after this show, let's you and me sit down and talk about maybe making you head of our digital communications department."

"Yes, sir. Actually, there's one more thing before I go."

"You name it, Norman. That was one of the best ideas I've heard in ages, so right now, you could ask for just about anything, and I'd say yes."

"How about one million dollars?"

"Excuse me?"

"Not for me, sir. For the show, as a reward. I also want to offer a cash prize of one million in case anyone can share credible information that leads us to locating Lance Cutler during the show."

"Oh. One million dollars for millions of new viewers? Sure thing. Consider it done. I'll find one of our sponsors to write us that check."

"Thank you, sir, thank you very much."

"No, Mr. Social Media Savant, thank you. Go get on the phone with our communications team and get that post out there. You may just bring us the greatest ratings in television history."

Having confirmed my suspicions about Jerry, I now had to turn my attention to that night's broadcast. I called Cliff to check in as I got in the car, and he said that Operation Boom headquarters were moving to a vacant house across the parking lot from the bowling alley. I confirmed the address and then asked for some space to focus on the TV show.

I called Marc to make sure he and Jeffrey were set to pick up Tom Lexington for his surprise lunch date. I reminded him that for the plan to work, Lexington needed to understand his life and the safety of his family would be in danger if he disclosed any information he'd learned from Carter.

Getting revenge on Lexington was going to be fun, but I realized I could have even more fun at the expense of the TV special. Why stop at scaring one show participant when I could scare two? If I could get Lexington and Skip both talking nonsensically, the show would run off the tracks. I came up with an offer I thought would be too hard for Skip to refuse—an offer that would keep him and his family safe and his involvement with the attempted murder of his friend Lance Cutler a secret.

I gave Lance a call. "Want to have a little fun?" I asked. "Be ready in fifteen minutes."

After that, I checked in with Jeffrey.

"Good timing, bro. Violet and I just finished up with Lexington's wife."

"Did Violet get the video?"

"Yeah, she got it. No audio, just video of me terrifying a poor woman. Why exactly did I do that again?"

"It's all part of my plan, Jeffrey. I promise it will be worth it. Can you have Violet text that video to Marc and me?"

"No sweat. Hey, if I don't talk to you before tonight, break a leg on the show."

I hung up with Jeffrey just as I pulled into the hotel parking lot. Out ran a man who looked nowhere near as well put together as the Lance Cutler images the news broadcasts shared. His hair was a mess, and his face was covered in stubble. He wore a pair of dark sunglasses and a trucker's ball cap under a beat-up hoodie. Basically, he looked like someone who'd spent the last thirty-something hours holed up in a motel.

"Where are we going?" he asked as I pulled out of the motel parking lot.

"We're going to go see Skip."

"That son of a bitch! Why didn't you tell me? I would have brought something to kill him with!"

"That's why I didn't tell you. We don't want him dead. Just scared."

"Scared? Why's that?"

"Lance, there are a lot of moving pieces right now, and I promise I will explain them all in detail. If anyone deserves to know what's going on, it's you, but right now, we need to worry about Skip. He and I are scheduled to appear on television tonight with your mother."

"That conniving bitch."

"Yep, that's the one. Anyway, I need Skip to know that I know what he tried to do to you and that you're still alive to tell the tale. Skip still thinks he can go on living his life filled with fraud and corruption and not be punished for his misdoings. When he sees you outside his door, he'll realize the lifestyle he's used to is over."

"But why can't I make his *entire* life over? That bastard tried to kill me. I want an eye for an eye."

"Lance, I understand that, but may I remind you that you in fact are not dead. He wanted to kill you; now you want to kill him. There, an eye for an eye. Now as I was saying, you are welcome to rough him up a little bit, show your anger and your rage toward him. Go for his neck or go for his balls—I don't care what you do. I just need him breathing when you're done with him."

"Then what?"

"Then I will offer him and his family the chance to enter witness protection and start a new life for themselves, freeing him from any prosecution related to his shady behavior or from the chance of you coming back to finish him off."

"Why do we want him free? He should have to pay for what he did."

"Oh, he will, Lance. The lavishness he's grown accustomed to will be gone, and he will be arrested on sight if he ever sets foot in the greater Chicago area or if he tries to enter law enforcement again."

Lance shrugged, seemingly coming around to the idea. It was clear he was still troubled, though.

"Why are you going to offer him witness protection so easily? Shouldn't he have to work or do something for us before getting that gift?"

"Great minds think alike, Lance," I said devilishly as I pulled out my notebook and tore out a sheet of paper. "For him to get witness protection, he has to say these things on air tonight. If he says anything not on this approved list, the deal will be off, and he'll have to deal with the consequences."

Lance looked at the list and chuckled. "This is some stupid stuff, Blaze. He's going to look like a dumbass on national television."

I nodded in agreement as I pulled into the driveway of a mansion. This was not something a cop's salary could afford. You would think Skip would at least pretend to hide that he was bringing in money on the side, but then again, this was a guy who paid to have his best friend killed. We parked next to a cherry-red Ferrari that must have cost well over $250,000.

"But what about my mom?"

"My focus now is on attacking this show," I said. "That network is trying to profit off of your situation, and Skip and a man named Tom Lexington are trying to profit off the two of us. Lexington will be getting similar instructions later today, and with the two of them sounding like lunatics, the show will fall apart. The last thing the voters would want is a candidate associated with this train wreck. For now, though, let's go tell your friend the good news that you're still alive."

"It sure is good news," Lance said as he got out of the car. "But after I'm done with Skip, I don't think he'll feel the same way."

20

Sarah Cutler stood in her oversized walk-in closet and weighed her options of what to wear for that night's *Looking for Lance* special. She had to find the right balance between grieving mother and powerful politician. If she wore black slacks like she usually did, she'd come across as too masculine and not motherly enough. Bright colors would show too much cheer at a time when she was distraught over the disappearance of her son, and heels too high would come across as too sexy. She settled on an ankle-length beige skirt, white blouse, and dark blazer with pockets, where she could keep tissues for when the time felt right to cry.

Kent called just as she started to get dressed. "Hey, I'm not going to be able to make the show tonight," he said. "You're going to have to do it alone."

"What? Kent, this is for our son. What could be more important than that?"

"Sarah, I just can't go on TV."

"Fine. What about that threat of yours? You said I had forty-eight hours, and we're well past that point."

"Forget about that now, Sarah. All that matters is the safety of our son," Kent said, keeping Lance's condition to himself. "Go find our boy."

He hung up before Sarah could say another word.

"That wuss," she muttered as she pulled on her skirt. "I knew he was all talk, saying he'd expose me. He's probably too scared of crying and making a fool out of himself on television."

She finished buttoning her blouse and realized her good fortune. With Kent no longer there beside her, Sarah had more freedom to exaggerate her stories, particularly when it came to her relationship with Lance.

Everything was coming together to make this a crowning moment for Sarah. Skip and she had an understanding about what to say and what not to say. Veteran journalist Tom Lexington would be there to hold Matt Vanner's hand and make sure the cocky host didn't pull any more surprises like last time. Mayor Paulson would be there, and his presence would unofficially serve as an endorsement for her candidacy.

Sarah looked at herself in the full-length mirror. She started coming up with stories she could tell about how close she and Lance were. She practiced making a believable cry and delivered her closing line about the importance of love and family and how, if she had indeed lost her beloved son, she wanted to do everything in her power to make sure no other mother in the city experienced the same loss. She grabbed a tissue and dabbed at the corner of her eye. As she pretended to cry, she looked at her reflection.

"This may look like my darkest night," she said, "but it will be my brightest yet. This is my night. This is my moment."

It was early afternoon when Vince and Reggie met up with Cliff, Dan, and Stubs at the bowling alley. Cliff said the bomb experts had walked the grounds for a few hours and had plenty of questions about the arrangements for the evening. Vince, pleased with his colleagues' initiative, got to work leading them through the facility.

The building itself, he explained, had been owned by Tony Santori for a little more than four years. At first, it was a legitimate business, but business was slow, and Santori quickly moved on from it. The alley was not all that big, just sixteen lanes, but it was the rest of the building that made for a perfect evening dinner party. Above the bowling alley was a long ballroom, with a smattering of smaller rooms to one side, including two dining rooms, a kitchen, three storage areas, and two bathrooms. Vince showed the group where the VIPs would be eating, then led them back into the ballroom.

"Do we know where everyone's going to be?" Stubs asked.

"I've got a seating chart all set up," Vince said. "The wildcard right now is whether Blaze, Mary, and Eli can get Feldman here and keep the extra people away. Other than that, we should be in good shape."

"That's great," Cliff said. "Now let's figure out where these bombs are going to be placed."

Lance and I laughed almost the entire way back to the motel from Skip's house. We joked about how when Skip saw Lance standing outside the door, he must have thought he was seeing a ghost—until that ghost gave him a beatdown. Lance had barged in and shoved his former friend and partner to the floor. Skip got a beating he wouldn't soon forget, although his face was spared for the show.

"Think it worked?" Lance asked as we closed in on the motel.

"I think it worked and then some," I replied. "You were perfect. I'm pretty sure Skip will stick to his script. Be sure you watch. It will be an experience."

"It's not like I have anything else to do."

"That reminds me, there are a bunch of magazines and a deck of cards in the backseat. There might be a mermaid coloring book and some crayons my granddaughter left back there too. Feel free to take it all."

"Thanks, Blaze, and thanks for looking out for me."

"It's my honor, Lieutenant. I'll be in touch tomorrow. Until then, stay out of sight."

―――

Jeffrey and Marc pulled up to Tom Lexington's house promptly at 2 p.m. Lexington ran out of his house, his shirt half tucked in and his suit jacket flapping behind him like a kite in the wind. He hopped into the back of the car, panting to catch his breath.

"Sorry to keep you waiting, Marc."

"No worries, Tom, we just got here."

"Oh. I don't even know what time it is. I've been running around like a madman for the last thirty minutes. I spent the morning going through questions with Vanner for the show tonight, and our rehearsal went long. I was already feeling behind schedule, and then I got home, and there was this vague note from my wife saying she wasn't happy and that we needed to talk but that she was taking the grandkids out for a while. I tried calling and calling, but she wouldn't pick up her phone, and I have no idea where she is, and then I remembered you were coming, so I had to change as fast as I could. And now I just need a little breather and a chance to relax."

"Hopefully lunch will help you to do just that."

"I sure hope so. I feel bad about everything that's happened between me and David these past couple of days. It's big of him to set up this lunch before the show tonight. He is certainly a standup guy."

"Well, he's excited to see you. For now, just sit back and relax."

Lexington leaned back in his seat and closed his eyes. Every time it looked like he was going to doze off, Jeffrey made sure to ask him a question. They varied from the serious, like how he got into journalism, to the ridiculous, like if he was a tree, what kind would he be. They all accomplished the same goal—they kept a clearly fatigued and worn-out Lexington awake. Before he knew it, they had arrived at their destination.

"Morry's Deli? This is where David wanted to meet?"

"He said there'd be no place better for you to be right before your big TV appearance."

Marc and Jeffrey escorted Tom into the deli. One of Feldman's Deli Boys was waiting for them and said Mr. Lexington's lunch guest was waiting in a private room.

"You're not eating with us?" he said, turning to Marc.

"You go ahead. We'll catch up in a bit."

Marc and Jeffrey waved goodbye as Feldman's guard led Tom into a back hallway. The guard took him to a small room no larger than a broom closet, plopped him down on a folding chair, and closed the door on the way out. Four feet in front of Tom sat Solomon Feldman, who twirled a pistol on his finger and smiled at a fresh wall of mayonnaise.

"Hi, there, Tom," Feldman said, still twirling the gun. "You and I need to have a little chat."

The rest of the Boom squad left the bowling alley, but Vince remained to meet with Tony's preselected staff. He felt bad these men who loyally served Santori would leave Wednesday night in body bags. Cliff made it seem easy to sacrifice innocent lives, but Vince had more trouble with the notion of killing people who didn't need to die. He had made peace with the fact that none of these men were innocent—they'd all done dirty deeds for Santori over the years, and so to destroy the Santori regime, they, too, must go.

Vince met the staff at the appointed time and walked through their assignments. Each of the five men listened carefully. One, though, seemed troubled.

"What's your name, son?" Vince asked.

"Manuel."

"How long have you worked for Mr. Santori?"

"Four years, sir."

"And what do you do for him, Manuel?"

Manuel stared at the ground.

"Don't worry, Manuel, we all work for Mr. Santori here. No need to be ashamed."

"I'm part of a street gang. We sell all types of hardcore drugs to addicts. Mr. Santori's always been good to me. He gives me a bonus whenever I bring in a new customer. I feel bad doing it—always have—but it's the only way I can provide for my family."

"Family?"

"Yes, me, my wife, and our two boys. I'm just thinking about them and really miss them, that's all."

That was not what Vince wanted to hear. "You'll be home to them soon," he said, knowing that would not be the case. "You can make them proud by doing this job just as well as you can. Can you do that for me, Manuel?"

Manuel nodded in agreement.

While Lexington was with Feldman, Marc and Jeffrey rushed back to spread a tarp across the backseats. Jeffrey then pulled the car around to a back alley, where they sat and waited. After twenty minutes, a garage door opened, and two Deli Boys carried an unconscious Tom Lexington to the limo. Lexington looked like he'd taken a bath in mayonnaise as glob after glob dripped off his limp body. The Deli Boys sat him up in the backseat, and Marc buckled him in. As Marc closed the door, Solomon Feldman came out with a handful of towels for his Boys.

"What did you do to him?" Marc asked Feldman in astonishment.

"Just what Blaze said to do. I told him I knew he was planning to reveal secrets about me on television tonight and that I didn't appreciate that. I showed him the picture Blaze sent me of the guy in black talking to his wife, and I told him that if he wanted them to stay safe, he'd not only need to keep my information secret, but he'd also have to only talk about nonsense on the show tonight. One mention of me, or for that matter a halfway relevant question, and his family would pay the consequences."

"Why's he unconscious?"

"Just to be sure he wouldn't say anything bad, we hopped him up on a variety of drugs we had lying around. He should wake up some time soon, but he's going to be in for a trip of a lifetime."

"And the mayonnaise?"

"That's a little inside joke between Blaze and me."

A small part of Marc felt bad for Tom, but just a small part. He thanked Feldman for his help, made sure Lexington was buckled up tightly, and then joined Jeffrey up front.

The two fist bumped as Jeffrey started the car. "To Team Blaze," Marc said.

"To Team Blaze," Jeffrey repeated. Together they laughed as they drove away from Morry's Deli.

My phone buzzed as I pulled into my garage.

"Detective Blaze here."

"Blaze, it's Vince."

"Oh, hey, Vince. Now's not a great time—I've got to get ready to head over to the broadcast studio."

"I'll be quick. I've got a problem, and I'm hoping you can help me come up with a creative solution."

Does the FBI solve any of its own problems anymore?

"What's up, Vince?"

"Well, I met with the staff members who are supposed to be working Wednesday night, and, well, it's way too small of a group. Santori only assigned five guys for the night, but we need more workers. The problem, as you know, is anyone who we bring in is ultimately going to be brought in to die."

"Yeah, we probably shouldn't put that part in a help wanted ad."

"Exactly. So my problem is figuring out how to recruit people Santori would trust and who beats to the same deceitful lowlife drummer as the rest of these families. Any ideas?"

"Hmm, let me think on that for a minute. I'm getting out of the car right now. Give me a few seconds."

As I walked into the house, I tried to think of who would be willing to work a job like that at a moment's notice whom Santori would trust. The door closing was like a light bulb going off for me.

"Vince, are you still there?"

"I'm here, Blaze. Got anything?"

"Do you remember Andy Wong, that guy who was selling stolen goods and nearly got caught a few days ago?"

"Do I remember him? I was the one who had to tell Santori that Wong got greedy and almost got caught."

"I can imagine Tony wasn't too happy about that. What better way for Wong to get back in Santori's good graces than by working his farewell bash? I know part of his crew got arrested, but I'm sure he's got other guys he could bring."

"Blaze, that's good. Wong will think he's forgiven. Santori will think Wong is remorseful—"

"And if all goes according to plan," I interrupted, "they'll both be dead before they realize they were wrong."

"I love it, Blaze."

"Happy to help. Now please tell any other FBI folks looking

for assistance to leave me be for a few hours. I've got a national broadcast to get ready for."

"Will do, Blaze. Have fun."

I left my phone in the kitchen as I went to the bedroom to get dressed for my TV debut. I looked in the mirror after slipping on the coat of my nicest suit and thought not only was I acting like a damn good detective, but now I looked like one too. Mary and I were supposed to drive to the studio together, but she still wasn't home, and I had to get going.

I grabbed my phone and saw I had two voicemails. The first was Tony Santori saying Tony expected me at the club the next day at 2 p.m. with the name of the fucker who killed Mel in the steam room. If I didn't show up with that information, I would have failed Tony and would be expected to return Tony's money before Tony personally killed me.

The second message was from Patrick, who was whispering in an excited way, "Hey, Detective Blaze, it's Patrick, you know, your neighbor?" *Does that dweeb still think I don't know who he is at this point?* "Call me as soon as you get this. I got to the studio early, and, boy, do I have some news for you about the show tonight. Call me."

Just as I deleted his message, Mary walked in the front door.

"Oh, nice of you to stop by," I said sarcastically.

"Don't start, David. You knew I was with Donny Pearlman. That's the last time I ever want to make a deal with that jerk again."

"Well, take that bunny tail off your ass, and let's get to work."

"What do you think I've been doing?"

I gave her a shrug.

"Give me five minutes," she said as she went to get dressed.

I called Patrick back while I waited.

"Hey, boss, thanks for calling back so quickly."

"What's up, Patrick? I'm just heading out to the studio now."

"Good. I've been here for a couple of hours, and it totally paid off."

"What do you mean?"

"Well, you know how originally I was going to hack into the network's system to disrupt the censoring capabilities?"

"Yeah, were you able to do that?"

"I didn't have to. Five minutes after sneaking my way into the studio, I befriended the beeper himself."

I was pretty sure I knew the answer to my next question, but I had to ask just to make sure. "Patrick, remind me, what's a beeper again?"

"Good one, boss. He's the person who beeps."

Ask a stupid question, get a stupid answer. "So what?"

"Well, boss, this may come as a surprise to you, but being a beeper is not the most glamorous of jobs. It takes a lot of skill and responsibility, but you never get any thanks for it. When you watch the credits for a TV show, you never see *beeper* listed. Beepers can also go days, even weeks, without work. At school, we don't even have a beeper."

"Patrick, what's your point?"

"Well, this is my new friend Bob the beeper's first day at this studio. He didn't want to work, but it had been five weeks since his last beeping job. The problem is his wife is pregnant—very pregnant. Like, might-have-her-baby-any-minute pregnant. The last place he wanted to be tonight was here, but he'd already agreed to the job. So I offered to help him out."

"How's that?"

"I told him I had broadcast experience and would be happy to step in so he could go be with his wife. So right now, he's at the hospital, and I'm Bob, official beeper for tonight's *Looking for Lance* special."

I smiled at the kid's creativity. "Patrick, that is beautiful. I couldn't have drawn it up any better myself. So that means we're all set? You'll be able to make it so there's no beeping and all the bad stuff stays in the broadcast?"

"Boss, not only can I keep the bad stuff in, but I can keep the good stuff out. What gets beeped will be entirely up to me."

"Great job, Patrick. I have to say I'm proud of you."

"Aw, thanks, boss. I've got one other surprise for you too."

"What's that?"

"If I told you, then it wouldn't be a surprise."

"Patrick, what are you planning?"

"Got to go, boss. You'll have to wait and see."

Matt Vanner put down his handheld mirror and stood to stretch, knowing this show was his ticket to the national news desk, even if he was cohosting with Tom Lexington. Vanner gained so much notoriety for how he took down Sarah Cutler on his show that his ego had doubled in size—an impressive accomplishment for someone who'd already thought so highly of himself.

"After tonight," he said out loud, "the fans and executives alike will be chanting my name. Matt Vanner. Matt Vanner. Matt—"

He stopped mid-chant. *Matt* was too informal if he wanted to be on the big stage. Walter Cronkite was never Walt, and Peter Jennings wasn't Pete. Matt decided that when he negotiated the new contract that would undoubtedly come after the show, he'd make sure to add a clause that he be referred to as *Matthew* moving forward.

Satisfied with himself, Vanner grabbed his phone and texted Lexington to see if he'd call him *Matthew* on air tonight. He waited, but there was no response.

"Has anyone seen Lexington?"

That was the first thing I heard as I walked up to the control room at MGBC studios. There was a little more than an hour left before the show when a short man with an oversized blazer and unfortunate combover frantically came out, asking around to find the show's cohost.

"Excuse me," I said, knocking on the control room door.

"Who are you?" the man asked, barely glancing in my direction.

"I'm Detective Blaze. I'm here for the show."

"Who?" he said, still not looking at me.

"De-tect-ive Blaze," I slowly enunciated. "You know, one of the guests on the broadcast?"

"Oh, right. Sorry, Blaze. Things are a little crazy over here. I'm Norman Yellin, the guy in charge of this whole production."

"Nice to put a face to the name, Mr. Yellin. Anything I can do to help out?"

"If you could find Tom Lexington, that would be great."

"I'm happy to ask around."

"No, it's okay, Blaze. Why don't you go over to Conference Room B down the hall. The other talent is there. I'll be over in a minute."

I appreciated being called part of the talent, even if Norman didn't recognize me. I took a quick glance around the control room before leaving. The room had a perfect view overlooking the audience and stage, and there, all the way to the right in the front row, sat Patrick, practicing pushing down on the bright red button in front of him.

I left the control room and walked down the hallway to Conference Room B, where there was a long table flanked by the so-called talent. I met a guy named Sherwin, who said he was psychic, and someone named Gerald, a hostage negotiator who said something about not yanking his chain. I sat down across from Frank Skepper, who refused to look in my direction. There was also a woman named Bethany, but before we were properly introduced, Norman Yellin came steaming in.

"Okay, folks, everyone take a seat. We've got some last-minute changes we're working through at the moment."

"Yes, I did see there was a sense of chaos around this broadcast," the psychic said.

"Right," said Yellin. "Anyway, we've had a couple of last-minute cancelations we weren't counting on."

"Cancelations? Need me to negotiate with them?" Gerald the hostage negotiator asked.

"No, but thanks. Kent Cutler, the father of Lieutenant Lance Cutler, was apparently too distraught to come on TV, which isn't a huge loss since we still have Sarah Cutler. The bigger blow is I just heard Mayor Paulson had to back out due to his ongoing health issues. We were hoping for a ratings boost by having him make his first public appearance in months."

"Ratings boost?" asked Bethany, apparently a grief counselor whose last name was Goldstein. "Is the goal for tonight ratings or to find a missing son and devoted police officer?"

"Yes," Yellin responded. "Of course the goal is to find Lance Cutler. Unfortunately, I just checked in with our network statisticians, and they told me there is an 88 percent chance Cutler is dead."

"I could have told you that," the psychic said under his breath.

"The audience doesn't need to know that, though. It is our job to make viewers think there's still a chance he is alive."

"Isn't there still a chance?" Gerald asked. "There was this one time I helped free a little girl who was kidnapped, and it took the kidnappers three whole weeks before delivering their ransom note."

"Sure, there's a chance," a clearly frustrated Yellin said, "but the reality is it's not likely."

"What's not likely?" said a man in his early thirties who

walked into the room wearing a navy suit with a baby-blue shirt. In the middle of the diagonal stripes on his tie were the initials *MV*.

"It's not likely that Cutler is alive," repeated Yellin, who recognized Matt Vanner's voice and didn't feel the need to properly acknowledge or introduce him.

Vanner decided to do that for himself, beginning a lap around the room to shake each person's hand as he said, "I'm Matthew Vanner. Thanks for coming on and helping us with the show."

He made it halfway around the table when Yellin cut him off. "Matt, sit down and shut up. We don't have time for that. Now tell me, have you heard from Lexington?"

"No," Vanner said as he sat at the far end of the room. "He should be here by now."

"Thank you, Captain Obvious," Yellin said. "We've already lost Kent Cutler and Mayor Paulson, and now our cohost is MIA."

"I'm sure there's a logical explanation," Vanner said. "If there's one thing I know about Tom Lexington, it's that he's always professional."

"Well, right now he's being a professional pain in my ass," Yellin said. "Now, listen everyone. I shouldn't need to tell you this, but we're going to have a lot of eyeballs on this broadcast tonight."

"Yes, there's a lot of buzz about it on social media," the psychic said, "something about giving away a hundred thousand dollars to one lucky viewer."

"Now that's pretty impressive," Yellin said. "Did you sense that?"

"No, I have a teenage daughter who told me."

"Ah, well Sherwin the psychic is right. We have a social media contest going where one lucky viewer will win a hundred grand if we're able to locate Lance Cutler during the show. The social buzz we've generated today has brought in thousands of new followers as well as millions of dollars from our sponsors, each of whom wants to have their name front and center on the broadcast when we find the missing lieutenant. We also said we'd offer one million to anyone who could provide a credible tip on Cutler's location. Ten sponsors have already come forward and given us the reward money."

"So you're giving away ten million?" the grief counselor clarified.

"No, just the one million."

"But what happens if you have to award the prize money? What sponsor's name are you going to put with it?"

"I'm not worried. I just said it's highly unlikely Cutler is alive anyway."

"Isn't that deceitful?" the counselor asked.

"It's called business, lady," Yellin said. "We do still have to kiss the asses of those sponsors, though, and we need to sell the idea that Cutler might still be alive. So, Sherwin, if you can hear some heavy breathing or see footprints or something, that'd be great. Gerald, let's make sure you say there's a fifty-fifty chance he's still alive."

"Why would we do that?" the psychic asked.

"I just told you we already got an extra nine million in sponsorship money. Help me out a little, and I'm sure we can find a way to get some of that money into your bank accounts."

I couldn't believe how upfront Yellin was about this being a ploy to make money and not to actually locate Lance. I had been feeling guilty about sabotaging the show, but after Yellin's speech, I had no problem with embarrassing the network a bit—and getting paid to do it. I was looking forward to hearing Skip recite the lines I'd given him. But what in the world had happened to Lexington? Marc and Wilt should have had him there an hour ago.

"Okay, people, I've got to go talk to Sarah Cutler and tell her that Paulson dropped out and give her the projections from our statisticians."

"Where is Mrs. Cutler?" the grief counselor asked. "I was hoping she and I could talk before the show."

"She's in her private dressing room," Yellin said. "She said she was too emotional to be with the group but that she's looking forward to joining you all on stage. Stay here. I'll be back soon."

Yellin was just about at the door when Vanner stood and shouted, "I just got a text from Tom. He said he's excited to see a great show."

"Does he remember he's supposed to *be* on that great show?" Yellin shouted. "Tell him to get his ass down here right now."

I excused myself to go to the bathroom. Once there and sure there was no one else with me, I called Marc.

"What the hell happened to you guys?" I whispered. "Where are you?"

"We're coming, we're coming," Marc said. "Feldman gave Lexington a cocktail of drugs that knocked him out. He should be waking up any moment, and we can be there in twenty minutes."

"But Marc, the show starts in fifteen."

"Find a way to stall."

"Marc, I can't stall millions of viewers. You need to get here now."

"We'll be there. Don't worry. Did Vanner get the text?"

"Was that you posing as Lexington?"

"Yes, sir," Marc said proudly.

"Nice job. Keep it up."

I made it back to the conference room shortly before Yellin returned.

"Vanner, any updates?" he asked before making it into the room.

"I wrote him that Kent Cutler and Paulson are both out," Vanner said, "and I gave him the updated format for the show, with me starting off with a question for each panelist, and then he'll be able to follow up."

"And?" Yellin pressed.

"And he said, 'Ten-four,'" Vanner responded.

"His ass better be here soon," Yellin said. "It's time to get you all on set and miked up. Follow me."

Yellin led us downstairs and onto the stage, where we were given little microphones that clipped onto our shirts and earpieces so we could hear instructions from the control room. We were then shown to our seats so the control booth could test the sound and make sure all the cameras were in the correct position. Vanner was furiously texting Lexington. The grief counselor Bethany Goldstein was looking all over for Sarah Cutler, wanting to introduce herself before the show. Sarah's seat was empty on set, as was Lexington's.

Suddenly, Sarah Cutler appeared from behind the set to a raucous ovation. Sarah somberly waved and acknowledged the crowd as she walked onto the set and sat down as a sound man attached a microphone to her blazer.

"Three minutes, people, three minutes to showtime," a producer shouted.

Amid the chaos of getting the final touches ready for the broadcast, Norman Yellin took a second to stand back and recognize what he'd created. Standing next to one of the cameras, he marveled at the full audience and what turned out to be an impressive assembling of individuals, particularly given the tight time constraints. A production assistant ran over and said the MGBC social media post about the show had generated more than 300,000 likes and more than a million shares, making it far and away the most viral post the network had ever put out. That news brought a smile to Yellin's face.

"Norman Yellin, you've done it," he said to himself. "You're going to make TV history."

"Two minutes to showtime, everyone. Two minutes."

Yellin looked back at the stage and quickly realized he had a problem. Tom Lexington's chair was still empty.

"Hey, you," he said to the production assistant. "Go run up there and take that empty chair off the set. Quick, do it now!"

The assistant ran and got the chair as Yellin hustled to get back up to the control room, ready to watch his precious performance. As the lights went dark and the producer counted down from ten, Yellin could only think of one thing. Where the hell was Tom Lexington?

21

The studio went dark as all of us on stage heard a voice in our ears count down to the start of the show. A single white spotlight shone down on the front of the stage, where a white guy with dreadlocks in his early twenties was standing with a guitar. He wore an all-black suit, a pair of bright white high-tops, and a lime-green nose ring, but the outfit and jewelry quickly became afterthoughts as he solemnly plucked at his guitar. The guy was good, stringing together chords with ease as he used music to pull at our heartstrings. He played a slow ballad that was heartfelt and powerful, drawing us in and setting the tone for what was to be an emotional evening.

At least that was the plan.

"Where the hell am I supposed to sit?" came a shout from the side of the studio.

Tom Lexington had arrived.

We actually smelled Lexington before we saw him. He reeked from Feldman's mayo shower, had clumps of mayo still in his hair, and his sport coat looked like he'd walked through a car wash and forgot to get dried off. As taken aback as we all were by his arrival, Lexington was more bewildered by the removal of his chair. He found a folding chair leaning against a wall, grabbed it, and made his way on set, where he plopped himself and his chair down right in the middle of the stage, no more than eight feet behind the guitarist. He crossed his right foot onto his left knee and sat back, appearing ready to take in the rest of the guitarist's performance.

"Go to delay, go to delay," we heard Norman Yellin shout in our ears, directing his plea to whoever in the booth was in control of implementing the five-second delay standard in all live broadcasts. We could only hear one part of the conversation, but the way Yellin screamed, we didn't need to hear anyone else's voice. "What do you mean the delay's not working? Then go to commercial, dammit. Just cut to commercial as soon as this hippie finishes."

Despite the intrusion and foul odor, the guitarist kept playing. He hit the crescendo and finished the song, letting the final chord drift off into a silent studio. The spotlight went off, and we were left in darkness.

"Go to commercial," Yellin shouted. "Now! Now! Cut to commercials."

Nothing happened. The studio remained black as confusion took over the control room. I peeked up at the booth, the only source of light in the entire studio, and I saw Patrick acting just as confused as everyone else. Amid the chaos, I'm pretty sure I saw him wink my way. No one knew what was happening and why they couldn't go to commercials, but Yellin quickly realized the show had to go on.

"Cue the lights. Get the stage lights on," he said into everyone's ears. "Vanner, we're live. Just start us off, and we'll get to a commercial break as soon as we can. Panelists, please be careful with what you say. There appears to be no tape delay, so please, please, watch your words."

The stage lights went on, and viewers around the world saw seven people on stage, six of us in a half circle and Tom Lexington in a folding chair in front of us all, partially blocking Sarah Cutler and psychic Sherwin Kite from the camera's view. Lexington wasn't set up with a microphone and earpiece yet, so he had no idea what was happening.

"Oh, for fuck's sake, someone go get Lexington out of the way of the camera," Yellin yelled.

A production assistant crawled onto the stage and whispered to Lexington that he and his chair were blocking some of the panelists.

"Too bad," Lexington said out loud as he folded his arms and stuck his chin out. "You all forgot a chair for me, so this is my new chair. And I'm not leaving it!"

Since he wasn't miked up, the viewing audience couldn't hear what he was saying. Instead, they just saw a man with globs of goo in his hair and a sopping sport coat having a conversation with what appeared to be an imaginary friend.

The production assistant looked up at the control booth, confused as to what to do next.

"Just move him," Yellin demanded.

A second assistant came on stage, and together they picked Lexington's chair up with him in it. As he moved, his odor spread across the stage. We each covered our noses as Lexington was put where his original chair had been.

"Vanner, start the damn show," Yellin shouted. "And keep your composure, everyone. No one outside of this building can smell Lexington, so stop with the facial expressions. We'll spray the room during a commercial break."

The melancholy mood set by the guitarist was gone, and it was Vanner's job to get the train back on the tracks.

"Good afternoon . . . I'm sorry, good evening, ladies and gentlemen, and welcome to *Looking for Lance*," he began. "Decades ago, the nation was glued to the radio and newspapers alike after American icon Charles Lindbergh's infant son was kidnapped. Years later, Americans watched in shock as Patty Hearst, heiress to the Hearst media fortune, was abducted and subsequently became a member of the Symbionese Liberation Army. It is our hope that tonight's broadcast will also go down in history. Over the course of the next ninety minutes, we're going to try to unravel the mystery of what happened to Chicago Police Department Lieutenant Lance Cutler, who went missing five days ago. We'll hear from a star-studded panel of experts, who will share their perspectives and offer insights into the psyche of Lieutenant Cutler and help piece together the puzzle of why, and hopefully where, this distinguished officer has vanished. Along the way, we'll hear stories about Lieutenant Cutler from some of the people who knew him best—sorry, I mean who *know* him best. Our assumption, or, rather, our hope, is that Lieutenant Cutler is still alive, and perhaps we might even be able to locate him by the end of the show. Speaking of that, if you have any information about Lance Cutler's whereabouts, please call the hotline number shown on your screen."

"Oh, shut up, Matt, and get on with it," an agitated Tom Lexington blared from the other side of the stage.

He still didn't have a microphone or earpiece, but now that he was closer to us, sitting just a few feet to my left, his voice could be more clearly picked up by our mics.

"I taught you better than that."

Vanner went red with embarrassment. "Right," he said hesitantly. "So who is Lance Cutler? I'm honored to be sitting here beside his mother, Sarah Cutler, who will tell us all about her son momentarily. But first, we have a montage to show."

The audience was treated to a three-minute video featuring images of Lance Cutler from the time he was a baby, up through his Little League playing days, then college, then on the force with the CPD. Thirty seconds before the video ended, Yellin got back in our earpieces.

"Okay, everyone, we got the commercial situation figured out. As soon as this montage finishes, we'll cut to commercial."

The video ended, and the commercials ran. An announcement rang out through the studio. "Two minutes, folks; two minutes till we're back live."

The chaos that had been in the control room now spilled onto the stage, where everyone was yelling at everyone else while trying to steer clear of Lexington, whose stench was getting worse by the minute. Gerald and Sherwin were both pissed they weren't introduced right off the bat and took their frustrations out on Vanner, who was angry at Yellin for not having the tech situation figured out earlier. Yellin, meanwhile, was screaming at Lexington for his unprofessionalism and demanded he leave the stage.

"Norman, my boy, you can yell at me all you want," Lexington said as he leaned back on his folding chair with his hands behind his head. "I ain't going nowhere."

Sarah Cutler kept her head down throughout the fracas. She had some words she wanted to say, but she knew there were voters in the audience, and she didn't want a camera to accidentally catch her saying something she'd regret. She opted for silence. Yellin, on the other hand, opted for yelling.

"Security," he shouted. "Remove Tom Lexington from the studio immediately!"

"Sir?" a twenty-something said as she tapped on Yellin's shoulder.

"What?" Yellin shouted back, turning to see the young woman quiver while holding a tablet in one hand.

"I know it's not my job to tell you what to do—"

"You're damn right!"

"But sir, I wouldn't take Lexington off the show. Social media is loving his oddness. We already had a big following thanks to your contest idea, but we're getting more mentions by the second with people wondering what's up with 'the clever oily old guy.'"

"I don't care right now. This is my show, and I want him out of here. Security!"

When I heard that order, I knew it was time to step in. With less than a minute before the show returned from commercials, I jumped out of my seat and grabbed Skip, who was trying to stay out of the way during all the commotion.

"Norman, Skip and I must step in here and defend Mr. Lexington," I said. "As you may remember, my contract clearly states that there will be two hosts, and if you remove Tom, I will be forced to leave the stage as well, and I'll bring Skip here along with me. Good luck having tongue-tied Vanner over there explain what happened to Lance's best friend and me to an already confused audience."

"Now hold on, Blaze. Let's not make rash decisions."

"Exactly. Don't kick Lexington out without hearing his side of the story. I'm sure there is a perfectly logical explanation for his appearance and odor. Maybe it was a big accident."

"You think this was an accident?" Yellin said, gesturing toward Lexington, who was still leaning back in his chair.

"Thirty seconds, people. Thirty seconds until we're live," shouted a producer.

"Fine, Lexington stays. But you're on a short leash," Yellin said, looking at the cohost. "Somebody get Tom a mic and an earpiece. And someone find a towel to clean up his hair during the next break."

An assistant quickly outfitted Lexington with a mic and an earpiece as Skip and I went back to our seats. As I began to sit down, I felt a tap on my shoulder. It was Sherwin the psychic.

"Detective Blaze," he said, "stay away from water."

Before I could ask for more explanation, the producer shut us all up. "Five, four, three, two, one—"

The audience lights dimmed as Vanner sat up straight to welcome viewers back to the show.

"Welcome back, everyone. It's time to meet our distinguished panel. First, sitting to my immediate left is Sarah Cutler, the mother of Lieutenant Lance Cutler and the current frontrunner to be the next mayor of the great city of Chicago. Mrs. Cutler, thank you for being here, particularly during this trying time. It must be awful to not know what's happened to your son."

"Yes, Matt, it is awful. No mother should ever have to feel what I'm feeling right now." She turned her attention from Vanner to the camera. "I am here as Lance's mother, but I am also here to tell the residents of this great city that if you elect me as your next mayor, I promise I will rid this city of its awful crime pattern so no one has to experience the agony and suffering I'm going through right now."

"Thank you, Mrs. Cutler," Vanner said. "We can get back to the issue of your candidacy in a little bit, but first, let's meet the rest of our panelists. Sitting next to Mrs. Cutler is Dr. Bethany Goldstein. A renowned psychologist and grief counselor, Dr. Goldstein is also the author of five books, including her latest, *Go Away, Grief*. Dr. Goldstein, thank you for being here."

"It's my pleasure," said the doctor, who must have easily been twice the size of Sarah Cutler. "And thank you for mentioning my book, Matthew. I actually have a section in it that's about the exact situation we're here to talk about."

"Cut the crap," Lexington cut in, leaning forward in his chair. "You don't have a chapter about a police officer disappearing and his mother, who is a prominent politician, going on television to try to find him. Or do you?"

Dr. Goldstein's face turned red. "Okay, well, not the exact situation, but I explore the strength it takes to tackle the emotional and physical abuse we all go through when demons take over our souls."

"Demons, huh?" Lexington said. "Okay, I'm intrigued."

Satisfied with the answer, he went back to his reclining position, his hands back atop his mayo-covered head.

"Right," Vanner said, trying to steer back control of the conversation. "Dr. Goldstein, have you ever dealt with another instance of a parent not knowing the whereabouts of their child?"

"Well, no, not exactly. But I can only imagine the grief Sarah here is feeling," Dr. Goldstein said, reaching to hold Sarah's hand.

The camera picked up this small comforting gesture, and so did Vanner. He knew even a handhold between strangers could be golden content for viewers, and he wanted to build on it.

"With that in mind," Vanner followed, "what would you say is one word that best describes Mrs. Cutler?"

Dr. Goldstein, still holding Sarah's hand, thought through the question. "Brave. That would be my word, Matthew. Sarah Cutler is a brave woman."

Out of nowhere, the audience burst into laughter. I looked up and saw the electronic "laugh" sign brightly lit, assuredly thanks to some more technical wizardry from Patrick. I refused to look at the control room, but I did notice a few large men wearing security shirts leave the set and head toward the elevator, likely going to help unravel the ongoing technical mishaps.

"Thank you, Dr. Goldstein. Next we have Detective Fredrick Russell Skepper, better known as Skip. You worked in the same Chicago Police Department precinct as Lieutenant Cutler, and you had the honor of being his best friend growing up, isn't that right?"

"Yes."

"Is it fair to say you two were inseparable growing up?"

"Yes."

Vanner needed more than one-word answers from Skip, so he opted for a more open-ended follow-up. "That must mean that as a kid, you spent a lot of time at the Cutlers' house. What was life like there with Lance? And what's an anecdote or two you have about spending time with our potential future mayor here?" Vanner asked, gesturing toward Sarah Cutler.

Skip was silent for a second, then gave Vanner just what he wanted. "Sarah was like a second mother to me. But more than that, she's been someone I could always turn to when I had a problem. Whenever I was sad, Sarah would hold me tight to her chest and not let go, and let me tell you, that brought me so much comfort."

This time, the correct emotional cue sign came on, and the audience *awwe*d at the anecdote. Vanner was proud he got Skip to open up. His last question to Dr. Goldstein worked well, so he decided to continue the approach.

"That's sweet, Skip. Tell us, what's one word you would use to describe Mrs. Cutler?"

"One word? Let me think." Skip began counting on his fingers and mouthing words to himself. "Just one word?"

"That's right, Skip. One word," Vanner clarified.

Skip went back to counting, thinking, and mouthing. Ten seconds went by. Then twenty seconds. For forty-five seconds, there was silence as the camera focused exclusively on Skip looking down at his hand, working through possible descriptors. Yellin shouted at the cameraman operating camera 2 to show something other than Skip looking down.

"Come on, man," Yellin cried. "If the person talking isn't interesting, show what they're talking about."

Camera 2 switched to focus on Sarah Cutler as Skip continued to think.

"Oh, for the love of God," Lexington cut in, "just pick a word!"

"Well," Skip finally said, "there are hundreds of things I could say about Sarah Cutler. Can I do two words instead of just one?"

"Fine," Vanner said. "What two words do you think best describe Sarah Cutler?"

Skip sat upright, cleared his throat, and looked straight at the mother of his former best friend.

"Great tits."

Taking Yellin's advice, camera 2 panned down so hundreds of millions of people could stare at Sarah Cutler's less than voluptuous breasts. Lexington almost fell out of his seat laughing, while I barely held in my own laughter, proud of Skip for his creativity in following my instructions to embarrass Sarah. Sherwin the psychic stared blankly at the camera, while Gerald, the hostage negotiator, took a look at Sarah and nodded in agreement. Skip smiled gleefully as the jaws of both Dr. Goldstein and Sarah dropped in shock.

"Camera two," Yellin shouted. "Stop focusing on her boobs! Show something else, anything else. Go to Vanner! Come on, Matt, get this thing back on track!"

"Um, okay, moving on," Vanner said, frazzled but doing what he could to try to regain control. "On to our next guest. Gerald Scherer is an avid cyclist who once competed for Team USA in the Summer Olympics. He used his notoriety and effective communication skills to become one of the foremost hostage negotiators in the world. He's successfully negotiated the release of American prisoners overseas and has talked dozens of people off the ledge—sometimes literally. His latest book is a national bestseller. Thank you, Gerald, for joining us."

"Don't yank my chain," Gerald scolded Vanner.

Vanner stiffened and looked like a schoolboy being reprimanded. "I'm so sorry, sir," Vanner apologized. "I didn't mean to imply that—"

Gerald let out a boisterous, bellowing laugh. "No, kid, *Don't Yank My Chain* is the name of my new book. I wanted to make sure people knew the title so they could order it online." He turned from Vanner to the cameras. "That's right, ladies and gentlemen. Buy my book today and not only will you learn about my illustrious career, but you'll also gain tips to help win any argument, whether you're quarreling with your spouse about doing the dishes or debating with friends about the best baseball player of all time. Kids, you can use my tips, too, when asking for a higher allowance."

Vanner was still frozen with fear. Lexington, on the other hand, literally fell out of his seat laughing that time.

"Oh, he got you good, Matty boy." Lexington laughed as he slowly got up and settled himself back into his folding chair.

The "laugh" sign once again came on as the audience broke out in laughter.

Vanner's cheeks couldn't have gotten redder. He had no control of the show and couldn't believe his trusted mentor was making things worse. The best option was to continue moving forward.

"Anyway," Vanner began, trying to focus on salvaging the show, "next to Mr. Scherer is Sherwin Kite. Mr. Kite recently won a nationally televised talent competition for his psychic abilities. Mr. Kite, if you please, can you demonstrate your psychic talents for us?"

"I'd be happy to, Matt," Sherwin responded.

He turned and stared intently and seriously at the camera. Then, out of nowhere, he began a little jingle.

"Some call my skills magic; some call them a gift. Others say I'm crazy and have gone slightly adrift. But I can see into the future, and it's not controversial. It's time for this show to go to commercial."

All of us sat speechless. Not surprisingly, it was Lexington who eventually broke the silence with a roaring laugh that nearly sent him out of his chair again.

"Holy mother of God, where did you all find this shithead?"

Vanner cut in. "I think Mr. Kite is right. We'll be back after a brief commercial break."

"Haha." Sherwin shouted, "I told you so!" as the show cut to a break.

The lights in the studio went on, and Vanner darted toward Lexington.

"What the hell's gotten into you, Lex? Why are you embarrassing me on national television? This was supposed to be my moment."

"Kid," Lexington said, reclining in his chair, "you brought

this one upon yourself. You're supposed to be the ringmaster of this circus up here. If you can't control the animals, they'll eat you alive."

"I would have at least thought you'd try to help me out."

"You want my help? Okay, when we come back on, I'll be sure to loft some softballs your way to hit out of the park."

"Thank you. Just some basic respect would be nice."

Norman Yellin stormed onto the stage. "What in God's name is going on up here, people!? This is supposed to be a show about Lance Cutler. You all barely mentioned him. And, Skip, what the hell? 'Great tits'? Really? Pull your shit together. And speaking of shit, Lexington, you're now on a very short leash. The combination of your *shithead* remark and Skip's obsession with Mama Mammaries over there is about to get us censored by the FCC!"

"I'm sorry, what did you just call me?" Sarah Cutler said.

The conversation was interrupted by the network's social media manager. "Mr. Yellin, Mr. Yellin, we've done it. Right now we're the top trending story in the country! You've got a viral sensation on your hands."

"What?" Yellin said.

"That's right. We're the most talked about story in the country. I heard you say we might get censored, but if we don't, we might become one of the most talked about topics globally."

"People are enjoying what they're seeing?" Yellin said, perplexed.

"They can't get enough of it, particularly Tom Lexington. Listen to these: 'Love that nutty hair-paste guy.' Or this one: 'Looking for a new drinking game? Take a shot every time that gooey-looking Lexington laughs. Double shots if he falls out of his chair.' And listen to this one: 'It's about time a TV station had the balls to deliver news the way we want to hear it.'"

"The people love me. What can I say?" Lexington said confidently.

Just then, a fellow assistant came running toward Yellin. "Mr. Yellin, Mr. Yellin, early reports show we've passed one hundred million viewers. Only the Super Bowls, Richard Nixon, and the moon landing had more viewers than we've got right now. Congratulations, sir!"

"Thirty seconds left, everyone. Thirty seconds until we're back live," the producer shouted.

Yellin didn't know what to do. His dream had turned into a train wreck of epic proportions, but it was getting the eyeballs he promised. If Vanner could somehow steer back control, they just might be able to salvage the show while millions were tuning in.

"Okay, people," he said to us on stage, "we've got more eyes on us than ever before. Let's get back to focusing on Lance Cutler, okay? We can still make this production a success, but I need you all to be on your best behavior. Can you do that? And, Vanner, be my captain, will you? Steer us straight."

"Will do," Vanner said.

"Aye, aye," Lexington said with a salute toward Yellin, who was running back to the control room.

"Five, four, three, two, one—"

"Welcome back to *Looking for Lance*," Vanner began. "We strayed a little off course there, but now I'd like to dig into the details about the disappearance of Lieutenant Cutler."

"Hey, Matt, Matt, over here," Lexington said, waving his hands in the air.

"Tom, I'd really like to move forward with some questions."

"That's what I wanted to say. You forgot to ask the psychic and the negotiator what their one word would be to describe Sarah. That was your idea, wasn't it?"

"I really don't think that's necessary," Vanner said.

"I thought you wanted me to help you out," Lexington said. "Fine, I'll just guess their words." He thought for a couple of seconds.

"As I was saying—" Vanner began.

"I bet they both would say *potential*."

Vanner, taken aback, forgot his charge and instead got curious. "Potential?" he said. "Why?"

"Well, as good of a psychic as Sherwin is, I'm sure he's always on the lookout for new clients. With Sarah there about to be in the mayor's office, that could mean potential for a lot of future gigs."

Sherwin nodded his head. "That's true. I am a very good psychic. In fact, I've done more birthday parties and *bar* and *bat mitzvahs* than any other psychic on the North Shore. But that's not all."

He reached into his jacket and pulled out two golden balloons. He put each to his mouth, then twisted and turned them until he had a full-size crown. He offered it to Sarah, who politely declined.

"Want to learn more? Email me at psychicmitzvah@aol.com."

"Okay, I'll give you that one," Vanner said to Lexington. "But why say *potential* for Gerald, our hostage negotiator?"

"Because he's potentially getting laid tonight," Lexington said with a wink. "Hostage negotiators aren't just talking people off a cliff; they're talking ladies into their bed."

The audience roared with laughter.

"He's not lying," Gerald bragged as he gave a shifty smile and a big thumbs-up to the camera.

I could only imagine how many guys watching across the country saw that thumbs-up and immediately changed their online dating profile occupation to *hostage negotiator*.

"That's it, I'm out of here," Sarah Cutler said, standing up and throwing her microphone and earpiece into her chair. She stormed off the stage, furious and humiliated.

"The tight ass has left the building," Lexington shouted.

"Commercial! Go to commercial," Yellin shouted in our ears.

"And we'll be right back," Vanner said sheepishly.

Patrick's wizardry struck again, though, and the show couldn't break. The cameras were still focused on Vanner, who was looking around in a daze of confusion and disarray.

"Are we still rolling?" he asked.

"Apparently," Yellin said through our earpieces. "Vanner, be my captain. Right this damn ship now, or you're going down with it!"

Yellin threw off his headset and ran to stop Sarah from leaving the studio.

Vanner had no idea what to do or say. More than 100 million eyes were on him, and he was speechless.

"Umm, Ms. Goldstein," he said, turning toward the grief counselor, "have you ever experienced anything like this before?"

Even I knew that was an awful question. What was she supposed to say? "Oh, yeah, this kind of teenage humor at the expense of a mother who is grieving for her missing son and running for office happens all the time"?

"No, Matthew," she said tersely, "I've never seen anything like this before."

She, too, stood up, put down her mic and earpiece, and walked off stage.

"The hefty ass has left the building," Lexington shouted.

Vanner looked like he'd gone into shock. What the hell was he supposed to do? Meanwhile, Yellin found Sarah backstage and pleaded for her to return to the set.

"Sarah—"

"It's Mrs. Cutler to you," Sarah interrupted.

"Fine. Mrs. Cutler, I know this hasn't turned out exactly how we thought it would."

"You think? I've gone from the sympathetic motherly candidate to the tits and ass candidate thanks to you and those clowns. This was a mistake."

"Mrs. Cutler, if I may, the only mistake will be if you don't go back and fix what's happened. If you leave now, you're right; you will be the tits and ass candidate. But you have the power to control the narrative. Get back on stage and take control for yourself. Show the public you can handle embarrassment, that you can laugh at yourself and turn the other cheek—sorry, no pun intended."

Sarah could have smacked Yellin then and there, but she knew he was right. The only way for her to show her authority was to take it from those bozos on stage.

"Fine," Sarah said. "I'll do it but not for you and not for this godforsaken network. When I become mayor, I'm suing the hell out of you and your company."

She took a breath and walked back toward the stage, but before she got there, she was body-blocked by Bethany Goldstein.

"Now listen, lady," Goldstein said as she pointed a finger inches from Sarah's face. "I'm sorry your son is missing, but this show isn't only about you. I've been peddling my book at mom-and-pop bookstores across the Midwest, and this is my big break. I'm here to sell grief, but I can't do that without you on stage."

"You listen here, missy," Sarah said, putting her own finger in Goldstein's face. "I don't care about you or your book. I bet your book is a piece of garbage anyway."

"Excuse me?"

"You heard me. And how dare you talk to the future mayor of Chicago like that? I'll have you banned from this great city when I'm elected."

"No loss for me. I live in a small town in eastern Ohio. But I'll tell you what, you conniving shrew. If you don't walk back on that set with me right now, holding my hand, I'll go out there myself and say you're a griefless bitch who was involved in her own son's disappearance."

That threat struck a chord with Sarah. How did this know-it-all about grief know that Sarah was connected to Lance's demise? She recognized she was walking a fine line.

"Why do you need to hold my hand?" Sarah asked.

"Chapter three in *Go Away, Grief* is all about physical connection and support, and the primary example I provide is holding a victim's hand and the power it can have to help overcome grief. So what's it going to be? Am I going to hold your wrinkly hand on TV, or am I going to tell the world Sarah Cutler couldn't care less about the fate of her son?"

Back on set, Vanner pleaded at the camera. "Now can we go to commercial, please?"

With no response in his ear, he realized it was up to him to try to salvage the show.

"Okay, Detective Blaze, I'd like to try to get into the specifics of the case at hand. You've spent some time investigating the whereabouts of Lieutenant Cutler. Can you shed some light on what you've been able to find out so far?"

"Thanks for that question, Matt. I'd be happy to talk about my latest findings. Before that, though, I wonder if I can ask my own question."

"Sure," Vanner said as he threw his hands in the air. "Why not?"

"Great, thanks. Apparently, Tom Lexington has become the star of the show, at least in the eyes of our viewing audience."

Hearing this, Lexington instinctively raised his hand and waved to the camera.

"Now perhaps he's sparked your curiosity because he certainly sparked mine. You all can clearly see something is not right with this man. There are wads of who knows what stuck in his hair, his face is crusty, and his clothes somehow still look to be sopping wet. What you folks watching can't tell is he also reeks like rotten eggs and sour milk—"

"You said you had a question, Detective Blaze," Vanner interrupted, trying to find some semblance of control.

"Yes, sorry. My question is quite simple. Tom, what the hell happened to you?"

"Funny you should ask, Blaze. It's actually a rather humorous story," Lexington said. "In order to say it, though, I have to use the C-word, and I'm not sure I'm allowed to do that. My wife definitely doesn't like it whenever I use that word."

"No, no, no! A thousand nos," Yellin shouted into our ears after just making it back to the control room.

"I think it'd be best if we move on," Vanner said. "Back to my original question—"

"What do you all think?" Lexington said to the studio audience. "Are you all curious why I look like this?"

The crowd shouted cries of approval.

"Okay, I'll tell you," Lexington said with a devilish grin.

"Oh, for the love of God, we're going to get cut off by the FCC," Yellin said to no one in particular. "Everyone in the broadcast business knows the words that can't be said on television, and the C-word is right on top."

He realized he had to take matters into his own hands.

"You, beeper," he said to Patrick. "Get out of the way. I'm manning that button myself. No way I'm letting us get thrown off the air because Lexington wants to go and use the C-word."

I peeked up to the control room and saw Patrick graciously move out of his seat as Yellin sat down. One hand was over the beep button, and the other was at his mouth as he nervously chewed his fingernails. With no ability to put the broadcast on delay, Yellin had to anticipate when Lexington would say what he shouldn't say. That need to predict could be nerve-wracking when only a few dozen people are watching, let alone 100 million.

Lexington sat up in his seat and looked directly at the camera.

"As I mentioned, my wife doesn't like it when I use the word *beep*. She tells me there are too many *beep* in our neighborhood already."

Lexington heard the beeps and got a little distracted but tried to push on.

"Personally, I don't know what the big deal is. I like *beep*. Hell, I love *beep*."

The fourth beep was too much for Lexington.

"Okay, what the hell's going on? Who's beeping me out?" he asked incredulously. "Vanner, is that you?"

Vanner held up his hands as an innocent bystander. "It wasn't me."

Lexington looked around. "Who the *beep* is beeping me out? They just did it again!" He got up and quickly questioned each of us. "Was it you, Skip?"

"It wasn't me," the cop responded.

"What about you, Mr. Ladies' Man?" he said to Gerald the negotiator.

"Not me," Gerald said.

Lexington briefly walked off set to find the culprit, and as he left, camera 2 followed him. Lexington was the show's golden goose, and the cameraman wasn't going to let him out of his sight. Lexington walked around in utter confusion, then returned on stage, briefly checking under some of our chairs in case the mysterious beeper was hiding there.

"What *beep* is beeping me out?" he said as he stood up. "Dammit, they just did it again!"

Lexington walked toward the curtain to see if the beeper was hiding there. He pulled one side of the curtain back to find Sarah Cutler and Bethany Goldstein in some sort of cat fight, with Goldstein trying to grab Sarah's hand while Sarah kept pulling it away.

"Well, look who I found," Lexington said proudly.

The grief therapist and mayoral candidate froze as they realized the spotlight and camera were on them. Goldstein reached for Sarah's hand, grabbed it, and held it tight as the two walked back to their seats.

"Look at this happy family," Lexington said as he sat back in his chair while the two women got their microphones and earpieces readjusted. "Now, what was I talking about?"

"I believe you were talking about Costco," I cut in, knowing his story better than he did since I was the one who came up with it.

"Right, the C-word," Lexington said. "I wasn't sure if we were able to mention a brand on air if they weren't a sponsor."

Yellin let out an audible sigh into our ears. I peeked at the control room and saw him give Patrick his seat back. Yellin stood just behind him in case he needed to pounce on the button unexpectedly.

"Anyway, like I was trying to explain, I was rushing out the door today and realized I needed lunch. I grabbed two pieces of bread, some turkey, and some lettuce, but it wasn't until I was in the car driving that I realized I forgot the mayo. I passed by a Costco." Lexington paused and looked up, seeing if he would get beeped again. "I ran into Costco to grab some mayo. They don't sell much in small quantities there, so I had to get an enormous container. I'll admit it was a little goofy to buy a sixty-four-ounce container just for my one little sandwich, but have you ever eaten a turkey and lettuce sandwich with no condiments? It's so plain. Am I right?"

The other panelists had no idea where this bizarre story was going, so they just nodded in agreement. I, meanwhile, was shocked that everyone was engrossed in this cockamamie tale.

"I bought my half gallon of mayo and got in the car," he continued. "I forgot to grab a knife to spread it, so I figured I'd just pour a small bit onto the sandwich. Well, to make a long story short, the container slipped out of my hands." Lexington stood up and motioned toward himself. "The rest, as they say, is history."

Lexington sat down to a stunned silence. Worn out from his tale, he closed his eyes and within seconds was fast asleep.

"Excuse me, Matt," Sarah interjected. With Lexington knocked out, she realized this was her chance to take control of the show. "May I please speak?"

"Yes, please, Mrs. Cutler. Go right ahead."

"Thank you," Sarah said, smoothing out the crease in her skirt before earnestly looking up at the camera. "Ladies and gentlemen across the country and around the world, I am sorry you've had to be witness to such utter foolishness tonight. This was supposed to be a serious effort to determine the whereabouts of my dear son, Lance, not some mockery of me and primetime television. Now I am under the impression that more than one hundred million people in the United States alone are tuned in right now; perhaps that number is now up to a hundred fifty million. Maybe you're watching to see if Tom Lexington will fall out of his chair again, or maybe you want to hear another man on this stage sexualize me. Whatever your reason, you're watching now, so I make this plea to you: If you know anything about where my boy, my only child, Lance Cutler, is, please call and let us know. He's been missing for five days, and I'm barely hanging on. To be the brunt of such childish jokes this evening certainly has not helped my mental state, but I'm pushing on in honor of Lance. If it takes me becoming the laughingstock of a nation to find my boy, I'll do it, and I'd do it again."

Parts of the studio audience started to clap as Candidate Cutler began picking up steam. Tom Lexington, meanwhile, was snoring away.

"That's just what I do," Sarah continued. "I fight for what I believe in, and I'll do whatever it takes to make what's right happen. I taught that lesson to Lance as a young boy, and it's something I've honed throughout my career. And if the great people of Chicago vote for me to be their next mayor, I will bend over backward for them and push day and night to make their lives better, easier, and safer."

Cries of "Safer with Sarah" started to ring out from the crowd over the sound of Lexington's drawn-out sleeping snorts.

"That's right! This city will be safer with Sarah," she continued. "I have the utmost respect for our current mayor, but Chicago needs someone who will make safety their top priority, and Mayor Paulson hasn't done that. But I will. I will stand up against the city's biggest crime lords, and I will not back down, not to intimidation and not to threats. I will stand up against them on behalf of the city and its beautiful people. I will stand up against them and say that their time ruling Chicago has come to an end. I will stand up against them and say there is a new boss in town, and her name is Sarah Cutler."

Applause exploded from the audience as Sarah received a standing ovation.

"Mrs. Cutler, thank you so much for that stirring speech," Vanner said, "and for bringing us back to the place we meant to be all along."

"You're welcome, Matthew. It's what leaders do."

Vanner either didn't catch Sarah's dig at him or chose to move past it. "I have to ask, though. If—and please note I'm emphasizing the word *if*—Lance is not located, or if he in fact has already lost his life, will you still run for mayor?"

"That's a great question, and I appreciate your care in how you worded it," Sarah responded.

She looked down at the ground and wiped at her tear duct as the studio became silent. I had to give the woman credit, even I was feeling bad for her. I quickly realized that was how she'd gotten the public to eat out of her guilty hands. She knew how to play people's emotions like no one I'd seen before, and there she was, taking an absolute joke of a show and using it to strengthen her candidacy. I didn't like her, but I was starting to feel a bit of respect for her.

"You know, Matthew," Sarah went on, "I've prayed to God every night since Lance disappeared, hoping and begging for his safe return. It hasn't happened yet, and as you said, maybe it never will. At this point, I can't control that. What I can try to control is whether any other mother is forced to deal with the anguish I'm feeling. There is no pain greater than the loss of a child, or so I've been told. For that to happen because crime has gone unpunished in this city is inexcusable. If Lance is dead—and I pray he's not, but if he is—I'll spend the rest of my life wondering if there was something I could have done to keep him safe. What I can't live with is ignoring a chance to keep other mothers and their children from facing this same fate. So, Matthew, to answer your question, yes. Yes, I will continue my run for mayor even if my boy is gone. I will continue because I believe I can make a difference. I will continue no matter how many immature men like Frank Skepper and Tom Lexington I have to encounter. I will continue because this city needs a hero, and that hero is me. My name is Sarah Cutler, and I am ready to be the next mayor of Chicago."

The audience erupted in a standing ovation, startling Tom Lexington awake. Dr. Bethany Goldstein reached toward Sarah in an act of solidarity and support, but Cutler brushed the doctor's hand away. Sarah stood up, detached her microphone and earpiece, and dropped them both on the floor. She put one hand over her heart as she mouthed *thank you* to the camera, glared at Lexington, then turned and walked off the stage, leaving the panelists, studio audience, and hundreds of millions of people stunned in silence.

"What a cunt!"

And with those three words, the screens of nearly 200 million people in the United States suddenly went black. The show had been cut off.

There was no precedent for this type of cancelation midshow, but those in the business were always taught that if a show was ever blacked out, the screen would stay black for a few seconds and then be replaced by a generic infomercial that would run on repeat through the planned entirety of the broadcast. But in his final act of technical voodoo, Patrick found a way to sabotage that plan. Instead of seeing a demonstration of a knife that could cut through metal or a blender that doubled as a microwave, the *Looking for Lance* viewing audience was treated to a John Denver Christmas special in the middle of February.

Three words changed the careers of many on stage that night and perhaps strengthened Sarah Cutler's voting base. Sherwin the psychic would surely get more gigs, and Gerald the negotiator would undoubtedly have many active nights. If Vanner were ever to make it on TV again, it'd be from the streets of one of the country's smallest markets, not some national show like he'd hoped. The network's staff would all be investigated for the technical sabotage but likely survive.

As for the person who expressed themselves so loudly, they would never find work again. Their name would not be forgotten, though, because for generations to come, people would talk about those three words uttered by Dr. Bethany Goldstein.

Mary was waiting in the car outside the studio. I got in, and we drove away in silence. For five minutes we drove, both of us staring straight ahead. Then, at a red light, Mary turned to me.

"Costco? Really?"

We laughed hysterically, welcome relief from the stress of everything else. Tears started rolling down both our cheeks as we took turns recreating the best moments from the broadcast debacle.

"Did you really make that nice man say Sarah Cutler has nice tits?" Mary asked.

"I may have had a hand in that," I said with a shrug. "But Skip is not a nice man, make no mistake about it."

"I'm sure you had your reasons. Exactly how much of that shitshow was your doing?"

"To be honest, I don't know," I said with a laugh. "Lexington's appearance was thanks to an associate of mine, but even I couldn't have scripted all that nonsense."

We continued laughing as we recreated Lexington searching for the beeper. Mary pretended to look under my seat and accidentally swayed out of her lane. A police car happened to be behind us and pulled her over.

The officer approached Mary's window for her license and registration, but when he saw me, he shouted to his colleague, "Hey, Larry, it's Detective Blaze!"

Larry came rushing over to stand next to the first officer.

"Detective Blaze, it's an honor," Larry said. "We're proud to have you as one of us. Thanks for all you do. You two go ahead and have a great night."

22

It was hard to sleep restfully after making a mockery of a television broadcast while also planning a mass mutiny—a genocide of evil people. I had tossed and turned all night, thinking about the goal behind Operation Boom and wondering if this was in fact God's mission for me. Was I doing what God wanted, or was I trying to be God myself? Was I playing God, or was God playing me? If only I could get a sign confirming the Almighty was truly on Team Blaze—a comet flying across the sky or an abrupt burst of thunder would do the trick. Until then, I had to make a choice, and I chose to move forward with Operation Boom.

I tiptoed to headquarters to think through what seemed to be the two biggest challenges on my plate: how to get Solomon Feldman to Boom and how to justify Boom itself. It seemed like ages ago, but it was just yesterday morning that I had the idea to put together my own broadcast for Wednesday to demonstrate why Boom needed to happen. Seeing firsthand how much it took to put a show together—and how easily it could fall apart—I knew I needed help. The problem was whomever I asked for help would need to know what it was the Boom Squad and I were planning. I didn't want to put that kind of pressure on Patrick. He'd done incredible work the previous night, but being a part of Boom could ruin his life.

Unsure how to move forward with the video, I switched my focus to Feldman, though, again, I struggled to see how to voluntarily get him to the Boom site. I was hitting a creativity wall, and I wondered if that was because I didn't believe in the mission. I'd never been a man to doubt myself. The reason I was so successful in business was my confidence in myself and my ability to sell anything. But was Boom too outrageous to sell?

Mary came in and kissed my cheek. Seeing my frustration, she suggested we go for a morning walk—away from the eyes of the FBI—to relive the highlights of the last night and work through whatever was bothering me.

Once we were outside and away from our FBI surveillance team, I reminded her how we needed to get Feldman to Boom without him knowing what was going on.

"Okay, let's think this one through," she said as we casually walked the neighborhood. "What do we know about Feldman and Santori?"

"We know they hate each other's guts, and each thinks he's the top dog in this city. We know they think the other was responsible for killing Mel Weinberg, when really neither had anything to do with it."

"That's good. What else?"

"They've both killed and hurt more people than either of us can imagine. Oh, they both made agreements with Sarah Cutler to not harm the other in exchange for more control of the city."

"Keep going. Let's get everything we know out there, and then we can piece the puzzle together."

"We know that Eli and Vince, the most-trusted associates of each, are turning on them as part of Operation Boom. Well, and we know Santori is fleeing the country Wednesday night."

"Anything else?"

Nothing immediately came to mind.

"Okay, so let's look at the pieces," she said. "We have Santori leaving the country. We've got both men cutting deals with the future mayor for more power. And we've got both out for revenge."

We walked silently as we let that last point hover over us.

"Do Feldman and Santori ever talk to one another?" Mary asked.

"I can't believe they do. Why?"

"What if we made up a conversation between them?"

"What do you mean?"

"We could tell each the other said something, and there'd be no reason for them to doubt it. After all, we have access to the people each man trusts the most."

"How does that help get Feldman to the bowling alley though?"

We both stared out ahead. One minute went by. Then two. Then five. Suddenly, Mary slapped me on the arm.

"I've got it! What do you know about all Jewish men?"

I turned to her, perplexed. "We're circumcised?"

"Focus, David, focus. What else?"

I had no idea where she was going with this. Frustrated with my ineptitude, she answered her own question.

"Jews like a good deal," she said.

"Now, Mary, that's a gross stereotype that—"

"David, how much did you pay for the suit you wore last night?"

"I don't remember, but it was buy two, get one free."

"And how about those shoes you're wearing?"

"I got these babies for 40 percent off," I said proudly.

"I rest my case. Anyway, what if we have Santori offer Feldman a deal?"

"A deal on what? And why would Santori do that?"

"A deal on his operation," Mary exclaimed. "We could tell Feldman that Santori is skipping town because he killed Mel or because he thinks the FBI is on to him. The reason doesn't matter; it just needs to be convincing."

"Okay, so we tell Feldman that Santori is skipping town and offering to sell his business at a reduced rate," I said. "Won't Feldman want to check this out for himself?"

"Of course, but we can have all communications run through Vince," Mary said. "After all, Santori trusts Vince implicitly, and you could direct the whole conversation."

"And Santori never needs to know a thing about it," I realized.

"Exactly."

We walked silently again as we thought through her plan.

"Mary," I finally said, "that's brilliant. But for it to work, we need Vince and Eli on board."

I called the two men as we continued our walk. Both thought the idea was absurd, but neither had a better solution, so they were in. Eli told me Feldman was having his weekly lunch with his top dogs to discuss plans for the week and the harm they could cause. He said Feldman would be at the deli all afternoon, and I could come by to help facilitate a conversation between Feldman and Santori, which would really be a call between Feldman and Vince. I got off the phone and gave Mary a hug.

"Thank you," I said. "This detective work is a lot more effective with you as my partner. And a lot more interesting."

"Looks like you have a few messages there," she said as she saw my phone.

I hadn't noticed the three voicemails until then. The first was from Marsha Lexington, thanking me for whatever I did to help loosen her husband up.

"At first when I watched my dear Tommy on TV last night, I was embarrassed," she said. "But the more I listened, the more I found myself laughing. Before long, I was crying from laughter. David, my Tommy is always so uptight and rigid. Whatever you talked to him about or did yesterday, you made him fun. I'm not sure I've ever laughed like that in my life. So thank you, Detective Blaze. Thank you."

The next message was from Lance, who was worried his mom came out looking like a victim instead of the selfish devil she was. The last was from Tony, who changed our meeting time to two the next afternoon.

"Don't be late," Tony said, "and bring the damn bastard who killed Mel Weinberg—or else!"

Instead of contemplating what *or else* meant, I texted Jeffrey with another favor. *Hey buddy, you know Skip, the cop from last night's show? Can you get his family in an hour and take them to the FBI offices downtown?*

No problem, he replied.

I texted Skip that he had an hour before his ride arrived.

"Anything else I can help with?" Mary asked.

I realized that all my brainstorming about the video broadcast had been just that—brainstorming—so I tried to quickly catch her up on my thinking.

"People are going to want answers about Operation Boom," I said. "If we're able to provide those answers before the questions are asked, we might just be able to explain the whole thing. If it's done right, hopefully the public will see we had no choice other than to kill all these bad guys. I just hope the recording can get done in time."

"Why not broadcast it live?" she asked.

"If it was live, we'd have the authorities on us in minutes. We'd be called insane, and the whole Boom operation would be busted before it ever made a spark."

I gave her the rundown of how I thought we could put the broadcast together and then asked what she thought of the plan.

"Two days ago, I would have said you were crazy," Mary said. "After all you've done, I know not to doubt you. If you think it will work, then I'm on board."

I'd never felt more connected to her.

"The problem is I'm going to need a lot of help—technical help," I said.

"Good thing you know a tech wizard." She grinned. "Give the kid a call."

I thought about my reservations of including Patrick but ultimately called him on speakerphone. He answered on the first ring.

"Hey, boss, that was one hell of a show last night," Patrick began. "When are we going to do it again?"

"Hey, Patrick, you did Team Blaze proud yesterday. We couldn't have pulled that off without you."

"Happy to be a part of the team. So what's next?"

"That's why I was calling. I have a new project I'm working on that could really benefit from your expertise, but I'm worried it's not right for you."

The kid's tone quickly changed. "Screw you, boss. Didn't I earn your trust yesterday? Didn't I show you I can take on any challenge?"

"I'm worried it's too dangerous, Patrick."

"My middle name is Danger. I can't believe you still don't trust me. If you don't want me on Team Blaze, I quit!"

Patrick hung up as Mary and I looked at each other, stunned by his brashness. Was that the same dweeb who still slept in a bunk bed in his parents' house? Thirty seconds later, he called back.

"Hey, boss, sorry about that. Kelly was in the room with me, and I wanted to show her I can be tough. I didn't mean to be rude, and I'm not quitting. And just between you and me, my middle name isn't Danger. It's Whitney."

"It's okay, Patrick, but I need you to listen. This next project is serious. People are going to die because of it."

There was silence on the other end of the phone.

"Boss," he finally said, "if you're still fighting evil, then I want to be fighting alongside you."

"Are you sure, Patrick? I don't want you to ruin your life."

"I'm sure."

I walked him through my thinking and said we needed to be discreet but ultimately needed to get this video before the world. He listened patiently, never making a sound as I explained the dangerous task.

"Oh, shit, Kelly's coming back. I gotta go. I think I have an idea, though. I'll text you later."

With that, Patrick once again hung up on us. Mary and I looked at each other and smiled as we came up to our house.

"The things we do for those we love," she said with a wink.

Sarah was pleased with her team's handling of the night's debacle. The Cutler campaign issued statements on her behalf acknowledging her disappointment in the behavior of her fellow panelists and dismay that the show did not bring out new information about her missing son. The team also emphasized Sarah's closing speech and said it demonstrated her ability to overcome obstacles and do what she knew was right, qualities that would benefit the city and its residents if she were to become mayor. Finally, to allow Sarah to focus on finding her son, the campaign announced she would be canceling her scheduled events for the next two days.

She might have kept her composure on air to deliver her final remarks, but more than twelve hours later, Sarah was still stewing. She wondered what the hell had happened and whom she should be most upset with: Tom Lexington, the name-calling grief counselor Dr. Goldstein, Matt Vanner, or Skip. She knew Skip to be unpredictable, particularly recently, but to talk about her breasts on national television—what was the point?

She tried calling him, but his phone was off. With her schedule now empty, she asked her driver, Oscar, to visit Skip's house and tell him she wanted to talk.

I began the drive to Morry's Deli with my mind hopping between the upcoming Boom broadcast and how to orchestrate a fake sale of power between the two dirtiest men in Chicago. I hadn't heard back from Patrick, but I knew I'd need interviews. I was going to need Marc, Jeffrey, and Wilt to collaborate to make that happen. Since I'd talked to the others more recently, I called Wilt to tell him about the project.

"Hey, Wilt, I haven't had a chance to fill in the whole team yet, but I'm working as part of a secret operation to hunt down a collection of bad guys Wednesday night."

"Secret operation? Sounds mysterious."

"The problem is we need to make a video that justifies our actions. I've made a lot of big sales in my life, but this will be the biggest. I need to convince the world it is right to remove these despicable people from the planet. I want the world to be the judge and jury of how history will be written."

"Wow, that's intense. You're really going to kill someone? I'm always happy to help, David, but I have to tell you, my recording skills aren't the greatest."

"Don't worry. I don't need you behind a camera. I need you to help get the people who are going to be in front of the camera."

"Okay, good. I can do that."

"Give Marc a call. He has a copy of Mel Weinberg's notebook, which I'm sure has the names of victims in it. Between that and the info he and Jeffrey got from Tom Lexington, you guys should have plenty of people to reach out to."

"Hey, speaking of Mel, did you ever figure out who killed him?"

"Yeah, but it's not relevant."

"Not relevant? David, who killed him?"

"I promise I'll tell you, but right now I need your undivided attention."

'Fine, go ahead."

"I need you guys to get as many people as possible to be willing to go on camera and say how they've been hurt by Tony Santori and Solomon Feldman or anyone who worked for them."

"Sounds fun," Wilt said.

Fun was not the word I'd have chosen, but I was glad he was on board. I got off the phone with Wilt just as Patrick called me back.

"Hey, boss, so you still want to make a show, right?"

"Yeah, Patrick, we need to justify Operation Boom."

"Okay, cool. I've got a couple of cameras for filming, and Kelly's willing to help out. Do you have people who are going to be interviewed?"

"Yep, the rest of Team Blaze is coordinating that now. Give Marc a call, and he can fill you in. Are you sure Kelly is okay with this? Does she understand the risk involved?"

"Yep, she's in. She'll do anything to make her résumé reel stand out. I'll call Marc and get the details. Just one more question. Who is going to be your host?"

"My host? I haven't thought about it."

"Well, you need to, boss. The only way to keep people's attention is to have someone who can sell them on what they're about to see."

"Good thinking, Patrick. I'll work on that. Here's one question for you. How are we going to get this on TV?"

"Oh, don't worry. I already have that figured out."

"You do? How?"

"Do you want to know, or do you want to be surprised like yesterday?"

I wanted to know, but I was pulling up to Morry's Deli, so I gave the kid the satisfaction of not telling me yet.

"I gotta run, Patrick, but thanks for the help. Tell me later."

With the broadcast coming together, it was time to shift my attention to Feldman and Boom. Outside the deli, I texted Eli to ask how much he thought his boss would be willing to pay for Santori's operation.

36 million, Eli wrote.

What? It's got to be worth well over $50 million.

36 million. Not a penny more.

I sat back in my seat. Did I just negotiate for more money on a made-up deal? Once a businessman, always a businessman.

I called Vince to outline our plan. Then before getting out of the car, I did something I rarely did. I closed my eyes and prayed. I prayed to God I was doing the right thing. I prayed the world would understand why Boom needed to happen. And I prayed this game of telephone would actually work; otherwise, I'd be seeing God sooner than I intended.

My stomach grumbled as I walked into the deli. Eli immediately saw me and asked me to join Feldman and his Boys in their private area.

"Take a seat, Blaze," Feldman said, motioning for me to sit with his other hefty soldiers at the table. "It sounds like we have a lot to talk about."

I looked at Eli.

"I told them about the message you gave me," Eli said, "about Santori having troubles and needing to sell everything off his Chicago operations before fleeing the country."

"Yes, we do have to talk," I said as I grabbed a poppy seed bagel. Starving, I reached for the cream cheese and smoked salmon, unaware the rest of the table was staring at me. "Oh, you want to talk now?"

"Of course, Blaze," Feldman said. "Why is Santori selling, and why is he coming to me?"

I took a quick bite of my bagel because I feared I wouldn't get another chance for a while. It was time to lie like I'd never lied before.

"Well, Sol, as you know, Tony Santori hired me to identify Mel Weinberg's killer. After extensive investigation and interviewing, my team and I discovered that, in fact, it was Tony Santori himself who ordered the hit."

"I knew it," Feldman shouted. "I told you that son of a bitch was responsible."

"You did, Sol, I remember. Anyway, I reported my findings to Santori and told him that if I was able to put the pieces together, it was only a matter of time before the police did too. The police are also aware of Santori's responsibility in that car explosion on Wacker Drive last week."

"Yeah, but it's not like this is the first time Santori's killed anyone. What's so different this time?"

"Quite honestly," I said with no honesty behind it, "I think it's just the timing. One of his men saw the FBI canvasing the West Coast Club recently, and I think that spooked Santori. I also don't know if you're aware, but he and some of the other leaders of hotshot Italian families come together every ten years to toast each other's successes. It's a tradition that dates back generations. Anyway, their next meeting is Wednesday, and I think Tony saw it as a sign that this could be his farewell sendoff. My understanding is he's selling off his entire empire and plans to leave town after the dinner and never return."

"So why me?" Feldman asked. "Why would he sell Chicago to me?"

I looked at Eli, who was listening as intently as the rest of the other top Deli Boys.

"Well, Sol," I began, "I don't want to brag, but it's actually because of me that he's selling Chicago to you."

"You? How?"

"Selling the business apparently was already on his mind. When he heard what I had to say about his role in the steam room murder, he looked at his side man, Vince, and said he needed a clean break from the company. He told Vince to negotiate the sale of everything he owned to a family back in New Jersey. Vince asked Santori if he was sure, and Santori said he had no choice. Then Tony got up, looked out his window, and said, 'I'm going to miss this great city. Chicago's been good to me. I hate to sell it to some jerk back East who won't care about it the way I did.'"

With my salesman face, I continued feeding Sol everything he wanted to hear.

"I heard that as my opportunity. 'Mr. Santori,' I said, 'you don't need business advice from me, but if you care so deeply about this city, why not sell your ownership to someone who has as much appreciation for it as you do?' Santori turned and stared at me, offended that I could insinuate someone cared about Chicago like he did. He asked who I had in mind.

"And that's when I said you," I continued, pointing to Feldman. "I told him about your long history in Chicago and how much you and the Deli Boys took pride in this city. I acknowledged that it meant selling to his biggest enemy, but here's where I think got him. I said, 'Mr. Santori, wouldn't you rather Chicago be in the hands of someone who will look after and care for the city rather than a guy from the East Coast who may never set foot in the Midwest?' Santori thought about that for what must have been five or ten minutes, just me, him, and Vince together in a roomful of silence. Eventually he turned to Vince and said, 'Make it happen.'"

Feldman grabbed a piece of salmon with his fork and slowly chewed on the fish, never taking his eyes off me.

"But Blaze," he finally said, "why did you suggest me?"

"I told you, Sol, you can always trust me to do the right thing."

Feldman finished chewing and picked up his glass of orange juice.

"Gentlemen," he said to his other Deli Boys, "join me in toasting Detective Blaze. He is one of a kind, and now he is one of us." He turned toward me. "To Blaze, our lantzman. *L'chayim.*"

I, too, raised a glass in my honor. I had Feldman convinced. Now I had to sell him on the sale.

"So what's next?" Feldman said. "How do we get this purchase underway?"

"I was told negotiations will go through Vince. I have his number. If you'd like, we can start the process right now."

"Do it. Eli, let Blaze call from your phone and put him on speakerphone for us."

I took Eli's phone and hoped this charade would work.

"Hello, is this Vince with the Santori family?"

"Who is this?"

"This is Detective Blaze. I have you on speakerphone and am here with Solomon Feldman about the discussion you, Mr. Santori, and I had earlier today."

"Ah, yes. Mr. Feldman, thank you for taking the time to talk. I assume this phone call means there's interest in the sale."

I looked at Feldman, who nodded his approval. "Yes, Vince, Mr. Feldman is certainly intrigued."

Vince began a long monologue about the virtues of the Santori family, followed by a laundry-list breakdown of where their profits came from—extortion money, gambling debts, drugs, and so on. He then asked Feldman to imagine how much more power he would have if he was able to combine his own operation with that of Santori's. Feldman was focused on what Vince was saying, but I had to show I was Feldman's advocate and looking out for him.

"Vince, that's all well and good," I interrupted, "but you don't need to convince Mr. Feldman of why this is a good deal. What we need to know is how much it will cost. What's Tony looking for in exchange for his empire?"

"Fifty million."

Feldman's eyes widened in surprise. I had hoped that would be his reaction.

"Don't bullshit me, Vince," I said. "There's no way Mr. Feldman is paying that much. Tell Tony Santori to find someone else to buy his business. Feldman will control the city even without this deal."

"Screw you, Blaze. How much is Mr. Feldman willing to spend?"

I took the tip Eli had given me and answered without looking at Feldman. "Thirty-six million."

"You can't be serious," Vince said.

"I am absolutely serious."

"Blaze, come on. Tony Santori is owed ten million in gambling debts alone this month. He's not going to sell everything he owns for thirty-six million."

"Like I said, then tell him to go find someone else."

I looked up and saw Feldman nod his head with approval and pride.

"Who the hell are you even working for, Blaze?"

"Not Tony Santori. He's skipping town, so I'm switching sides. I'm looking out for my lantzmen. Now here's our final offer. We'll pay thirty million, but Santori can keep those ten million in gambling debts. So it's like he's getting forty million for the business."

"Tony is not going to like that."

"Well, Vince, you know what I have to say about that. Besides, time is money, and from what I understand, Mr. Santori is running out of time. We don't need this deal. We're happy to walk away."

"Relax, Blaze. Let me figure out how to present it to Tony, and I'll be back in touch."

"We're here at Morry's Deli and not going anywhere. You know how to find us."

I hung up the phone. I hadn't even handed it back to Eli when a slow clap began from Solomon Feldman himself. The others joined in, and within seconds, I was receiving a standing ovation from the group. Feldman walked over and patted me on the back.

"I had my doubts about you, Blaze, but not anymore. That was negotiating at its finest, one of the most beautiful manipulations I've ever seen."

"Ain't that the truth," I said proudly as I shook Feldman's hand. "Ain't that the truth."

While Vince was negotiating the fake sale of Santori's organization, Santori himself was sprawled out on his leather couch, watching a documentary about his idol, Al Capone. Santori had watched the movie dozens of times, but this time, he viewed it from a different perspective. All the other times he'd studied the legendary Capone, he'd focused on the accomplishments—his control over others, his ways of intimidation, his overall power. This time, though, Santori's attention was on Capone's downfall, from his arrests and trials to his multiple imprisonments and ultimate demise. Once Capone went to jail, he was never the same. Santori did not want the same thing to happen to him. He'd flown on the side of cockiness for years, but knowing Jermaine had spotted the FBI outside the West Coast Club, Santori figured his days of freedom were numbered—unless he fled. He wanted to live out his life the way his idol was never able to.

When the movie finished, Santori got up and went to his desk, where he'd started a list of talking points for his speech that would precede dinner on Wednesday. He wanted to acknowledge each of his attendees and their accomplishments since the last gathering ten years before. From there, though, the spotlight would be on him. Santori had itemized details about his proudest achievements, and from there, he wanted to devote the bulk of his time to what it meant to build a legacy. After his speech, he would raise his glass and lead a toast before the customary singing of "Siamo una Famiglia." He'd been trying all day to figure out a powerful closing line to end his speech before the toast, and after watching the movie, he had it. He grabbed a pen and jotted down his parting thought, reading it out loud to make sure it sounded right.

"I've spent my life inspired by Al Capone. History will ultimately compare us, but let me be clear: Capone is no Santori. He got caught. No one will ever catch Tony Santori."

Vince called us back at the deli, and I nonchalantly picked up the phone.

"So, Vince, do we have a deal?"

"Blaze, I presented Mr. Feldman's offer to Mr. Santori, and his exact words were to 'tell that fucker to go fuck off for having the fucking nerve to try and fuck Tony Santori with such a fucking lowball offer.'"

"Five *fucks* in one sentence," I replied. "That's impressive."

"Let me finish," Vince said. "I told Mr. Santori that I agreed Mr. Feldman's number was low, but I also reminded him he's not in a powerful position to negotiate right now. Once he calmed down, he recognized I was right. So here's what we can do. Mr. Santori is ready to agree to the deal in principle, but there are a few stipulations."

"We're listening."

"Mr. Santori wants all cash, all in hundred-dollar bills. The money is to be delivered Wednesday night at a private event Mr. Santori is hosting, and Mr. Santori wants Mr. Feldman to be the one who delivers it. The agreement will be formalized with a handshake between the two men. No handshake, no deal."

I looked at Feldman, who nodded his approval.

"Vince, Mr. Feldman accepts Mr. Santori's proposal."

Vince was silent for a full ten seconds. "Detective Blaze," he finally said, "I'll be in touch with the details and location for the drop-off."

"Does that mean we have a deal?" I asked.

"Yes, Detective Blaze. We have a deal."

Sarah Cutler appreciated the calm that came with her now-quiet day, although she was a little surprised just how quiet it was. She hadn't heard from Kent since he'd backed out of the TV appearance, and she realized it had been days since she'd heard from Solomon Feldman or Tony Santori. She tried reaching out to Annette but couldn't connect with her. Content with being alone, Sarah flipped through some old magazines while an old football game played on TV in the background.

A knock on the door disrupted the calm. It was her driver, Oscar, who said no one was at Skip's house. He said a courier had handed him a letter addressed to *Madam Mayor* as he returned to Sarah's building.

"Thanks, Oscar," Sarah said as she took the letter. "Why don't you take the rest of the day off? I'm not going anywhere."

Sarah waited for Oscar to leave before opening the envelope.

Dear Madam Mayor,

I've arranged with Detective Blaze to go into witness protection with the FBI in exchange for information about my corrupt past with the Chicago Police Department. I'm sure they'll want to know if Lance was involved, so you can assume your son will go down with me. Speaking of your son, I wonder if they'll ask if I know anything about his whereabouts or who might have any information about what happened to him. Think I'll mention your name? If the

FBI comes knocking on your door, you'll have the answer to that question.

I don't know where we'll be relocated, but I know we will be safe. The same can't be said for you, Sarah. That grief counselor was right. You truly are a conniving bitch, and someday soon, your shady dealings are going to bite you in the ass. I hope you are elected mayor just so your fall from grace will be even greater.

Time's running out, Madam Mayor. Time to do what's right.

Skip

Sarah balled up the letter and threw it across the room. She paced around her condo, frantically thinking through Skip's note and what its implications would be for her. Suddenly, she stopped.

"If Skip is in witness protection," she said, "then he can't deny anything I say."

Sarah walked over to the living room and stared out her condo window over the city she hoped to soon control. With no Skip, Sarah could control the narrative about Lance. She knew the longer the public wondered about Lance's fate, the more questions would arise. She had to bring closure to the question of what happened to her son.

Her mind raced as she spent the next hour brainstorming different scenarios. She settled on a story that she received a call from Lance's kidnappers, who confirmed her boy had been shot and killed. She would arrange for her campaign team to put out a press release and a quote from her about how her heart was broken and how devastated she was to lose her only son.

She'd then have her team schedule a memorial for Lance to publicly remember him and help her reemerge from the live broadcast embarrassment. She'd use the memorial as a way to rededicate her campaign to fighting for safety. Lance's death could wind up being what pushed her over the top in the minds of voters. Who would vote against a mother who'd just lost her only son? Even though she'd no longer be looking for Lance, she'd say she would always be sure she was *leading* for Lance.

She called her campaign manager to break the news and get the wheels of her plan in motion. The staffer started sobbing and asked how she could help. Sarah said she wanted the memorial on Wednesday—the sooner, the better.

"Do you want the morning or the afternoon?" the manager asked through tears.

"Let's do the afternoon," Sarah said, thinking an afternoon speech would certainly be the lead story on that evening's news.

"I'm truly sorry for your loss, Sarah. Lance was a good man."

"He was," Sarah said. "Now it's my job to make sure he's never forgotten."

Satisfied, she hung up with her campaign manager and called Kent.

"Sit down," she said somberly. "We need to talk."

"What's wrong?" her husband asked.

"It's Lance, dear. I just got a call confirming our worst fears. He's dead, Kent. Our boy is dead."

Kent was taken aback. He was one of the few people on earth who knew Lance was in fact alive—at least he *thought* Lance was still alive.

"How could that be?" he asked.

"Apparently, he was kidnapped and held captive by some radical group that didn't want to see me win the election. They thought his disappearance would force me to suspend my campaign. They spent the past five days torturing our boy, but when they heard what I said last night about continuing to run no matter what happened to Lance, they decided to test me. They shot him dead, Kent," she shouted hysterically, "and it's all because of me!"

Kent had talked to Lance two days earlier. There was no way what Sarah said was true, but he had to give her credit for her morbid storytelling. The question was why she was lying. What was she trying to gain? Rather than call her bluff, Kent decided to play along.

"No, it can't be. It just can't be," he cried. "Not our boy! Our baby boy!"

"I know, Kent, I know," Sarah said, pleased with how gullible her husband was. "Now you know why I have to run for mayor. I have to honor our son."

Kent sniffled as he pretended to regain his composure. "Yes, I understand. That's what our poor Lance would want you to do. If you backed down, you'd be called *soft* for the rest of your life."

Sarah was caught off guard. She thought Kent would have blamed her for Lance's death. *He must just be in too much shock right now.* "Thanks. Maybe you're right. But Kent, our son is gone."

"I know, and there will be a time to mourn. You can't beat yourself up, though. You need to stay strong. This city needs to see you be tough in your darkest hour. And I'll be right by your side whenever you need it."

Where is this side of Kent coming from? Sarah wondered. "Thanks, Kent. You have no idea how much that means to me. My campaign team is going to organize a special memorial for Wednesday. It would be great to have us unified and stand together as two mourning parents."

"Of course," Kent said. "Just send me the details. I'll see you Wednesday."

The two hung up with very different reactions. Sarah was stunned at Kent's kindness. Was this the same man who threatened to expose her for covering up the steam room murder less than a week before? Was this the man whom she desperately wanted a divorce from? Maybe this was the beginning of a new chapter for them, Sarah thought. Maybe lying to him was a good thing. Maybe they had a future together after all.

Kent hung up the phone and stared at it, imagining Sarah's face was looking back at him, and said the only three words that came to mind: "What a bitch."

Kent then called Lance to give him a heads-up about Sarah.

"Dad, I told you not to call unless it's an emergency," Lance answered.

"I think this qualifies. The news is going to break soon that you're dead."

"What? I'm not dead."

"I know that, but your mom doesn't, and she's up to something. She just called and told me this made-up tale about you being kidnapped and tortured and murdered because she wouldn't stop running for mayor."

"That woman is unbelievable."

"Don't I know it. Anyway, I played along because I don't want her to know the truth, but just be careful. There's going to be a lot of media talking about you tomorrow."

"Okay, thanks, Dad. I'll make sure to lay low. In the meantime, I'll relay what you told me to someone who I'm sure can figure out what Sarah is up to and how to get back at her."

"Who's that?"

"Detective Blaze."

23

We *have a problem.*

That was the text message that woke me up Tuesday at 5:15 a.m. The message was from Cliff and had no other context with it. Was one of our Boom members having cold feet about the operation? Had the bowling alley already blown up? The options were infinite. Before I could roll out of bed and write Cliff back, my phone buzzed again.

We have a situation.

That text came from Lance, again with no context. Which was more pressing, a problem or a situation? Just then, another text came in, this one from Eli.

We have an issue.

I sighed. *For the love of God, people, give me some more information. And why is everyone writing so early?* I crept into the bathroom, where I knew the FBI couldn't track my conversation. *So we've got a problem, a situation, and an issue.* I didn't know which was most important, so I went in reverse alphabetical order—that seemed just as good as any other option. Situation first, then problem, then issue.

"Hey, Blaze, congratulations," Lance said when I called. "You're talking to a dead man."

"Good morning to you, too, Lance. What do you mean?"

"Have you seen the news yet?"

"No, I just got up, thanks to you."

"Sorry about that. Anyway, listen to these headlines. *Missing Chicago cop confirmed dead. Lance Cutler murdered by kidnappers. Sarah Cutler heartbroken by death of her son.*"

"Lance, what is all that about?"

"It's about my mother being her typical self. Why she made up this story, I don't know, but I'm positive it was her."

"I don't doubt you, but how can you be sure?"

"My dad told me late last night. Sarah called and gave him this BS story about how she received word from my alleged kidnappers that they'd killed me because she wouldn't end her campaign."

"Wait, your dad knows you're alive?"

"Yeah, I called him a few days ago just to let him know. That's why he and Mayor Paulson backed out of that stupid broadcast you were on."

"You know, I wondered about that. They saw that Sarah was going to use them and the show to boost her campaign."

"Exactly. My guess is that's the same thing she's trying to do with this story now, but I was hoping you could help figure that out."

I didn't have time to take on another project, but how could I say no to a dead man? "Of course I'll help you. But first, what did your dad tell your mom when she said you were dead?"

"He played along. He wanted to find out her agenda and figured it'd be easier if he pretended he didn't know the truth."

"Your dad's a wise man, Lance. Listen, I've got to handle another problem and issue, but let me think on this one. We might be able to use Sarah's lies to our own advantage. Keep your head down, and I'll check back in later today."

"Thanks, Blaze. We can't let her run this city."

Situation handled, at least partially. Now on to the problem.

"Good morning, Cliff," I said as I called our Boom leader. "What's the problem?"

"Blaze, we need ears."

This is what he woke me up for? "What do you mean?"

"We need ears in the room. For Boom. We need to know when Santori gives his celebratory toast so we can have the bombs go off. It's not like Vince or Reggie can call us from the inside."

Cliff was right. With all the focus on the logistics of getting Feldman to Boom, I forgot to think about the logistics of making Boom go, well, boom. Granted, I would think the bomb experts would have been focused on that, but apparently they needed some assistance.

"Okay, so what kind of ears are you thinking?"

"We need some sort of electronic device that will allow us to listen in on the conversation," he said. "That way, when Santori gets ready for his toast, we'll be ready to detonate the explosives."

"Okay, so we need a bug. Some digital tool to let us monitor what's going on inside."

"Exactly."

Jerry, my electronics wiz, owed me a favor anyway. Here was a perfect way for him to cash that in.

"I'm on it, Cliff. I've got the perfect person who can help."

Problem solved. Now on to the issue.

"Hey, Blaze, I wasn't sure if you'd be awake already," Eli said as he answered the phone.

"It feels like I've already had a full day at the office. What's up?"

"Feldman's getting anxious about tomorrow and going to Santori's chosen site. He feels he's doing Santori a favor by agreeing to the deal and the least Santori can do is come to the deli to make it official. He's worried Santori is going to double-cross him."

"Ugh. Hasn't Feldman ever had to go anywhere else to secure a large deal before?"

"Not since I've been around him. He's always made everyone come to him. He doesn't like being told what to do or where to go. It makes him feel like he's not in control. When he's at the deli, he owns the place."

"I understand, but tell him it will be worth it. Say you were concerned, too, and called to find out more. Tell him Santori is hosting other Italian family leaders for a big dinner tomorrow and wants to show Feldman off to his fellow mafia patriarchs."

"Okay, that should work. Thanks, Blaze."

It wasn't even 6 a.m., and I'd already handled a situation, solved a problem, and fixed an issue. Whether or not it would be a good day was unclear, but one thing was certain: it was going to be busy.

Tony Santori woke up early, anxious for the next day's immaculate celebration. The attendees were coming from across the country to break bread and share their latest victories, but Tony couldn't give a damn about what everyone else accomplished since the last dinner ten years before. This dinner was going to be all about him. The last time the family leaders gathered, Tony hadn't even set foot in Chicago. Back then, his focus was following in his family's footsteps back East and maintaining the status quo. But Tony quickly grew up and realized he wasn't okay with the status quo. He wanted more, and he got it. The power and control he'd acquired in a relatively short amount of time in Chicago was a feat that should have been admired and celebrated. He would make sure of that.

Tony walked into his dressing room, a room he'd decorated with floor-to-ceiling mirrors on all four walls. He put on one of his favorite black suits and meticulously folded his pink handkerchief into his front coat pocket. He looked at himself from every angle, checking his slicked-back hair for any unkempt strands.

"I am a fucking model of perfection," he told himself. "And tomorrow night, everyone in that room will know it."

Tony wanted Wednesday's dinner to be a night no one in attendance would ever forget, and to do that, he needed everything to be perfect. He trusted Vince and his handling of the event, but he wanted additional eyes to make sure there were no surprises. His cousin Enzo was flying in late that night from New Jersey. Santori called and told him to man the bowling alley all day Wednesday to make sure nothing suspicious happened. With Enzo lined up, he called Vince to give him the heads-up.

"Good morning, boss," Vince answered. "Tomorrow's the big day."

"No shit," Santori responded. "Enzo is going to be at the bowling alley all day tomorrow just to make sure everything goes according to plan."

"Why do we need Enzo there? You don't trust me, boss?"

"I trust you, Vince; otherwise, I wouldn't have given you the fucking job in the first place. I've got a lot riding on tomorrow night and want to make sure everything is perfect. Enzo isn't there to look over your shoulder or take responsibilities from you. Think of him as an extra set of eyes. A living security camera, if you will."

A living security camera was the last thing Vince wanted to have around the bowling alley, but he knew it was useless to push back.

"Okay, boss. When's Enzo getting there?"

"He's getting into Chicago late tonight and heading straight to the alley. But don't worry about him, Vince. You just worry about yourself and your tasks. And speaking of tasks, why hasn't Detective Blaze found the steam room killer yet?"

"I don't know, boss. I'm sure he's close."

"I don't know, Vince," Santori said, his voice rising with anger. "Something's not feeling right about him. He better show up to our meeting with the killer; otherwise, that old man won't live past this afternoon."

Vince couldn't get Tony's description of Enzo out of his head: a living security camera. The always calm Vince drove to the bowling alley as soon as he'd heard from Santori, frantically wondering how the Boom team would get everything in place. The plan was to plant the explosives in the early-morning hours on Wednesday, but with Enzo scheduled to get to the bowling alley later that night, the Boom team had to call an audible. Vince called Cliff to break the news.

"What do you mean we have to get everything in place today?" Cliff responded. "We're not ready."

"You're going to have to be," Vince said. "Once Enzo is here, I can't cover for you guys. Everything in the building's got to be in place by sundown tonight."

"Vince, there are too many moving pieces here. We're still going through our arsenal of weapons, and we haven't figured out where Feldman is going to be or how to keep him and Santori from seeing each other. You're asking me to fly a plane while still building it."

"Cliff, I hear you, but we've got no choice. You, Dan Baum, and Stubs must get in today and do the best you can. I'm at the alley now, and it's quiet. The tables are being set up later today, and we're having linens delivered, but otherwise there shouldn't be many people coming and going. Get what you can and get over here fast. Take lots of notes on where you place everything, and we can go over it as a team tonight at the Boom meeting."

"I don't like this, Vince."

"I don't either, Cliff, but if we don't get things in place today, Boom will go down as a bust."

Marc, Wilt, Jeffrey, and Patrick operated like a well-oiled machine—identifying, contacting, and assembling victims to testify on camera about crimes committed by many of the scheduled attendees at Santori's Wednesday night bash. Wilt combed through Mel Weinberg's journal, while Patrick created an algorithm to quickly scour through Carter's confession and tag any names he'd mentioned. Patrick then compiled the names and contact information for Marc, who explained the project to the victims and tried to convince them to go on camera. Jeffrey stepped in wherever was needed and also offered the use of his garage for filming.

By ten o'clock Tuesday morning, there was a line of a dozen people standing in Jeffrey's driveway, waiting to tell their painful tale.

"Bring in the first one," Marc shouted.

In walked a short white man in work boots and jeans who was about forty. His face was rugged, and a few strands of blond hair crept out from under his black hood. He sat in the makeshift studio Patrick and Kelly had assembled.

"Good morning, sir," Patrick began as Kelly adjusted the lighting. "Please, go right ahead and tell us your story."

The man stared blankly at the camera for a few seconds. "Eight years ago, I was in a bad place," he began. "I was living in New Jersey at the time, and my wife and I were expecting our first child. Her pregnancy was awful. She was so sick, she had to stop working, which meant I had to take on a second job just to try to keep us afloat. Even with that extra income, it wasn't enough, and we fell behind on our mortgage and utilities. We needed fourteen thousand dollars, or else we would lose our house. My wife was bedridden, and there was no way I could get a third job and still function. That's when I heard about a special kind of lender. I spoke with a representative of this guy, who said he could make my debt disappear. The deal sounded too good to be true, but he sold me when he said the lender was in a family-owned business and understood the importance of protecting those you love. I had no other options. I said okay.

"When I got my paychecks the next week, I was stunned to see I got raises at both jobs. With that extra money, I began to think paying off our debt might actually be possible. But it wasn't," the man said as he fought back tears. "It was never going to be possible."

The man bent forward and began to cry as Patrick continued filming. "That night, I got a phone call asking if I liked my financial surprise. I said yes and asked how I could ever repay them. That's when I was told I now owed a man named Tony Santori forty-five thousand dollars by the next week. I said there was no way I could find that kind of money in time, and they said they'd burn my house down and take the insurance money instead. I tried to reason with the man. I even offered to sell the house and give him the forty-five thousand then, but that would obviously take time. That's when I heard the seven words that still haunt me to this day: 'Tony Santori is not a patient man.'"

The man took the collar of his sweatshirt and wiped his eyes and nose. "I went to work the next day and had no idea what to do. Midway through my shift, I got a call from a neighbor telling me to come home right away. There were sirens in the background. I asked what was going on, and he just told me to come quickly.

"When I got there, I saw my house awash in flames. I cried out for my wife, but the paramedics told me they couldn't rescue her in time. My house was gone; my wife; my unborn child; even my dog, Sparky, all gone in minutes."

Sobbing, he stood up and walked away from the camera. "I'm sorry. I can't do this."

Wilt consoled the man and led him out of the garage. Marc felt bad about bringing up such an ugly memory, but this was the job he'd signed up for, and time was of the essence.

"Next," Marc called.

"Hi, everyone, my name is Barbara," a woman in a pink puffy winter coat said as she sat down.

Barbara's body said she was in her late twenties, but the wear on her face made her look twice as old.

"I used to go by Babs, but I gave up that name seven years ago when my twin sister, Nancy, went missing."

Barbara pulled a pack of tissues out of her pocket.

"Nancy always was the smarter of the two of us. She wanted to become a nurse and was fascinated with the medical world. I used to joke that she was a doctor junkie—little did I know how true that would end up being. Anyway, she was in her first year of junior college when she met a foreign guy training to be a doctor. One fall day, Nancy disappeared. So did the wannabe doctor.

"I'll make a long story short. The guy was a front man in a prostitution ring. My sister was drugged and raped, then sold as a whore on the black market. That went on for weeks—really months, I guess. We never heard from her until a random Tuesday about two months after she went missing. She called my cell phone, and when I answered, I barely recognized her voice. This was my twin, and yet even I had to ask who she was. Her voice was raspy with no energy behind it. She was broken and barely coherent. The only two words I could clearly understand were her last ones: *Solomon Feldman*.

"We received notice a few days later that Nancy was dead. Her body was shipped back to us, and an autopsy was performed. It was determined she died of a drug overdose—this was a woman who'd never touched an illegal substance once before being kidnapped. She didn't even drink alcohol. We received condolences from hundreds of people. We even got a form letter from the president of the United States.

"But we didn't want letters; we wanted retribution. We wanted Solomon Feldman to pay for what he did to Nancy. But as soon as we mentioned his name to the police, the officers literally backed away from us. 'Sorry, ma'am,' they said to me and my family. 'Feldman is big trouble, but we can't touch him. Besides, we've got nothing on him.'

"That was it. They wouldn't look into him anymore or even take our calls. For a while, I was angry at the police, but then I realized my anger should really be directed toward Feldman. And that's why I'm here. I've been told there's a chance Feldman could go up in flames. All I can say is I hope he does, and I hope he rots in hell. Find that son of a bitch and slaughter him. Do it for me and do it for Nancy."

"Thank you, Barbara, for being so forthcoming," Marc said. "Next."

The next person to sit down was a six-foot-tall Black man with broad shoulders and a single gold stud in his left ear. Four years ago, Perry Berkshire was a rookie quarterback for the Chicago Bears and started the season with eight straight wins. He threw for twenty-one touchdowns and no interceptions, and he ran for another seven scores. He had the city thinking about the Super Bowl when all of a sudden, he vanished. No one knew where, and no one knew why. There were rumors he had a drug problem or that he got the daughter of a famous politician pregnant, but the story the public agreed on was he got a case of the yips, and the pressure of being quarterback in such a big market was too much to handle. Word was he had a nervous breakdown and disappeared to Wyoming to live in the woods.

"Mr. Berkshire," Jeffrey said, coming over to the camera, "it's an honor to have you here. I was at your second career start. You made the other team's defense look silly. What'd you throw for that game, three hundred and twenty-five yards?"

"Yes, sir. Scored two TDs with my feet too," he said with a small grin. "That's not what I'm here to talk about, though."

"Of course. Please, Mr. Berkshire, go right ahead."

"My name is Perry Berkshire," he said as he looked right at the camera, "and I'm here to tell my story. My *real* story. I've heard talk that I became some woodsman or ran off with the governor's daughter. None of those are true. The truth is I never wanted to leave in the first place. I still remember it like it was yesterday."

Perry looked off past the camera as if he were watching his past play out before him.

"I was at a community-service event, helping paint the outside of a local school building. We'd just won our fifth game of the season, and everyone was getting excited about how we were doing. Anyway, I finished at the school and was getting into my car when I felt a tap on my shoulder. Now, I'm a large man, but the dude I saw when I turned around made me feel tiny. He had at least three inches and easily one hundred pounds on me and clearly was a man I did not want to make angry. He said he worked for Tony Santori and that Santori was proud of how well we were doing as a team. I thanked him and asked if Tony wanted an autograph or something. The man said no. What Tony wanted was for us to stop winning by so much. The point spreads were getting wider by the game, and it was apparently getting harder for him to make money off of us.

"I told the man I couldn't shave points to help a gambler, but he made it clear I should reconsider my stance. I said I'd think about it, and we went our separate ways. Fast forward to that weekend, and we were playing Kansas City. We were favored by twenty points and up by eighteen with two minutes to go in the game. We were driving down the field and getting close to field-goal range. It was third down, and we needed two more yards to make our kicker feel comfortable. I snapped the ball and saw an opening to run through. I probably could have gotten the yardage, but instead, I held on and took a sack, the first one I'd suffered all season. We ended up punting, and the clock ran out during Kansas City's next drive. Everyone was happy we'd won our sixth straight game, including me, but in the back of my mind, I wondered if I took that sack for Santori.

"I talked to my dad about what happened, and he suggested I go to the police. I took his advice and was greeted at the local station by an officer, Frank Skepper, who clearly was more interested in my autograph than my story. He didn't seem worried about what happened. In fact, he personally thanked me after saying he and some guys on the force won fifteen thousand dollars thanks to me.

"I hoped the whole thing would go away, and for the next two weeks, it was quiet. Then the Wednesday after we won our eighth game, I got an anonymous text that said we were favored by thirteen points in our next game and that I better be sure we didn't win by more than twelve. I wrote back and said I couldn't do that. Five minutes later, I received another text, reminding me I didn't want to get on Tony Santori's bad side. Two minutes after that, another text came through, this time with a picture of my girlfriend and a warning: *You wouldn't want anything bad to happen to her, would you?*

"Seeing that picture of my girl rattled me. I pretended to be sick that weekend and sat out the game. We won by seventeen, but I figured I was safe. After all, I didn't play. How could I be held accountable? But I was wrong. The next night, two men broke into my home. One guy was built like a linebacker and held a gun to my girlfriend's head. The other guy was short and fat and clearly took orders from the linebacker. The second guy pointed a gun and told me to sit at my dining room table and do exactly as he said. He turned to the linebacker and said, 'Carter, you sure this is what you want?' Carter responded by saying, 'This is what Tony Santori wants, and no one questions Tony Santori.'

"That bastard Carter brought my girl over to the table to get a front-row view for what was to come. The short guy told me to put my hands flat on the table and not move, or my girl was dead. As soon as I did, he pulled a hammer out of his pocket and went to work on my thumbs.

"I never touched a football again," Perry said as he held his hands up to the camera to show the gruesome result of his assault. "He crippled my thumbs. He crippled my life. He crippled my future."

In Vince's haste to figure out how to get the explosives in place, he completely forgot about the other news Santori had given him. Santori said Blaze was a dead man unless he showed up with Mel Weinberg's killer at their afternoon meeting. Vince didn't know if Blaze knew the culprit, but he knew the detective should at least be warned.

He pulled out his phone and sent a four-word text message—four words meant to get Blaze's attention and give him a heads-up that his life could be in danger. It was the fourth four-word message like that sent to Blaze that morning, but without question, this one was the most serious:

We have an emergency.

24

Tony Santori's excitement over Wednesday's celebration dissipated as he thought more about Detective Blaze. With Santori planning on leaving the country in thirty-six hours, he needed to know who killed the bastard in the steam room. He'd hired Blaze to find the killer, and the old man hadn't delivered. He thought back on their interactions and realized the detective never gave any indication he was making progress on the case. All Blaze ever said was he was getting close and he'd have information to share soon. The two were supposed to meet that afternoon, but Tony couldn't wait anymore.

"That two-timing fucker," Santori roared as he slammed his fist on his desk. "I bet he hasn't even been working on finding the killer. I bet he took Tony's money and thought he could just keep blowing Tony off. Well, he's got another thing coming. No one takes advantage of Tony Santori and lives to talk about it."

Santori got up and furiously walked to the door. "Jermaine, get the fuck in here," he shouted. Santori was pacing when Jermaine walked in. "That fucking detective double-crossed me," Santori roared.

"Who? Blaze? I like that old guy," Jermaine said with a smile. "You know, he and I were talking about basketball—"

"I don't give a flying fuck what you and him were talking about, Jermaine. Now shut up and listen."

Jermaine's smile disappeared as his gaze dropped to the floor.

"That fucker took Tony's money and hasn't done what Tony paid for. If he thinks he can get away, he's got another thing coming."

"What do you mean, boss?" Jermaine asked, still staring at the ground.

"I mean that when he comes here this afternoon, I'm going to kill him."

"Boss, don't you think that's a little extreme?"

Santori looked curiously at Jermaine, then paced again. "You're right," he said. "If the FBI is already on to me, I probably should keep my nose clean. You, on the other hand . . ."

"Me what?"

"You could kill him for me."

"Wait, what?"

"Of course. If you kill Blaze, he'll pay the price for lying to me."

"But what about me?"

"Dammit, Jermaine, when did you get so soft? I'm trying to tie up my loose ends before getting out of town. If it's that big of a deal, I'll give you some of the cash I was going to give Blaze. Will that shut you up?"

"But I thought—"

"See, that's what I mean. I don't have you here to think. I have you here to be my muscle. Is that understood?"

Jermaine didn't answer. Santori, aghast, walked right up to Jermaine, so close his nose was nearly pressed against Jermaine's chin.

"I said, is that understood?"

Jermaine looked down at his boss. "Yes, sir."

"Good." Santori walked back toward his desk. "Now, all this talk about thinking made me realize there's one other loose end that needs to be tied up. I can't leave the country and risk anyone revealing any of my darkest secrets. I know you and the boys would never think of talking to the feds, but there's one other person I'm not sure I can trust."

"Who's that?"

"Betty."

"Betty?"

"Did I stutter? Yes, Betty. As CEO here at the club, she knows everything about how my operation was built and functions. Let's bring her up and confirm her loyalty. I need to know she won't talk once I'm gone."

Sarah Cutler could not remember the last time she'd spent two consecutive days out of the spotlight. Other than a morning call with leaders of her campaign team, Sarah's day was spent by herself. One of her speechwriters was crafting a eulogy for Lance that Sarah would read at Wednesday's memorial, while Sarah herself was putting together planned remarks for the media that would follow the service. Most mothers would have probably preferred to focus on the speech about their lost son than on campaign promises, but Sarah had already proven she was not like most mothers. She was interrupted by her campaign manager, who said the media were getting anxious and wanted a new statement from Candidate Cutler.

"Tell them to let me mourn in peace," she said. "Everything they need to know will be revealed tomorrow after the memorial."

Betty knew what kind of monster Tony Santori was, but she'd looked the other way for years. Ever since she learned that Santori was to blame for the senseless murder of Henry Jackson last week, though, she'd wondered if she'd let him go too far. Henry was more than a friend to Betty—he was like family. She had no idea why he had to die, but all she could think about was his two children and how they'd never see their father again. She remembered how hard it was when her dad went to prison—all the birthday parties he missed, the family dinners that never felt complete. Those kids would never see their father again, and it was because of Tony Santori, but Betty felt that indirectly it was because of her. Since then, she'd tried to avoid Santori at all costs, but he'd just requested her presence, and when he called, you came.

Betty walked up the hidden stairs of the WCC and realized something was wrong. The place was almost deserted, which was unusual for this back hallway. Secondly, Jermaine, who was standing outside Tony Santori's door, was clearly distracted. Usually he'd jokingly hit on her with some goofy pickup line like "Hey, babe, your dad must be a boxer because you are a knockout." Today, though, he didn't even lock eyes with her. She patted him on the arm.

"What's up, sugar?" she said to Jermaine.

Jermaine looked away. "Boss wants to see you."

"Jermaine, what's going on?"

Before he could answer, Santori opened the door. "My dear Betty, come in, come in," he said joyfully.

Joyful was not a word Betty would have ever used to describe Tony Santori, and she knew him better than most.

"Hi, Tony," she said as she entered his office. "What has you all smiles today?"

"Is it that obvious I'm in a good mood?" he said with an even bigger grin. "Jermaine, come join us and please close the door behind you."

Betty turned and watched Jermaine enter the room, close the door, then stand against it, his eyes never leaving the floor.

"Come, join me," Tony said, sitting down on his couch. "Betty, my dear, how long have we known each other?"

"Too long, Tony, too long," she said with a nervous grin.

"Ha, that's true. It does seem like we're all getting older, yet you still look so young and beautiful. I bet you could run this place for decades if you wanted to. As for me, I know that I'm getting up there in age, and I've decided to retire."

"Good for you," she said. "What made you decide now's the right time?"

"You know," Tony said as he looked around his office, "you get to a certain point in your life when you just have a feeling. I don't know how to explain it. It just feels like now is the right time."

"I'm really happy for you, Tony," she said, realizing she might soon be free of him. "What are you going to do?"

"I'm still planning that out, but I'm leaving town tomorrow. Speaking of retirement, I wanted to ask what you knew about Detective Blaze."

"You mean David? He's been a member of the WCC for years. He's a character, particularly with this whole Blaze act. But I consider him a dear friend. We've gone out for lunch dozens of times over the years. Why do you ask? Does it have to do with his incessant snooping?"

"Well, Betty, the reason I asked is I wanted to know how heartbroken you'd be when he dies."

"David die? I don't think I've ever seen a seventy-year-old in better shape than him. He's got lots of years ahead of him."

"No, he's going to die, and it's going to be in the next couple of hours."

"What?" Betty jumped to her feet. "Why is David going to die?"

"Because David took fifty thousand dollars from Tony Santori and is trying to play Tony for a fool. Now, please, sit back down."

Betty couldn't think straight as she sank to the couch. She couldn't stand by and watch Tony murder another one of her friends. But what could she do?

"Tony," she finally said, "I can't let you kill David."

"You can't let me?" Santori laughed, standing just so he could stare down at Betty. "Let me remind you who actually runs this club. This is my house," he yelled, "and I decide what happens!"

He grabbed Betty by the collar and flung her to the floor. He stormed over to her quivering body and kneeled over her.

"I'm deciding that Detective Blaze is going to die, and you're going to watch it." Santori leaned down closer so that his mouth was inches from Betty's ear. "And I'll let you in on a little secret," he whispered. "After I kill that son of a bitch, I'm going to kill you."

Santori got up and began to walk away.

"Now you wait just a minute," Betty said as she got up off the floor, her voice rising in partial anger and partial fear. "I've been loyal to you and your family for years. I lost count a long time ago of the illegal things I've watched you do, and never have I said a thing."

"And Tony appreciates that, Betty," Santori said, motioning for Jermaine to come toward them. "But with me retiring, I can't risk you becoming a traitor. That attendant who got himself killed in the Wacker Drive explosion, he was a traitor. Blaze is a traitor too. Tony can't stand traitors."

"You don't trust me, Tony?"

"I don't trust anybody. It's nothing personal. Now, Jermaine will take you away so you can wait for your boyfriend to arrive."

"You sick son of a bitch," Betty yelled as she charged at Santori, fists clenched ready to hit him.

Before she took two steps, Jermaine's arm was wrapped around her neck. She flailed, trying to get out of his chokehold, but his grip was too tight. Soon, she was unconscious, falling limp against Jermaine's large body.

"Take her across the hall. And you know what, Jermaine? Fuck waiting for Blaze. Go find him and kill him. Then come back and deal with Betty. Do you understand?"

"Yes, boss."

"And, Jermaine?"

"Yeah?"

"Make sure no one can find their bodies."

"Yes, boss."

I was on my way to the West Coast Club to meet with Santori when I got a call from Patrick, who was raving about the interviews he'd recorded so far.

"Blaze, these are some powerful testimonials we're getting here," he said before even saying hello.

"Yeah? Tell me about them."

"Boss, I don't think I could do them justice. This production of ours will surely justify getting rid of these awful men. Kelly said she couldn't imagine so much evil could exist in the world and is definitely on board with helping in any way she can."

"So how are we going to get this in front of everyone?"

"I thought you wanted to be surprised. Just know anyone in the world in front of a screen tomorrow night will witness this broadcast and hear these gut-wrenching stories."

He spent the next fifteen minutes telling me who cried, whose stories were the most compelling, and how it was going to be hard to narrow down what makes the final production. He got me thinking about how powerful it is to hear someone's story from their own mouth, which gave me an idea.

"Patrick, I gotta run. Keep up the great work."

I hung up before he could say anything and called Lance Cutler. I told him about our video project and the role I was hoping he'd play.

"Blaze, I'll do whatever you need," he said.

"That's great, Lance," I said as I pulled into the WCC parking lot. "Don't forget to tell your dad."

A call from an unrecognizable number caught my attention, and I told Lance I had to get going.

"Hello?" I said to the mysterious number.

"Detective Blaze," a frantic voice said, "did you just pull into the West Coast Club parking lot?"

"Perhaps. Who wants to know?"

"It's me, Bryan."

"Bryan?"

"You know, the WCC manager. I slept at your house a few nights ago on my birthday."

"Oh, Bryan! Hey, how are you doing? How did you know I'm at the club?"

"I'm watching you on camera fifty-six. I was about to call you anyway, and then I saw you pull up. Something's wrong. I don't think it's safe here. You need to leave."

"But Bryan, I have a meeting scheduled with Tony Santori."

"Then definitely don't come in. I think Santori's up to something. Go find somewhere safe, then call me back, but go now before it's too late."

I took a quick look at my phone to see if there was any clue about what Bryan was talking about. That was when I saw Vince's warning: *We have an emergency.* Convinced something was up, I sped out of the lot before Santori's men could spot me.

I pulled into a parking lot beside an abandoned office building a few blocks away and called Bryan back.

"Are you somewhere safe?" he asked.

"I hope so. What's going on?"

"Detective Blaze, it's Betty. Something's happened to her."

"What do you mean?"

"She and I were supposed to meet at 12:30 p.m., and she is a stickler for promptness. It's now 2 p.m. and still no word from her. No email, no text, no nothing."

"Bryan, you made me bail on my meeting with Santori for this? I'm sure there's a logical explanation."

"That's what I thought, but then I went back and looked at our security cameras. Nobody knows this, but camera twenty-seven gets a glimpse at some hidden stairs that lead to Mr. Santori's private office space."

Little did Bryan know I was well acquainted with camera twenty-seven. "Okay. So what?"

"I saw Betty walk down the back hallway at 1:05 p.m. and go up those stairs, but she never came back. I think she's in danger."

"Okay, Bryan, you did the right thing in letting me know. Let me make a couple of calls. Sit tight."

I hung up with him and immediately called Vince. No response. I texted him, asking what the emergency was, but again, I heard nothing back. My concern for Betty was growing by the second. Yes, we had our differences in opinion over my recent presence at the WCC, but she was a friend, and she helped protect me. I owed her. If she was in trouble, I had to save her. With Vince unresponsive, I called Cliff Stanley.

"Cliff, do you know where Vince is? There's an emergency."

"You're telling me. Dan Baum and Stubs were not too happy to hear about it."

"Hear about what?"

"The emergency."

"If Baum and Stubs were upset, I don't think we're talking about the same emergency."

"Vince called me this morning and said we had to get all

the bombs in place today. Santori's got one of his goons flying in from New Jersey and staying at the bowling alley tonight, which means we can't put the explosives in place tomorrow like we originally planned. Why? What emergency were you talking about?"

"I think Betty, the CEO of the West Coast Club, was taken hostage by Santori. We need to save her."

"No, we can't mess up any more of our plans. We're already scrambling as it is, and we can't let Santori realize we're coming. We need to let this pass, Blaze. Boom needs you to stay away."

"But Cliff, she might die."

"And that will be sad, but there are casualties in war, Blaze. She'll die for the greater good."

"But she doesn't have to, Cliff. We just need to—"

"Blaze, I've got too much on my plate right now as it is. Santori will meet his maker tomorrow. Think of it as redemption for him taking Becky."

"It's Betty, Cliff. Betty."

"Whoever. I'm sorry, Blaze, but we've got to keep our eyes on the bigger picture. I'll see you and Mary tonight."

Cliff hung up. I understood why he'd said what he said, but I couldn't sit back and just let Betty die. I had to do something. Before I could think of anything, I got a text message from an unknown number: *We need to talk. Meet me at Truman Boxing Gym in 20 minutes. Two lives depend on it, including yours.*

Who is this? I wrote back.

I'm the person who's supposed to kill you. Stop asking questions and get moving.

Not wanting to upset this mystery person, I hightailed it over to Truman Boxing Gym. On the way, I called Mary to update her on Betty, Santori, and this new meeting of mine.

"Blaze, what are you thinking? You can't go meet your murderer!"

"What other choice do I have?"

"Not go," Mary screamed. "They're going to kill you!"

"If they wanted to kill me, why would they say we need to talk? Don't worry. I'm sure everything will be fine. I'll go and then meet you at the Boom house across from the bowling alley for tonight's meeting."

"That's assuming you're alive for the Boom meeting."

"Right, let's go with that assumption. I love you, Mary."

"I love you too, David. Please come back to me alive."

Walking into the boxing gym was like walking back in time. There were three rings, a handful of punching bags, and a bunch of free weights, but what gave it the nostalgic touch were the hundreds of black-and-white photos and promotional posters adorning the gym's walls. There weren't any pictures of recent fighters—these walls were saved for the legends, guys like Jack Johnson and Jack Dempsey, Joe Louis and Sugar Ray Robinson. The far wall had a tribute to Muhammad Ali filled with snapshots of his younger days, back when he was so fast he could turn off a light switch and be in bed before the room went dark. I always liked Ali's confidence. I tried to channel a small bit of it as I prepared to go face to face with my apparent killer.

A couple dozen guys filled the gym. There were sparring matches going on in two of the rings, and most people were focused on those. It was alongside the far ring where I saw who I was there for. The man who was supposed to kill me leaned against the ring, staring at the wall in front of him.

"Jermaine," I shouted in exaggerated delight. "What's up, big man? How you been?" I tried giving him a fist bump, but he left me hanging. Clearly, he was troubled. "You looking at Ali's pictures? Man, could that kid fight."

"Amen. What I'd give to have seen him in the ring."

"It was magic."

Jermaine turned and looked at me. "You saw him fight?"

"Never in person, but I watched all his big fights on TV—the

Thrilla in Manilla, the Rumble in the Jungle. Watching him box was like watching Superman fly out of a phone booth. You just had to root for him."

"That's crazy. You know, Blaze, you're something else. In another life, you and I could have been brothers, between your love of basketball and your respect for Ali. Who knows what else we have in common?"

"Why do we need another life for that to happen?"

"Well, Blaze," he said, looking down, "like I said in my text, I'm supposed to kill you. But between you and me, I don't want to."

"That's another thing we have in common. I don't want you to kill me either. Now what's this about a second life being at risk?"

"Well, after I kill you, I'm supposed to go back to the WCC and kill Betty too."

"Why?"

"Because Tony wants me to."

I paused to think through the situation. "What about what you want, Jermaine?"

"What do you mean?"

"It seems like Tony thinks you're some brainless thug, but I'm sure you have your own thoughts, don't you? What is it that you want to do?"

"I know I don't want to spend the rest of my life in prison."

"That's a good start," I said, recognizing I might be able to get Jermaine to turn on his boss. "But what do you want? What do you want to be?"

He paused to think. "I want to show the world I can make decisions for myself. I want to be someone who makes a difference. I want to be a winner like Maxie."

"Who's Maxie?"

"Maxie Dougan. He was my hero in and out of the boxing ring."

"I've never heard of him."

"He never made it far as a boxer, but what I loved was he always viewed himself as a winner, even if he got knocked out or lost. His attitude was that if he showed up and gave his all, then he was a winner."

"Sounds like a smart man."

"He was. Still is. I ran into him a couple of years ago; he's CEO of some big corporation. He's apparently giving with his time and his money, and he said we should reconnect some time if I ever wanted to do winning work. As we split, he pulled a silver dollar out of his pocket and flipped it to me. I asked him what it was for, and he looked me in the eye and said, 'Remember, Jermaine, you can always be a winner.'"

Jermaine pulled the coin out of an inside jacket pocket and showed it to me.

"Looks like a normal silver dollar," I said in confusion.

"Flip it over," he said.

I did and discovered it was a two-headed coin.

"See what I mean?" Jermaine said. "If you want, you can always be a winner. You just have to know how to control the game. That's what I want, Blaze. I want to be a winner."

"Jermaine, I'm so glad to hear that. Because if you don't kill me, I can help you make a difference. I can help make you the winner you want to be. The trick is you're going to have to do something Santori doesn't like."

"Besides not killing you?"

"Yeah, and it has to do with his extravaganza tomorrow night."

"What is it?"

"Jermaine, can I trust you?"

He looked around to make sure no one was eavesdropping on our conversation.

"Yeah, Blaze, you can trust me."

"Well, tomorrow night while your boss is toasting his own

good fortunes, Solomon Feldman and his Deli Boys are going to make a surprise appearance at the bowling alley."

"Blaze, are you crazy? I'll have to kill them on sight."

"Just hear me out. I'll take care of Feldman. I just need you to get him and his Boys in the building."

"What if somebody sees me with them?"

"As Santori's head of security, no one will question your motives. Just say it's a going-away surprise for your boss. All I need from you is to usher them into a private room and make sure Santori doesn't know they're there."

"Blaze, that doesn't make any sense."

"Do you trust me?"

"I don't know. You're asking me to go behind Tony's back."

"The alternative is you kill me now, which, personally, I'm not a fan of."

Jermaine stayed quiet. "What will I need to do after that?" he finally asked.

"Nothing. Just make sure they don't get out of the room. Then go about whatever you were supposed to be doing."

"I'm supposed to be outside with the hired security making sure no one gets into the building."

"Hired security?"

"Yeah, whenever there's a big gathering like this, we have our own security, but we also hire out a third-party organization for added manpower."

"Interesting. Anyway, that's it. All you need to do is keep Feldman where he is."

"And what do I tell the boss about you and Betty?"

"Say you searched me out and put two bullets in my head. Then say you went back and got Betty, took her out to the lake, shot her, and tossed us both in the water."

"I guess that could work. But what should I actually do with Betty?"

"That's a good question. When does Santori leave his office for the night?"

"Probably in a couple hours."

I thought through our options. "Okay, this just might work. Wait until he's gone, then quietly sneak her out of the club. Take her home and tell her not to turn on any lights and to stay there until she hears from me."

Jermaine was quiet as he thought through the plan.

"You know, Blaze, that sounds so crazy that it just might work."

"You'd be surprised how many times I hear that. So are you on board? This means looking Santori in the eye and lying to him. Can you do that?"

Jermaine shimmied his shoulders as he stood up straight.

"I can do that, Blaze."

"And you're not going to kill me?"

Jermaine laughed a deep, hearty laugh. "No, Blaze, I'm not going to kill you. I like you too much. You know, after the boss leaves the country, I'll be looking for work. Think you'd maybe have an opening on Team Blaze for me?"

"That's a thought for another day. For now, though, let's keep our arrangement secret. I'll text you a code message to let you know when Feldman is about to arrive."

"What will the message say?"

I looked for inspiration at the wall where Jermaine was fixated. After a few seconds, the perfect codewords came to me.

"Float like a butterfly," I said. "That will be the message."

Jermaine nodded and gave me a quick fist bump. "I get it, Blaze, just like Ali. Float like a butterfly—"

"That's right," I said, "and sting like a bee."

25

I saw Mary standing outside the Boom house across from the abandoned bowling alley and watched her let out a sigh of relief.

"I've been standing here for twenty minutes wondering if I'd ever see you again," she said.

"Relax," I said with a grin. "I told you there was nothing to fear. Now come on, we've got a Boom meeting to get to and a lot of plans to talk through."

We walked inside and were immediately struck by the silence. A card table was in what could have been the house's living room, and around the table sat Eli, Reggie from the FBI, Dan Baum, and Stubs, each lost in his own thoughts, mentally preparing for the task before them. Vince and Cliff were whispering in the kitchen when they saw us walk in.

"Blaze, Mary, good to see you both," Cliff said as he smiled and shook our hands. "Come, join the rest of the group and let's get this final Boom meeting started."

We took our seats around the table. I tried to greet Stubs and Dan, who were both to my right, but they were still staring off in the distance. I turned to follow their focus, and that was when I saw the single sheet of paper taped to the wall. I suddenly understood why everyone was silent. Written in dull black ink but in big, capital letters were the words *our last night*. The simplicity was powerful. True, this was our last night meeting together, but this was also our last night living the lives we were used to. Boom would change everything. Today, we were strategists with a plan. Tomorrow, we would hopefully be deliverers of justice. Today, we were citizens. Tomorrow, we would be vigilantes.

"Good evening, everyone," Cliff said to the still-silent group. "I see you're already deep in thought. That's good. We have a tall task before us. This mission is risky, and it will be dangerous. If you're not scared, you're not human. Now, before we get into specifics, there are a couple of things I want to say."

He reached into his pants pocket to pull out a notecard with scribbles on both sides.

"Oh, for the love of God," Stubs said, "did you write a speech?"

Vince and Dan Baum both snickered as the rest of the group came out of its collective trance.

"Shut up, Stubs, just let me get through this," Cliff said, clearing his throat. "Tonight we are gathered on the precipice of history. At this time tomorrow, we will be mere moments from orchestrating one of the greatest acts of human fortitude that will bring closure to many and questions to many others. Each of you has brought a certain skill set and talent to the team, and without any one of you, we would be unable to perform the covert actions we've agreed to undertake. This idea of blowing up a room full of bad guys came together in a matter of days, but I believe each of us has waited our whole lives for this opportunity, whether we knew it or not. I believe we were destined to come together for this purpose, and let me say I am damn proud to be your leader and on this journey with you."

Cliff turned his notecard over.

"Tomorrow, we will write our names in the history books. We should go down as the Brave Boomsters who chose good over evil. Tomorrow night, Tony Santori will die. Solomon Feldman will die. The leaders of the Torralini family will die. Andy Wong,

Lorenzo Rossi, Angelo Romano, and Dino Maramona will all perish. By taking their lives, we are giving life to thousands of others. When people go to sleep tomorrow night, they will rest easier because the world will be a safer place, and that will be because of you."

Cliff looked up from his notes. "Know that to me," he said, choking up, "you are all heroes." He cleared his throat and raised his voice. "And remember, nothing will stand in the way of our destiny."

He put his notecard away and looked to his audience, waiting for some sort of acknowledgment. The silence was deafening. I guessed Cliff used notes so his own nerves and uneasiness about our plan didn't show. It was the eve of destruction, and I thought all of us were at least a bit terrified of what we'd committed to. Cliff realized the applause he was waiting for wasn't coming, so he moved on.

"Now, on to logistics," he said. "I believe everyone here is aware our timeline for planting the explosives was rushed, but thanks to Stubs and Dan Baum, we got everything in place. Guys, why don't you come up and tell us about what you were able to do?"

Cliff pulled over a rolling whiteboard with a blueprint of the bowling alley and a few dozen red circles drawn on it.

"Let's talk explosives," Stubs said as he rolled over to the whiteboard. "With the expedited timeline, Dan and I grabbed whatever we could find at Cliff's barn, and we were able to plant twenty-eight explosives throughout the bowling alley, which you can see on the blueprint here marked with red circles. Many of them are located in this private dining room off of the main banquet hall, where Tony Santori and the other family leaders will be breaking bread."

"And taking their last breaths," Cliff interjected.

"That's the plan," Stubs said. "We have fifteen explosives scattered around the room, meaning anyone in the room when they go off will be blown to smithereens. We had to get a little creative with the placement of the bombs, but they are all now securely hidden in different potted plants as well as in the centerpieces placed along the table where the group will be eating. We also have seven bombs dispersed throughout the banquet hall and three bombs on each of the two sets of stairways leading from the hall."

"Stubs, I have a question," I said, raising my hand. "What about Feldman? He and Santori can't see each other, so where will he be?"

"Oh, thanks for the reminder, Blaze," Stubs said. "We drew on this map before we went back to deal with the explosives for him. Dan, will you come add those on the blueprint for me?"

Stubs handed a red marker to Dan Baum, who began drawing circles over a small room on the opposite side of the building.

"Feldman and his Deli Boys will be sequestered in this room across from the bowling lanes," Stubs said.

"It used to be the arcade back when the bowling alley was actually functioning," Vince declared. "There's still a pool table in there."

"There won't be when we're done with it," Stubs said. "We planted two explosives underneath that table, and there are four others in position around the room."

"Speaking of Feldman, I have a question for Blaze," Vince said. "How are we going to get Feldman in the building?"

"We're not," I said. "Jermaine is."

"Who's Jermaine?" Reggie asked.

"He's Santori's top security man," I explained. "If you saw him, you might think he was a human wrecking ball, but I've come to know him as a gentle giant."

"Gentle giant?" Vince said. "You sure we're talking about the same Jermaine? And why the hell would he let Feldman in?"

"Who cares why," Cliff interrupted. "The point is it gets Feldman in the building."

"Exactly," I said. "Now, Stubs, just to confirm, with the added bombs for Feldman, we have thirty-four explosives altogether, correct?"

"That's right," Stubs said. "As extra precaution, we also brought in a few barrels of gasoline strategically positioned around the building, just to add some extra flames to the blast."

"The barrels fit with the rustic theme I told Tony I was going with for the event," Vince added.

"Right. Anyway," Stubs continued, "we also installed a listening device in the private dining room that will allow someone stationed here in this house to listen to what Santori and his guests are saying. That way, we'll know when it's time to get our party started."

"That's right," Vince said. "Tony will invite everyone in the dining room to be seated and then deliver a speech about how great he is. It shouldn't be more than fifteen minutes. Once he's done, he'll invite everyone to raise their glasses in a toast, and when those glasses go up, Boom goes down."

"Boom, boom, bang, bang!" Cliff shouted, trying to build up the energy in the room.

Eli raised his hand. "When you say, 'Boom goes down,' how will it actually happen? What will set the explosives off?"

"I can take that," Dan Baum said. "As a self-proclaimed wizard with explosives, I was able to connect the bombs wirelessly to one system. I've known from the start that would be how we'd arrange for the explosions, but what I didn't know was what the trigger would be. Fortunately, as we rummaged through Cliff's collection, we stumbled upon this beauty."

He walked over to the hall closet and pulled out an old blasting machine with a T-handle to push down.

"Just like what Wile E. Coyote used to try to catch the Road

Runner in Looney Tunes," Dan continued as he struggled to carry the device over to the group. "Now you can look but don't touch. Once we push this handle down, it sends a signal to the whole system, and those bombs will light up the night sky."

"That's what I'm talking about," Cliff cheered as we all stared at the rusty, ancient-looking contraption.

"And you're sure it works?" Eli asked.

"Oh, yeah, it works," Dan responded. "We tested it out at Cliff's barn just to make sure the signal worked. And it did. I hooked this beauty up to all types of electronics over there. I turned on the lights, even heated up some popcorn in the microwave with it, all without connecting its mechanism to a single wire. Everything is done remotely."

"That's incredible," Mary said.

"The problem is its range," Dan continued. "When we were testing in the barn, everything in the system was close together. If we pushed the lever down here, I don't know that it would actually set the system off at the bowling alley, so we'll need to be closer. Stubs and I talked through different options, and the best solution we came up with is to hide it in a cardboard box near the dumpsters by the building's back entrance. I'll dress like a homeless guy and sit near the box. Then when I get the signal, I'll blow the whole place up."

"How will you get the signal?" I asked.

"Actually, your boy Jerry hooked us up," Cliff said. "When he brought the bug for us to plant in the dining room, he also threw in a dozen earbuds so we could all communicate with one another."

"That's great and all," Reggie said, "but those of us who will be in the bowling alley obviously can't wear earbuds, so how will we get the signal to get out before being blown up with the bad guys?"

Silence again fell over the group. I looked around the room and saw Stubs and Dan Baum looking at the ground. Eli's eyes were closed. Vince stared blankly at the paper taped to the wall. They all clearly knew something that Reggie, Mary, and I didn't.

"Guys?" Reggie repeated. "How will we get the signal?"

More silence.

"Reggie," Cliff finally said, "you've brought us to the rather uncomfortable portion of the meeting. As you all saw, I wrote the words *our last meeting* on the wall behind me. The last time I saw combat, I was in Iraq. There was a buddy of mine who—"

"Cliff, I appreciate your tales of battle and all," Reggie said, standing up from his chair, "but right now, I don't want stories. I want answers. What are you saying—or not saying?"

"He's saying that some of us are going to die inside with the bad guys tomorrow," Eli said, his eyes still closed.

A hush once again overtook us all. I hadn't realized any of us were going to die for this mission. Apparently, neither did Reggie.

"Oh, hell, no, I'm not dying in there!" Reggie shouted as he pushed his chair onto the floor. "No way, not me. I'm getting the hell out of there before the bombs go off."

"You can't do that, Reggie," Cliff explained. "Giovanni Torallini specifically requested you be in the dining room with him, standing by his side—well, behind him, as is custom. Each of the family heads in that room will have their most-trusted aide with them. If you were to leave, it would create suspicion."

"I don't care. Torallini doesn't need me supervising him as he eats. He's a big boy."

"Thank you, Reggie. I think we all understand that," Cliff said. "But this is about respect."

"Respect! You want to talk about respect? How about respecting my wishes and making it so I can live past tomorrow? Why don't you worry about that respect?"

"Reggie, it takes lives to save lives. There are casualties in war."

"But we're not in a damn war," Reggie yelled. "This isn't some destitute town in the Middle East. We're talking about a bowling alley in the Chicago suburbs."

"It's still a war," Cliff screamed. "A war against evil!"

Reggie had no response, so he stood and stewed, his arms crossed against his chest. If he had no other ways to voice his frustration, he would at least continue to show it.

"Speaking of war," Dan Baum interjected, "I feel it necessary to be transparent about the explosives we're using."

"What about them?" Mary asked.

"Stubs and I are used to working with top-of-the-line, military-grade devices," Dan said, "and, well, that's not exactly what's in our arsenal for this operation."

"What are you talking about? Those are all military-grade," Cliff said.

"Yeah, but the last time they were top of the line was decades, maybe centuries, ago," Stubs said. "I think some of those relics date back to the damn Civil War. Cliff, your collection is great and all, but for our purposes—"

"Now wait just a minute," Cliff interrupted. "That collection is one of the finest in the country. I told you all at the last meeting that the Smithsonian was acquiring some of my more valuable pieces."

"That's great, Cliff," Stubs said, "but I don't think the Smithsonian was planning on using them as explosives. We are."

Cliff brushed off Stubs's remark. "Look, it's not like we can go to the store and ask for more modern bombs over the counter. This is what we've got to work with. Now, Dan, please carry on."

Dan continued. "Like I said, I connected all the explosives to the T-handle."

"And what about Feldman?" I asked. "Will that Wile E. Coyote detonator of yours set off his bombs all the way on the other side of the building?"

"Hell, yeah, it will take down Feldman," Cliff enthusiastically shouted, trying once again to fire up the group. It didn't work.

"Actually, no, Cliff, it won't take down Feldman," Dan clarified. "As Stubs mentioned before, we had already set up the explosives for the building when we remembered Feldman. We had to create a second system for him, and the bombs on that network are connected to this little guy." He pulled a tiny remote out of his pocket, no bigger than a credit card. "It's got great range and can spark an explosion from over a mile away."

"Wait a minute," Mary said, "if that remote is so great, why didn't you set all the bombs up to it or buy a second remote for the other system meant for Santori? That seems a lot more reliable than that old relic," she said as she motioned to the T-handle. "At least those remotes were created this century."

"In hindsight, that probably would have made more sense, but we'd already established the network with the T-handle and didn't have enough time to recalibrate everything."

"Besides, there's nothing like using the classics as a way to honor those who defended our lives and freedoms before us," Cliff said, still trying to win back the crowd.

"Anyway," Dan continued, "we're going to need someone to push the remote to detonate Feldman's bombs. I can't very well push it and the T-handle down at the same time."

"I'll do it," Stubs said.

"Great, thanks, Stubs," Dan said as he handed him the remote.

There was a brief spell of silence as the group watched Stubs examine the remote before putting it in his pocket.

"What if the bombs don't work?" Mary asked straightforwardly.

"They will," Cliff said.

"But what if they don't?" Mary repeated.

"They will," Cliff shouted. "There is no other option. This is what we have to work with. And they *will* work. You've just got to believe."

"Wait a minute," Reggie said, his fists clenched so tight his knuckles were turning purple. "You've got me going on a suicide mission, and your advice is to 'believe it will work'? Have you gone insane, Cliff? If this doesn't work and Torralini finds out I was involved, he'll kill me himself."

"Sounds like it's a lose-lose situation for you," Dan said.

"Fuck you, Baum, and fuck this whole operation," Reggie said. "This is not what I signed up for. There's got to be another way."

"There's not, Reggie. Look."

Cliff flipped over the whiteboard to show another blueprint of the building, this time with the red circles for the bombs and a slew of black circle stickers spread out all over the map.

"Each black circle represents a person. A person who tonight is breathing but who tomorrow will not be."

"Oh, yeah?" Reggie asked, walking toward the board and running his hand through his slicked-back hair. "Which one is me?"

Cliff pointed to a circle in the private dining room.

"This one?" Reggie clarified. He then peeled the sticker off the board, crumpled it, and threw it in Cliff's face. "I can't believe you, Cliff. Am I the only one of us you were planning to kill?"

"You are not the only one," a calm Eli said, his eyes now open. "I assume that I, too, am destined to die tomorrow."

"Eli, no," I blurted.

"Blaze, it is okay," Eli smoothly said. "I am at peace. If dying will help us bring down these tyrants, then it will be worth it."

"Eli is right," Cliff confirmed. "Stubs, Dan, and I talked through a dozen different scenarios of how to get Eli out, but every time, it just felt too risky. He will be locked in a room with Feldman, and there will be no way to get him out."

"I appreciate that consideration, Cliff," Eli said. "Really, though, I'm okay with this."

"I'm not," Reggie continued. "Why, if I were in charge, I'd—"

"Oh, for the love of God, shut the fuck up already, you damn greaseball," Vince said as he, too, stood up. "You're not in charge, and you know what? Thank goodness. If you were leading us to battle, we'd already be dead."

Reggie stopped in his tracks. "What did you just call me?"

"You heard me," Vince said. "Now shut the hell up. I'll be standing next to Santori tomorrow and dying right along with you, and you don't see me putting on a pity party."

Reggie charged at Vince before *pity party* was out of his mouth. Reggie's only advantage was the element of surprise as he plowed shoulder first into Vince's chest and drove him to the ground. Reggie connected on three punches to Vince's face before the surprise wore off and Vince took control.

Mary and I looked at one another. Three nights earlier, we were blown away by the impressive credentials of our fellow Boomsters. Now, what was once an inspiring group of experts seemed more like an incompetent group of children.

Vince, still underneath Reggie, punched his fellow FBI agent in the kidney, then used his strength to flip Reggie onto his back, gaining the upper hand as he sat on top of Reggie. He pulled his hand back and was ready to connect with Reggie's cheek when a blood-curdling whistle rang through the house.

With my hands over my ears, I turned to see Mary standing with two fingers in her mouth. Before the first Boom meeting, I'd never heard that sound ever come out of her mouth. Hearing it for the second time, I prayed I'd never have to hear it again.

Cliff pulled Vince off Reggie, Vince's fist still clenched and ready to strike.

"Why don't we take a five-minute break?" I suggested.

Before anyone could answer, Reggie was gone, lighting a cigarette as he stormed out the front door. The group circled Vince, making sure he was okay.

"I'll go talk to Reggie," I volunteered. I leaned over to Mary before I left. "Do you still have that basket with stuff for the grandkids in the back of your car?"

"Of course," she said. "Why?"

"Go run and grab it, please. I think it may come in handy."

Mary looked perplexed, but rather than push back, she got up and walked out the front door with me behind her. While she went to her car, I saw Reggie leaning against the house's wrought-iron fence, a cloud of smoke blowing away from his face. He used his non-cigarette hand to smooth out his hair, which was disheveled from the altercation.

"Oh, hey, Blaze," he said as I approached. "Sorry about the scene back there."

"Don't apologize, Reggie. I understand not wanting to die. I am a fan of living myself."

"Vince and I have been on the same side since our training days. We're a team, and I shouldn't have done that."

"I hear you, Reggie, but still, I understand why you'd be upset about . . . you know, well, dying."

"I know I put up a fight, but between you and me, I get it—the whole sacrificing for the greater good. I just don't like how they're going about this."

"Who?"

"Cliff, Stubs, and Baum. Those war nuts believe they're living on borrowed time, yet me, Vince, and Eli are the ones destined to meet our maker tomorrow. Why? Why does it have to be that way?"

"Well, Reggie, it sounded like—"

"It sounded like Cliff's too focused on vengeance, not justice."

"What do you mean?"

"I mean that Cliff has lost track of the goal. I joined this mission because Vince told me we were going to make the world a better place for the innocent. But Cliff and his bomb boys are being reckless, and they're more focused on killing everyone than being strategic and limiting the deaths to those who are in fact guilty. Did you see all those black stickers? What good is making the world better for the innocent if those same innocent people die? If I need to die for this to work, I'll do it. I'll be brave like Eli, but if I'm going to do that, I want to know this plan will go off without a hitch. I'm not having this 'just believe' crap that Cliff is trying to sell. If I'm going to die, all the bad guys need to die too."

Mary returned and told us the meeting was starting up again.

"Look, Reggie," I said as we started for the door, "I don't know what to say, but I do know we need to operate like a team. If we're fighting internally, there's no way we'll succeed."

"I agree," he said. Then he leaned in toward me. "That was a pretty good tackle, though, am I right?" he whispered.

"It caught me by surprise."

"Vince too," Reggie said with a grin. "In all seriousness, Blaze—and I don't actively promote this, but I've struggled with anger management issues for a while now. That's why I did what I did to Vince. When he called me a *greaseball*, I lost it. We all have our triggers. People making fun of my hair is mine."

"Got it. Never say anything about your hair if I want to live."

I smiled, trying to lighten the mood. Reggie looked at me and laughed. *Mission accomplished.* I put my arm over his shoulder as we walked back into the house. As we entered, Mary handed me a basket filled with colored pencils, stickers, and a few toy cars. I grabbed the stickers and winked as I handed her the basket.

"Okay, everyone, let's get back to business," Cliff said as we found our seats. "Now, we need to talk about body count. As you can see by this board, there will be a number of fatalities."

He paused to nod at Eli and Vince but opted not to look at Reggie.

"Cliff, I have a question," I said, raising my hand. "When we first started talking about this plan, my understanding was we were taking down a handful of bad guys, maybe a couple dozen at the most. Looking at your schematic there, we're now talking about killing upward of fifty or seventy-five people. Who are all those people, and do they all need to die?"

"They're casualties of war, Blaze," Cliff responded.

"Yes, I've heard you say that before, but do they need to be? Take, for example, those fifteen black dots scattered along the perimeter of the building. Who are they?"

"That's the general security team hired by Santori to keep unwanted people out of the building."

"Wait, general security?" Eli cut in. "How come we haven't heard about them?"

"*General security* is a bit of a loose term," Vince said. "Candidly, this is one of the Santori family's stupidest traditions. I just learned about it myself earlier today, but apparently back in Jersey, whenever the family would have an important meeting, they'd hire outside security personnel to protect the meeting location. One day, one of the family elders pointed out that these highly trained security experts could easily turn on the family and rob them, take them hostage, or kill them—or all three. That's when Tony Santori himself, who was probably in his twenties at the time, said they should just hire actors instead. Instead of having actual security, he thought just having people who looked the part would do the trick and keep them all safe."

"You're joking," Eli said.

"Scout's honor," Vince continued. "Santori called me earlier today and shared that very tale and told me I had to get a group together. Fortunately, I found a local improv group available on short notice that specializes in role playing. They said they even had props to help sell the act. They had a catchy name—The Roundhouse Rebels. No idea what it means, but I liked that it had *rebels* in it."

"You've got to be kidding me," Mary cut in. "That's Carissa's group."

"Carissa?" I said. "Carissa who?"

"Carissa Castelellanos."

The seven of us stared at Mary, collectively wondering who the hell Carissa Castelellanos was and why she mattered to us.

"Is she some stripper too?" Stubs crassly joked.

"No, you misogynist twit," Mary snapped back. "First of all, I was a pole dancer, but that's beside the point. I met Carissa after I gave up the pole and discovered I could use my flexible legs in other ways."

I had absolutely no idea where Mary was going with this, but I was intrigued, as were the other six men in the group.

"Back then, I discovered I was a natural at taekwondo, and after a few years of training, I earned a spot at the World Taekwondo Championships. It was there I met Carissa, who was also competing. That woman had a body like a Greek goddess, but good God, could she kick the shit out of her opponents. She took home the silver medal but probably should have won gold."

"How did you do?" Reggie asked.

"I was damn near last." Mary sighed. "I was aggressive but could never connect on any of my spinning kicks."

"Wait, what the hell is happening here?" I cut in. "First pole dancing, now taekwondo—who are you, Mary?"

"I'm a woman with a past, Blaze, just like you. Well, maybe not just like you, but you know what I mean."

"I don't mean to interrupt this counseling session," Cliff cut in, "but can we get back to Boom?"

"Of course," Mary said. "My point was that I know Carissa. I can warn her that she's risking her life by taking on this assignment. Once all of Santori's guests are in the building, we can have her and her team leave the scene, cutting down our number of fatalities by fifteen."

I was still wrapping my head around Mary's adventuresome past, but her plan was good.

"Cliff," I said as I looked at his blueprint, "can we update the map to help differentiate who will be where tomorrow night and, more significantly, who will live and who will die?"

"Be my guest," Cliff said, "but all I've got are black circles."

"No problem, I've got my own supply."

I reached into my pocket and grabbed the sheets of stickers meant for my grandkids. There were three sheets with princesses on them and one with yellow smiley faces. I replaced the general security stickers with princesses.

"Now, Cliff," I continued, "where are Vince and Eli on this map?"

I took off their black dots and replaced them with smiley faces and added a smiley face where Reggie's sticker had been—they were the good guys, after all.

"Vince, are any of the staff innocent?"

"I don't know," Vince answered. "Obviously, Andy Wong isn't, and I assume all of his men have checkered pasts."

"What about the guys you met with before?"

"I'm not sure. There was one guy named Manuel who I had a good feeling about despite the fact he said he was a drug dealer. There was something different about him."

"Who cares?" Cliff cut in. "So what if Manuel or any of the other staff dies?"

"I care," I said as I replaced five more black dots with princesses. "We don't need to kill potentially innocent people. If they're innocent, they deserve to live. And if not, they can be handled by the normal due process of the law."

"I don't know if they're innocent," Vince reiterated.

"Do you have Manuel's number? My team can do some digging into him."

Vince gave me the worker's number.

"I still don't get it," Cliff said. "What's the point of this?"

"The point," I said, "is these princesses are innocent. They have the right to live."

"I want to be a princess," Reggie muttered under his breath. We all looked at him. "What? You know what I mean."

"Sure, maybe they have the right to live," Cliff continued, "but so what? What's the difference between killing fifteen or so people and killing fifty?"

"The difference is we can justify killing the fifteen. We'll be hard pressed to convince the general public that Operation Boom was for the greater good if we murder dozens of innocent people."

The room was once again silent. Dan Baum looked at Cliff.

"Blaze brings up a good point," he said. "How are we going to justify all of this?"

It was a question Cliff had not considered. It was also one he didn't care about.

"Our actions will speak for themselves," Cliff said. "Once the public realizes who all these bad people were, they'll realize we had to take these drastic actions."

"But how will the public know?" Reggie asked. "How can we be sure they'll know why we're doing this?"

Cliff was losing his audience once again. This time, I was ready to rescue him.

"You asked how the public will know, Reggie," I said. "The answer is we're going to tell them."

"How?" he asked. "Particularly if I'm dead?"

"The Blaze team has been working behind the scenes to produce a video explaining just how evil these men are. They've shot interviews with more than a dozen victims who personally explain how they were tormented by Santori, Feldman, and some other people in attendance. The testimonials are raw, powerful, and compelling. Soon after the bowling alley goes up in flames, one of my associates will hijack the TV airwaves and distribute the video for the country to see."

"You can do that?" Reggie said in amazement.

"I've learned," I said as I looked at Mary, "that with the right resources, you can do anything. Oh, and speaking of resources, we'll have an extra set of hands helping us out tomorrow night."

"Dammit, Blaze, this isn't an open-invitation party," Stubs shouted.

"I understand, Stubs, but this person is an expert in deception and I think will be a valuable addition to the team."

"That's not your call, Blaze," Cliff said, raising his voice once again. "I'm the one in charge here."

"I'm sorry, Cliff, I meant no disrespect. So do you want me to tell Lieutenant Lance Cutler he's not welcome, or will you?"

"Lance Cutler?" Stubs said. "The dead cop?"

"That's the one, although I can assure you he is in fact very much alive."

"Alive?" Cliff said. "But how?"

"A magician never reveals his secrets," I said as I winked at Eli. "Just know that Lance is on board and willing to help. He'll be here tomorrow afternoon, as will two of my team members in case any of you would like to be included in the video. You're not obligated to speak, but if you want to share your reasons for joining this illustrious team and following through on this operation, that will be your best chance. Cliff, when do you want us all here?"

Cliff sat, dumbfounded by my surprise announcements.

"Cliff?" I repeated. "What time are we meeting?"

"What?" he finally said. "Um, let's meet here at 3 p.m."

"Perfect," I said. "I'll make sure my team is here and ready to film. Now I think we should all get some rest. Cliff, did you have anything else you wanted to say?"

Cliff should have known to expect the unexpected from me, yet he still sat with a stunned look on his face. "No, that's it."

"Great," I said. "Meeting adjourned."

I reached out to Mary and escorted her to the door as the rest of the group got up from their seats. As I opened the door for my taekwondo-kicking, pole-dancing sweetheart, I overheard Stubs talking to Cliff.

"He turned Santori's top security guy, cut our death count down, developed a way to justify this whole stunt, and somehow helped hide from the world the fact that Lance Cutler is in fact alive," Stubs said. "I hate to say it, but maybe Blaze should be leading this operation."

I looked back as Cliff continued to sit with a blank look on his face.

"Maybe he should," Cliff said. "Maybe he should."

It was nearly midnight when Jermaine's cell phone rang with a call from Tony Santori.

"Is it done?" Santori asked.

Jermaine knew the question was coming. He pulled out the script Blaze had given him and began reading it back to Santori. He wasn't used to lying to his boss, so he wanted to be sure he did it right.

"Yeah, boss," Jermaine began. "I told that old man that no one fucks with Tony Santori and gets away with it."

"And what did he say?"

Jermaine kept reading from the script. "He said he should have known better. He said he never should have tried to pull a fast one on you and that he now realized that in a world divided by good and evil, the true champion, the person who stood higher than all others, was you, boss, the one and only Tony Santori."

"Damn straight. Then what?"

Jermaine almost read *pause for dramatic effect* until he remembered that was a cue for him from Blaze. He paused.

"Then what, Jermaine?"

"Then I put a bullet in his brain."

"That's my boy, Jermaine," Santori shouted. "Bye bye, Blaze. That will show him what happens when you mess with Tony Santori."

26

Sleep evaded me for much of the night. How could I sleep knowing what was to come in less than twenty-four hours? I'd been a killer salesman all my life, but soon I'd become a salesman who killed, and that thought was not easy to fall asleep to. I finally gave up and tiptoed to headquarters, groggy yet energized to mentally prepare for the biggest day of my life.

I had apparently gotten some sleep during the night because I'd missed a phone call. I checked my voicemail and heard Betty, who whispered so quietly I could barely understand her.

"Hi, David, it's Betty. Listen, I'm supposed to be laying low, and I'm doing that right now, literally. I'm lying on the floor behind my couch at home, but I had to call and thank you. You saved my life last night. I don't know how you convinced Jermaine not to kill me—all he said was I better thank my lucky stars that I know you.

"David, I've spent the last two hours thanking those stars. I was sure I was going to die, but I'm still here, and I'm still alive, and that's because of you. I've decided to come clean and tell the police about the illegal activities at the WCC that made a lot of greedy people a lot of money, beginning with Tony Santori. That bastard was going to kill me, so I'm done protecting him. I'm sure I'll end up with some jail time for my role in his illegal activities over the years, but I'm okay with that. I feel like my life was saved for a reason, and now I'm trying to figure out what that reason is. Whatever the answer, it's all because of you. So thank you, David. From the bottom of my heart, thank you."

Well, that was surprising. I wondered if the world would be as thankful once Boom was complete and our actions were explained. With time to kill before the real killing began, I decided to look back at my detective pamphlets. It felt like it had been months since I cracked any of them open, but the reality was it had only been ten days since I first acquired them. I opened a pamphlet about asking tough questions but quickly got distracted. I put the brochure down and closed my eyes. I couldn't get that number out of my head. Ten days—that was it.

My whole life—scratch that, my whole world—had changed in less than two weeks. I went from being lost with no purpose to preparing to take down the Italian mafia and Jewish mobsters. *God sure works in mysterious ways.*

Just then, Mary startled me back to reality.

"David Blazen, come here right now," she shouted.

Apparently not everyone was thankful for my actions.

I followed the sound of Mary's voice to our bathroom, where I found her away from the FBI bugs, soaking in a warm bath, tears running down her face.

"What's wrong, Mary?"

"Close the door," she said before blowing her nose.

I did as I was instructed, then turned and sat on the floor next to the tub. We didn't speak for almost a minute as I waited for her to make the first move.

"David, I'm scared," she finally confessed.

"Scared of what?"

"I'm scared about tonight. What if something happens to you? Or me? We were supposed to live out this beautiful retired life together, but what if one of us doesn't make it out of Boom alive? Last night, I almost had a heart attack at the thought of never seeing you again."

"But I came back, didn't I?"

"That time you did, but what if this time you don't? Or I don't? What if this time we dig ourselves too deep of a hole, and even you can't find a way out for us?" More tears came rushing down her face. "David, I don't want to die," she whispered, "and I don't want to be a widow."

I reached over the tub and dried her cheeks with a towel. "You won't die, Mary, and you won't be a widow—at least not today."

She cracked a small smile. "It just feels like there are too many moving pieces," she said, "and I'm scared we won't be able to juggle them all."

"That's why we have a team, Mary. We have a team, we have a plan, and by George, we're going to follow the plan to a T. Santori gives toast. Santori goes boom. Feldman goes boom. Bad guys die. Good guys live. Easy peasy, lemon squeezy."

"Are you sure, David?"

"I am. Now dry those eyes. You've got nothing to worry your pretty mind about."

Mary smiled more as she looked at me. I reached my hand out for hers, and there we sat, together in silence. Finally, Mary locked eyes with me once again.

"David?"

"Yes, dear?"

"This is not what I envisioned retirement looking like."

"Me neither. I never realized that retirement could be so exhilarating. Or thrilling."

"Or entertaining. Remember you traipsing around the backyard in nothing but my trench coat?" She began to chuckle at the memory.

"That was nothing," I said with a smile. "How about when we

stumbled upon Patrick and his girl getting frisky in the backyard?"

We laughed at the memory.

"That was a good one," Mary said, "Oh, how about our Valentine's Day houseguests? Remember Bryan walking around shirtless and clueless?"

The laughs were becoming louder and harder to control.

"We've had some very strange people in this house recently," Mary continued. "Remember when Lance and Eli joined us in bed?"

"At least they had clothes on," I said, "unlike Jerry as he traipsed through the back channels of the WCC to commit murder."

The laughs kept coming as we kept one-upping each other with ridiculous memories.

"How about Wilt inside the smoky crematorium, smuggling out a piece of a dead hitman?" Mary said. "What was the name of that place again?"

I couldn't get the answer out without laughing. "Holy Mother of Baby Jesus Crematorium."

"That's right. That was ridiculous," Mary said as tears began to drip down her face.

"You know what the most ridiculous thing was, though?" I asked.

We looked each other in the eyes, our cheeks soaked with tears of laughter. We paused, then shouted the answer out at the same time: "Mayonnaise!"

Nothing could be more ridiculous than Tom Lexington doused in mayonnaise and being stoned on national television. We both laughed at the memory for a bit. I wiped away my tears as Mary leaned her head against the back of the tub.

"Mary," I said, "in all seriousness, I want to thank you. I know it was hard to be around me after I retired, and then these past couple of weeks have certainly been, well, interesting. I know you had your doubts, but the fact that you stuck by my side means more to me than you'll ever know."

"Aw, Blaze, don't mention it. You've definitely made life more interesting."

"You have, too, Miss Pole-dancing Taekwondo-er. Any other past jobs of yours that I don't know about?"

"I think that's it, but you never know," Mary said with a smirk.

"Seriously, Mary. Thank you. I couldn't have done this without you. Whatever happens tonight with Boom, know that I will always be grateful for having you in my life."

Mary leaned over the tub to give me a kiss. "Right back at you, Blaze."

Sarah Cutler grabbed a modest black dress and a simple strand of pearls to wear to her son's memorial. Whether it was fake or not was of little consequence to Sarah—she'd already earned a victory by running damage control after that TV spectacle. The fact people were talking about her with sympathy instead of satire was a PR win if there ever was one. This memorial would be her crowning achievement. She'd reenter the public spotlight as a new candidate, one emboldened by the loss of her son and determined to fight the city's pathetic crime record head on. After the memorial, she would speak to the press about her refusal to walk away from her campaign and her newfound energy to fight for justice—no matter the price. Her goal was to show strength amid sorrow.

Sarah and her campaign team had orchestrated every detail of the day, from the type of flowers at the church to the photo slideshow that would be displayed. The *Looking for Lance* broadcast had focused on images of Lance throughout his life; this memorial would only show pictures of him with Sarah. Yes, this was to be Lance's memorial, but it was not designed as a tribute to him as much as it was a tribute to the loss of Sarah's son. Everything about the event was to help shape her image. Her reputation. Her legacy.

Sarah met her husband, Kent, at the back entrance of the church.

"Thanks, Oscar," she said to her driver as she got out of the car. "See you after the show—I mean, service."

"Good luck, Sarah," Oscar said. "I hope you find the peace you're looking for."

The church was filled beyond capacity thirty minutes before the afternoon memorial was scheduled to begin. Idle chatter echoed off the church's vaulted ceiling and stained-glass mosaics on the walls. In the front of the room stood a twenty-five-foot sculpture of Jesus atop a marble wall. Even for the nonreligious, the scene was breathtaking.

Moments before the service began, Sarah peeked out from behind the marble wall and admired the standing-room-only crowd. Whether these people were there for Lance or for her made no difference—her campaign team would be sure to say this gathering was clearly a show of support for Sarah's mayoral candidacy.

Kent found Sarah and put his hand in hers.

"Are you ready for this, dear?" he asked, his voice shaking.

You weak little man, I was born for this, she thought to herself. She squeezed her husband's hand and nodded. "Let's do this."

The two walked out from behind the white wall, and the room went silent. They walked down the steps of the altar and found their seats in the first pew. Knowing everyone's attention was on her, Sarah played to the moment and hugged Kent.

Kent was taken aback. If he hadn't known this whole thing

was a show, he might have actually been convinced Sarah felt remorse. Neither was sure of the last time they shared an embrace like that. The hug lasted a few seconds. Then they separated and turned toward the front of the church, their hands finding one another's once again. As Father Zayas walked to the podium, Kent and Sarah each had the same thought: *Let the show begin.*

Mary and I walked into the Boom house and were impressed by the sense of calm among the group, a stark contrast from the previous evening's behavior. Stubs was joking with Dan Baum, who was wearing baggy pants, a torn trench coat, and an olive-green bucket hat. A bushy gray beard lay on his lap. Cliff was showing Patrick and Kelly his Buzz Saw machine gun, suicide vest, and grenade.

"What are those for?" Mary asked.

"These beauties? They're just background props for my interview. I thought it would help sell my story of being a preeminent historic weapons connoisseur."

"They look great, Mr. Cliff, sir," Patrick said. "I think I've got everything I need here. All I need now is the host's intro video."

Patrick and Kelly both looked at me. So did Cliff. And Mary. *Shit.*

Perfect. That was the word that kept coming to Sarah's mind throughout the memorial. Everything about the performance was perfect. From Father Zayas's emotional eulogy to the photo montage of Lance's life with Sarah, every little detail was playing just how Sarah had hoped. The father thanked those in attendance for showing their love and support for the Cutler family, and he acknowledged that seeing how many people cared about

Lance would surely help Sarah and Kent deal with the loss of their son. Sarah, a tissue ready in her hand, dabbed at her dry eyes and nodded in agreement.

The service lasted just over an hour. Afterward, attendees were invited to the church's front steps, where a podium was set for Sarah's big speech. Sarah, not wanting to beat her audience, opted to stay seated at her pew "in reflection" as the church emptied out. Through it all, Kent sat by her side.

"Lance would have liked this," Kent said to his wife, "particularly that anecdote about you teaching him to always keep his eye on the prize."

"I think he would have liked it," Sarah said, opting not to look at Kent. "I'm sorry if it sounded like I was the only one who made him who he was. Obviously, you were an instrumental part of his upbringing."

"Obviously," Kent said, trying to fake compassion for a few more minutes. "We all know you gave him his drive, though. There's no questioning that."

"That's true. Thanks for understanding, Kent."

Kent just smiled. The front doors to the church were closed, but through them the couple could hear cheers of "Safer with Sarah" ring out from outside.

"Sounds like your crowd is waiting," Kent said. "Go give the people what they want. I'll be right behind you."

Sarah found Kent's hand and gave it a squeeze. Then she got up, straightened her dress, and confidently walked through the empty church. She reached the front doors, took a breath, and pushed the doors open to find a throng of thousands calling out her name.

"Lead us, Sarah!"

"Win it for Lance!"

"Fix this city, Sarah!"

"Sarah, we love you!"

Sarah looked out at the crowd and waved. She walked up to the podium and took in the view. This was her moment. This was what the whole charade was for. Sarah had all the support she could ever ask for right there. Those people believed in her cause, or they at least felt sympathy for her. Either way, they were hers now. All she had to do was continue pulling at their heartstrings.

Sarah had practiced her speech dozens of times the past few days and made sure it was as emotional a delivery as she'd ever given. Each time she'd rehearsed it, she tried to make herself cry. She knew an image of her crying as she spoke about her fight against violence minutes after memorializing her murdered son would quickly become iconic, like Truman holding up the newspaper with *Dewey defeats Truman* plastered on its front page. Despite her best efforts, she couldn't force any tears, so she resorted to the next best thing—elongated pauses in her delivery. If she couldn't bring tears out, she could at least pretend she was holding them back.

And that was exactly what she did.

"Ladies and gentlemen, thank you for coming out to honor the legacy of my dear boy," she began.

The crowd erupted in applause. Sarah read the audience and saw an opportunity. She stepped back from the microphone and covered her face with both hands as if the magnitude of the moment was too much to handle.

Kent watched Sarah hide her face and saw his own opportunity. He quickly stepped to the podium.

"Yes, thank you all for coming. Now, please, my wife and I need to mourn in private."

"What the—"

Before Sarah could finish her sentence, Kent had his arm around her and was ushering her away from the podium and down the stairs toward a black limo.

"Kent, what are you doing? I need to get back up there!"

"Slight change of plans, dear," he said as he pushed their way through the crowd of reporters.

"Sarah, are you suspending your campaign?" a reporter asked.

"Sarah, what about Lance's killers?" another shouted out.

"Sarah! Sarah! Sarah!"

Sarah had no idea what was going on. She wanted to fight back against Kent, to slip out of his grasp and run back to her podium and her adoring supporters, but she knew the photos and video from this moment would be seen the world over, so the last thing she wanted was to come across as hostile or physical with her husband. She kept her face down and pretended to be too overwhelmed to answer any questions. She wanted to give her fans the speech of a lifetime. Instead, they got one measly sentence.

"Kent, what the hell is going on?" she said under her breath as they cleared the stairs. "That's not even my car. Where's Oscar?"

"Like I said, dear, there's been a change in plans."

Kent opened the back door to the car and politely helped his wife in. He slammed the door, then rushed to the front passenger seat, where he hopped in, never looking back as he got into the car. The only thing those close to the limo could hear was his brief instruction as he closed the door.

"Okay, Jeffrey," he said, "get us out of here."

"Who is doing the intro video?" Patrick asked.

I gulped. "I guess I am, kid. Come on, let's go outside and get this out of the way."

"David, what are you going to say?" Mary asked.

I thought for a moment. "To be determined," I said with a wink.

"I'll stick around and get some more background video in case we need it," Kelly said.

Outside, I gave Patrick a little nudge as he carried his camera and a tripod.

"Dammit, kid, why didn't you tell me we needed an intro?"

"Sorry, boss, I just assumed you'd have something put together."

"I appreciate that. And it's fine. Where do you want to shoot this?"

"Down the block on the sidewalk will work. I want to have the bowling alley in the background while you're talking."

"You never told me, how are we getting this on the airwaves anyway?"

"It's thanks to you, actually."

"What do you mean?"

"I don't know if you remember, but years ago, you taught me a very important life lesson. We were standing in your backyard, and in a very authoritative way, you said, 'Patrick, I want to tell you something my father taught me when I was your age. It's nice to be important, kid, but it's more important to be nice.'"

"Wise words indeed, but what does that have to do with us now?"

"You remember my buddy Bob the beeper?"

"The guy you subbed for at the TV station? Yeah. So what?"

"Well, it turns out his wife went into labor during the show, and thanks to me taking his spot, he was able to be by her side when their child was born."

"That's sweet, but I still don't see the connection."

"His brother works for a network and owes Bob a favor. Bob owes me a favor, so, in turn, his brother owes me one."

"And did you tell them what we're doing?"

"Not really, but I said it could be dangerous. They both said they want to get out of the industry anyway, so they're cool with helping us out. I've been sending them footage as soon as I get it, and they're helping piece together the final product."

"Patrick, I don't know what to say."

"Well, you better think of something quick. I'm just about ready for your intro."

As Patrick fiddled with the camera, I tried to come up with something intelligent to say. I thought about my first reaction to hearing about Operation Boom. I thought about the bad guys who soon would gather inside the bowling alley. I thought about my mission to bring justice to evil.

Then my mind started to drift. I thought about my career as a businessman and my second career as a detective. I thought about little Summer celebrating after playing Candyland. I even thought about poor Calvin Talbert and his private detective certificate hanging framed on my wall.

"Okay, boss, I'm ready when you are."

"What the hell is going on, Kent?" Sarah shouted as she slammed on the divider separating the front and back of the limo. "That was my moment! My goddamn moment to seal this election, and you took it from me!"

"Just like you took something from me," said a familiar voice from behind Sarah.

She slowly turned to find Lance, the son she had just spent an hour memorializing, getting up from a crouched position on the floor, hidden under a black blanket she hadn't seen in her rush for answers. Her jaw dropped.

"What's this?" Lance said as he sat up and made his way toward Sarah. "Is the next mayor of Chicago speechless?"

"I, I'm just s-stunned to see you," she finally said. "I thought you were dead."

That statement was in fact true. In all her posturing about Lance's murder and framing it in her own best interest, Sarah had never actually considered the possibility that Lance was still alive. Lance sat two feet from his mother, his eyes locked on hers.

"Don't you have something to say to me?" he said.

Sarah's mind was racing, and she didn't hear Lance's question. She was in full-on candidate mode and quickly tried to piece together who was part of this stunt. Clearly, Kent had a hand in it, but who else? Skip had told her Lance was dead. Did he know the truth all along? She hated not being in control of the situation, but whatever Lance's end game was, her best plan of attack was to go on the defensive. Like her father had taught her, if you're ever caught doing something you're not supposed to, deny, deny, and then deny some more.

"I said, don't you have something to say to me?"

"What do you want me to say, Lance?"

"I don't know. 'Good to see you're alive. Sorry for lying to the world and using your alleged death for my own personal gain.'"

"Lance, how could you say such a thing? I would never use my only child's death to push my agenda. I've been mourning your death like any good mother would."

"Bullshit. That's the biggest load of bullshit I've ever heard, and I've heard a lot from you over the years. If you're such a good mother, why haven't you even tried to hug me?"

Sarah started to inch toward him.

"Nope, don't try it now, Sarah. You had your chance. I know how your mind works. You're too focused on yourself to even recognize that your only son is alive and sitting right here in front of you. I bet right now you're trying to figure out what my plan is and who all is helping me. I bet you're bitter about not being able to sell some new campaign slogan to all those people back at the memorial."

"Fine, Lance. You want to play this game? I'll play. You're damn right I'm bitter. I would have secured the election with the speech I had prepared. I had thousands of supporters there for me."

"You're wrong, Sarah. They weren't there for you. They were there for *me*. Sure, they may have some sympathy for you, but they weren't there to support Candidate Cutler. They were there to mourn the loss of a good man."

"A good man, huh? Is that what you are, Lance? I thought you were a dirty cop."

"I was. You're right. I did things in the past that I'm not proud of, but I've learned from them, and I'm ready to change my ways. And that starts with you confessing."

"Me? Confess what?"

"For starters, how about the steam room murder?"

"You mean suicide."

"No, I mean murder. The murder you told me to cover up."

"Yes, I told you to cover it up, and that's just what you did. Thank you. Are we good now?"

"No, I don't need you to confess to me. I need you to confess to all those fans of yours."

"Are you crazy? I've got those twits right where I want them. I've got so much sympathy stocked up I could tell them anything, and they'd believe me. The last thing I'd ever do right now is tell them the truth."

"Then I will. I'll come out publicly and show the world I'm very much alive and that it was you who orchestrated my apparent death, the latest in a long line of inappropriate actions spearheaded by you and your campaign."

"Good luck with that, Lance. Sure, people will be happy you're alive, but it will be your voice against mine. And you may be my son, but as you've seen, I have no problem making up any story I need to about what you've done. I'll tell all about the money you and Skip absconded with and the crimes you've committed. I'll make up so many tales and bury your ass so deep in them you'll wish you actually were dead."

"I really am a son of a bitch, aren't I?"

"Cute, Lance, real cute. Call me a bitch if you want. Just be ready to call me the next mayor of Chicago too."

"What about your dirt? The crimes you've committed. The questionable alliances you've formed."

"I don't know what you're talking about."

"How about your secret meetings with Solomon Feldman and Tony Santori?"

"How do you know about those? I mean, I don't know what meetings you're talking about."

"Nice try, Sarah."

"So what? Yes, I met with both men. Feldman has been a financial supporter of mine for years, and Santori, well, I had to tell him there was about to be a new sheriff in town and he better fall in line with me or else suffer the consequences."

"So basically you're saying you're corrupt, and this whole 'safer with Sarah' bullshit is just that."

"It's not bullshit; this city will be safer with me. That was dickhead Paulson's downfall, if you ask me. He made friends with the good guys, and sure, it made him popular, but he had no friends among the Santoris and Feldmans of the world. I befriended the two of them and offered them money and power the likes of which they'd never seen before. With the three of us in charge of Chicago, we'll show the city we're fighting crime while mastering it at the same time. Is that corrupt? You're damn right. But is it smart? You're damn right."

The two sat in silence as the limo continued out of downtown and toward the western suburbs.

"Where are we going, anyway?" Sarah finally asked.

"Why did you ask me to cover up the steam room murder?" Lance asked, ignoring her question.

"Because you're weak, Lance, and I knew you'd do anything I ask. I love you for it, but it's always been your weakness."

Lance stared at her in silence.

"Now, if you wanted a piece of the action, I could get you in with Feldman and Santori. Together we can come up with some story about how you escaped from your kidnappers and have returned to fight crime alongside your mother. I could get you a seat in the city government, or we could put you back on the force. You name the job, and I'll make it happen. Having an in with the police would be really helpful, and, together, you, me, Feldman, and Santori could make more money than we've ever dreamed of. Or we could come up with another story. Or, hell, we can just keep pretending you're dead, and you can do a lot of behind-the-scenes work. You say the word. Tell me what you want, and I'll make it happen."

"I told you, I want you to confess. Detective Blaze is making a video that will air on national television tonight, and I want you to go on and tell the world how awful you really are."

"Detective Blaze? That nitwit? He's been a detective for about as long as we've been on this car ride. No one will take him seriously."

"They will when he shares the proof he has on you."

"Proof? What proof?"

"Proof of your meeting with Feldman. He knows the driver who picked you up after you met Feldman."

"So what? I could just say I was at a pawn shop across the street to sell off this worthless wedding ring of mine."

Lance was silent.

"Face it, kid. You've got nothing on me. Now, I appreciate you trying to act all tough back here, but enough is enough. It's time to remember who's really in charge, and that's me. Now, here's what's going to happen. You're going to tell the driver to turn this car around and take me home. You have until then to decide what you want your future to look like, whether you want a seat in the city offices or a job with the police."

"And what if I don't want to partner with you three criminals?"

"Well, I'd say you could live out your life in solitude, but after this display today, I don't think I could trust you to keep quiet."

"Meaning what?"

"Meaning if you don't join us, we'll make you disappear. Permanently this time."

"Are you saying you'd kill your own son?"

"I'd do anything to become mayor. Now turn this car around."

Lance knocked on the divider separating him and Sarah from Jeffrey and Kent. The screen lowered as the car pulled to a stop.

"We're all set," Kent said.

"And good timing," Jeffrey added. "We're here."

"Where?" Sarah asked.

"Remember I said Detective Blaze was putting a video together? The final interviews and footage are being shot right over there."

Lance pointed toward the Boom house, where a camera and tripod were set up on the front sidewalk.

"I already told you, I'm not saying a damn thing on camera," Sarah said.

"Oh, don't worry," Lance said. "You already did."

He pulled out a tiny camera attached to his shirt button and an equally small microphone off the limo's ceiling.

"Give me those," Sarah said as she lunged at the electronics.

She grabbed them out of Lance's hand, tossed the two devices on the ground, and stomped on them repeatedly.

"You're too late, Sarah," Lance said. "That camera transferred the footage live, and the video's already been recorded. It's set to air for the world to see later tonight."

Sarah was once again speechless.

Lance smiled as he got out of the car. Before closing the door, he leaned back in to see his mother still shocked and silent.

"On behalf of one nitwit detective and this son of a bitch, we thank you for your honesty."

27

"Good evening, ladies and gentlemen," I said into Patrick's camera. "My name is Detective Blaze, and do we have a show in store for you tonight. This will be a unique type of broadcast. There will be no commercials, for we want no disruptions during our message. We apologize for interrupting your regularly scheduled program, but this was the best way for us to get our story out to the world, unfiltered and in our own words. Now, I've already said a lot of *we* and *our*, and you're probably asking yourself, 'Who is he talking about?' Well, the team I speak of is unlike any other I'd ever encountered. We call ourselves the Boomsters, but many of you would call us heroes. I sure do. We are an elite team of eight individuals—seven men and one woman—made up of veterans, law enforcement, and crime solvers. Our mission? To rid the world of evil. I know that sounds like a lofty goal, but tonight, you'll see our plan executed before your very eyes."

I paused. "*Executed.* That's an interesting word, for some people will call our upcoming actions an execution. Others will call them brilliant—and necessary. It's up to you to decide which side of the fence you're on. You see that bowling alley behind me?" I said, pointing over my shoulder. "In just a little while, you, the public, will watch that building go up in flames. Inside that building are some of the nastiest criminals this country has ever seen. Murderers. Drug dealers. Thieves. Nasty, nasty people. They have been, and always will be, worried about themselves, first and foremost. Who are these people I speak of? The infamous Tony Santori, along with notorious criminals like Solomon Feldman, Andy Wong, the Torralini brothers, and others who have wreaked havoc on our society.

"These are crooked men who for years have found loopholes in the legal system and made millions of dollars while devastating the lives of thousands, maybe millions, of people. There's no way to know the true number of people impacted by these men, but there is a way to estimate the number of lives saved by completing tonight's mission. That estimate is one hundred thousand people. That's right. Men, women, and children who would be in financial ruin, be addicted to drugs, or be dead if these men continued their current path. Add to that the loved ones and friends, and the chain of harm is virtually endless. How do we know that? The Boomsters connected with multiple statisticians who performed probability models and data analyses, and each independently came to that conclusion. Get rid of a couple dozen people and save all those souls. Would you do it?

"Keep that question in mind as you watch. Now, that's enough of me talking. Allow me to introduce you to some of my fellow Boomsters responsible for tonight's activities. You're going to see a series of interviews from them, as well as victims of some of the perpetrators in that bowling alley. First up, the man who came up with the idea of Operation Boom, FBI Special Agent Cliff Stanley. Oh, and just to be clear, the FBI has no knowledge of this operation and has not sanctioned or endorsed it in any way. Let's roll the tape."

I stood still and waited for a cue from Patrick.

"How was that?" I finally asked.

"Boss, that was perfect," he said as he gave me a solo round of applause. "I think I got everything I needed. I can show you the playback if you want. It's your call."

"Thanks, Patrick. There's actually a different call I need to make. Why don't you head back and help Kelly out?"

I patted the kid on the shoulder and pulled out my phone. I walked down the block toward the Boom house. *Pick up, pick up*, I thought to myself.

"Hello?"

"Eli, good. I was worried it was too late."

"We're just about to leave the deli. What's wrong?"

"Nothing is wrong, Eli. I just . . . I just wanted to say goodbye."

"That was kind of you, Blaze. I know we didn't get a chance to talk last night. I want to thank you for all you've done."

"Thank me? You're sacrificing your life for the greater good. We should all be thanking you."

"I'm doing what I was meant to do, Blaze, just as you are. This will be me pulling a figurative trigger, and I will do it proudly for my fallen brothers back in Israel. Now, I'd love to continue talking, but I need to go before Feldman gets suspicious. Hopefully, God arranges for me to see you again in a better place."

"Just hopefully not soon."

"Agreed," Eli said with a laugh. "Thank you, Blaze. Thank you for making the world a better place."

He hung up, leaving me wondering what God had in store for me.

Sarah Cutler was in shock over what had just happened, and for the first time in her life, she didn't have a solution. She was done. That tape would end her. It would reveal her true self to the world and ensure no one ever gave her an ounce of sympathy again.

Tony Santori stood proudly at the bowling alley's ballroom entrance with a glass of champagne in his hand and a look of confidence on his face.

"Welcome, welcome, please come in and get comfortable," he said as his guests arrived. "Thank you all for coming to my celebration."

"Your celebration?" Giovanni Torralini said. "Aren't we celebrating all of us?"

"Well, yes, of course," Tony said. "You know tonight is about all of us—about our pasts, our presents, and our futures."

Giovanni gave a half smile and nod as he and his siblings walked past Santori. With Reggie by his side, he grabbed a glass of champagne and walked to one corner of the room.

"Something's not right, Reggie," Giovanni said. "I don't like this."

Reggie didn't like it either. He was still not thrilled about dying, but he'd run out of better options. His only job was to make sure everything went according to plan.

"What do you mean, boss?"

"I think Santori is up to something."

"Like what?"

"I don't know. Just keep an eye out for anything suspicious."

Cliff Stanley stuck his head out the front door of the Boom house.

"Blaze," he emphatically whispered. "Get in here. It's almost go time."

Before I got to the door, I heard my name again.

"Blaze. Blaze!"

I turned and found Lance jogging toward us.

"Blaze, we got her. We got my bitch of a mom on tape."

"That's great, Lance. Where is she now?"

"Still in the limo with my dad and your brother."

"How'd my brother get a limo? Never mind, we're a little busy right now."

"Great, let me help."

I looked at Lance. I didn't know what else he could do for our mission, but there was no time to argue.

"Sure, come join the team."

Lance and I walked into the house and found the group huddled together—Cliff, Stubs, Dan Baum, and Mary circled up shoulder to shoulder. Patrick was walking around the circle, getting some sort of fancy 360-degree footage of the group as Kelly zoomed her camera in on Cliff. Lance and I added ourselves to the already tight circle.

"Good to see you alive, Lieutenant Cutler," Cliff began. "Now, listen, this is the real deal. No backing out. It's time to rid the world of these evil bastards."

"Cliff," I interjected, "before we go any further, can we have a moment of silence for our three Boomsters who are giving themselves up for the cause?"

"Good call, Blaze," Cliff said, his tone quickly turning somber. "Let us all remember the courage and bravery of our fellow brothers. They are paying the ultimate sacrifice so we can live in a world that is safer, less corrupt, and less scary. Let us honor them now as we dedicate our mission to them."

We all bowed our heads in silence.

"Now," Cliff said with a maniacal grin, "let's light that bowling alley up like a Christmas tree. "Boom, boom, bang, bang!"

"Boom, boom, bang, bang," we repeated.

"Boom, boom, bang, bang!" Cliff shouted.

"Boom, boom, bang, bang," the group screamed together.

"Let's do this! Everybody take a set of these," Cliff said, handing us each a set of earbuds. "This is how we'll talk with one another. They're all connected to one network, so everyone will hear anything you say. Dan, get your hideous beard back on and get ready to get over to the building. Stubs and I will be on lookout. Mary, Blaze, Lance, you guys sit tight. Get ready for the action to begin."

I didn't have to wait long. As Cliff and Stubs made their way over to the front window, my phone buzzed with a text from Eli saying he, Feldman, and the Deli Boys were five minutes away from the bowling alley.

I quickly texted Jermaine with the heads-up: *Float like a butterfly*.

No response. I texted again. *Float like a butterfly.* Still nothing.

What if Jermaine forgot? Or what if he'd told Santori? This whole plan could blow up in my face. I was getting ready to call him when I got a buzz back.

Sting like a bee, the text said.

That was close.

"Hey, Cliff," I called out with a sigh of relief, "Feldman's almost here."

Solomon Feldman leaned against the backseat of his limo, his arms sprawled along the seat top. He felt like a king on his throne, excited to expand his empire. Originally, he hadn't liked the idea of meeting anywhere but the deli, but he had a backup plan in case Santori tried to pull any tricks. Feldman had each of his Deli Boys bring two suitcases—half had the money; the rest were filled with guns.

"Are you sure you want to bring all these suitcases in?" Eli questioned as they approached the bowling alley.

"I'm sure." Feldman grinned. "If Santori tries to be a wiseass, he's going to end up a dead wiseass."

The car pulled up to the bowling alley, and out walked a large man dressed in all black. He opened the back door and stuck his head in.

"Mr. Feldman, I presume?" Jermaine asked.

"That's me. Who the hell are you?"

"My name is Jermaine, sir. I'm in charge of Mr. Santori's security. Please allow me to show you and your associates inside."

Feldman got out, followed by Eli and four Deli Boys, each with their suitcases. Jermaine walked them between two armed security guards and through the front door.

"What's the security for?" Feldman asked as they made their way inside.

"Mr. Santori believes you can never be too careful," Jermaine said.

"On that, he and I agree," Feldman said as he winked at Eli. "Where is Santori anyway?"

"He'll be with you in just a few minutes," Jermaine said, escorting them into a large windowless room. "Please wait here, and I'll get Mr. Santori. Feel free to play a game of pool or two while you wait."

"What about Blaze?" Feldman asked. "He's going to be here for the handshake, isn't he?"

"You know, I haven't seen Blaze yet. Let me find out where he is, and I'll get back to you."

Jermaine left the room and quietly locked the door.

"Okay, everyone, Feldman's in the building," Cliff said to the Boomsters. "Let's get in position. Dan, grab the detonator and get over to your perch by the garbage cans. Keep an eye out for those folks parading as security."

"Don't you think they'll be a little suspicious of a homeless man walking with an explosive contraption?" Dan asked as he lugged the blasting machine out of the closet. "Besides, this thing is really heavy. We didn't think about the transport part."

"Don't worry, boys," Mary said. "I'll get security out of the way."

"And here, let me help you carry that," Lance offered.

Mary texted Carissa as planned to get her team away from the building, and Cliff and Stubs both watched as the general security crew fled.

"Dan, the coast is clear," Cliff said. "Get going."

Lance grabbed the blaster.

"Careful with that thing," Dan shouted. "If that handle falls, the bombs go off!"

"Officer Cutler," Cliff said, "I don't think it's a good idea—"

"I need to do something," Lance said. "I can't just sit and watch."

Dan and Lance crept in the shadows across the street, through the parking lot, and over to the garbage can, where Dan had positioned a set of boxes to serve as his makeshift home. Dan assembled one of the boxes so Lance could place the blasting machine inside.

"Okay, we're set," Dan said. "Now get out of here."

Lance ducked into the darkness and jogged back to the house. Dan sat on the ground, his back to the building and the smell of rotten garbage all around him. He realized at that moment he couldn't have been happier.

Sarah was still stewing in the back of the limo when she saw Lance creeping in the darkness toward the Boom house.

"Kent, what the hell is Lance doing? Kent, are you there?"

Her husband didn't respond.

"Fine. If you're not going to tell me, I'll just have to find out for myself."

Sarah saw an opportunity and jumped out of the parked car, leaving Jeffrey and Kent to watch as she ran toward the Boom house.

Tony Santori pulled Vince aside as the guests mingled.

"Where's everybody else?" Santori asked. "Where's my attorney, Pearlman?"

"There must have been some delay with the bus that was taking them," Vince said. "I'm sure everything's fine."

"But we need to move things along. I don't want to fall behind schedule."

"Go ahead and start, boss. I'm sure they'll be here soon."

"I hope so," Santori said as he clinked a knife to his glass to get the room's attention. "Okay, everyone, thank you again for coming to my beautiful city for tonight's celebration. This is a night we've waited ten years for, so let's get it started. I invite you to join me in the adjacent dining room for our featured presentation, followed by a toast and dinner. It's sure to be a blast."

Giovanni immediately turned to Reggie. "Did you hear that? A *blast*? I don't trust him," Giovanni said. "He's got something up his sleeve. Stay outside and be on the lookout."

Reggie couldn't believe his luck. "Whatever you say, boss," he said, struggling to contain his excitement.

"They're filing into the dining room," Cliff said, peering through his binoculars and knowing everyone with earbuds could hear him. "It won't be long now. Our audio feed will include sound from the bug in the dining room. Dan, listen for my signal. Everybody else, don't say a word unless it's an emergency."

Tony Santori, the four Torralinis, Lorenzo Rossi, Angelo Romano, and Dino Maramona all took their seats, each with his trusted high-ranking associate standing three feet behind him. Vince stood behind Tony Santori and noticed Reggie was nowhere to be seen. Santori also noticed.

"Giovanni, what happened to your man?" Tony asked.

"He said his stomach was bothering him," Giovanni said. "I'm sure he'll be fine."

"Should we wait?"

"No, no, please, go ahead. I'll fill him in on anything he missed."

"Very well," Tony said.

He wasn't happy with another person missing his speech, but he had a schedule to stick to. He pulled his chair out and stood before the room, ready for his moment to begin.

Cliff, Stubs, Mary, and I all looked out at the bowling alley from the front window.

"Reggie figured a way out," I said to no one in particular. "That sly son of a bitch."

"Quiet, Blaze," Cliff said. "Santori's about to begin."

Reggie hid around the corner from the dining room until he was sure everyone had filed in. He wanted to skedaddle before anyone noticed he was missing. He briskly walked toward the front stairs and was nearly there when he heard a deep, booming voice.

"Hey, who the hell are you? And where do you think you're going?"

Reggie froze. He slowly turned and saw a large black man appear from a side hallway, gun pulled out and an all-business look on his face. Reggie had to think fast. Fortunately, he remembered the conversation at the last Boom meeting.

"Wait a minute, are you Jermaine?"

"How do you know my name?"

"I'm a friend of Detective Blaze. Have you seen him?"

"No shit, I'm looking for him too. I'm going to guard the front door. Want to come with me and see if he's still outside?"

"Jermaine, I would love to come outside with you."

"Gentlemen, a lot has changed in the world since we last convened ten years ago," Santori said to his criminal brethren.

"Yeah, we all got a lot richer," Dino Maramona shouted.

"Damn straight," said Tomas Torralini.

"Yes, we sure have," Tony continued. "Dino, I've admired your drug trafficking over the years. And, Lorenzo, you and the Rossi family have had some incredible successes thanks to the Yankees and some shrewd gambling. And Angelo, how you've made such a killing with prostitution has always perplexed me. And then there are the Torralinis. I'm sorry Junior didn't make the trip, but please pass on my regards to him as well as my congratulations for your family's continued financial victories.

"But tonight," Santori said, "tonight I want to talk about me. Because, I'll be honest, while you all have had some impressive successes this past decade, I can confidently say none of them has been as lucrative as my operation here in Chicago."

No one except Tony Santori appreciated that backhanded compliment.

"Don't get me wrong. I'm not here to boast. Well, maybe a little," he said with a grin. "But what I really want to do is share my secrets. I want to tell you how I grabbed this city by the balls and made it my own so that hopefully you can take a tip or two and apply it to your own lives. See, gentlemen, tonight I want to talk about legacy. I want to talk about who we are and, more importantly, how we'll be remembered."

Cliff continued watching from the window as he listened to Santori. A sly grin emerged.

"I'm glad we're recording this," he said. "This cocky Santori is going to give us all we need to clean up the city after he's gone."

We all listened intently as Santori detailed the strengths of each of his guests before going in depth about his patented Santori protection plan. Mary squeezed my hand tightly as we heard him talk about stealing millions from hardworking business owners and killing those who got in his way. When he said his guests could create similar plans and own their cities like he owned Chicago, our group glanced at one another. These men were clearly monsters, and we were surer than ever that we were doing the right thing.

"We've got to be getting close," Cliff said softly, the excitement and tension mounting. "It's almost time."

Mary tapped me on the shoulder and mouthed, "What about Manuel?"

Shit! In all the excitement, I'd forgotten to investigate whether he was a good guy. I decided to throw him a lifeline with a quick text message. I guess we'd find out if he was good or not.

Manuel, there is a bomb threat at the bowling alley and you need to get out now! Take your men and run out the back. Do it now if you want to live!

The house was silent. We stood stoic as we stared out the front window. A knock on the door startled us all.

"Who the hell is that?" Stubs snapped.

"I got it, I got it," Lance said. He quickly opened the door and found his mom staring at him. "Do you have some more confessions for the camera?" he asked.

"Screw you, Lance. I want to know—"

"Shut up, everyone," Cliff commanded. "We're only a couple of minutes away. We need to hear what's going on."

"That's what I want to know," Sarah said, walking into the house. "What's going on?"

I turned to see her tapping her foot with her fists at her waist.

"Ah, Mrs. Cutler, good to see you again. Great interview in the limo, by the way."

"You son of a bitch," Sarah said. "If I—"

"If you say one more word, I will kill you myself," Cliff shouted, turning and staring down Sarah.

"Excuse me?" Sarah said, aghast. "Do you know who I am?"

"I don't care if you're the goddamn queen of England. You need to shut the fuck up right now, or you'll blow this whole operation. You want to know what's going on? Here. Take these." Cliff tossed an extra pair of earbuds to her. "Now sit down, shut up, and listen."

Sarah wanted to stand up for herself, but this was not the time. She unpacked the earbuds, pulled up a folding chair, sat down, and heard the unmistakable voice of Tony Santori in her ear.

Andy Wong saw Manuel and the waitstaff drop what they were doing and run from the kitchen. He wondered where they were going and decided to follow them. The group appeared to be escaping from the scene. Why? Wong didn't know. Clearly, something was going down, and if there was a chance to escape, he figured he'd take it.

Wong kept his distance and didn't see which way Manuel and the waitstaff went once they left the building, but he didn't feel a need to wait and figure it out. He made a beeline down the sidewalk and sprinted around the corner, putting the bowling alley and his past behind him.

"Where the hell is that general security team?" Jermaine bellowed as he and Reggie made it outside. "They're supposed to be stationed right here."

"That's strange," Reggie said. "Maybe they saw something suspicious. I'm sure it's not a big deal."

"I don't know," Jermaine said. "Something doesn't feel right."

"Where the hell is Santori?" Feldman asked, pounding on the pool table. "I don't like waiting."

Eli said nothing.

"Eli, something's not right," Feldman continued. "What's taking so long? And where the hell is Blaze?"

"I don't know, Sol," Eli said. "I'll text Blaze now, but I'm sure Santori will be here soon. There must be a logical explanation."

"There better be," Feldman said as he grabbed a suitcase and opened it. "Otherwise, these guns are going to see some use tonight."

Eli knew the bombs must be coming soon. They'd been sitting in isolation, playing pool and thinking about their alleged newfound riches, for at least twenty minutes. He pulled out his phone and pretended to text Blaze. He'd prided himself on being a man who'd never pulled a trigger on another human being. In war, it was his downfall, but that night, in that moment, his silence and perseverance would be more powerful than a single trigger could ever be.

Eli was ready to leave this world. He closed his eyes and in his head thanked God for the gift of life.

I felt a sense of pride as I stood waiting in silence in front of the window with my fellow Boomsters. If there were ever to be a monument built in our honor, this image of us looking out at the bowling alley could very well be the design of the sculpture—good looking out at evil, waiting with patience for the bombs to detonate.

As the clock ticked down to Boom time, I felt an uncommon urge to pray as this whole experience weirdly brought me closer to God. I took out my earbuds and crept to the back room for a moment of solitude. I kneeled on the couch and stared out at the clear black sky. Then I closed my eyes and quietly spoke to God.

"Dear God, it's your buddy Blaze here. I know we've had an interesting relationship over the years, me and you. I don't know if it was your doing at Mel's funeral when I saw my spirit rise before me, but that out-of-body experience showed me that making the world a better place—a safer place—is my true calling. I know I've looked for signs from you to make sure what we're doing here is right, but deep down, I know it is. I know murder is wrong, but I believe that killing those who would kill others is justifiable. I don't know if it says that exactly in the Bible, but I believe that taking this action is right. I hope you agree."

"Blaze, get in here," Cliff shouted from the front window. "It's almost time."

"Goddammit, hold on," I shouted. "Oops, sorry, God," I whispered. "I didn't mean it that way. Listen, I gotta run. I know I'm doing the right thing, but if you could show me one sign, you know, just for confirmation, that'd be great. Thanks, God."

I ran back to the front window and put my earbuds in. Tony Santori was still yammering about how great he was. Then, as we looked out the window, the most unexpected thing happened. It began to rain. Sheets and sheets of pouring rain cascaded down from a cloudless sky.

"What the hell? It wasn't supposed to rain," Dan Baum shouted from behind the dumpster. "There's not a cloud in the sky. I'm no meteorologist, but that's not supposed to happen."

Mary nudged my arm as she took out her earbuds.

"David," she said, "remember that psychic from the broadcast? Didn't he tell you to stay away from water? What if this is a sign we shouldn't be doing this?"

I took out my earbuds and kissed her forehead.

"No, dear, this is the complete opposite. This is God telling me what we're doing is right. I asked for a sign, and he's giving it. I'm positive we're doing the right thing."

"And that, my friends, is how I became the king of Chicago," Tony Santori continued, "a man among boys, a legend who will be revered by all."

"You sure do think highly of yourself," Giovanni Torralini said.

"You're right, Giovanni, I do. And you know what? I've earned the right to do so. I took the lessons I learned from my predecessors, and I built on them. I am who I am today because I was determined to be the best, but I also acknowledge I am where I am because of my past. And with that in mind, allow me to lead us in our age-old tradition of a premeal toast. Everyone, please raise a glass."

"Here we go, Boomsters, it's showtime," Cliff said. "Get ready for my signal."

"A toast to our past, a toast to our present, but most importantly, a toast to our future," Santori said. "We are the chosen ones. Our families admire us. Our communities fear us. We are the masters of our own fate. To family. To prosperity. To us.

"And if you don't mind," Santori continued, "I'd like to add a final note to our toast. Then we can all sing 'Siamo una Famiglia' and enjoy a festive feast. I just talked all about legacy. One man whose legacy I've always admired is Al Capone. I admired the hell out of that man. I modeled my life, my style, even my personality after him. But as I've gotten older and more retrospective, I've realized that while Capone and I have our similarities, there is one glaring difference. History will ultimately compare us, but let me be clear: Capone is no Santori. He got caught. No one will ever catch Tony Santori."

"Now, now, now," Cliff shouted. "Light them up . . . light the bastards up!"

Stubs emphatically pushed and pushed the button on the remote clicker controlling the bombs in Feldman's room, while Dan shoved the T-handle down. As the handle hit the blasting box, a thunderous boom erupted from the bowling alley, and a yellow blast lit up the night sky.

As a cloud of smoke formed over the alley, we all heard Dan Baum's frantic voice shouting in our ears: "Goddammit, something's wrong!"

28

From our vantage point in the Boom house, it was clear something was wrong. The bomb meant for Feldman and controlled by Stubs went off without a hitch, and that corner of the bowling alley where the Deli Boys were erupted in flames. But the bombs meant for Santori still hadn't detonated.

"For fuck's sake, Dan, push the detonator down," Cliff shouted.

"I am jackass, I am," Dan yelled. "Something's not right. I've pushed the handle down a half dozen times, and nothing's happening. I think it's this godforsaken rain. It's messed with the connection."

"That detonator survived World War II. It should be able to handle a little moisture."

"Well, Cliff, I'm telling you it's not working. So you can either continue with your damn history lesson or help me figure out a plan B 'cause this box is a dud."

Tony Santori and his guests ducked for cover at the sound of the explosion.

"What the fuck was that?" Giovanni Torralini shouted.

"Hell if I know," a stunned Santori said. "Vince, what the fuck was that?"

Vince was equally surprised. He assumed the blast he'd heard were the bombs meant for Feldman, but why hadn't the ones for Santori's group gone off?

"I don't know, boss," he managed to say. "This venue was supposed to be perfectly safe."

"Well, it wasn't," Giovanni yelled.

"Shut up," Santori barked. "Now, listen, we could stay here and argue, or we can get the hell out of here!"

"Holy shit, was that a bomb?" Jermaine shouted, turning to see the back part of the bowling alley up in flames as rain continued to pelt him and Reggie. "I knew something was wrong. Where the hell did that security group go? I've got to find Mr. Santori and make sure he's safe."

Reggie knew he couldn't let Jermaine get to Santori, so he pulled out his gun and aimed it at his companion.

"I can't let you do that, Jermaine."

"Easy now, Reggie, calm down," Jermaine said. "What the hell is going on?"

Before Reggie could answer, he saw Dan emerge from around the far corner, cursing the rain as he threw rocks at the building.

"Dan!" Reggie shouted. "What happened? Why didn't the bombs go off?"

Jermaine heard *bombs* and pulled his own gun on Reggie.

"Okay, you son of a bitch, get those hands in the air. You, homeless guy, get over here and put those hands up. I don't know who the hell you are, but whatever you're planning, I'm putting a stop to it."

The sudden flash of rain stopped abruptly as I watched the scene unfold through Cliff's binoculars. I knew I had to step in to keep the master plan intact—and everyone alive.

"Dan! Dan," I shouted. "Tell him you're working with me. Tell him Blaze knows what's going on."

Dan did, then turned toward the Boom house, staring at us from across the parking lot.

"He said he wants to talk to you," Dan said.

I watched Dan take out his earbuds and toss them to Jermaine, who caught them one-handed while still pointing the gun.

"Hello?" Jermaine said. "Blaze, is that you?"

"Hey, Jermaine, I'm here," I responded. "Those guys are good, I promise. They won't harm you."

"Blaze, they have a bomb," he said. "They're trying to blow up this building."

"I know, Jermaine. So am I, and I need your help."

"Blaze, have you gone mad?"

"Jermaine, do you want an escape from Santori? Do you want to free yourself from his grasp and protect the world from his evil ways?"

"Blaze, I don't understand."

"Dammit, Jermaine, do you want to be a good guy or a bad guy?"

"Good, Blaze. I want to be a good guy."

"That's good, Jermaine. You're picking the right side. Now, listen, there are a lot of bad men who are going to try to escape out that front door. I need you, Reggie, and Dan to hold it down. Fire at anyone you see."

"What? Blaze, I'm not going to shoot at—"

"Jermaine, I can't argue with you now. This is your moment! You want to be a winner like Maxie Dougan, right? This is how you do it. Stand guard and make sure no one gets out that door. You do that and you'll go down a winner."

"But what if Mr. Santori comes out?"

I paused before slowly enunciating my answer. "Then blow his brains out. You can do this, Jermaine. Now go!"

Jermaine looked at Reggie and Dan for a moment before he took out the earbuds and tossed them to Dan.

"Come on," Jermaine said. "Blaze has a job for us."

Tony Santori opened the private dining room's door and was met by a thick cloud of smoke. The group quickly ran out of the room, coughing as the fumes filled the banquet hall. Giovanni pulled a gun out with one hand as he rubbed his eyes with the other.

"What now?" Giovanni asked.

"Let's split up," Santori said. "It sounded like the bomb came from the back of the building. You lead the group out the front door where you all came in. Me and Vince will head to the back and get to the bottom of this."

Cliff Stanley looked at the building going up in flames and swore he was back in Afghanistan. The blast of the bomb and the ensuing chaos took him right back to war-torn battlefields of his past. But that was his past. He needed to focus on the present. He turned and gave me a nod of approval.

"That was quick thinking, Blaze, but those three can't take everyone by themselves. Besides, what about the back door? What if the bad guys try to escape out the back?"

"Then we'll have to stop them," I replied, thinking at breakneck speed.

"With what?" Stubs called.

I turned toward the makeshift kitchen. "Those," I shouted. "Cliff's artifacts."

"That's not enough," Cliff said. "No way we can outgun them with a gun, a vest, and a grenade."

"We're gonna have to," I continued. "Who wants the grenade?"

"I'll take it," Stubs said.

"I'll run the machine gun over to Reggie so he's got more firepower for the front door," I said.

"What about the back?" Cliff repeated. "We need someone to man the back door."

"I'll do it," Lance volunteered, "but I don't have a weapon."

"Here," I said, pulling Mel's gun from its holster, which I brought in case of an emergency. "Take this one."

I tossed the gun like it was a set of car keys. Fortunately, Lance was sure-handed as he caught and pocketed it. He ran to the door and opened it for Stubs, who wheeled out with the grenade secured between his thighs. Lance followed close behind as the two crossed the street and into the bowling alley parking lot.

"That just leaves the vest," I said.

The room went silent. Cliff, Patrick, Kelly, Mary, and I were the only possible candidates, and no one was overly excited to die for the cause. Just then, the door burst open as Kent Cutler charged in.

"What the hell is going on?" he asked. "Did you all see that explosion?"

No one noticed Kent's arrival.

"I'll do it," Mary said. "I'll wear the vest."

"What!?" I screamed. "Absolutely not, Mary. There's no way I'm letting you die."

"That's sweet, dear, but someone needs to do it. I haven't brought much to the team so far, so this can be my grand gesture."

"Mrs. Blaze, no," Patrick called from behind the camera.

"It will be painless," Cliff said as he grabbed the vest. "And you will be a hero."

"Stop! You can't do that."

Mary turned to Kent Cutler, a man she'd never met before.

"You can't kill yourself. You clearly have a life. You need someone who's got nothing to live for." Kent looked at his wife. "Sarah will do it."

"Excuse me?" a stunned Sarah countered. "And why would I do that?"

"Because you have a one-way ticket to hell with your name on it," Kent said as he grabbed the vest from Cliff and took it to Sarah. "And the faster you get there, the better this world will be."

"Kent Cutler, have you forgotten who you're talking to?" Sarah said.

"No. I'm talking to a woman who has never loved anyone other than herself. Not her constituents. Not her husband. Not even her own son. I also haven't forgotten the recording Lance got of you confessing all your sins. You're going to jail, Sarah, and you're going for a long time. The only way out is to sacrifice yourself right here and right now."

"This is all very touching," Cliff said, "but if we're going to deploy this vest, we need to do it now."

Sarah looked at her husband and the suicide vest. She looked at Mary and me. She hated to admit it, but she knew Kent was right.

"Fine," she said, grabbing the vest. "I'll do it."

Vince knew this building better than anyone, and he couldn't figure out why Santori sent the group toward the front stairs. Yes, the blast came from the back, but it would have been way faster to go toward the opposite hallway and down the back stairway.

"Vince, are you coming?" Santori yelled.

"Right behind you, boss," Vince yelled.

Just then, a spark from the fire fell and caught Vince square in the face. He ducked down, desperately trying to brush the embers from his skin. The sting was unbearable, but he had to fight through it.

"Boss? Boss, where did you go?"

Manuel's associates were two blocks away from the bowling alley with no plans of turning back. Manuel, on the other hand, was being drawn back to the burning building.

He didn't know who had sent that text message warning him of the explosion, but he figured there was a reason his life was saved, and he guessed it had to do with Mr. Santori. Yes, Mr. Santori made Manuel do a lot of bad things over the years, but he also gave Manuel a life. He helped him support his family. And now Manuel had a feeling Mr. Santori needed his help.

While his fellow waitstaff continued to flee from the burning bowling alley, Manuel turned and sprinted back toward the growing flames.

I grabbed the Buzz Saw and headed for the door as Sarah was getting the vest adjusted. I didn't know the proper etiquette for running with a machine gun, so I hoisted the thing over my head with both hands and sprinted across the street and through the parking lot. I saw Jermaine, Reggie, and Dan standing forty feet or so from the bowling alley's entrance, each with a gun pointed at the front door.

"Reggie! Reggie," I shouted.

The three men turned, their guns pointed at me.

"Hey, guys, relax. It's me, just bringing extra ammunition."

"Thanks, Blaze," Reggie said, taking the machine gun out of my hand, "but this may be a little overkill."

"I don't know, Reggie," I said, thinking fast. "Did you hear what those guys said about you?"

"What guys?"

"Santori. Lorenzo Rossi. All the guys in the dining room. They were making fun of your hair."

Reggie's body stiffened. "They did what?"

"That's right," I lied. "Your boss himself, Giovanni Torralini, called you a greaseball. And now they're all trying to escape out that front door."

"The hell they are," Reggie screamed. "No one calls me a greaseball and gets away with it. No one!"

He turned and started firing aimlessly at the building. Cliff had told us the gun could fire twenty-five rounds per second, and seeing it in action, I believed him.

"I'm not a fucking greaseball," Reggie shouted, firing over and over at the front of the building.

Jermaine and Dan, unsure what to do during Reggie's rampage, turned their guns and focused on the front door. I sprinted back through the parking lot, wanting to get as far away from Reggie and that gun as I could.

The smoke hadn't yet engulfed the building's entrance as Giovanni Torralini led the group of criminals down the front stairs. He was halfway down when hundreds of bullets battered the front wall. They all ducked for cover and sprinted back up to the second floor. Giovanni peered out the single window at the top of the stairs to see who was firing and couldn't believe his eyes.

"Reggie," he said to himself. "What the hell are you doing?"

Just then the window he was looking through shattered, sending Giovanni to the floor as scraps of glass rained down on him. Smoke quickly spread toward the open window.

"That son of a bitch is trying to kill us," Giovanni said.

"What are we going to do?" his brother Tomas said as he cowered against the wall.

"I'll show them no one turns on Giovanni Torralini and gets away with it."

He counted to three, then stood up and fired back at Reggie and Jermaine. He got five shots off. Two missed, and the other three got Jermaine—two in the leg and one in the chest—knocking the colossal man to the ground.

The smoke from the explosion was its thickest in the back stairway and up through the second-story hallway. The back door to the bowling alley had been blasted off with the explosion, and smoke was pouring out when Lance arrived. He quickly surveyed the area and found no one. Seconds later, Vince burst through the smoke and put his hands on his knees, desperate to feel fresh air on his burnt face. Lance saw him and raised Mel's gun.

"Who are you?" Lance yelled.

Vince stopped suddenly, putting one hand in the air as the other rubbed at his eyes.

"Lieutenant Cutler? Is that you?"

"I'm asking the questions," Lance shouted. "Who are you?"

"I'm Vince—I mean John Sedgwick. I'm with the FBI and am part of the Boomsters."

"Oh," Lance said, lowering his weapon. "Sorry about that."

"No worries," he said as he exhaled. "Where's Santori?"

"I haven't seen him."

"Dammit, I need to find Santori."

Vince turned, took a deep breath, and ran back into the building.

Sarah was in a daze from the moment she walked out of the Boom house, suicide vest securely strapped to her chest. Her eyes were locked on the bowling alley, the fire spreading on the far side of it as she walked through the parking lot, her thoughts on how quickly she'd fallen off her self-built pedestal. That afternoon, she had been preparing for the biggest speech of her life. Now she was moments away from ending her life. The highest of highs to the lowest of lows in a matter of hours—and all because she had been so focused on herself.

Only in the face of death did she acknowledge her own greed. She couldn't believe she had the audacity to stage her own son's funeral just to gain some votes. And now that she knew Lance was alive, she felt embarrassment and shame like she'd never experienced before. Kent was right. She was an awful person, and she deserved to die.

That realization crushed Sarah. She had failed as a candidate. She had failed as a mother. But really, she had failed as a human being. As she walked toward her death, the sound of oncoming sirens getting louder by the second, Sarah did something she'd never done before in her life.

She cried.

I made it to the front yard of the Boom house when screams from Stubs ripped through our ears.

"Goddamn wheelchair. I hate this piece of shit!"

"Stubs," Cliff called, "what's wrong?"

"My wheelchair is stuck in a damn pothole!" Stubs shouted. "If I try to force my way out, this grenade is going to fall out of my lap and send me—and only me—off to an afterlife. I need to get closer."

I turned and saw Stubs in the middle of the parking lot. He and I hadn't seen eye to eye on a lot of things, but this man was a hero, no doubt about it. And right now, he needed help.

Sarah was mere yards from him but didn't seem to notice. Mary and I both called to get her attention.

"Sarah! Sarah!"

"Sarah?"

Lance wasn't sure why someone was calling his mom's name. He thought she was still in the Boom house. He took a quick step away from his post in the back of the building and peeked out into the parking lot, where he saw Sarah walking, wearing what looked like a suicide vest.

"Sarah! Sarah," Lance shouted.

There was no response. Confused and surprisingly concerned, Lance tried a different approach.

"Mom! Mom!"

He didn't know the last time he'd called her by that name. Neither did Sarah, who stopped suddenly and turned to see her son standing near the building. They were one hundred yards away, but the earbuds made it sound like they were next to each other.

"Mom, what are you doing?"

Sarah wiped a tear from her cheek and looked defeatedly at her boy.

"For once in my life, Lance, I'm doing what's right." Lance began to run toward Sarah, but she held up her hand and told him to stop. "There's nothing you can do to stop me, Lance. I have to do this. Take care of yourself and take care of our city."

"But Mom—"

"That's enough, Lance. I need to do this. I'm sorry for all the pain I caused you. Please know that though I failed to show it, I've always, always loved you."

Sarah took her earbuds and threw them on the ground. She'd said goodbye to her son. Now it was time to say goodbye to the world.

With Sarah not responding to my call, I turned and sprinted back to help Stubs. The man was a decorated veteran, a hero whose bravery had saved thousands of American lives. Even if most people didn't know his story, I did, and I could not let it end in a parking lot pothole.

"Stubs, give me the grenade," I called as I sprinted toward him. "I'll toss it into the fire."

"Hell, no, Blaze. Just get me out of this damn hole."

"It's okay, Stubs, just give it to me."

"No! I've lived with the guilt of watching my brothers die in Afghanistan for damn near twenty years, and I won't sit back and watch more die tonight. I'm responsible for this grenade, and I'm escorting it through the front door. Now get my fuckin' chair free!"

Sarah turned and saw us. She was no more than twenty feet away.

"What the hell are you boys doing?" she said as I freed Stubs's chair.

"We're saying goodbye," Stubs said. "Thanks for the help, Blaze. Now get out of here."

"Stubs, don't do this."

"I have to."

"No," Sarah said as she held her hand out to Stubs. "*We* have to."

I'd never seen such self-sacrifice before. I knew Stubs was a hero, but for the first time, I saw Sarah being one, too, as she put the good of others before herself. The two were inspiring. I stood motionless in the parking lot, watching their courage, and tears began to form in my eyes. Sarah saw and leaned in toward my ear.

"Look out for Lance for me," she whispered. "And, Blaze, this city will need a new leader, someone who can take care of it and look out for its best interest. Think about it. You could do a lot as mayor of Chicago."

Before I could say anything more, she turned, took Stubs's hand, and continued toward the bowling alley.

"David?" Mary said through our earbuds. "Did she just say you should run for mayor?"

Torralini stopped shooting, either because he was dead or out of ammo, Reggie thought. He put down the machine gun and joined Dan by Jermaine's side. The big man was lying on his back in a pool of water as blood spilled from his leg.

"Jermaine! Jermaine, are you okay?"

"I think I'm good, but I don't know how. I felt a bullet hit my chest, and I swore I was dead," Jermaine said through clenched teeth.

He reached into his chest pocket and found his lifesaver. He pulled out Maxie Dougan's two-headed coin and saw there was a massive indentation in the middle from being struck by a bullet. Jermaine looked at the coin and smiled.

"Tell Blaze I'm a winner," he said. "Tell him Maxie's coin just saved my life."

Reggie looked up and saw Stubs and Sarah Cutler approaching, one holding a grenade and the other in a suicide vest.

"What the hell is going on?" Dan cried from Jermaine's side. "Stubs, what are you doing?"

Stubs and Sarah had no time to explain the plan. Stubs saw the Buzz Saw and told Dan to be ready.

"For what?" Dan cried out.

Stubs and Sarah continued until they were twenty feet from the darkened lights above the bowling alley entrance. He looked up at her and she down at him, their hands clasped together. Stubs heard sirens and knew they were running out of time.

"If we're going to do this, we've got to do it now."

Sarah squeezed Stubs's hand. "I'm ready."

"Dan," Stubs called, "cover us!"

Dan and Reggie opened fire on the building, giving the two just enough time to get through the front door.

"Vince, where the fuck are you?" Santori yelled.

Vince heard the call from the bottom of the back stairs and sprinted up through the smoke, taking the stairs two at a time. He got to the top and saw the silhouette of his boss standing in a side doorway.

Santori turned just as Vince appeared, his eyes bloodshot and his face burned.

"There you are," Santori yelled. "I've been looking all over for you. Come on, there's a secret escape through here."

Vince heard those words and knew it was time to come clean. He'd given six years of his life to Santori, and he was willing to die to take the monster down. Vince pulled his gun and aimed it at Santori.

"Tony," he said coldly, "I can't let you leave this building."

Santori stared into Vince's bloodshot eyes. Ten feet separated the two men, but Santori never felt farther apart. He quickly realized Vince must have been responsible for the bomb going off. This was the man whom Tony had trusted with his life—and there Vince was, looking to take that very life. The rage at being betrayed boiled up through Tony as the smoke and flames spread around him.

"You fucking bastard!"

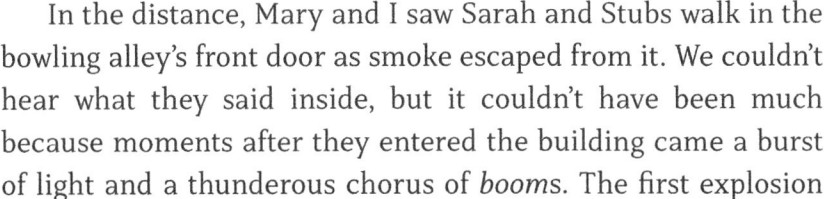

In the distance, Mary and I saw Sarah and Stubs walk in the bowling alley's front door as smoke escaped from it. We couldn't hear what they said inside, but it couldn't have been much because moments after they entered the building came a burst of light and a thunderous chorus of *boom*s. The first explosion came from the front, and it set off a chain reaction of deafening blasts as bomb after bomb went off, igniting dozens of fires and enveloping the building in a cloud of smoke.

Together, Mary and I stood outside the Boom house, speechless at the scene before us. Walls quickly caved in as flames spread throughout the building. I reached my hand out for Mary's, and we watched the smoke drift through the evening sky.

"Boom, boom, bang, bang," Cliff shouted as he bounded out the front door like a kid on the last day of school, disrupting our serene silence. "Holy hell, that was incredible! We did it, Blaze. We got them sons of bitches, every last one of them!"

Just then, a single gunshot rang out. I turned to see Cliff fall in agony as he grabbed his shoulder, writhing in pain and cursing up a storm. I turned back to see a pistol inches away from my face, the barrel aimed right between my eyes.

"Almost every last one," said Andy Wong, the man whose smuggling operation I'd thwarted as my first real case and who clearly hadn't forgiven me. He was the one who tried to have me killed behind the cleaners—and he was apparently ready to finish the job.

"This was all your doing, wasn't it?" he asked. "You were the reason my men and I were asked to work here tonight, weren't you? It wasn't Santori who wanted us here. It was you!"

"Mr. Wong," I said, my hands up in the air, "let's be civilized. Can we put the gun down and talk about this like grownups?"

"Civilized? You just tried to kill me! You killed all of my associates. You blew up a damn building with who knows how many people inside. You want me to be civilized?"

He had a point. Meanwhile, Cliff was rolling around on the ground, screaming like a madman as he tried to apply pressure to his shoulder.

"Shut the hell up, or the next bullet shuts you up for good," Wong screamed. "As for you, Detective Blaze, I'm going to have to think up something fun for you. Part of me wants to kill you nice and slow, make you suffer in pain. Maybe I'll kill your girlfriend here first, make you watch her die. Or maybe I'll just shoot you now and get it over with. So many choices."

"Drop it, Wong," a voice called out.

Andy Wong turned to find Lance standing twenty feet away holding Mel's gun, the blazing building behind him casting a frightening backdrop.

Before Wong could do anything, Mary pushed me to the side and did a spinning roundhouse kick, knocking Wong's gun from his hand. She then jumped and did a flying sidekick into his chest that knocked him to the ground. Lance ran over and put his knee on Wong's back, holding him in place.

"Blaze, you got some handcuffs?" he asked.

I patted my pockets, not sure why I thought handcuffs would have magically appeared.

"I've got some," Cliff managed between groans.

I ran over and grabbed them, then brought them over to Lance. As Lance cuffed Wong, Patrick and Kelly ran out of the house.

"Mary," Patrick cried, "that was incredible! Will you teach me that move?"

Mary looked at me, then at Patrick. "It's *Mrs. Blaze*," she said with a wink. "And sure."

"Did you get that all on tape?" I asked.

"Every second of it," Kelly responded. "We've got it all."

"The public will love that flying kick," Patrick said. "Hell, I might need to take up taekwondo."

A dozen police cars and fire trucks stormed into the bowling alley parking lot.

"Patrick, I think it's time to start the show," I said.

"And I think it's time for you guys to get out of here," Lance called.

Mary and I were happy not to stick around. We thanked Lance for his help, then turned toward the Boom house.

"What about me?" Kent called from the front door, careful not to step on Cliff.

Lance saw his dad and ran up to give him a hug, both unsure how to feel about losing Sarah.

"Come on, Dad, let's go home," Lance said.

"Let Jeffrey take you home," I called. "Kent, thank you again for convincing Sarah to do what was right. She'll go down as a hero."

"Thanks, Blaze. Is there any way we can keep her confession out of the broadcast to maintain her image?"

I realized we didn't need to bury her after her heroic sacrifice. Plus, she did give me a pretty powerful endorsement.

"You have my word," I said. "Her secret is safe. Now excuse us, but we really need to run."

"Blaze," a hoarse voice called. It was Cliff.

I ran up to him and leaned in close so he didn't have to strain when he talked.

"Where's Vince?" Cliff asked me.

I turned to Lance, who closed his eyes and shook his head. I turned back to Cliff.

"He died for the cause, Cliff. I'm sorry."

"Don't be sorry, Blaze. You did good," he said. "You did real good."

"We all did, Cliff." I gave him a light fist bump. "Boom, boom, bang, bang."

"Boom, boom, bang, bang," he said between cries of pain.

I turned and grabbed Mary's hand, and together we ran toward our car and drove away, leaving the burning bowling alley, our fellow Boomsters—both living and deceased—and a bunch of dead bad guys behind us.

We were two minutes into our drive when my phone rang. It was Tom Lexington.

"Blaze, what have you gotten yourself into?" he asked. "I was watching my DIY home repair show, and it just got interrupted by some home movie with you talking about Boomsters. What's going on?"

"Just keep watching, Tom. You'll like the ending."

"Blaze, give me something."

"Santori's dead. Feldman's dead. The Torralini family, Lorenzo Rossi, Angelo Romano, Dino Maramona. All dead."

"How in God's name did you pull that off?"

"Tom, it's been a long day."

"At least give me a quote."

"Tom, here's my quote: 'The good guys won. Justice prevailed.' That's all I've got for you now. So long as I'm not arrested before the morning, give me a call, and I'll spill the whole story for you. I'll give you all the insider info you want, and you can be the world's trusted source for the biggest story in decades."

"Thanks, Blaze. Anything I can do for you?"

"Yeah, in the morning before you call me, call Metro City Internet College and tell them Detective Blaze thanks them for their pamphlets. Also, see if they have any about entering politics."

"Why?" Lexington asked.

"Because *Mayor Blaze* has a nice ring to it."

EPILOGUE

On February 28, Mary and I were supposed to be relaxing and drinking margaritas on the sun-soaked beach in Mexico. Instead, we sat alone in the Oval Office, waiting to meet with the president of the United States.

It'd been two weeks since our Valentine's dinner—when Mary told me about her surprise travel plans to get me out of my retirement rut—and one week to the day since Operation Boom was successfully executed. We didn't know how the public would handle our extreme actions to protect the greater good, and based on the past week, the public hadn't been able to make up its mind.

The video justifying our actions was seen live by millions of people and quickly became the most-watched video ever on any social media platform. Boomster supporters called it clear proof of why what we did was necessary. Those who felt we were in the wrong said the video was all the proof they needed—not only did we admit to committing murder, but we showed how we did it. Case closed.

But it wasn't that easy.

None of us were arrested, though Lieutenant Lance Cutler advised us to remain under voluntary house arrest, a move Cliff Stanley supported. The thought was we would stay out of the limelight while the justice system tried to figure out what to do with our situation. The problem was no one wanted to touch our potential case. The public began calling it *Boomsters versus Evil*, but the reality was, to that point, no charges were filed, and no case existed. That wasn't stopping people from talking about it, particularly Tom Lexington's *NorthShore News*. What in reality was a small local newspaper quickly became the envy of news organizations the world over because it kept publishing scoop after scoop about the Boomsters and the mission—stories no other journalist was having luck uncovering.

That was because no other journalist had the relationship with me that Tom Lexington had. He and I had been through a lot the last couple of weeks, but while our relationship was challenged, our respect for one another grew. While under house arrest, I had made it a daily routine to call him from the bathroom on my pink phone—just in case the FBI was still snooping on me—and give him new details that hadn't made our broadcast.

He'd written a powerful exposé about the under-the-table arrangement between Tony Santori and the West Coast Club thanks to hundreds of documents Betty had handed over to the FBI and IRS. Betty turned herself in to the authorities, content with doing jail time for her role in the operation as control of the WCC was handed over to club manager Bryan Randall. Lexington went on to chronicle Santori's rise and fall, capped off by a full-page feature, "The Two Worst Men in Chicago History: Tony Santori and Al Capone."

One of Lexington's most entertaining pieces was about Jermaine, who was still in the hospital dealing with complications from surgery to remove the bullets in his leg. I told Tom about the Maxie Dougan story and how Maxie's coin had saved Jermaine's life. Lexington did some digging and was able to connect with Dougan, who was the CEO of a multibillion-dollar organization.

Dougan was touched by the story and visited Jermaine's hospital room, where the two had talked for hours. They reminisced about Dougan's fighting days, and Lexington got a great photo of them holding Jermaine's bullet-dented coin. Dougan offered to cover all of Jermaine's legal fees and said there was a job waiting for him whenever he was healthy and done with any charges filed against him. Turned out Jermaine was a winner after all.

Lexington had also run an emotional Q&A with Lance about his mysterious disappearance, his return to the Chicago Police Department, and the loss of his mother, leading mayoral candidate Sarah Cutler. Lance and I had worked together to craft a narrative that was not entirely false yet also steered far enough away from the actual truth. For example, when he was asked what he was doing while the world was looking for him, Lance said he was off on a spiritual retreat to reexamine his life priorities and whom he considered trusted friends. He said he was honored and appreciative that the police welcomed him back to his post, and he was looking forward to serving the city and making it safe, the way his mom had envisioned.

As for Sarah Cutler, she went down as a hero. The public never heard her confession, though I did ask Patrick to make sure he saved the recording—just in case we ever needed it. For all her campaign's BS about the world being safer with Sarah, the reality was we were all safer thanks to her igniting the blast that made Operation Boom go boom.

Lexington wrote about the other "victims" of Boom besides Santori—the bad men who may or may not have deserved to die. He wrote about the four Torralinis and their control in California, and he chronicled the careers of Lorenzo Rossi, Angelo Romano, and Dino Maramona. Though Andy Wong didn't die in the blast, he'd likely spend the rest of his life in prison, thanks in part to Lexington's detailed account of his operations.

Tom had also launched a fun daily feature called "Hold the

Mayo," where he'd riff about anything on his mind that day. His best work, though, came as part of his new "Mad Men or Bad Men" series, where he profiled each of the Boomsters. He started Friday with a moving piece about our fallen Boomsters, talking about Vince's sacrifice and his undercover work, Stubs's determination to honor the friends he lost in Afghanistan, and Eli's courage to bring Solomon Feldman to the venue. Saturday's story was about Reggie, followed by a Sunday feature on Cliff, who was put on administrative leave while things got sorted out. Monday's story tracked Dan Baum's career trajectory and Tuesday's focused on Mary's philanthropic work over the years—omitting anything about her more colorful past.

That left the current day's feature, which was about me. I didn't want the spotlight because that wasn't why I had gotten into the detective business. So I made sure much of the piece documented the contributions of Team Blaze—Marc, Jeffrey, Wilt, Patrick, and Kelly. I told Tom my goal in becoming a detective was twofold: on the one hand, I really just needed something to keep my mind occupied, but just as importantly, I thought I could make a difference. The top headline in the morning's newspaper said just that: "Blaze: 'I Thought I Could Make a Difference.'"

I didn't have time to read the story, but I had grabbed the newspaper as Mary and I were rushed out of the house by the Secret Service to board a private plane to Washington, DC. We hadn't been told where we were going; we were only instructed to dress nicely. And that was how we ended up in the Oval Office, sitting mere feet from the Resolute desk and staring at a blue carpet adorned with the seal of the president of the United States.

"Why do you think we're here?" Mary asked.

Before I could answer, a door opened, and in walked the president himself, followed by a pair of aides. We immediately stood up as he approached and reached out to shake our hands.

"Detective Blaze, Mary, thank you for joining me here in the White House," he said. "Please, have a seat."

We both sat down as the president took a seat on the couch across from us. On the coffee table was the *NorthShore News*, which I had brought with me from home but still hadn't read. Embarrassed for leaving it out, I tried to grab and hide it before the president noticed, but I was too late.

"Hey, is that the *NorthShore News*?" he said as he picked up the paper before me. "I love this paper. That Tom Lexington, what a riot."

The president took a couple minutes to flip through the pages as we sat in silence, watching him peruse the news. He finally flipped back to the front page and quickly skimmed the story about me.

"So, Detective Blaze, you thought you could make a difference," he said.

"I did, sir," I said.

"Sean, Rachel, can you give us some privacy for a minute?" he said to his aides.

The two nodded and exited, leaving Mary and me alone with the leader of the free world.

"Well," he said once he was sure we were alone, "you sure did make a hell of a mess."

"Sir, if you don't mind—"

"Please, let me finish," he said. "We're seeing rallies and protests all over the country supporting or vilifying your actions. Hundreds of thousands of people in big cities and small towns alike are showing up in town squares and downtowns to cheer for your innocence or demand your arrest. Justice was served, but it's how you got there that has divided people. Just yesterday, one hundred and fifty thousand people in your hometown of Chicago gathered, with half the crowd calling you heroes and half claiming you're villains for making a mockery of the judicial system."

"I did hear that, sir," I began, "but if you can—"

"I said please let me finish."

"Yes, sir."

"Now, Blaze, you've put this country in a precarious position. I've been informed that hundreds of lawyers and judges across the nation have expressed zero interest in hearing a *Boomsters versus Evil* case, should one ever develop. Yesterday alone, I had not one but two justices contact me to say they would recuse themselves should your situation ever make it to the Supreme Court."

"Why would they do that?" Mary asked.

"One of them lost a nephew to the Torralini family, and another apparently had a previous financial relationship with the Santori family, and they did not want their ruling tainted by their past."

"What do you think, sir? If you don't mind me asking," I said. "Did we do the right thing?"

"All I'll say is whether people think you were vigilant or vigilantes, you saw a problem and tried to deal with it," he said. "It was unconventional. Hell, it seems like everything about you is unconventional."

"I'll take that as a compliment, sir."

"I've also been in contact with FBI director Thomas Mangold, and he is working on securing funding to rename a portion of the J. Edgar Hoover building in honor of John Sedgwick, the undercover agent you knew as Vince. I've also been asked for my opinions about the design of a new memorial honoring the men and women who served in Afghanistan, and I'm going to propose that your fellow Boomster Stubs be prominently featured."

"Thank you, sir, those are both incredible recognitions for two incredible men."

"No, Blaze. Thank you," he said as we reached across the coffee table to shake hands. "Now how about an autograph?"

"I'd love one, sir."

"No Blaze, I promised my grandson I'd get yours. He wants to be a crime stopper just like you."

He handed me my copy of the NorthShore News. I grabbed a presidential pen off the coffee table and signed on top of the article about me.

To the president, I wrote. *I hope I made a difference. And to the president's grandson, you can make a difference too! Detective Blaze.*

"Thanks, Blaze. Now if you'll excuse me, I have to go to another meeting, but I wanted to meet you and share my appreciation for your work."

We shook hands again. Then Mary and I watched the president exit the Oval Office. While we waited for someone to come in and tell us where to go next, I had an unfortunate realization.

"That crook," I whispered to Mary. "He stole my newspaper."

I grabbed one of the presidential pens and pocketed it in exchange. Just then, the president reappeared.

"Oh, Blaze," he said, startling me.

"I'm sorry, sir," I said, holding up my hands. "I know I shouldn't have taken the pen."

"What? Oh, don't worry. Take as many of those as you like. We've got thousands of them. Apparently, a junior staff member who worked here back in the seventies got hustled by a traveling salesman and bought two hundred thousand pens in honor of the country's two-hundredth anniversary. We're still making our way through them."

"You know, I thought they looked familiar."

"What?" the president asked.

"Never mind. That's a story for another day."

"Very well. I realized we didn't discuss how to fix this Boom situation."

"Yes, sir, that's true. What do you recommend?"

"Write a book, Blaze. Tell the world your story and let the public decide if what you did was right."

"Yes, sir, I can do that."

The *NorthShore News* was not usually read in the Cayman Islands, but for the past week, its website was the only one visited by the computer housed in the private office of a guarded villa that looked out over the Caribbean Sea. Every story about the Boomsters was read and analyzed, and each was finished with the same refrain.

"Fuck you, Blaze, you lying piece of shit. Fuck you!"

Manuel sat by as Tony Santori indulged in another round of cursing at the computer. Personally, he didn't know why Santori continued to torture himself by reading about what happened, but he wasn't going to question his boss. After all, it was Tony Santori who had saved Manuel's life. He had run back into the bowling alley to find Santori, but it was Santori who'd found him. Santori led him into a side room where the closet hid an emergency escape slide. Since the building was Santori's, he knew all about the undisclosed exit locations. Manuel had slid down just as Vince pulled his gun on Santori. As for Santori, he jumped for the slide just as the roof blew off from the explosives, leaving him with several burns across his face.

Manuel felt good about his decision, about helping the man who'd given his family so much. Santori, meanwhile, was as far from good as could be. His closest confidants had turned on him. His fellow family heads had been executed. And his operation was being investigated by the IRS and FBI. And in Tony Santori's eyes, there was one man responsible for it all.

"Fuck you, Blaze," he shouted again, slamming his fist on his desk. "You thought you could make a difference? You thought you were getting justice? Fuck justice. I want revenge!"

Now that you've finished reading this book, it would mean the world to me if you would leave your thoughts about it on your preferred retail platform. If that platform is Amazon, you can scan the QR code or visit the link below, sign in, and leave a review:

https://amazon.com/gp/product-review/B0CGTT89HB

Thank you,
David Marks

Made in the USA
Monee, IL
08 November 2024

69674954R00312